# EBONY
# GATE

# EBONY GATE

# GATE

## *The Phoenix Hoard, Book 1*

## JULIA VEE
### *and*
## KEN BEBELLE

**TOR**

TOR PUBLISHING GROUP

NEW YORK

EBONY GATE

Copyright © 2023 by Sixth Moon Press LLC

A Tor Book
Published by Tom Doherty Associates / Tor Publishing Group
120 Broadway
New York, NY 10271

www.tor-forge.com

Tor® is a registered trademark of Macmillan Publishing Group, LLC.

Library of Congress Cataloging-in-Publication Data

Names: Vee, Julia, author. | Bebelle, Ken, author.
Title: Ebony gate / Julia Vee and Ken Bebelle.
Description: First edition. | New York : Tor Publishing Group, 2023. |
Series: The phoenix hoard ; book 1
Identifiers: LCCN 2023007708 (print) | LCCN 2023007709 (ebook) |
ISBN 9781250837431 (hardcover) | ISBN 9781250837448 (ebook)
Subjects: LCGFT: Magic realist fiction. | Thrillers (Fiction). | Novels.
Classification: LCC PS3622.E424 E26 2023 (print) |
LCC PS3622.E424 (ebook) | DDC 813'.6—dc23/eng/20230313
LC record available at https://lccn.loc.gov/2023007708
LC ebook record available at https://lccn.loc.gov/2023007709

Our books may be purchased in bulk for promotional, educational, or business use. Please contact your local bookseller or the Macmillan Corporate and Premium Sales Department at 1-800-221-7945, extension 5442, or by email at MacmillanSpecialMarkets@macmillan.com.

First Edition: 2023

Printed in the United States of America

0  9  8  7  6  5  4  3  2  1

# EBONY
# GATE

# HUNTING GROUNDS

Midnight in Golden Gate Park was mostly quiet, just the distant sounds of city traffic and my grunts of exertion as I dragged the yeti corpse to my Jeep. The damp nighttime fog had driven out both locals and tourists hours ago, leaving me enough privacy to deal with the beast before it decimated the local bison herd.

I paused at the end of the bison paddock to take a break, my breaths pluming in the cold night air. When Ito-san had called, I had answered, unable to shake off generations of respect for one's elders. It didn't matter to Ito-san that I was retired. Ito-san was one of the older generation of Lóng Jiārén here in San Francisco, and still considered me the Blade of Soong. For two years I had tried to forge a new life without bloodshed, but Ito-san still called on me for monster cleanup.

The hibagon poaching the bison herd was monster disposal, the perfect job for a Blade—even a supposedly retired one. Ito-san managed to play on my love for this town and my desire to stay in the good graces of his clan. Most Jiārén clans here didn't want to associate with me. So for Ito-san, I always said yes. Which is how I found myself lugging this beast across Golden Gate Park in the dead of night.

Getting a two-hundred-pound headless yeti corpse into the Jeep was giving me a leg workout. I grunted and heaved, and with a final shove, it smacked onto the plastic liner I'd set out earlier. The slap of the body against the plastic splashed sticky hibagon blood against my face.

*Drip, drip, drip.*

*Hot blood sprays across my face, stinging my eyes and painting my vision scarlet. A handful of pearls hit the ground, the gems brushed with crimson, the clicking sound like dead bones rattling in a cup. My blood-sticky hands raise my sword over my head and her steel sings a ringing song of misery.*

*A girl's high-pitched scream echoes in my ears. "Butcher!"*

My breath rushed out of my chest and I dry-heaved, my hand on the back of my Jeep, the cool San Francisco night once again surrounding me. It seemed that whether my eyes were open or closed, the bloody landscape of my past could still fill my sight. Bad enough that my nightmares ran with blood, but now even my waking hours weren't safe.

With a final shove the beast's shoulders cleared the back bumper and I slammed down the hatch. The door clicked shut over the hibagon with barely an inch to spare. Good thing I'd already cut its head off.

Coiling my long hair into tight braids had done nothing to shield it from the spraying blood when I beheaded the beast earlier. Swaths of drying blood flaked off the front of my black haori jacket and stained the embroidered silver phoenix on my chest a rusty red. I opened the driver's door to my Jeep and despaired at the pristine upholstery.

Between tonight's bloody mess and the fiasco at the museum earlier tonight, my qì was tied up in knots. The new donor, some big-shot venture capitalist from Seattle with more good looks than sense, had chewed up hours of my time fussing over his collection of swords. And then we'd finally gotten to the last sword.

I unhooked the black trash bag holding the yeti's head from my waistband and tossed it in the passenger-side footwell with entirely too much force. The bag made a wet squelch as it landed.

How in all the heavens had Crimson Cloud Splitter landed in this Júwàirén's hands? The fool thought it was a lost work of Kunimitsu. I knew better, but I couldn't reveal why. I'd let my business partner placate the wealthy donor while I bit my tongue. Unfortunately, my silence had cost me a future evening as my partner, Tessa, had agreed to table the issue until a later time. Once I finished monster corpse disposal, I would have to turn my attention to the ancient sword. It was too notorious to leave in the wrong hands. Which meant it would have to end up in my hands, at least temporarily.

I untied my own swords and carefully laid them both along the center console. I would clean them as soon as I got home. Shaking off my frustration, I climbed in and tried not to notice how the wet fabric of my pants squished against the driver's seat.

Now I needed to get rid of the body.

When you needed to purify a magical corpse, no questions asked, the Herbalist was your best bet. Others called her the Herbalist, or Grandma Chen, if they were regulars. I called her Popo. I'd known her since I was a toddler and my side gig hunting monsters had brought me to the back entrance of her shop in the Inner Sunset district on more than one occasion. My other option was Oliver Nakamoto, head of the temple near Japantown. Between the two, it was no contest. The snooty Head of the Nakamoto Clan and I couldn't stand each other.

Popo had eschewed the magical environs of Lotus Lane adjacent to Chinatown for the sprawling Inner Sunset, which was also thankfully closer to Golden Gate Park.

This short drive to Popo's was just long enough for the yeti blood on my hands to dry into flaky specks that fluttered down the dashboard and forced me to question my decision-making for the past two years. Why did I keep saying yes when the old-timers called? I sighed. I needed the goodwill. It hadn't been easy starting a new life here after my actions at Beijing's Pearl Market. The Jiārén here did not welcome the Butcher living among them. Magical monster cleanup had garnered me some modest amount of goodwill with the locals.

I tried not to gag at the smell of the corpse in my Jeep as I drove to the Herbalist's back entrance. I needed to learn to say no to these gigs the same way I'd been saying no to my father's endless litany of requests for the last two years. San Francisco was my home now. This tiny city with all its light and shadow spoke to me in a way that Tokyo never had. I wanted to stay here and I wanted to live a life that didn't require me to remember that I'd been the Butcher of Beijing. To that end I had slowly carved out a niche in my artifacts business. I just needed to stay out of the death-dealing business.

The next time Ito-san or one of the old-timers called to ask to me to take care of some rampaging beast from the Realm, I had to say no.

The front of the Herbalist's homeopathic remedy spa was half lit. Even with only security lights I picked out white leather–upholstered spa recliners lined up like New Age sentries against a long mirrored wall. The interior was spotless, trendy spa meets sci-fi movie set, the decor peppered with water features and greenery. I hadn't visited in some time, but I hoped Popo was working late, prepping her elixirs and potions for the next day. I drove the Jeep to the back of the building.

I parked in the rear, killed the engine, and leaned back, closing my eyes for a moment. As my thoughts drifted, the music of San Francisco's burgeoning magic called out to me, lulling me into a stupor. It almost caught me this time but I bit down on my tongue, jolting myself awake. The coppery taste of blood filled my mouth. San Francisco was getting harder to ignore. Like a needy toddler, the awakening magical consciousness of the city clamored for my attention. I was trying hard to convince it to go look elsewhere. So far, no luck.

I got out of my Jeep and gauged the distance to the door against the biting fatigue in my legs. Start dragging now, or later? Once again, perhaps my decisions for the past two years hadn't been the greatest. On the other hand, if I hadn't made my choices, the blood soaking my clothes right now would be human blood.

I'd given up everything—my place in the Soong Clan, the proud lineage of the Blades before me, and my love, Kamon Apichai. All of that so that I could live without bloodshed and death.

Here I was free. Free to say no to killing.

Despite the cost, I knew I'd made the right choice. The right choice didn't make my loss less painful.

Movement in the shadows around the back door of the spa tickled at my senses and pulled me out of my navel-gazing. Instinct kicked in and brought my body to complete stillness, my eyes and ears scanning for threats.

Dark shapes moved around the door, four young men, whispering to each other, laughing, and reeking of cheap cologne and machismo. I grabbed my swords and crept toward the door, my soft-soled boots quiet on the asphalt. I tied on my swords as I moved forward, my hands going through the motions with the ease of years of practice. Sword of Truth, the sword of every Soong Blade before me, I tied to my back, respect for the sword I would never draw again. Hachi, my wakizashi, I tied to my hip.

As I got closer my eyes adjusted to the darkness of the shadows and the shapes resolved into four guys in black nylon tracksuits, huddled around Popo's back door. The jackets had an embroidered golden dragon clawing its way around the right bicep. The guys wore their hair long and gelled back, with no part. I knew exactly who they were. In better light, on the backs of their jackets I would find the stylized character for thunder, with a large number nine wrapped around it. It felt wrong, and my annoyance with these low-level thugs rose to the fore.

These guys were Clan Louie Claws. Street-level enforcers, usually kids with píng-level powers at best, used to run protection rackets and as cannon fodder.

And definitely outside of their usual hunting grounds. Were they hassling Popo? My annoyance ratcheted up to anger. Popo didn't have a lot of muscle around to deal with nonsense like this. She ran a spa. Not exactly a place that needed a bouncer. Also, I was just trying to get a corpse processed and these idiots were making extra trouble for me on an already long night.

I came to a stop just inside the shadows and growled, the sound low and deep in my chest. The whispered conversation died and the boys whirled toward the sound of my voice. If nothing else, they'd learn a valuable lesson in situational awareness tonight.

"Siu pangyou, even dragons respect territory boundaries."

With that one word, *dragons,* I signaled to these kids that we were all Lóng Jiārén, descendants of the Eight Sons of the Dragon and heirs to their power. As Jiārén, we came from a world of violence and Dragon talent that was best kept in the dark of night and in quiet alleys like this one.

Jiārén had infiltrated nearly every major city on the Pacific Rim. When they reached San Francisco they had settled into Lotus Lane, a hidden nook on the outskirts of Chinatown, as well as the surrounds of Japantown. These baby Claws belonged on Lotus Lane. Not sure what they were doing way out here. Anticipation at schooling them sent gooseflesh down my neck and burned off my fatigue. The night was young, I could fit in some entertainment.

Of course, there were four of them to only one of me. Those odds hardly seemed fair—but I was feeling generous and wanted to give them a bit of a chance.

After a moment of hesitation, the boys spread out, facing me in a ragged semicircle. The smallest one looked barely old enough to drive, his round face already shiny with sweat. Round Face pulled a leaf-shaped knife and held it at chest level in a trembling hand. Cute.

The husky boy on my left, the senior Claw by the sash tied around his arm, backed the smallest one down with a stern look and turned to me, his thin mustache drooping as his lip curled into a cocky sneer. "Siu ze, it's dangerous to be out alone this late at night. Maybe we should walk you home. You never know what kind of monsters might be around."

Okay, now he was pissing me off. I understood what was happening. A young woman of average height taking on four men in a dark alley. I'd been underestimated nearly my entire life, but it irritated me when people referred to me as *little missy*. Like I was some ignorant upstart.

My palm itched, my hand drifting to my sword. I'd teach this kid a lesson. One I'd taught many times in my years as the Blade of Soong. Mustache Boy might be taller and wider than me but he was about to learn what my deceptively lean build could do. He took a few steps forward, lazily draping his hand over the curved grip of a short sword held inside his belt.

Auras flickered to life from the other two boys and the scent of ozone and cinnamon washed down the alley. The boy with the knife licked his lips, his eyes darting back and forth between me and his friends.

The boys had dim auras, but the scents told me everything I needed to know. Few could smell Jiārén talent like I could. In fact I knew exactly zero people with my peculiar talent. It wasn't something I advertised, and it was handy in situations like this. As I suspected, their talents were only píng class, nothing to write home about. No kinetics, no combat-grade talents like my father or my brother. Maybe some low-level influence. Typical foot soldiers. "You boys are pretty far from Lotus Lane. Do your parents know you're out so late?"

Mustache Boy rippled his fingers on his sword hilt as if debating whether to draw it. "Claws go where they want."

His eyes drifted back to Popo's back door. "Lotus Lane is getting cramped, y'know? A dragon needs to stretch its wings."

He smiled, showing his very white teeth, canines filed down to sharp points. "If the old lady wanted to stay safe, she should have stayed in Tran territory. There's no one to watch over her out here."

The Trans had arrived in San Francisco in the seventies. The Louies had established themselves here before the Great Quake, and were understandably upset at the arrival of the upstart clan. It had only taken a few years for tensions to come to a boil, breaking out into open clan warfare that had nearly consumed all of Chinatown.

By the eighties, the Bā Tóu had had enough and sent my mother to the city to forge a truce or start rolling heads. Bā Tóu got what they wanted and a truce had been hammered out. You'd understand if you met my mother.

The Trans took the piers and ports, controlling the shipping for all magical transport in and out of the San Francisco Bay area. The Louies retained Lotus Lane and the lion's share of banking for Jiārén families. The truce had kept the peace for four decades. But the Jiārén community continued to grow. Mustache Boy was right, Lotus Lane had gotten crowded. Popo was just the latest of many to venture away from familiar neighborhoods to make their fortune.

Unlike my mother, I had no reason to broker a peace. I was just trying to dispose of a body.

I walked toward the boys, my steps measured, my hand on the wakizashi at my hip. Threatening me was one thing, threatening Popo was another. My blood heated as I considered these punks shaking down a little old lady who ran a spa for protection money. "Suo zai. You should have done your homework. You're in another predator's territory now."

Mustache Boy pulled his sword from its sheath, the metal dull and nicked in the dim lighting. "This is no one's territory! The old lady made her choice when she opened up here!"

I smiled, baring *my* teeth now. "The Herbalist is family to me. She is Jiārén. My Jiārén. This is *my* territory!"

I sidestepped out of the shadows, into the dull light of the streetlamps. I stretched out my arms, cracked my wrists, and rolled my shoulders. All showmanship I would never do had I expected this to be a real fight. But tonight I wasn't in the mood to be spilling blood and so I had to rely on something else to put this matter to bed—my reputation as the Butcher. Unlike my father with his combat-grade animator skills, and my mother with her Void-walking talent, I had no talent or gift to speak of. Instead, I'd earned my reputation the old-fashioned way—with training, practice, and the shrieks of my victims ringing in my ears.

I turned my body into hanmi, the half stance, and let my hand rest on Hachi, a short and brutally efficient weapon, good for cutting in close quarters like this alley. Hachi's tsuba was carved by a master, the round guard adorned with a red phoenix inlaid with blood jade. The blood jade was for show since I had about as much talent as a paper towel, but the value was extraordinary and an opulent display of the Soong Clan's status as a Hoard Custodian family.

If these fools didn't recognize the blood jade phoenix on the tsuba, they'd been living under a rock. The blood jade wasn't as flashy at night so I fed it the trace amount of qì I could muster and the feathers of the phoenix lit up, an eerie splash of crimson and gold light sparking in the dark alley.

Mustache Boy's breath caught at the display and I stared at him coolly. The look of fear in his eyes was familiar and gratifying. This one knew who I was. He'd badly underestimated his prey and been caught flat-footed. If I had to kill him, his gravestone would say, HE UNDERESTIMATED THE BUTCHER.

"Are you still sure you want to do this?" I tapped my fingers lightly on Hachi's grip.

The ozone and cinnamon vanished and the three older boys began backing away from me. Good to see I hadn't lost my touch.

Round Face stared at his friends, the shock plain on his face. "What gives? Come on, we can take her!"

"Johnny, shut up, just—"

Johnny Round Face took a step toward me, small knife held high, his eyes wild. "No! This is some trick, some test! I can do this!"

He lunged at me, knife swinging. I sidestepped and drew Hachi from my belt in one motion. The blade sang its high note in the evening calm. I whipped my sword across my body and struck the boy's wrist with the flat of the blade. He cried out and his knife dropped to the ground. I pivoted and followed the boy's motion past me, planting my boot in the small of his back and riding him down to the concrete. He slammed facedown into the asphalt, his breath exploding out of him. The other boys hadn't moved a muscle.

I rested the flat of my blade against the young boy's cheek as he lay beneath me, gasping for breath. I leaned in close, putting my weight behind the sword. The one eye I could see bulged, the whites huge and stark.

I ran my finger across his throat, my meaning clear. "Tonight's your lucky night, Johnny."

I yanked the collar of his shirt down, exposing his pale, sweaty neck. The broad Louie tattoo with its distinctive number nine curled across his shoulders and was still shiny and speckled with blood. This must have been his first night out. Hell of an initiation.

Suddenly the boy I was kneeling on looked very young, and very afraid. The adrenaline waned, and a wave of fatigue washed over me. I just wanted a hot shower and a good night's sleep, but I couldn't have these punks coming back later. I wouldn't be around every time some punk Claw decided Popo looked like an easy target. They'd started it, but I had to finish it. One more time I'd call on my bloody reputation and try to give Popo a little coverage from these punks.

The persona was easy to slip back into. Too easy. The formal words tumbled out with no effort at all and tasted like ashes and regret. "Despite your transgression, it would be most unlucky to spill your guts on the Herbalist's doorstep. You and your friends will remember that the Butcher is watching over her. Run along, Johnny, and tell everyone about this night—the night the Butcher let you keep all your limbs."

Johnny whimpered, the sound loud in the now quiet alley. I let him up and he scrabbled against the asphalt like a crab before getting upright. Mustache Boy and his cohorts started running and Johnny turned to follow. He gave me one last look, his eyes wild with fear, his panting breaths leaving puffs of air in the cool night.

Satisfaction at rousting these thugs had my lips curving upward before reason and shame flooded me. It was always like this. Fighting felt good. Their fear equaled respect and respect felt good. Right. Not one minute after I'd vowed in the car ride over to stop living up to the moniker of the Butcher of Beijing and I was tapping my sword and threatening pimply faced kids. The ones who called me the Butcher were right about me. I was still a monster.

Breaking my blade and hiding out halfway across the world for the last two years hadn't changed me at all.

# THE HERBALIST

Most alleys smelled like a gag-inducing mixture of grease, asphalt, and dumpster. Not the Herbalist's place. The back door of her spa was painted an auspicious red, and the stoop was pristine, likely power washed daily. Outsiders might marvel at how clean it was but Jiārén like me knew exactly why there was no odor behind Popo's shop beyond the lingering wisps of cologne from the departed Claws.

Popo's peculiar talent stripped all trace elements from a host and its surroundings, rendering everything odorless. And that was exactly why I was here. In her tender care, all traces of this hibagon would vanish, keeping our Jiārén quirks hidden from the outside world. That talent made her the Herbalist.

I scrubbed my hand on my filthy pants, trying to get the blood off, and then pulled out my phone and called Popo.

"Vitality Health Services is closed. Please call again during our normal business hours. We will be open at ten a.m.," a pleasant voice intoned.

Well, at least I'd tried to call first. I pounded on the door, two sharp thuds, because any more than two is impolite.

I waited. The alley was quiet now with the thugs disposed of.

I heard the soft shuffle of footsteps and then a click. I lifted my head up at the soft click and cursed at my carelessness. Shiny new cameras perched above the doorway. I'd let myself get distracted with the Claws and hadn't checked my surroundings thoroughly. It was good I'd retired from being the Blade—an oversight like that two years ago could have cost me my head, literally.

The door opened revealing a pristine white hallway lined with tall chrome utility racks filled with fluffy white towels. The aroma of cucumber wafted out, and tiny Popo smiled up at me.

She'd worn the same hairstyle for decades, a short bob with a tucked-under curl. She looked the same as my first visit when my father had brought me here as a young girl. Despite her age, her fair skin glowed with health and she wore a cozy-looking pink cashmere turtleneck. Her petite frame made me feel like a giant even though I was only a bit above average height. Her aura glowed a soft nimbus of warm yellow, hazy and wide. The Jiārén I ran with learned to lock down their auras early to prevent enemies from gaining any advantage over them. Popo's Vermillion Bird talent wasn't going to get her killed. Advertising that she was a gāo-level purification talent was good for her business.

"Hi, Popo, enjoy the show?" I gestured to the new cameras, a little salty now that I knew she had likely watched the confrontation from a bank of video monitors inside.

She craned her neck, making a show of checking the entire length of the alley. She gave me a sly smile. "Thanks for taking out the trash."

I resisted the urge to grit my teeth. "Sure. My pleasure."

She clucked and squinted at the area just above my head. "Does this mean you're finally our Sentinel? If so, it's about time."

Ugh. Not this again. I shook my head.

She sighed. "Well, I don't see why not. You're already doing all the work anyway, but with none of the benefits."

It wasn't clear to me that there were any benefits to being the Sentinel of San Francisco. Being at the beck and call of the Soong Clan had been hard enough. I'd already learned too many sharp lessons about the true cost of power. Yoked to a whole city of demanding magical elites? My neck chafed at the thought. No, thank you.

I stepped closer and loomed over her.

Popo stepped back, seeming to take in my bloody clothing. Her eyes traveled to my swords but she didn't comment.

"Did you bring me something?" Her dark eyes sparkled with interest.

Popo put up with watching me sweat and heave the hibagon corpse across the parking lot until I got the beast up to her doorstep. When I paused for breath at the back door, the expression on her face was equal parts disappointment, exasperation, and impatience.

As I mopped a lovely mix of my own sweat and hibagon blood off my neck, Popo sniffed and tapped a sequence of buttons on a panel just inside the door. I squatted down to pick up the corpse again when she waved her hand and shooed me away.

"Āiya. Enough."

I rocked back onto my heels and rested. In a moment, heavy steps approached from inside and a towering shadow appeared behind Popo.

Popo spoke without looking behind her. "Ah Péng, please take Emiko's specimen to the old freezer. I think it will need to be cleaned before we can work on it."

The shadow eased around Popo's petite form and unfolded out of the doorway. Péng "Bill" Fong checked in somewhere around six foot eight, with arms and legs thickened by years of heavy labor. His stained blue coveralls stretched tight over a massive barrel chest and gut. The white lab coat he wore over the coveralls stopped comically short at his waist, the buttons nowhere near closing. Despite his massive frame his round face was almost cherubic, and even at this late hour, he still had his trademark smile. Since his Chinese name literally meant *big,* I called him Big Bill.

Big Bill dropped to one knee next to the plastic-wrapped corpse and offered me a massive fist. "Hey, Emiko, working late?"

I grinned and bumped knuckles with him, my own fist looking delicately small for once in my life. "Yeah, you know how it is sometimes."

He slid his massive hands under the beast and grunted as he straightened up, lifting the corpse with no more effort than lifting a bag of groceries. His pale red aura flickered and the faint herbal smell of Big Bill's Dragon Limb talent washed over me. I'd seen it before, but it was still stunning, and I didn't know exactly how much of Big Bill's strength was his muscle, and how much was his White Tiger talent. Given that his aura had only small tinges of color around the edges, I leaned toward muscle rather than talent.

I ran back to my Jeep and grabbed the bag with the hibagon's head. When I brought it back to Big Bill he stuck out a pinky and I looped the bag handles over his meaty finger.

Big Bill turned and walked through the back door, calling over his shoulder, "I'll have it ready in ten minutes."

My shoulders sagged in relief. I was swearing off monster cleanup permanently. The last thing I needed was more blood on my hands or my nightmares getting any worse. I needed to keep my blade and my Jeep clean from Jiārén matters. The rich scent of blood wafted toward me as Bill turned away and I nearly stumbled as the stench scrambled my senses. Yes, this was definitely the last time.

Popo waved me in through the door. "Come on, it's been too long since you visited. I can show you the new lab while Ah Péng cleans up."

She opened another door, revealing a narrow hallway lined with more stainless steel shelves stacked with more clean linens. As we walked, Popo waved her hands before her and the illusion of the hallway fell apart like cobwebs.

The thing that had been bothering me finally percolated to the surface. "Popo, when did you install security cameras?"

Popo's slippered feet swished quietly along the floor. "Oh, two, maybe three weeks ago."

A little chill settled in my chest. "How long have those Claws been shaking you down?"

She barked a laugh and waved a hand. "Claws. Please. I don't know why Dai Lou allows them to call themselves that. They're just hatchlings. Dumb enough to think that going after an old lady will earn some of Dai Lou's attention."

Despite her casual laugh, lines of tension creased her face. She was disturbed but trying to downplay it. The annoyance I'd felt earlier at seeing the thugs at her back door came rushing back, overriding my normal reluctance to get involved.

"Popo, why didn't you call me?"

She turned to me, a sly look in her eye. "Oh? I thought you weren't the Sentinel."

I grunted. She had a point, why had I claimed her alley as my territory? Stupid. I'd turned down her invitation for Chinese New Year festivities to distance myself and now here I was offering up protection services. I needed my head examined. But that had been for a party. This was something else altogether—something I couldn't ignore.

"Popo, I'm serious. I don't have to be the Sentinel to help you run off some punk Louies poaching outside their lines."

She stopped and turned to face me. "Emiko. You need to be smarter than that. As much as I enjoyed your show outside, it's going to cause problems."

I swallowed hard. I hadn't thought about that. I thought I'd been helping her. I hung my head and started to apologize.

She held up a hand, cutting me off. "What do you think will

happen if you start beating up Louie Claws, even if they are beyond Lotus Lane? Hmm? How long will Dai Lou stand by and let a
young woman continue to cause the Louies to lose face?"

They were all about face. Reputation.

I thought about the logo the Louie Claws wore—the stylized
nine. Nine was an odd choice for any Jiārén clan. We cleaved to the
Eight Sons of the Dragon and never spoke the name of the ninth for
he was the betrayer and why we were cast out from the Realm.

Our entire society revolved around the Eight Sons. We had the
Bā Tóu who governed us, the Eight Heads, and we had Bā Shǒu,
the enforcers. Each Bā Tóu member acted as Custodian of a Hoard
cache. Unfortunately for me, my father was Bā Tóu and my mother
was Bā Shǒu. Duty to the Hoard and our eight Dragon gods governed our lives. So much so that I barely ever saw my mother as she
was always away on Bā Shǒu business. My mother was notorious
amongst Jiārén. If she paid your clan a visit, knocking on your door
was a mere courtesy—she had the power to rip into your Realm
Fragment and seize your Hoard treasure. Her Void-walking gift
was revered and reviled in equal parts. It also kept her hopping to
the tune of the Bā Shǒu as she enforced the Laws of Lóng Jiārén.

The Louies were Hoard Custodians and Ray Louie sat on the
Bā Tóu with my father, which is why I couldn't understand why
the Louie clan embraced the nine for its symbol. It made me wary
of the Louies, and I'd taken out my frustration on those Claws in
the alley.

It had been a mistake.

I wanted to say something, but she was right. Putting myself at
odds with the oldest Jiārén clan in San Francisco was stupid. If I
started making waves, I needed to be ready to deal with the consequences.

This was my father's realm, the political games, the maneu-
vering, the whispered deals. My father excelled at using everyone in our clan to his best advantage, including me. After my

first spectacular failure my parents had dropped me off with the Jōkōryūkai. Six years with Ogata-sensei had transformed me from awkward teenager to one of my father's sharpest weapons. But when all you had was a sword, every problem looked like a neck.

Popo reached up and cupped her hand along my jaw, the touch more tender than any human contact I'd had in a long time. "Emiko, you've had a hard life, and I think coming to San Francisco hasn't made it any easier. Your swords alone cannot protect you or me from what is coming."

The shift in her tone took me off guard, but before I could ask she resumed walking down the cool white hallway. "You should make some friends. You have been here too long to not have more friends."

"I have . . . a . . . friend." My business partner counted as a friend, right?

Popo turned the look on me again. "The Tran twins went to Lóng Kǒu with you, didn't they?"

My recollection of the Trans was a little fuzzy. The Tran twins had been a year ahead of me and a powerhouse from their very first year at Lóng Kǒu, their Azure Dragon talents amply showcasing the Jiārén belief that we could shape our world to our will. Based on my parentage, I had also entered as an Azure Dragon, but I had little else in common with the Trans. Fiona with her French fashion and Freddy with his showy talent. I had to walk over the bridges to get to the Lóng Kǒu halls. Too pedestrian for Freddy Tran. He had to use his talent and make it look like he was flying over the lake. "Um, we didn't exactly run in the same circles."

"And that matters, why?"

Again, I didn't have a response that bore speaking aloud. Hoard Custodian families and their offspring were all accustomed to a great degree of success in all aspects of their lives. My failure from Lóng Kǒu had been just the first of several unexpected disappointments for my parents. The Trans had sailed through Lóng Kǒu at

the top of their class, as befit the heirs of a Hoard Custodian family.
I doubted the Trans remembered anything about me other than my
bloody tenure as the Blade of Soong. Not that any of this mattered
to Popo.

Popo's face showed the self-satisfied smile of meddling matri-
archs the world over. "Good. It's settled then. Go reintroduce yourself to the Trans."

I mumbled my assent, wondering how our talk had wandered so
far afield, and why Popo was taking such an interest in my social
life now.

Popo continued, "Don't worry about me, Emiko. You and I are
much alike. They always underestimate us." She smiled and patted
her side. Through the fabric of her sweater I saw the outline of a
small pistol holstered under her left arm.

It didn't surprise me that she owned a gun, but the fact that she
was carrying right now was a little disconcerting. I hadn't considered how dangerous it might be for Jiārén to live and work in parts
of the city that weren't controlled by the clans. We knew how to
avoid scrutiny from Júwàirén, outsiders. No-look spells shielded
our weapons, our storefronts, and most of our activities so that outsiders saw what they expected to see.

It was tragic that the biggest threat might be from our own people.
I doubted that Popo would fire the gun in anything but the direst
of circumstances, but it bothered me that she needed to take things
into her own hands. Just having the gun exposed her to risking Dì
Èr Tiáo, the Second Law. The second most important law among
our people forbade us from killing each other unless justified. Unsurprisingly, powerful families like my own were very good at jus-
tifying a wide range of our actions. Popo, however, didn't have the
backing of a Hoard clan. I understood her needs, but I wasn't sure
what I could do about it.

My brooding brought us to the end of the hallway. The illusion had
disappeared completely and the walls were mere concrete, covered

with gray industrial paint. In spite of its appearance, the hallway still smelled antiseptically clean. An unfamiliar door barred the end of the hallway.

Popo caught my elbow in my moment of hesitation. "Don't worry, this is just the new lab."

She opened the door and we passed into a small air lock where clean, water-scented air rushed around us. Popo's talent was comforting, familiar, and removed any contaminants before we entered her lab. I exited the lock and stopped, stunned at the sight before me.

She laughed at the look on my face. "Yes, it has been a while, hasn't it?" Her dark eyes twinkled with delight.

I closed my mouth and tried to take it all in. The lab was tidy, small, but clearly laid out with function in mind. The walls and floors were pristine white. LED strips gridded across the ceiling bathed the room in cool light. Stainless steel countertops ran the length of the room. Light glinted off glass and steel everywhere I looked. Popo's lab made the Apple Store look like a low-rent thrift shop.

The tables carried a mysterious array of boxy machines and fluid-filled beakers. One counter held nothing but spinning centrifuges. A young woman about my age kept a watchful eye over them and made meticulous marks on her clipboard. She glanced up at us and her eyes widened in alarm. Maybe it was the swords or maybe it was all the hibagon blood. I probably didn't smell great, either.

Popo took my arm and gently guided me through the lab. "You should visit more often. I'm sure I can find something for your blocked meridians."

I barked a laugh, almost a sneeze. "Wow! I had no idea. Popo, this is amazing!"

Popo brushed off the compliment. "It's nothing. Just keeping up with the times. Do you know how hard it is to find apprentices who can break down a carcass? Or even find one who wants to?"

She waved an arm at all her high-tech equipment. "This was as inevitable as death and taxes, dear. I just chose to not get left behind."

I nodded and saw Popo in a new light. My estimation of her had gone up tremendously in the last five minutes. Apparently Lóng Jiārén were not all as feudal as my father. The Soong estate had two faces. One we showed the public, a sprawling mansion lodged in the hillside of Atami in Shizuoka prefecture, about an hour and a half from Tokyo. Peel back the curtain and those keyed to our blood could enter our Realm Fragment. There my father ruled his domain like an emperor from a lost era.

We exited the lab through a heavy door on the opposite wall and entered a room where the air was thick with humidity. Low tables held rows of hydroponics bays basking under matching rows of grow lights. Exotic-looking plants of all colors and shapes filled the planters to bursting.

I stopped next to a squat tree with delicate pink flowers. As I brushed my fingers over the peach blossoms a gentle tingle of power tickled my fingertips. I looked back to Popo and raised my eyebrows.

She shrugged. "One of my oldest projects. Still haven't found the right growing conditions, but I'm getting closer every year. Can you imagine if I can get it right?"

If Popo could cultivate Immortality Peaches she would instantly become the most famous herbalist in history. Even my aunt Lulu with her prodigious talents couldn't produce those. I wasn't sure success in this arena would be a good thing. But worries about mythic peaches dropped away as we approached the door exiting the grow room. This door was heavily built, like the others, but seemed to radiate power and menace, if a door could somehow be intimidating.

Because this one was a Door.

Jiārén might look like Wàirén, but we were different. Jiārén came from the Realm, a world drenched in mystical Dragon power. Our people lived under the power of those dragons, and our constant exposure changed us over the eons, until we were all living embodiments of Dragon power.

Two millennia ago, the betrayal of the Ninth Dragon brought down the Cataclysm that forced our ancestors to flee to our new adopted home. We survived and managed to bring small pieces of home with us. Not keepsakes, but actual Fragments of our home world, accessible through Doors, keyed to our talents. These Fragments were isolated islands of the Realm, separated from each other by an endless Void of chaos and primal power. The only way to cross the Void was with the help of a Door.

I knew of exactly one person who could cross the Void without a Door, but I didn't like to think about my mother and her dark talents.

As I looked, the border around the Door flickered, the frame seeming to waver like heat haze in the desert. Of course. I should have remembered Popo had a Door. I gritted my teeth. I could do this. It would be ugly, and embarrassing, but I'd live.

Popo took hold of my hand and squeezed. I closed my eyes for a moment, centering myself. I opened my eyes and found Popo still looking at me, her bright eyes intent. I took a deep breath and blew it out slowly. "Okay, I'm ready."

She placed her hand on the knob and her aura flared, surrounding her body with a halo of warm yellow light. I'd always thought of Popo's aura as a friendly color. Maybe because most Vermillion Bird talents weren't combat oriented, focused instead on alchemy and energy purification. The scent of clean running water filled the hallway as her talent swelled and activated the Door, opening a passage to take us from this world to her Fragment of the Realm. The Door swung open, and raw energy blazed from the open doorway like heat from a blast furnace. The chaotic color and not-space of the Void between worlds filled my vision like static on a dead television. Vertigo gripped me, upending my balance.

With almost no aura of my own to buffer the maelstrom of raw energy around me, Crossing to a Realm Fragment was always a brutal experience. Imagine the most intense sensory overload, combined with stomach-churning nausea. Jiārén who used Doors sparked their talent before the Crossing, using their aura as a shield to blunt the worst of the onslaught. As the Broken Tooth of Soong Clan, the talentless dud, I had no such luxury. The furnace-bright power slammed through the Door and fried me.

The Void between worlds was an endless, roiling sea of chaos and potential, the raw power that birthed gods and worlds. I stepped through.

# BACKROOM DEALINGS

Crossing squeezed my insides out like a tube of toothpaste. Popo's hand clutched mine and my feet landed on solid ground. Gravity found me again and my legs collapsed. I barely caught myself with my hands before the bile raced up my throat and spewed out of my mouth. I coughed and hacked, the acid burning my sinuses. I hated Crossing to a Realm Fragment.

For most Jiārén, traveling to a Fragment was liberating. In the Fragments of our home world, our talents could run free, the dragon within us unfurling its wings. In a Fragment, we were not bound by notions of political or geological boundaries. We did not identify with nations. We were Jiārén, descended from the very dragons themselves.

In our new world we kept our power hidden from prying Wàirén eyes. Returning to the Realm, even just a piece of it, returned us to our natural state of being where we didn't have to hide our talents from outsiders. Me, not so much. Realm Fragments only reminded me of my failure as a daughter and my failure to the clan.

Popo patted me gently on the back as I regained control of myself. I blinked the tears away, appalled at the large puddle of sick I'd just spit up onto her spotless floor.

"Popo, I'm so sorry—"

"Mo si, mo si. Āiya, get up, girl."

She grabbed me under the arm and helped me to my feet. Wow, she was a lot stronger than she looked. She reached up and brushed some stray hair away from my face, her mouth curling into a beaming smile. "I didn't work this long and hard to still have to clean the floors. Come. I'll send someone along to clean up."

We finally reached the walk-in freezer that I still associated with Popo's talent. It looked much as I remembered it, albeit smaller, and much cleaner. Creaking chains hung from the ceiling, ending in pointed meat hooks large enough to hang a full-grown bull. The chains were spotlessly clean. Glass jars lined the east wall from floor to ceiling, all curiously empty. I remembered this room as Popo's repository, where she stored raw materials before processing. I wondered where everything had gone; Popo never threw anything out she thought might be useful someday.

The real treats hung on the north and west walls. A dread assortment of stainless steel cleavers, bone saws, blades, hooks, and extra lengths of chain, each implement clean and bright, the handles worn smooth from decades of use. Enough implements to make even the most dedicated sadist happy.

About the only nice thing about the frigid locker was that it kept the smell to a minimum. Tonight's special, my hibagon, lay across two steel work tables Big Bill had pushed together to hold the massive carcass. Popo stood across the table from me, her breath puffing out in pale white mist. She donned a heavy work apron and pulled up her sleeves, revealing a wide white jade bracelet on her wrist. She whipped out blue nitrile gloves, pulling them on with a snap and covering the bracelet. A small, bone-handled knife appeared from the front pocket of her rubber apron and made quick work of the plastic bags, laying my handiwork out for us under the harsh LED lights. I admired the knife briefly. Japanese ceramic, probably as sharp as my swords.

Popo's gaze slid over the carcass, her sharp eyes missing nothing. Without preamble she lifted the beast's head, taking a deep whiff of the matted fur. I gagged.

"This one will be a lot of purification work, I may not be able to salvage the organs." She dropped the head with a plunk. Her hands roamed over the hibagon's torso, poking and prodding, feeling for the internal organs, identifying and quantifying them as surely as any MRI. She spoke softly, without looking up from her work. "Did the city ask this of you?"

I stifled a groan. Why was everyone so interested in me taking another job? "No, Popo. Ito-san asked for me. I'm not the Sentinel."

She tutted quietly under her breath as she continued her examination. "Such a shame. Your mother would be so proud of you."

I highly doubted that, but decorum dictated that I keep my mouth shut. My mother had expressed many things about me, but pride in her elder daughter had seldom made the list. There were only eight Sentinels, and even if I became the ninth, which I did not see happening, my mother would be the first person to point out that I was the wrong person for the task. My father on the other hand would be extremely pleased that I was doing something he considered worthy and would no doubt take all the credit for it if I did assume the mantle of the Sentinel.

But San Francisco's magic had been getting harder and harder to tune out, like an obnoxious neighbor's late-night party. Odd sensations, almost like premonitions, bled into my perceptions at random times. Last week the sensation of rolling ocean waves had nearly toppled me from a ladder. Other times I'd been nearly overwhelmed by the press of a surging crowd of pedestrians, even though I was alone in my bed. It was irritating at best, maddening at worst.

All I could find in my research about Sentinels was about as reliable as a wiki entry. Cities with enough magical mass gained sentience after many years. Sentient cities chose someone from the local Lóng Jiārén community to become its Sentinel, a proxy for the city's prerogatives. No one understood the selection process. Sentinels weren't like Superman, flying over the city in a blaze of glory, but everyone just accepted that they existed. Sentinels kept their lore secret, which only grew their legends.

I had no idea what it meant to be a Sentinel. The cost, the responsibility, how much it could wreck my carefully rebuilt life were all unknowns. Every fiber of my being told me to run screaming in the opposite direction of the Sentinel mantle.

Popo took my silence for unease because she changed her tactics. "Your father is well?"

I nearly laughed. I hadn't seen my father in two years, since I'd left Tokyo. Our last video call had been three months ago. I was clearly an ungrateful offspring. My father texted me often and I usually ghosted him when he called. As far as I could tell from calls with my brother and texts from my father, he remained healthy as a horse, and his machinations in the Bā Tóu Council continued unabated. "He's well."

Popo turned to me, a knowing look in her eye. "You should visit him more often, Emiko. I'm sure he misses you terribly. Your mother, too."

This was not where I wanted this conversation to go. "Work's just been really busy, Popo. I mean . . ." I held my hands out, indicating the hibagon. As if I were being swamped under an invasion of yeti. I mean, I *had* been busy. My salvage and reclamation niche had proved lucrative.

Popo tutted and studied me a bit longer. "You look so much like your mother, but you have your father's build."

I winced at the backhanded compliment. My mother was slim and elegant, and half a head taller than my father. Me, not so much. I had never attained my mother's height, topping out instead at five and a half feet. Though I was lean on top, my lower body was as muscled as a champion ice skater. My mother possessed the classically beautiful face of all the Hiroto women, creamy fair skin, straight small noses, and delicate chins. I didn't see the resemblance, but then I also studiously avoided my mother.

Popo turned back to her inspection of the yeti corpse, her expression giving nothing away. I had a sneaking suspicion Father would be hearing about this visit. After another minute of quiet poking she seemed satisfied with her findings and stood, groaning as her back straightened. "Still, I'm glad you came to visit."

She continued, "I won't charge you anything for the purification work, however, it takes a lot of work to dispose of a creature of this size—"

Her pause was an invitation to start bargaining. She'd take it off my hands! I wanted to shout to the heavens. The prospect of dragging it back to my Jeep was unbearable.

"—but I'll need two hundred dollars from you to help pay for Ah Péng to carve it up."

Really? It was after midnight. She wanted this song and dance now? It wasn't about the money—it was about advantage. I could never allow myself to be seen as a mark. Not even with Popo. I bowed my head, speaking deliberately. "Popo, I can't possibly pay you to break down the carcass."

She sighed long and low, her disappointment in me obvious. "I am old and not as strong as I used to be and you expect me to carve up this beast by myself?"

I scoured my memory frantically to up my bargaining game. "You can afford to pay Big Bill to do the hard work because you're going to make a killing on this. The freeze-dried liver from the hibagon will give a boost to earth elemental talents."

Her deep-set black eyes lit up. "Soong siu ze, how many earth talents do you know in San Francisco?"

So now I was just *little missy*. She was doing that on purpose, trying to rile me up. It's true that we didn't have many earth talents here—too many unstable soils. But she was toying with me because I knew she had clientele all over the world.

I gestured to the hibagon's enormous body. "Look at the size of this thing! It will yield a lot of product. Yang Si-fu in Singapore speaks highly of the quality of your products."

Popo cocked her head and watched me, a small smile playing on her lips.

I blundered on. "I'm sure that Yang Si-fu and his family would be grateful for your skill in rendering this ingredient for them."

She patted me gently on the arm. "I may not be able to guarantee the purity of this product."

Now she was just fishing for compliments. "Popo! Don't be so modest. You are the best purifier on this continent, if not the world. I trust you to render the ingredients perfectly."

She preened for just a moment before resuming her sport. "I do work hard on my purification, which means I am more tired and must rely on Ah Péng to assist me after."

I bit my cheek to kill the urge to sigh. I was bone-tired, and the chill of the locker made my thoughts sluggish. My business partner, Tessa, and I had an early morning appointment with Professor . . . Professor . . . Some professor at the university. I still had to track down the hibagon's den, too, after that. But it was clear that Popo was just warming up.

I reached for my jade pendant, stroking it absently. Its weight and shape comforted me as I tried to work out how to best finish with Popo so I could go home.

"Popo, you're right. I've been terribly inconsiderate of you. I can't possibly leave you this specimen. I will take it to the Nakamoto Clan for a cleansing fire ritual." The fire ritual would cremate the massive corpse but I would have to answer a ton of questions and dealing with the imperious Oliver Nakamoto annoyed me. But the Nakamoto Clan was willing to do business with me, and Popo knew it.

She threw up her hands in alarm. "Do you know what time it is? Far too late for a young woman to be going into that part of town. I will take it off your hands for five hundred dollars."

Her markup would be twenty times that—per ounce. $500 for a

night of sitting out in the cold and dragging this monster across the park was practically like getting robbed. But Popo would have me haggling in the meat locker for another hour if she had her way. I needed to get to the point.

"The least I can do is help you break it down, Popo."

I grabbed the biggest cleaver I could reach off the back wall. I swayed a bit under the weight as I unhooked it. Wow, I was really tired.

If I hadn't been looking for it, I think I would have missed her eyelid twitching. But she was a veteran of this kind of thing, and other than the eye twitch, her poker face didn't slip.

"No need, no need. As you said, I can have Ah Peng help me with that. Why are we arguing over a few dollars? We are Jiārén! Let's go up front and I'll get you your money. We missed you over New Year's! I still have your red envelope here for you! Come, I'll show you out through the front."

I followed her out of the freezer, hanging up the cleaver on my way out. I wasn't quite home free yet, I still had to get through the Door.

Popo took my hand and squeezed gently, her crinkling eyes once again full of grandmotherly kindness. "Ready?"

I took a deep breath and nodded. She turned the handle and my vision blurred, the door and walls around us melting into meaningless noise. Vertigo grabbed me again and threatened to sweep my legs out from under me until Popo squeezed my hand again. I squeezed back and the world righted itself. Her voice came to me, faint, like I was listening through layers of dense fabric.

"Step through . . ."

For the second time in an hour I found myself on my knees, spitting up bile onto the pristine spa flooring. I crawled out of her broom closet and let her close the Door behind me.

"Emiko, are you okay?"

I groaned and sat up. Slowly. I'd pushed too hard. Dragging that stupid hibagon through the park. Then two Crossings in the space of an hour. My qì was drained. I could feel the city again, its magic tingling in the soles of my feet. It was strangely comforting after the thick haze of the Fragment.

Popo reappeared with a small ceramic cup in her hands. She pushed it at me and made me drink. The bitter liquid scalded my tongue but it soothed the tightness in my chest as it went down. I finished the cup and thanked her. She nodded in approval when she saw that I'd drained the cup and then handed me a small chaser. The little bright pink cylinder of haw flakes brought a smile to my face and I ripped open the package to pop the small candy disks in my mouth. It made me feel like a little kid again coming to her shop with Father.

She took my right hand and soft warmth spread into my palm from her fingertips. She turned my hand this way and that and then clucked. "Emiko, you need to take your magnesium."

I shrugged.

Her eyes crinkled into a smile. "Here you go."

She pressed a small red envelope with flowing gold script into my hands. I wouldn't open it, but I could tell she'd paid me more than $500. I mean, she was still going to make a killing on everything she'd harvest from the carcass, but at least I'd tried to participate in the time-honored tradition of bargaining. As tired as I was, I had acquitted myself decently and was happy to let her have this round.

Then she tucked a small brown apothecary-style glass bottle with a silver label in my pocket. "It will help you sleep and heal your cuticles."

I thanked her with a small bow and headed to the door. The lights went out behind me as I exited the spa. The alley was dark and quiet now—no evidence remained of my earlier skirmish with the Louie Claws. I patted the bottle in my pocket and wondered if I had bottled water in the car. I couldn't care less about my cuticles but I sure could use some sleep.

It was late when I exited the Herbalist's storefront on Irving Street. Popo had stuffed twelve hundred-dollar bills into the red envelope. That would definitely cover gas and my dry-cleaning bill with plenty left over for groceries and tea. I looked at the bottle she'd given me. Magnesium. Huh. I'd have to try it. Maybe it would help with the nightmares. Dreamless sleep was a rare commodity these days.

Ignoring the stains on the driver's seat, I got back into my Jeep and let my head fall back against the headrest with a thump. A hot shower was going to feel so good.

Two Crossings had drained me. This was part of why I had left the family business. Hard to be the Blade when you were barfing your guts out. The main part had been all the killing, which had come all too easily to me. I scrubbed at my cheek, remembering the hibagon's hot blood on my skin. And . . . maybe . . . I'd gone a little too hard on the Louie kids. Two years since breaking my sword and I was still falling back into the same old patterns.

Being the Blade meant never having to second-guess my actions. The Head led the clan. The Blade served the clan. My father only needed to point and I carried out his will. Often that meant swinging Sword of Truth, the ringing steel drowning out the cries of our enemies. Only now, without the chilling clarity of the sword and the voices within, could I wonder if they had ever been our enemies at all. Maybe they were only my victims, and pawns in my father's machinations. Pawns like me.

I thought about what Popo said, too, about the Louies. I'd avoided conflict with the Louie Clan primarily by staying out of their way. It wasn't hard since they controlled most of Lotus Lane and many of those merchants refused to do business with me. It had forced me to expand my network of suppliers. My father had a congenial enough business relationship with Dai Lou, but I went out of my way to avoid asking my father for help or a favor. With men like my father or Dai Lou, it was best not to get into debt.

As if on cue, my phone buzzed.

I took my phone out of my pocket for the first time since entering the spa. Another text from Father. He was uncanny.

**Daughter. You have not called.**

My father would try again soon if guilting me to call him out of filial piety failed. My fingers hovered over the glowing phone screen, the blank reply space silently mocking me. I had ghosted him three times. Experience told me to expect a text from my brother soon. One thing I did not have to worry about was my mother trying to reach me. She hadn't spoken to me since I'd broken Sword of Truth two years ago. A chill walked across my heart and the darkened parking lot suddenly seemed ominous and foreboding. This late at night the only others out were a couple of homeless listlessly pushing rickety shopping carts. Getting home to Dogpatch and behind my protective wards sounded like an excellent idea.

With the activity of the evening concluded, the text from my father reminded me how my whole clan was an ocean away. Keeping busy meant I didn't think about eating in the kitchen with Uncle Jake and Lulu Āyí and joking with my father's soldiers. I didn't have to see their disappointment that I was no longer their Blade. My father and mother had given me two bites at the apple and I'd disappointed them both times. I didn't expect a third shot at redemption.

I clutched my jade pendant for comfort, the sharp edges and ridges of the carved foo lion a familiar worrying ground for my fingers. I hesitated only a moment before closing my eyes and humming a familiar tune. My meager qì flowed into the stone and activated the talent contained within. A wisp of green smoke curled around my pendant and the welcome smell of sawdust and white pepper hit my nostrils.

Two hundred pounds of foo lion appeared sprawled across the front seats and center console, forepaws digging mercilessly into my battered thighs. The beast shook his massive crimson head, fluffing out a golden mane of curling hair. His jaws opened and he yawned hugely, pink tongue flicking out and licking the tips of deadly curving canines. The lion's eyes fixed on me and his mouth opened again, tongue lolling out and laving across my cheek.

"Ew! Gross, I'm covered in blood!"

Bāo ignored my protests and nuzzled closer, mashing his face and mane into my neck. My arms reacted automatically, circling around his warm body, my hands digging deep into his thick mane. I squeezed him tight, the comforting rumble of his purr vibrating against my chest.

Some people have cats. I have a lion.

I stayed like that for a long moment, holding Bāo until the homesickness passed. He sensed when it had passed and wriggled out from under my arms. I yelped as he pressed down on my legs, his claws popping out and stabbing my thighs. I batted him playfully across the head and wrestled him into the passenger seat. The seat belt wouldn't fit on him, but I trusted that he would be able to survive any trouble I might find between here and home.

"What do you say, boy? Go home and take a nap?"

Bāo yawned again and sat back, giving me a look that asked why I wasn't driving already. I hadn't whistled him up in months, and the first thing he wanted was a nap. Lion or no, he was still a cat.

# GRAPPLING

*Drip, drip, drip.*

*Bright red blood trickles from my father's eye, slewing sideways across his ashen skin. It makes a track that ends at the point of his cheekbone before dripping to the paved steps. The smell of sawdust and pepper is so thick in my nose that I think I may choke on it. I can barely breathe through the smell. White smoke drifts down the stairs, wispy fingers reaching for me.*

*Sound crashes around me, Lulu Āyí's racking sobs and Uncle Jake's grunts of pain. My body shakes, tossed left to right, and I float up and out of my body.*

*I am small, so small, and the pool of blood around my neck grows larger by the moment. I am lying at the steps to the front house, beneath the pair of stone lions that bracket the front door. I love these lions, especially the one with the orb under his paw. Father is lying on the steps, too, and something is wrong with his eyes.*

*Sugi, my father's favorite animate, a large wooden wolf, shakes me in her jaws like a rag doll. The pain is bone deep. I stare up at the large lion. I wish he would save us.*

*Blood sprays.*

*Uncle Jake cries out in pain. His hand is in Sugi's mouth, trying to wrench the wolf's mouth open. Blood runs down his wrist from where the wooden fangs have pierced his skin.*

*My mother stands behind him, dressed in black, dressed for work, as always. She doesn't make a sound, just watches. Her hands are balled into fists inside her pockets.*

*Lulu Āyí is on her knees, sobbing into her hands. She's wearing her favorite gown, the one with the embroidered lotus flowers, and I want to tell her to get up, or the blood will stain the fabric. I reach for the lion, my hand small against the giant stone pedestal. Help us, please.*

*Sawdust and pepper shocks my senses again and my father's talent crackles in the air around us like impending lightning. Mother's eyes widen as Father's talent breaks into the open like a balloon bursting. One of the stone lions cracks with a sound like a tree splitting. An animal roar drowns out Āyí's cries and my mother turns away. A blur of red and gold rushes across my vision.*

*The sharp smell of burnt ginger pierces the sawdust and pepper like a ray of light and panic seizes my heart. I only know one thing that happens when I smell ginger. It is the smell of my mother leaving. I try to cry out but I cannot make a sound. My vision darkens around my mother, clad in black, shadows curling around her like smoke. She is shaking and clutching something in her hands. Blood drips from her fingertips.*

*Drip, drip, drip.*

*Uncle Jake bellows in pain and Sugi's jaws tighten around my neck. A lion roars above me.*

Years of training kept me from gasping as I rose through the haze of sleep, my heart thundering hard enough to hurt my ribs. I opened my eyes, which felt glued together. My arm was numb. When I could see, I realized I was lying on the hard bamboo floor of my living room and staring up at my ceiling fan. The alarm on my phone was going off. I didn't remember setting it. I didn't remember falling asleep, either. Around me lay an array of polished Tibetan singing bowls of varying sizes. Guess I'd fallen asleep in my sound circle. Not quite as restorative as qigong but the sound circle had helped.

I let my back relax against the floor and exhaled slowly, willing my heart to slow. My jaw hurt and the tightness along my jaw and neck told me I'd been grinding my teeth again. Revisiting my childhood was rarely pleasant, and this particular memory was one of the worst. The details blurred in my mind, the edges softening as sleep fled from me. I'd only asked my mother once about this dream, and she had made it clear that there was nothing to discuss. Ever. Her demeanor as she answered had been just as cold as she had been in my dream, and I had broken out into a cold sweat trying to meet her eyes.

When I tried to cover my face with my hands and wallow in my self-pity, I found my right arm pinned. I turned over to see Bāo's gigantic crimson head lying on my arm, his flowing gold mane spilled across the bamboo flooring. No wonder. His head alone had to weigh forty pounds. But his presence did the trick as always, banishing my dark thoughts and bringing me back to the present. I rolled into him and scratched him behind the ear.

"Bāo. Please give me back my arm."

He gave a soft huff in response and licked my face. Ouch! The rough feel of his tongue exfoliated my cheek better than any high-end Korean face scrub.

To my relief, he lumbered up and freed my arm. Bāo prowled around me on silent paws as I shut off the alarm on my phone. It was 5:15 a.m. The only light through my windows came from the streetlamps. My hips and shoulder blades creaked from the hours I'd been unconscious on the hardwood floor. I groaned and considered skipping out on my Brazilian jiujitsu class.

Before that indecision could take root, I rolled into a seated position and got up. There was no fighting it, years of Ogata-sensei's routine wasn't going to let me go back to sleep.

My place in the Dogpatch wasn't in the ritzy part of the city, but the cost differential had allowed me leeway to remodel the small Craftsman-style property to my security standards. I could have had a smaller place in the hip Potrero Hill district nearby but this mix of industrial and aging residential units in the less hilly part of town meant I could afford a double lot. All the money I made from my artifact and salvage work, which had been considerable, I poured into the security upgrades. My time as the Blade of Soong had made me a fair share of enemies. I couldn't afford *not* to put in the security.

The double lot meant I had a house in the front and a smaller cottage in the back. I used the front house as my office and IT cabinet, and relied on Júwàirén security to protect it. I'd painted the front house gray with white trim and installed a heavy security door with a reinforced frame. I painted the door bright blue to meld earth and water for feng shui. There was no reason a door couldn't stop a tank and look nice at the same time.

Bulletproof glass filled all the window frames, also reinforced. Over a stretch of two sweaty weeks I had ripped out the interior walls at likely breach points and reinforced those areas before replacing the drywall and repainting. While I had the walls open I had run heavy-gauge cable to the newly reinforced window and doorframes, giving me the option to electrify them at need.

A large concrete planter of black bamboo sat on the porch, next to a shoe rack for people to remove their shoes, and a collection of cute animal slippers that awaited any visitors.

The last upgrade was a work in progress. I'd already reinforced the downstairs bathroom into a small panic room, again with a heavy security door. The last step was to dig a bolt-hole leading to the in-law cottage at the rear of my property. I was reasonably sure I could hold up against a SWAT team in the front house, but if things fell apart I would fall back behind my inner layer of magical wards. Hey, it's not paranoia if they're really coming for you.

I lived in the smaller cottage in the back, which was easier to ward with Jiārén techniques. It cost an arm and leg to renew the wards every few months. Enchanted dragon mouth water spouts on the corners of the roof led to storm drains, which led to underground pipes matching the footprint of my cottage. The water spouts kept the water circulating at all times, creating a calming aural backdrop of white noise. The current also pushed elemental energy through the pipes, creating a field effect similar to an electric current. The pipes spiraled outward until they traced the entire perimeter of my property, making ever larger circles of power around my home. In this way, I had a protective perimeter around the cottage. Around my small Hoard. The perimeter was both early detection and home defense because I did not have enough qì to activate a Door to a Realm Fragment. Instead I'd improvised and this setup also played up my small gift. Very few people had my houndlike ability to smell Jiārén talents, either, so the added benefit was the cycling energy created a soothing scent of mint with an undertone of lemon—the water elemental's signature.

A pair of stone foo lions guarded the doorway of the cottage, looking incongruous in the xeriscape rock garden that separated the two houses. Unlike Bāo, these guardians were not animated. They had cameras in their eyes, and the heavy bases of their statues held a reservoir of earth elemental power. I checked on the statues each month, making sure the power hadn't degraded. These were my last line of defense if everything else failed. I'd only get to pull this trigger once and if I did, I'd never be coming back here.

I'd broken into plenty of homes as the Blade. I'd used my hard-earned knowledge to build a system I couldn't break. Someone could probably break my system, but if I couldn't imagine it, at least I slept well at night.

I turned the shower on and let the pressure pound away at my skin. I scrubbed vigorously with my Japanese nylon scrub cloth. I bought these in bulk from the Daiso and wondered how anyone functioned without them.

The aches and pains faded in the morning routine and I made my way to the kitchen to boil water. I desperately needed tea. Then I needed to get my butt in gear to my Brazilian jiujitsu class at Big G's Gym. Out of eight BJJ gyms in the city, the one closest to my house offered a convenient early morning class.

Years of kodokan judo had honed my body and the BJJ kept my street-fighting skills from deteriorating. Brazilian jiujitsu worked well for my body type and most Lóng Jiārén weren't good close-quarters fighters. If I were missing my weapons, my body was my best weapon and getting a Dragon talent to the ground usually meant I would come out the victor.

I stretched, my back still twinging from hauling that hibagon carcass. After two Crossings last night I suspected this morning was not going to be one of my better BJJ rolling sessions. I pulled out my heavy black cotton gi while my tea steeped.

After class, I would head over to the Phelan estate's stored files to continue my research. My business partner, Tessa, was counting on me to bring it home. I was sure there was a Hoard artifact in Phelan manor but I had to prove it to the executor of the estate to get access. I had clients who would pay handsomely for a Hoard artifact—including my own father.

For Jiārén, the ability to accumulate Hoard artifacts was their greatest hope at increasing their Dragon talent. It wasn't a guarantee since very few could tap into the capricious energy, but it was worth everything to Jiārén families.

I savored my last moments of peace with the tea, then stood and downed the dregs. Bāo watched my movements from my bed. Of course the lazy lion had taken my bed. He leapt off, all feline grace, and nudged my hip. I scratched under his chin and then decided to let him stay home and play guard lion.

I looked at Sword of Truth, cradled in an elegantly carved rack in my room. She housed the spirits of the Soong Blades before me and those spirits had guided my hand when I carried out my father's orders. They were quiet now but sometimes I'd hear them in my dreams. When I'd broken her and severed my connection as the Blade of the Soong Clan, I should have left the pieces behind, too. But I couldn't bring myself to do it and she'd come with me to San Francisco. And then I'd given her a place of honor in my home. You'd think I was having trouble letting go or something.

I did have boundaries. I didn't bring my sword to the gym. The idea of leaving her unattended in my gym bag was just . . . wrong. I wanted to be normal, but I wasn't. Normal people didn't agonize over ancient swords of power, did they? I'd worn Sword of Truth on my back almost every waking hour of my adult life. It would get easier to leave her, eventually. I hoped. I would only be gone an hour.

At 6 a.m. sharp, the small class of four students and the instructor at Big G's started the intense warm-up and exercises of Brazilian jiujitsu. The sounds of our thumping against the mats echoed in the huge industrial warehouse. Most BJJ classes were in the evening to accommodate folks after work. The early morning session was for purple belts and up. I didn't have a belt pursuant to international BJJ rules, but after a grappling session with me, the owner of the gym agreed that I could be placed in this advanced class.

I fit in with these type-A morning people more than I had expected. There was Ellie, the blond soft-spoken stay-at-home mom from posh Noe Valley, who would train until she was dripping with sweat, then calmly towel off before she pulled on a cashmere wrap sweater to jet home to take her kids to school. She and I were close in size and it was a testament to BJJ that we could hold our own against the bigger students, Marshall and Jorge. There were usually a few additional drop-in students, but I'd been with the core group of students my entire two years of full-time living in San Francisco.

My instructor, Charlie, was built like a brick wall, but spoke softly enough for all his tough looks. He shaved his head daily and groomed his dark beard to a neat shape. From his meticulous grooming to the precise knots on his obi, everything about Charlie displayed control.

I envied that. I tried to emulate it. Fake it till you make it, right? I wore my long hair in two braids, coiled tight and low at the back of my skull. My gi was clean and neat. That was on the outside. Inside, chaos reigned.

As we prepared to start our drills, another drop-in student walked in. A booming voice, too loud for the quiet of the gym, interrupted my stretching. "Bom dia, Charlie!"

I'd just heard that voice echoing across the concrete expanse of the Pacific Museum yesterday.

The heavens couldn't be so cruel. No, please.

Despite my fervent prayers to all Eight Sons of the Great Dragon, the owner of the voice did not drop off into a gaping pit between the doorway and the mat.

Charlie looked up and beamed at the newcomer. "Olá, Adam!"

Adam, the wealthy donor from Seattle, strode in like he owned the place. Heck, maybe he did. He certainly had given a boatload of money to the Pacific Museum where Tessa worked. I cursed the skies and clouds that this man had intruded into my morning routine. It was bad enough that he'd eaten up my evenings with endless meetings over the sword exhibit. There were seven other BJJ gyms in this city. Was nothing sacred?

He was as tall as a tree and had the wingspan to match. The gi hid much, but there was no denying the latent power in his tapered physique. His slightly curly hair might have been pale blond when he was younger. He looked like a modern-day Viking. More importantly, he had a black belt tied around his trim waist. As my classmates were aware, that was usually a decade-long quest to earn.

Heat rose up the back of my neck and I clenched my hands into fists until my knuckles popped. It wasn't enough that he was good-looking and philanthropic with his money, he apparently had the dedication and self-discipline to persevere for a decade for his black belt.

He spotted me. His smile broadened and his clear blue eyes lit up with delight. "Emiko! Is this your gym?"

It was. It had been. Now I was rethinking it.

I unclenched my hands and gave him a curt nod.

Charlie saved me from having to make conversation by introducing Adam to everyone else and starting our warm-up. Adam's presence irritated me like a pebble in my boot but I threw myself into the workout to clear those thoughts. My body grew warm and loose and my mind sharpened as I fell into the familiarity of the routine.

For the last rolling session of the morning, Charlie paired me with Adam. I assessed his physique with a practiced eye. His eyes, blue and fierce, did the same to me. I eyeballed his muscled frame and guessed he had nearly twenty kilos on me.

A big man like this, I had to get down to the mat, fast. My advantage here was speed and the fact that I was much lower to the ground. He kept his hands loose but I knew from the slight flex of his fingers that he would grab me for a lapel drag. I assessed my submission strategy. I had to go low.

I lunged forward, low and hard, grabbed his right heel, and leaned in just enough against that same knee to overbalance him. The bigger they are, the harder they fall. With a grunt, he tipped and crashed against the mat. From there it was straight forward to the finish. We rolled, but my flexibility helped me evade his attempted arm bar. Get on top, stay on top. I grabbed his lapel and executed the bow-and-arrow choke. He was a beast of a man, strong and heavy. In any other situation he would overpower me with brute force. My only advantage had been surprising him early. But now I had him in position. I angled my hip and gave just one more crank. He winced and tapped out. A sense of satisfaction rippled through me. BJJ fundamentals for the win.

It was the fastest takedown of the session and he knew it. He rolled over onto his back and gave me a small salute. I grinned and offered him a hand up. He loomed over me, a sheepish smile on his face. I blinked. That was some smile and he hadn't even dialed the wattage up. He was handsome, and now that I wasn't assessing him as an opponent, it was distracting. I gave myself a little shake. I had to steer clear of distractions, handsome or not. This was exactly why I'd said no yesterday when he'd asked me to drinks after the museum meeting. That and the fact that I might have to rob him of an ancient sword soon.

Charlie squeezed my shoulder gently. "Nice work, Emiko."

Then Charlie turned to the new guy. "Adam, you have to work on getting low."

It was nice to end class on a high note. It's the small wins that drove me forward and kept me showing up week after week.

We walked to the benches, folks retrieving clean gear out of their gym bags and backpacks. As I ran a towel over the back of my neck, I thought longingly of coffee. One thing I had become an immediate fan of since living in the West was the utter and serious devotion to coffee the locals had. I wondered if I had enough time to wait in line for a strong cup of hand-poured brew, heavy with real cream and loaded with cinnamon. I pulled on my socks and black shearling-lined boots and guzzled from my water bottle.

Post class, there were about ten to fifteen minutes where the students chatted. Before class, the gym was cold and as students we tended to be very quiet, some of us barely awake. After a session, we were all warm and loose, buzzing from the endorphins so we relaxed together while we changed and dried off. We talked about our jobs and I mentioned my research and freelance work for the university. I omitted the part about how I researched ancient artifacts from another realm and hunted mythical monsters on the side.

Jorge, originally from just outside Rio de Janeiro, was in his mid-forties, and trim and wiry. He'd moved here for school and now managed an engineering team at a hot startup in town. He showed off pictures of his weekend home improvement projects, which included brewing beer and roasting a pig at his weekend place in wine country north of the city. I sincerely regretted turning down his invite to the neighborhood pig roast and said so.

Jorge laughed. "My wife, Liz, packed some roast pork leftovers for all of you. Well, except for Marshall. He got the vegan stuff."

My jaw nearly fell open in astonishment before delight suffused my face. "You brought us a pig care package?"

Jorge reached into his olive-green duffel bag. He handed me a small steel bento box. I sniffed appreciatively as the scent of roasted pork wafted out. Besides thanking Jorge profusely, I didn't know what to say. I was touched by his thoughtfulness. We had been working out side by side, three mornings a week for nearly two years and I had never brought Jorge anything. For the first time, I realized that when Jorge went home, he probably shared his morning adventures with his wife and kids. I didn't take this life with me into my other life. I wanted nothing in my Lóng Jiārén life to touch this small oasis.

I'd joined this gym to give some structure to my weeks. But maybe I'd gained more than just hours of rolling practice. Maybe I was finding the basis for friendship? I hadn't really made deep friendships or settled down here after two long years of hiding from my past. I stared down at Jorge's thoughtful gift. Popo was right, I needed to try harder.

I thanked Jorge and he pulled me in for a jovial hug and a hearty back slap. I patted his shoulder in return, feeling awkward. The Soongs were not huggers. Luckily, Jorge didn't seem to notice that I was overwhelmed by all this socializing.

Adam started chatting in Portuguese with Jorge, who responded in kind. Whoa.

Adam saw me looking at him, and shrugged. "I lived in Rio for a year. Picked up some of the language." I was grudgingly impressed. Portuguese was hard. I'd tried to learn a bit during my time in Hong Kong from my colleagues in Macao but I'd struggled with it, and then decided that fluency in three dialects of Chinese, along with Japanese, was going to be good enough for me.

As I waved goodbye to the guys, Adam did the same and we exited the gym together.

The sun was out now, promising a beautiful spring day in the city. The gym was housed in the industrial area, surrounded by broken blacktop and chain-link fencing. Though there wasn't much nature to be found, the San Francisco Bay surrounded us and the heartbeat of the city's magic pulsed around me, in the very air I inhaled. I could feel it even beneath my boots, a living hum that seemed to vibrate up my legs. I knew it wasn't like this for other Lóng Jiārén. I just didn't know why I was so attuned to the city's magic when I had no talent of my own. My lips flattened in annoyance. I concentrated on the other aspects of my life. My *normal* life.

I thought about my little box of roasted pig. It would go great with eggs when I got home.

"Good footwork today," Adam commented.

"Thanks." I did use my feet first, before my arms. A legacy from years of sword work.

I looked up at him, searching for a polite response. We'd changed out of our gi jackets. I'd swapped mine for San Francisco hipster camouflage, my ubiquitous black puffy microdown. Adam had changed into a gray zip-up hoodie that stretched snugly across his broad shoulders. His hair was dry now, the curls a dark blond. His eyes were round and blue, and intensely focused on me. The sunlight glinted gold on the stubble on his chin, and with his cheeks flushed from the earlier activity he looked masculine and irritatingly attractive.

Before I could form an appropriately neutral reply, he smiled at me. I wasn't prepared for the up-close impact of his inviting smile, the way his eyes crinkled at the corners, his long eyelashes casting a small shadow on his high sharp cheekbones. He was really handsome. And I was staring. Staring was bad.

Adam shifted his bag on his shoulder. "How about coffee?"

I almost snarled. I wanted, needed, coffee. I had been planning to get coffee around the corner. But I was not about to spend any more time with Adam than was strictly necessary.

"How about no."

"Are you not a coffee drinker? I'm sure they have tea there, too. We could discuss the Kunimitsu." His absolute confidence and ability to repel my rejection sent a hot surge of irritation through my veins.

"It's not a Kunimitsu."

Adam held up his hand and began ticking off items. "It has the wave-shaped hamon and the fish belly tang. The engravings of the burning dragon are a virtual twin to the Myōhō Kunimitsu."

I waved dismissively and ticked off on my own fingers. "It isn't signed. Kunimitsu and his sons always signed their work. It isn't dated, and it doesn't have the myōhō renge kyō mantra. Those are critical elements for the sword to be an authentic Kunimitsu and they are all missing."

There was more to it than that, but I was leaning on these to get Adam and Tessa to hold off on displaying this sword at the gala. The last thing I needed right now was a lost Hoard piece on display in a Wàirén museum. Word would spread and San Francisco would become the Wild West as every Jiārén clan on this side of the planet made a play for the sword. Even worse, some traditionalists would think that the First Law would mean silencing Adam and Tessa permanently. I couldn't let this happen. And I couldn't believe I was getting sucked back into Jiārén intrigues even here. My resentment for Adam dragging me into this doubled.

Adam's voice lowered, but lost no intensity for it. "I'll give you that. But even Professor Ōtsuka, who is a revered scholar in the field, has concluded that this sword is likely a Kunimitsu."

I shook my head. "She only confirmed that it is in the style of the Kunimitsu school."

Adam seemed to take a step back, his sharp blue eyes boring into mine. "I don't get you."

"What's not to get?"

His eyes narrowed. "You're not an academic, yet the museum has you on speed dial to vet my collection. You seem to know more about East Asian swords than anybody I've ever met, and yet in all my years of collecting I've never heard your name even mentioned in passing. Just where do you fit in with all this?"

When I sensed danger I tended to go very, very still, preparing myself to launch into motion. It took a conscious effort to shift my weight between my feet and give a light shrug. I hoped it looked nonchalant but Adam was dancing dangerously around the truth. I was an expert in Jiārén weapons, and I liked it better when people didn't know my name. "Maybe I should update my LinkedIn profile?"

Adam smiled at my quip and the stress lines in his forehead relaxed. "I don't mean to suggest you're not qualified. The sword collector community is probably bigger than I realized."

I slowly let the tension out of my spine and tried to smile back. It was more like baring my teeth. "The museum values your contribution to the collection. I'm just doing my job."

He dragged his hand through his curls. "I'm sure we'll come to an agreement on the sword eventually. I mean, it's not like I'm claiming something as ludicrous as the Lost Heart of Yázì or something."

My smile faded and I focused on him with laser intensity. Was he toying with me?

"What did you say?"

Adam cranked up the dazzling smile. Again. "You know, the

Lost Heart of Yàzì? Mythical stone of unknown origin rumored to house the soul of the Father of Dragons?"

I blinked. The Lost Heart of Yàzì was a Jiārén myth. How in the eight great hells had this guy heard of it?

With a tilt of my head, I struggled for a casual dismissal. "As fascinating as this mythology lesson is, I think your optimism over the sword is misplaced."

Adam's smiled brightened. "Maybe we could discuss it more over coffee?"

This guy's ego was incredible. Also, I had to remember that he had ruined my morning by showing up at my gym. I kept my voice even. "I'm not having coffee or tea with you, Adam. Just like I wasn't having drinks with you last night, remember?"

Adam bent his head, sheepish. "I just moved in this weekend, Emiko. I'm trying to get out and meet folks."

That aww shucks manner might work on other girls but I wasn't about to spend any more time with him than I had to. He was a mark, and I needed to remember that. "Try joining the yacht club."

Adam grinned at me, a thousand watts of brightness in the gray San Francisco morning. "That's next on my list. I'll see you Wednesday at class."

With a friendly wave, he walked off in the direction of the coffee shop, effectively making sure I couldn't now go there to get the coffee I was craving. Damn him to the eighth level of hell and the sixteen lesser hells beneath it. What should have been a restorative morning with a routine workout had turned into a high-stakes grappling session followed by a verbal sparring match. Even worse, he'd gotten too nosy about my credentials and name-dropped a mythical Jiārén artifact. He saw too much and he was a complication my life didn't need. I was going to have to deal with him sooner or later, and I needed to do it before he got my business partner killed.

# TALON CALL

I drove straight home, unnerved by my conversation with Adam. Or perhaps it would be more accurate to say I was unnerved by my reaction to him. It had been barely tolerable having the weekly meeting with him at the museum going over the weapons collection. Now he'd moved here and joined my gym. Why hadn't he stayed in Seattle? At least before I'd thought my exposure to the distracting man would be limited to the end of the exhibition.

There was no help for it. I'd have to scope out his security and requisition the sword. A guy like Adam would have insurance. Better to let some bumbling insurance investigators nose around than let the rest of the Jiārén collector community get wind of Crimson Cloud Splitter resurfacing. That did present a problem as to what in the heavens and skies above I would do with the sword after I secured it, but at least Tessa would be safe. One problem at a time.

I pulled up in front of my house, the day's tasks piling up mentally. I'd get Andie to give me some intel on Adam. As our IT specialist, and all things computer and search related, I trusted Andie to get her hands on even the smallest tidbit of intel on Adam. The fact that she also happened to be married to my business partner made it even more likely she would put a rush on this for me. Then, I needed to get cracking on the Phelan job. A score like that would pay my mortgage for a year, even after my partner Tessa got her cut.

She had all the respectable relationships. I had all the means and methods that were not available to more respectable folk and, of course, to Wàirén.

I'd start my research from my base of operations in the front house, and enjoy my newfound pork for breakfast. Maybe steep a nice pot of oolong since I'd been robbed of my coffee earlier. Pu'er might be even better. I wasn't going to let that blasted Adam steal any more of my morning or my thoughts. A small thrill of anticipation for the Phelan job restored my equilibrium. I was a talented finder and this was how I could grow my artifact recovery business. It was who I was becoming and how I could leave my past behind me.

Before I could grab my duffel bag and exit the Jeep, my chest clenched. Pain stabbed through my body and I doubled over, nearly banging my forehead into the steering wheel and gasping for breath. My eyes clenched shut and tears streamed down my cheeks. I took a breath, shallow at first, then deeper as the tightness in my chest slowly loosened.

I knew this pain. I'd felt this pain once before. It had led to starting a war with the Yakuza and the death of my cousin Tai. Skies, this was bad.

My phone rang and I answered the call without even looking at it.

"Tatsuya?" My voice sounded strained to my ears.

My little brother answered, his voice tight as well. "Yes. You felt it, too?"

I'd felt it as if heaven itself had opened up and struck me with a bolt of lightning, searing my guts with cold fire.

It was a Talon Call. No doubt about it with Tacchan's confirmation. Somewhere, someone had activated a Soong Talon. Someone had called in a blood marker against our family, an iron-clad debt that held our family's power as collateral. In my life, I'd dealt with Talons only a handful of times. Talent-wielding Jiārén modeling their lives after Dragon gods had few hard and fast rules that everyone agreed on. The Talons were one of those rules.

A Talon was a contract, bound by blood, Dragon power, and honor. It was a get-out-of-jail-free and insta-kill, all rolled into one tidy package. In two thousand years of Jiārén history, no one had ever denied a Talon Call.

I heard muffled voices on the far end of the call. After a moment my brother returned.

His voice was still shaken. "Father didn't feel it."

My stomach dropped. Talons called out to anyone who shared blood with the one who had sealed the Talon. If our father hadn't felt it, then . . .

Tacchan's voice cracked. "Mother."

Indeed. It seemed even while on another continent my mother was still able to find ways to screw with my life. My lips twisted into a bitter smile. A Talon Call resonated with the Dragon power in our blood, a connection that bypassed the physical world. My mother should have felt the Call. She wouldn't have phoned me but if she could have, she would have called Tatsuya in a heartbeat. He was the heir and she would never risk him. If she hadn't called him, it was because she was on the other side of the Void. Who knew when she would ever resurface?

That sealed it. I wasn't going to let her debts screw up my brother's last year in Lóng Kǒu. "I'll handle it, Tacchan."

It was unthinkable that my brother risk himself. He was the Soong heir—everything I was not. I'd fulfilled a Talon before. I'd been emotionally and mentally shredded after but I'd redeemed the Talon held by the Tanaka Clan. They weren't exactly happy with how I'd done it, but I'd done it. I could do it again.

A moment of hesitation. "Nee-san, be careful, please?"

Just like that, we were children again with Tatsuya toddling after me. "Nee-san! Nee-san!" As his older sister, he was my charge. For him, I mustered a cheery tone. "When am I not?"

I hung up before he could get the last word in. If he knew how messy Talon Calls could get he would never let it go. I grabbed my gear and all but ran to my front door. I wanted this over with. My hands shook with anger as I disarmed my wards and unlocked my door. I hadn't seen nor spoken to my mother in two years and now her blood had put me in debt to someone, again. What convenience had she or one of our Hiroto ancestors bought for themselves at my expense?

Two years of living here in San Francisco had done a lot for me. One was to give me distance from the clan. From my father. From my mother. I had never lived up to their expectations and then finally two years ago I had stopped trying. My Father was the Head of the Clan, and I was the eldest. By all rights, I should have been the heir. But I was a no-talent Soong, and my mother couldn't even bear to look at me. Thankfully for everyone involved, my brother Tatsuya had gāo talent, a rare combat-level animation gift. He was the future of the clan, and the beloved of my mother. Or at least, I had assumed that. But my mother wasn't here to protect Tatsuya now. It had to be me.

And even though I had run away from the clan, my father had never severed me. He called me often. He nagged. He tried to inveigle me back. It was exhausting and comforting at the same time. He still considered me valuable to the clan. I just wanted to change how I added value.

Unfortunately, this Talon Call meant the service I would give to the clan was the same I had rendered before—one that would demand bloodletting.

My gear hit the floor unceremoniously as I burst into the front house. The entry and living room of the front house had been converted into a reception area for clients. I made a beeline for the largest piece of furniture, a longevity table set against the wall. From under the table I pulled out a large, shallow golden bowl. A Chinese dragon danced around the interior of the bowl, laid out in mother of pearl. Sitting in the bowl was a slender double-edged knife. My family name was etched into the blade, and another dragon hammered out of silver twisted around the handle.

I set the bowl on top of the longevity table and grabbed my water bottle from my gear bag. As I poured a measure of water into the bowl I muttered a simple plea for a blessing from the Dragon Father. Granted, I was cutting a few corners, but the important part of the working was the next part. Like most gods, the Dragon Father just wanted to be paid. I pulled the blade from the water and stuck the tip of the blade into the pad of my left thumb.

The blade slid easily into my flesh, the edge so sharp there was hardly any resistance. I pulled it out and a fat drop of crimson blood welled at the cut. I squeezed my thumb, coaxing more blood from the wound, and held my hand over the bowl. The drop of blood quivered and fell into the water. Bright red fingers of blood trailed away from the droplet as it sank. It settled on the bottom of the bowl like a bloody pearl, refusing to mix with the water.

Another drop welled up and the sight of the blood falling from my pale hand triggered memories of a time I kept trying to forget. The bloody trails grew long, swirling around the bowl now, creating a spiral pattern, the Dragon legacy in my blood resonating with the call from the Talon.

I closed my eyes.

I opened my eyes and found myself in Golden Gate Park at night. I turned slowly in place, getting my bearings. My physical body was still standing in my front room, but whoever had activated the Talon had gone to the trouble of making our metaphysical meeting look like the park. On this plane, all the edges were softer, as if my eyes had lost a bit of focus. After a moment, I found him, standing next to a large bonsai tree outside the Japanese tea garden. With a thought, I moved through the darkness and appeared beside the bonsai. Dark shadows concealed the caller's face from me. As I approached he moved into the dim lamplight.

"Good day. Thank you for meeting me. I am Sugiwara."

My senses buzzed, reacting to the haze of black and gray around his head where his aura should have been. He towered over me, nearly seven feet tall, and a sickly sweet aroma rolled around him like morning fog. If his name was Sugiwara then I was a nine-tailed fox. Whoever he was, he wasn't human.

He was gaunt, with a pale complexion and severe features. At a glance he might be anywhere from thirty to seventy. Beneath his stately camel coat he wore a charcoal suit of exquisite tailoring. Sunken dark eyes peeked out from under a sweep of dark hair over his forehead. He wore a gray herringbone buggy cap. Very dapper.

I blinked and his image morphed. Power cascaded off his skeletal shoulders, wrapping his body in whorls of fine white mist. The mist drifted to the ground where it pooled around his feet. Long-fingered white hands emerged from the mist, held steepled in front of his chest. His eyes, now the deep red of congealing blood, gazed at me.

When you find yourself in the presence of a death god, it's good to remember your manners. I bowed deeply to the shinigami, fighting down the deep instinct to flee, and greeted him in Japanese.

He gave a slight bow in return before speaking. His voice was soft and his pronunciation precise. "I'm pleased to see you answering the Talon Call."

I nodded. "May I ask how you came to hold a Hiroto Talon?"

The shinigami's eyes narrowed and studied me for a long, uncomfortable moment. "I am acquainted with your mother."

His response confirmed my fear—it hadn't been some random Hiroto ancestor who had traded this Talon. It had been my conveniently absent mother. I struggled to keep my response neutral. "She travels widely."

Why in the name of the Dragon Father would my mother put us

in debt to a death god? What could have possessed her to risk our entire family like this?

I looked around us. The tea garden was closed and dark. We were the only two figures that I could see in any direction. No animals prowled the grounds, no birds flitted between the trees. Once I focused on it, I noticed that the trees were completely still. The shinigami had reproduced the park like an immersive photograph.

He still hadn't produced the Talon so I pushed us past the pleasantries. "What are we doing here?"

"I find I am in need of a mortal agent. You were convenient."

I kept my distance from the shinigami. "I'm honored. And you still haven't answered my question."

There were rules, traditions, expectations when the Japanese conversed with each other in formal settings. I knew I was trampling on all of them but my annoyance at my mother did not allow for this right now.

The shinigami's mouth pressed into a thin line. He swept an arm out, indicating the tea garden behind him. "The Ebony Gate is missing."

I looked in the direction he pointed, racking my memory for the garden's layout. I'd visited the teahouse many times but scarcely paid attention to the statuary and rocks. "The polished black wood slab?"

His eyes crinkled with displeasure. "Yes, it was inscribed with 'The Song of Izanagi-no-Mikoto,' a necessary measure."

I let out a low whistle. Many people prized ebony wood, the polished blackwood grown in the tropics and Africa. It was endangered, and nearly a hundred times more costly than the equivalent weight in oakwood. Ebony grew at slow rates, forming a dense and beautiful wood. A slab of ebony that size had to weigh a thousand pounds. The commercial value alone was enormous, let alone the historical value.

If it was inscribed, a difficult process with this type of hardwood, someone had gone to a lot of trouble to do it, then ship it all the way here to San Francisco. And if it was "The Song of Izanagi-no-Mikoto," there was only one reason for the inscription.

Izanagi-no-Mikoto was known for giving birth to the sun god Amaterasu from his left eye and the moon god Tsukiyomi from his right eye. Before that, he'd been married and his wife, Izanami, had given birth to the fire god, Kagutsuchi. The flames burned her and sent her to Yomi-no-kuni, the underworld. Izanagi had followed her there only to discover her angry undead state. He'd fled his zombie ghost wife and her allies, sealing the path to Yomi with a stone. "The Song of Izanagi-no-Mikoto" was one of creation and death, love and sorrow—and a curse.

I gawped at the garden entrance and looked again at Sugiwara-san. "You mean . . ."

I could hardly bring myself to say it. My mouth suddenly dry, I tried again. "Is there a . . . um . . ."

He nodded, a slow, exaggerated motion. "Yes, the Ebony Gate seals a portal to the world of darkness."

The inscription of "The Song of Izanagi-no-Mikoto" was used to ward off the ghosts of the underworld. The Ebony Gate was a seal on a portal to Yomi. And now the Ebony Gate was missing and all that dwelled in the land of the dead were free to enter the world of the living through the portal in the garden. Great.

He turned to me and his glamour burned away in a flare of smokeless flame. A column of white mist bloomed next to him and a short figure stepped out of the smoke. I didn't recognize the high-collared, embroidered robes, but the glossy white fur, pointed ears, and twitching whiskers were a clue. A cat.

More likely, a yokai. A demon in service to the shinigami, perhaps. The cat stood upright and stepped out of the smoke, its robe woven from shimmering green silk with gold embroidery. The delicate embroidery showed detailed scenes of screaming humans subjected to brutal punishment at the hands of horned demons. Oh, well, other than the macabre robe, the cat was pretty cute.

The cat stopped next to the shinigami and brought an impossibly large tome out of its robes. "Today's census, lord."

The book was bound in dark leather, with iron clasps locking it shut. The shinigami sighed and took the book, waving his hand over the locks. The book sprang open and the shinigami traced his skeletal finger along the open page.

As the shinigami read, the cat licked a bright pink tongue along its paw and flicked an ear. Wow, an adorable demon cat. The cat's whiskers twitched and its shining dark eyes found mine.

Flames danced within those shining eyes. I blinked. Not so cute.

After a long moment the shinigami held his hand up and an ivory brush appeared in his fingers, the brush tip wet with bright red ink. He made a column of neat marks on the open page and slammed the book shut with one hand before returning the locked book to the small demon.

"You see? The wheels of the underworld grind on, relentless, despite what may come. I am en route to renew the ward on the Ebony Gate. It has been ninety-nine years since I last renewed the ward. I will renew the ward. You will locate the Gate before the full moon."

I bristled at the shinigami's imperious command. "What happens if I can't?"

The cat leaned over, ears twitching, and whispered in his master's ear.

The death god cocked his head to the side, listening to the demon, his crimson eyes unfocused. "My associate tells me that even now, the portal to Yomi is open and the teeming hordes of hungry yurei who inhabit Yomi will find their way to your world."

The death god's eyes focused behind me into the tea garden. "But you must know this. You must have some understanding of what will be wrought if legions of yurei are unleashed on your city." He inhaled deeply, looking up to the sparkling city skyline around us. "Yes, even at this distance, I can feel the teeming life of your city. The yurei will be unable to resist. They will sink their fangs deep into the marrow of your city and drink until it is nothing but a husk."

It sounded bad when he put it that way. I wasn't going to let that happen. Still, something didn't smell right here. "Yes, legions of yurei that are supposed to be under your safekeeping. Surely you don't need a mere mortal like me? A powerful being such as yourself should be able to seal the portal."

Sugiwara-sama drew himself up to his full height and regarded me from half-lidded eyes. He snapped his fingers again and the little demon bureaucrat disappeared. "Hmm. Yes, your mother did say you would be difficult."

Another deep stab of resentment hit me in the chest. She should be here. It should be the legendary dark walker, Sara Hiroto, fulfilling the Talon. Instead she was on the other side of the Void, safely beyond this shinigami's reach, leaving me and Tatsuya to make good on our/her debt. I hoped the darkness hid the flush rising up my neck. "My mother is not here, I am."

The shinigami unfurled his hands and a dark ball of death energy sprang to life in his palm, a writhing sphere of inky blackness with tiny whipping tendrils along its surface. He passed the energy from hand to hand, little flickers of blue lightning keeping the ball from touching his hands. It was mesmerizing, and more than a little terrifying. As I watched, the shinigami began to speak.

"My power, like all things, has limits. In order to close the portal, I must bind my power to an anchor of sufficient quality and durability. The Ebony Gate was the seal, and together with its anchor it stood guard over this portal for hundreds of years."

He waved a skeletal hand and an image flared between us. The dark Gate rose majestic before us, the script a warning to all of the horrors that were locked behind it in Yomi. From within the ebony melted away and a shimmering red stone was revealed. Red with an inner gold light, curved and throbbing like a heart. Familiar to all Jiārén. My draw dropped. It was the largest single piece of blood jade I'd ever seen.

"The portal to Yomi is not simply a door we close and shut with a latch. The denizens of Yomi hunger to escape their fate and spend eternity clawing at the doors until their fingers are raw to the bone. I am the key that locks the door, but I must be selective about what I use to fashion the doors and how I anchor them."

He'd anchored the Ebony Gate with the Lost Heart of Yázì. It wasn't a myth after all—merely hidden from the living.

The shinigami's eyes burned a fiery red, the light burning through me. He crooned, his voice caressing. "Yes. I see now. Perhaps this is why your mother sent me to you. You have a gift, do you not? I believe you would be a sufficient anchor to close the portal."

The energy in his hands flared, spewing icy cold power in purple waves that made my stomach flop over. His words sent a shiver down my spine. "Yes, I could bind you into the Gate, turn you into statuary. It would be lovely. You would spend the next millennium keeping your city safe. What do you think?"

The death god smiled at me. It was not a comforting smile.

I willed my hands to stay relaxed at my sides as I held his gaze. I gave myself a moment to quell the rising bile in my throat, passing it off like I was considering his offer. "As generous as your offer is, I'm afraid I must decline. Surely there is another way."

The shinigami clapped his hands together and crushed the purple ball of energy between them. It made a low thump like someone dropping a heavy book and my ears popped. "As I said, my authority is limited. I cannot act with impunity in the mortal world. You shall be my agent. You know the city and your reputation precedes you. I know you will protect those under your aegis."

Sugiwara-sama shifted his posture slightly wider, just like I had seen my father do many times. Power poses. He reached into the billowing smoke of his robes and drew out a Talon. My eyes locked onto the familiar shape, out of place in unfamiliar hands.

Talons were poured from the purest of Hoard gold. The ingots had a cylindrical base, the top morphing into a single dragon claw. A bas-relief dragon was carved into the gold, wrapping around the base. The dragon's body twined its way around a crane, my mother's symbol. The goldsmiths who poured the Talons spelled the gold, making the tip of the Talon needle sharp. Even in the dark of night, I could see the faint red glow of the Talon. My shoulders slumped, even though I knew this was coming. The shinigami's skeletal fingers gripped the gold ingot, knuckles digging into the soft metal. The ephemeral tugging at the center of my chest intensified, nearly bringing me to my knees. That was the cost of my mother's blood on the Talon.

"Without the Gate, I will be forced to use the next best thing to seal the portal. That would be you. In the meantime, yurei will invade your city and consume the lifeblood of your people. I have no love for the living, it does not bother me one whit if your city lives or dies. I am only the Custodian of the Gates to Yomi. To fulfill your Talon Call, you will find the Ebony Gate and its anchor by the rise of the full moon tomorrow night or I will use your soul to restore order in Yomi."

Fire sparked in his eye sockets, giving me a preview. I looked up at the moon, round and shimmering behind the fog. Bad enough a Gate was missing, but now I had a deadline to get it back. How in the many levels of hell did I get roped into this? My eyes went back to the Talon in the death god's hands and the dark smudge of my mother's dried blood over the crane. Right.

The shinigami pointed at my left hand. "May I?"

I had zero desire to endure living death as a statue for millennia. Even if I declined, the shinigami would do it anyway. Hell's bureaucracy would grind on regardless of my wishes. At the same time, there was a reason we had so many stories of mortals pulling the wool over a god's eyes. I might be in a corner now, but that didn't mean I couldn't jump out of it later.

"I want to know the exact terms to satisfy the Talon."

Clouds of white smoke burst from the shinigami's skeletal hands and swallowed the light around us, plunging us into darkness. I had the sudden sensation of standing on the edge of a very tall, very fragile precipice. The shinigami's voice rumbled directly inside my head, causing my eyes to water. I steeled my legs, willing myself to stay upright as the death god's voice continued to thunder in my head. "For your mother's sake, I give you until midnight tomorrow to retrieve the Ebony Gate. I will have the portal sealed by then. Your Talon duty will be satisfied if either the Gate is secured or your soul is anchoring the portal to Yomi before I leave San Francisco."

The darkness faded and starlight leached back into reality. I wobbled like I'd just come off a roller coaster. What choice did I have? If I didn't answer, that left Tatsuya, which was unacceptable. He was the future of Soong Clan. It was my job to ensure that. "I will answer the Talon Call."

The shinigami took my left hand. I resisted the urge to yank it back. Hand-to-hand combat with a death god would be a bad idea.

He turned it over and the chill of his touch seeped into my bones. He scribed a sigil on my left palm and I nearly cried out at the sharp pain. Death energy bloomed around my hand, twisting tendrils of oily black smoke engulfing both of our hands. The power pulsed and faded, until only a soft blue glow remained. Like I had gone to a cool new nightclub and they'd stamped my palm instead of the top of my hand.

"It will lend you some small protection against the yurei through my mark. It is not full protection, but could buy you some time."

Well that was something, at least. It's not like the tools in my weapons bag would have much effect on the ghostly yurei.

"Clap your palms together twice and I will respond to your

call when you have found the Gate." He bowed, lower this time. I wished he could have just used a cell phone. A text would have been fine. Also, he seemed very confident I would locate the Gate and its anchor in time. I wished I felt the same.

He gestured expansively around the garden and dark smoke rose from the ground as the metaphysical construct fell to pieces. "I know that the daughter of Sara Hiroto will find the Gate. If you fail, you will satisfy the Talon Call with your afterlife."

The shinigami seemed to place a lot of weight on my mother vouching for me. That by itself churned up a lot of conflicting feelings, even without the threat of living death hanging over me. Before I could ask him anything else the death god evaporated into a haze of cloying black smoke. Typical.

# INTRUSION

I opened my eyes in the real world and found myself hunched over my spirit bowl, my face and neck covered in a sheen of sweat. The water was gone from the bowl and my blood was just a dried smudge at the bottom. As I cleaned the bowl and put it and the knife away, the smell suddenly hit me. A smell that did not belong, a smell that definitely indicated another Jiārén's talent. Ogata-sensei had determined early in my training that my meager talent was a significant tactical advantage. Much of my early training focused on memorizing the unique scents of different Dragon talents. I sniffed again and identified the faint tang of shoe leather and gunpowder. Yin talent. What on earth had possessed a ghost master to visit me? And, I realized with a sick feeling, did it have anything to do with what just happened?

I retrieved Hachi from my duffel bag and made my way to the back door. Staying just inside, I scanned my property then crept outside.

My yard between the front house and back cottage was modest but I'd worked hard to make it peaceful and secure. No tall trees or giant bushes to provide hiding spots. Small swirls of green-and-yellow-striped succulents bordered the rock garden to the east. A heavy stone bench sat in the sand garden to the west. I'd tried to recreate the small oasis of the Soong estate with that bench.

I crouched low and sidestepped the perimeter of the front house, inhaling where the odor was strongest. Someone had attempted my front door and the windows. I found a footprint amongst my plants and a smudge of bitter-smelling ash on my windowsill. They'd gotten smart to the wards at some point and stopped before setting them off.

I let out a piercing whistle, three short rising notes. From the rear cottage, Bāo responded with two short growls. All clear. I checked the perimeter of the back cottage to be certain. I heard nothing except for the sound of the water circulating from the dragon spouts and my own breathing. I smelled the usual mint and lemon tang . . . but there it was again, shoe leather and gunpowder. The water in the spouts still ran clear and strong.

Nobody had gotten into my personal living space but unease made my stomach tighten. I had many enemies, but few had been motivated enough to try me here on my home turf. Could this have anything to do with the Ebony Gate? Or maybe it was just a coincidence and an attempt to swipe my Hoard pieces. My lips flattened in annoyance. Unlikely.

My stone guardians should have the footage. My plans for a delicious porky breakfast and a bracing cup of Pu'er tea with my research had just gone out the window. Now I would be watching security footage and neurotically scanning my property for any unwelcome presents left behind.

I checked the back cottage. No bugs. No ephemeral nets or lassos left by weaver talents. My steps quickened as I checked the front house. He, she, or they had gotten into the front house. No doors were forced but I could smell them all over the house. The stench was everywhere—even the pantry. They'd opened my drawers, touched my mail, and handled my food. The server had blipped, sending an error report to my email. At least I had the time stamp. I checked the footage and found only an annoying blur of black haze. Cursed skies.

Whoever the intruder had been, they had to have been watching my house and they'd hit it after I went to the gym. And they'd been savvy enough to send a ghost master, someone who could direct a ghost right through my walls, bypassing my Wàirén security measures. Not just a resourceful enemy then, but also a smart one. I shivered at the thought, thankful I'd had Bāo with me while I'd slept last night in the back cottage.

Blessedly, Sword of Truth had been in the back cottage, where I slept. My chest hollowed out just thinking of what could have happened if they'd taken her.

With grim resolve I began cleaning the front house. I scanned it twice for bugs. I powered down the servers. I would need to talk to Andie about that. I threw out everything in the pantry except my emergency stash of Kit Kats. Thankfully they'd been protected inside a repurposed metal cookie tin. I lit incense to rid my house of the smell of the ghost. By eight thirty in the morning I was wiped out.

When I was finally satisfied I had eliminated all traces of the ghost intrusion, I went to my cottage to bring supplies to the front house. Namely tea. A nice floral jasmine would make the place smell right again.

After two cups of tea, I set my cup down with a thunk. I didn't have the energy for Father's questions but I couldn't put it off anymore. I phoned my father.

He picked up on the first ring. "Bao bei! It's been so long since you've called. Chen Tàitài and I were just talking about you." Guilt—not bad for an opening salvo. But my strategy for my father today was to ignore his attacks and press forward.

"Where's Mother? This is a Hiroto matter." This was a rhetorical question. We both knew she was beyond, in the Void space.

"She's been traveling. You know how it is. Bā Shǒu business."

As expected. Anger roiled in my chest, threatening to boil over. I did not want to hear my father make excuses for her. My own stupid fault for pointing out this was a Hiroto Talon. I cut to the chase and gave my father a brief rundown of my conversation with the shinigami. If he was alarmed by the appearance of a death god in my life, he didn't show it.

"We can't risk Tatsuya so I will recover the stolen Gate and its anchor."

"Of course. I have every confidence in your abilities."

Silence hung heavy in the air after that. I took a breath and willed the tumult in my chest to calm down. He was going to make me ask for it. Why would I expect anything different?

"But you have a suggestion." My voice flattened.

"I cannot intervene in a Talon Call sealed with your mother's blood. But you have the necessary resources at your disposal to answer this Call."

Of course, he wouldn't come out and say what he meant. Every interaction I had with my father was like this, a test to prove my worth. My brain raced through my weapons arsenal, the spelled tiles I kept on hand, the jewelry I had no use for, the Hoard pieces I kept but couldn't use . . . and then it hit me.

Father meant the Soong Talons he'd gifted me on my twentieth birthday. I had two in the safe.

My eyes closed at the irony. Father was telling me to use a Talon to get help in redeeming the Hiroto Talon. It was mortgaging the future to pay for past debt.

"You think I should use a Talon."

"If you place your pieces correctly, you can reclaim your mother's Talon and strengthen our bonds with another Hoard clan. The expense is well worth the risk."

This was how my father conducted business, schemes within schemes. Nothing done in two steps when he could do it in four and turn a tidy profit at the same time. No problem was so great that he couldn't find a kernel of opportunity within. But I had been trained to be a simple solution, the sharp edge held to soft skin. My father's schemes made my head swim.

If my father noticed the uncomfortable silence he gave no sign. "Do you believe anyone there is worthy of the Talon?"

My lips twisted into a bitter smile. Popo must be psychic. In the space of half a day of her telling me to visit the Hoard Custodian families here in this city, my father was hinting the same.

"Only the Louies or the Trans."

"Which one?"

I chewed my lip. The Trans were new in town. New, as in only the last few decades. The Louies had a century on them. But the Trans kept tabs on what Wàirén goods moved through the city. In contrast, the Louies controlled all of Lotus Lane and the surrounds of Japantown. Raymond "Dai Lou" Louie owned the bank and ruled the Jiārén of his territory with a silk-gloved fist.

My mother and father weren't going to suddenly appear to bail me out. I had to figure this out on my own.

"The Louies would know if there were rumors of a Gate."

"True . . ."

The pause in my father's voice reminded me.

"Father, the Gate is anchored by the Lost Heart of Yázì."

Silence met my words, broken only by a sound like cracking knuckles.

Finally he spoke. "Many third parties will be after this as well. Clans under the Black Tortoise can ensnare the unprepared. Do not disappoint me."

He was absolutely right. I should have thought of that. I ground my teeth in frustration. "Yes, Father."

"You may need two Talons. Call me when you make progress. I will await your update, Mimi."

With that, he hung up on me. In one sentence he had told me that Tatsuya's future as heir was so precious I could double down by using two Talons. Unheard of. Brought about by the fact my mother had done the unthinkable, by bargaining with a death god.

I closed my eyes and tried to center myself. This wasn't helping. I had to fulfill the Talon. I took a deep breath, pulling the scent of my jasmine tea into my lungs. The familiar aroma helped to clear my head.

I cleared the Phelan research off my desk. Money was nice, but being alive to spend it was more important. A massive heist of the Ebony Gate and the legendary Lost Heart of Yázì meant I needed to look at the big players. I pulled out my old dossiers on the Tran and Louie Clans on my phone and sat down at the kitchen table to prep for the day. I needed to make a plan.

The surer bet was to visit the Louies. They had ears listening behind every door in the city. Something as important as the Ebony Gate had surely tickled the ear of someone in Dai Lou's employ. On the other hand, the Trans handled all inbound and outbound Jiārén freight for San Francisco. If the thief was planning to move the Gate and the Lost Heart, they would need to move it through the Trans' system.

The Louies were charm speakers, their honeyed words able to soothe and reassure the most anxious of patrons and clients. Luckily for society they hadn't gone into selling insurance. Although perhaps it was more worrisome the Louies had gone into banking. They'd been in San Francisco for over a hundred years and had entwined themselves with just about every aspect of the city. In an area replete with new millionaires, the Louies had the kind of old money that tech CEOs only dreamed of.

The Trans were air talents, and a strong clan, to be sure. Their arrival had touched off a brutal decade of clan warfare. The majority of their strength resided in Asia, with their San Francisco operations led by Fiona, their French-tutored princess. Fiona was a force to be reckoned with, both in talent and in business acumen. Her only weakness was her youth. According to my intelligence, Dai Lou, over fifty years Fiona's senior, had never once deigned to speak with her.

This was how the Bā Shǒu Council resolved the turf war between the Trans and Louies over fifty years ago. Tired of watching the Jiārén foothold in San Francisco eroded by infighting, Bā Shǒu had sent the one person able to cow both the impetuous Trans and the arrogant Louies—Sara Hiroto, my mother.

My mother came to town and brokered a cease-fire the day she arrived. By the next day the deal that carved up the city had been hammered out and signed. The Louies got to keep the banking and merchant network and the Trans got all the export and import action from the ports. There was plenty of Jiārén money in San Francisco and this was how it got divvied up. My father was considered a minor interloper, what with his Soong jewelry stores, which was why he was so careful to preserve good relations with both families.

I leaned back in my chair and stretched, my back giving a satisfying pop. Cleaning the house had been a harder workout than the jiujitsu. Bāo padded in from the living room and rested his massive head on my lap, shamelessly fishing for pats. I stroked his red fur, and ran my fingers through his curly gold mane, finding his spot behind his ear and scratching. He purred happily, the sound making my chair vibrate.

"What do you think, boy? The Louies or the Trans? Who first?"

I'd spent the last two years studiously avoiding both clans. On purpose. Now I had to meet with them and say the right things. Bāo wriggled his head, trying to get my hand moving again against his ear. As he moved, the coin on his collar caught the light. A worn loop of leather went through the square hole in the coin, tethering the coin to Bāo's collar. Half the coin was discolored and oxidized and the other half was bright and shiny. The coin was imbued with my father's talent, a reservoir of power to animate Bāo at need.

Thoughts of my father crystallized my waffling. You paid respect to your elders first. And well, better late than never. I had until tomorrow night to fulfill the terms of the Talon. It was time to rip off the Band-Aid.

"Okay, Bāo. I'm going to visit the Louies." I held out my hand and waited for him to shrink down.

He circled around me, avoiding my gaze. His tail flicked in disdain. Then he went still and gave a low growl at the door. Seconds later the doorbell rang.

I checked the security camera. A petite blonde with frizzy curls tapped her purple Converse–clad foot impatiently on my porch. It was Tessa MacNeil, the other half of SOMAC Salvage. My business partner and my anchor to normalcy. Casual footwear notwithstanding, she was dressed sharply today in a fitted heathered-plum pantsuit over a sunny yellow camisole.

I let her in and she bounced over the threshold. "Emiko, why are you still in gi pants?"

She spotted Bāo and stopped. "And since when did you have a dog?"

I grimaced. "He's not my dog." Technically, he wasn't a dog at all. He was a lion. Also, he wasn't exactly mine. It was complicated. But Tessa was a Wàirén and she saw only what she expected to see. That was the gift of my father's animates.

"He's just here for a bit. Hey, did we have a meeting today?"

Distracted, Tessa looked toward the kitchen. "Oooh, did you make the fancy tea?" Tessa thought anything that didn't come in a Lipton bag was fancy.

I rolled my eyes and tried to figure out how to get Tessa out of the house so I could start tracking down the Ebony Gate. But it was hard to be rude to my business partner and closest-person-I-had-to-a-friend of the last two years. "Would you like some jasmine pearl?"

Bāo padded out of the room. No doubt I would find him lounging on my pillow later.

I grabbed a to-go mug and poured the tea in there. Hopefully Tessa would get the hint. "Here you go. I, uh . . . I need to take care of some stuff so I don't have time to chat this morning."

She paused mid-sip, and her eyes took on a wicked sparkle. "So, I heard Adam ask you out for drinks after our meeting. Is he not your type?"

I spluttered. "What? No. No, I don't date clients."

Tessa smiled at me over the lip of her mug. "Technically, he's just a donor to the museum, and the museum is your client."

Married people are the worst. Just because she and her wife, Andie, were blissful didn't mean she needed to play matchmaker for me.

She pretended to think. "I mean, you're going to be working very closely on the Kunimitsu sword, right?"

I clenched my jaw. "It's not a Kunimitsu."

It was much rarer than a mere thirteenth-century sword. Adam wasn't even here and his obsession with what he thought was the Lost Sword of Kunimitsu was putting everyone who'd seen it at risk.

My curt response just seemed to egg Tessa on. She plucked at the neckline of her camisole and fanned herself. "Oh, that's right. You two sure had a heated debate about that."

She wiggled her eyebrows. "You're both so passionate about ancient Japanese swords."

In spite of myself I grinned at Tessa's antics. The only person who'd ever joked around with me was Tatsuya, and that was infrequent now that he was at Lóng Kǒu. And she was right. We had gotten into it before I'd realized I needed to keep my mouth shut.

Tessa's eyes flew open and she pointed an accusing finger at me. "You do like him! I knew it!"

I wiped the smile off my face. "No. He's annoying. And full of himself. And too rich."

"Too rich? Who says that?"

I'd grown up surrounded by uber-wealthy Jiārén. It made me uncomfortable now to think about how much I'd taken for granted. In addition to being ultra-wealthy, Adam's other offenses were numerous. He was too good-looking, too fit, too personable, too astute, and too generous. Too much everything. I poured and drank the last of the tea. "He's just . . . He's too much. I don't need that in my life right now."

Further, the idea of dating anyone, much less a Wàirén who seemed set on annoying me at every turn, was so alien that I found myself at a complete loss. My last relationship hadn't ended well. In fact, I'd ended it. Badly. I wasn't the type of person who enjoyed doing things I was demonstrably bad at. Also, I needed to steal from him, which was a bad way to start a relationship. So, no.

Tessa got the hint and sobered up. "Okay, but in all seriousness, I do need you to move on Adam's sword. The Asian artifact exhibition starts in two weeks, and Adam's collection is one of the centerpieces. He's our point of contact for the family and they only agreed to donate the pieces on the condition that we include the Kunimitsu."

Her voice turned to pleading. "So, help a girl out? Please?"

Tessa was my partner and she deserved whatever help I could give her. I had a feeling that I wouldn't be able to convince Adam to remove the sword from the collection. For his own good. For everyone's good. That left fewer legal avenues. But all that would wait until after I survived my Talon Call. If I did. The irony did not escape me that I was trying to recover one stolen artifact only to live longer to steal another one.

"I'll get on it next. I've one last thing to clear off my plate and then I'm all yours. Oh, and our server's acting funny so I need Andie to take a look."

"I think Andie's working from home today so she should be free."

Tessa moved to the door, her hands wrapped around her mug. "So . . . we're doing pizza this Saturday . . . Andie's going to get fresh figs from the farmer's market . . ."

I made a face. "Figs have no place on pizza."

"Fine! I'll make her bite the bullet and buy some pepperoni. Will you come?"

Tessa and I had danced this dance before, but I couldn't afford to be any closer to her and Andie than I already was. "Sorry, I can't make it."

My partner paused, her hand on the doorknob, mood suddenly somber. "You always say that. Are we friends or just business partners?"

"What? Of course we're—"

"Because a friend would come over for dinner, Emiko."

"Really, Tessa, this time—"

"What?"

"I'm . . . going to be busy then." It wasn't a lie, but it felt terrible to say and the look on Tessa's face was salt in the wound.

As much as I enjoyed their company, the more distance I kept from them, the safer Tessa and Andie were. It was the price I paid for my past, but one I was willing to pay. "I appreciate the invite."

I did. It meant a lot to me. But I didn't see myself accepting anytime soon.

I sent Tessa off with her travel mug of tea and a promise that I would read her emails later. I texted the stalwart Andie.

**Server breach. Please check logs**

Three bubbles popped up and I could practically imagine the outrage sizzling through Andie's taps.

**I'll lock it down**

I gave Andie a thumbs-up.

We could debrief later. Maybe after I knew I wasn't going to become a garden statue.

# GUANXI

After a quick shower I donned a black long-sleeved Henley and went through my gear. My pants came in two flavors and two colors. Tight latex or tactical, and black or urban camo. I loved urban camo. I loved many things about the West, but urban camo topped the list. I looked longingly at the black latex pants but today was a tactical pants day. Specifically my fitted 5.11 cotton poly blend tactical pants with lots of pockets and a Teflon finish because who knew what kind of crazy nonsense I would be wading through today. I pulled on my black Chelsea boots, the Vibram soles my insurance plan for the guaranteed amount of walking I'd be doing.

I strapped on my weapons holsters and slid the familiar tools of my trade into them. I pulled on my custom gauntlets, tucking sharp ceramic shurikens in the sleeves. I shrugged into a clean haori, concealing my myriad weapons. My belt and swords completed my outfit for the day. With my weapons in place, my nerves settled, my mind calming.

My last weapon, my lion, still lazed in the sunshine on my hardwood floors. "Bāo."

Bāo flicked his tail at me lazily, not even deigning to look at me. He knew what was coming. You'd think a cat who spent most of his time as an inanimate pendant would spend more time moving when he was animated. I whistled a short tune, the notes descending, and a pale green glow surrounded my foo lion. His head popped up finally and his mouth stretched wide as he yawned, and then vanished. I picked up the jade pendant from the floor. The stone was still warm. I tied it around my neck, the weight of the jade reminding me that I wasn't totally alone.

In order to talk to the Louies, I'd need to bring something with me. Nothing as simple as flowers or a box of pastries, unfortunately. I pulled aside the bookshelf in my bedroom, revealing an unremarkable expanse of wood paneling. I traced my hand across the wood until I found the spot, and placed my palm on the hidden biometric scanner. A small maple drawer slid out and opened with a soft click, revealing gleaming gold figurines set into a black velvet–lined interior.

Two Soong Talons. These particular ingots were nearly two hundred years old and other than my swords, the only things of value I'd brought with me to San Francisco. All were cast in solid gold, but gave off the subtle red hue of Hoard pieces. The Soong Talons were nearly identical to the one I'd seen in the shinigami's hand, but mine were unmarked by blood.

The gold radiated a faint energy I perceived as a gentle press on my senses, like the air around me was being compressed. Most Jiārén went their whole lives without ever bartering a Talon. Unfortunately, I wasn't from a regular Jiārén family. Hoard Custodian families bartered their Talons when the stakes went beyond life and death. The threat to my immortal soul qualified. If I offered a Soong Talon to the Louies, they might keep it for a century before calling on the Soongs to redeem it. Or they could call it in next week depending on what they found most advantageous. I was trading one problem for another but I was betting that anything the Louies would want from my family was better than me in millennium of service to the shinigami.

I grabbed a Talon, closed the hidden drawer, and headed out to talk to the most powerful man in San Francisco.

# GOLD COAST

Once in my Jeep, I made for the exclusive mansions tucked away in Seacliff. The neighborhood changed dramatically as I left my small Craftsman home in Dogpatch and headed all the way across town to the wealthy enclave where the average home price was something in the range of ten million a pop. Seacliff was for *old* money. The Louies were old money, or as old money as you could get after the Chinese Exclusion Act of 1882.

The patriarch of House Louie probably didn't remember me. My father had brought me when I was five. Even then, Dai Lou had seemed ancient and larger than life, an old dragon retired comfortably on his mountain of gold. He'd ignored me for the most part, but seemed genuinely pleased with the gift my father had brought from the mainland. Dai Lou had recently stepped back, and his younger brother "Uncle" Jimmy seemed to be the operations guy now. Jimmy was often seen glad-handing local politicians and skillfully keeping the Wàirén in the dark about our Jiārén activities. I'd rather launch myself into sword-flying chaos.

When I finally found parking, I was a good walk from the Louie compound. Typical. I wondered if the Sentinel would have as much trouble finding parking. I killed the engine and stewed for a few moments as the engine ticked and cooled. The idea of visiting Dai Lou was generating a lot more butterflies in my stomach than I'd anticipated. When I'd come to San Francisco I'd been trying to cut off as much of my old life as possible. I'd ignored my father's multiple voice mails to visit Dai Lou and pay my respects. I squinted into the rearview mirror and eyed the gates to the Louie property and considered showing up two years late to "visit." Better late than never?

For once, I channeled my father and thought ahead to my meeting with Dai Lou. It would be less than polite to show up at his door wielding my swords. Possibly not quite sending the message I was aiming for. I sighed and stowed my swords in the false bottom in the rear of my Jeep, a custom space made exactly for them and a few other things. Sword of Truth would be safe enough.

I hoofed it all the way to the tall stucco walls that surrounded the Louie estate. Pagoda-style trims graced the top of the white stucco, but I couldn't see anything else as the wide plank double doors had to be eight feet tall and eight feet wide. Behind me the ocean waves lapped softly against the rocks. The homes here perched on the cliffside. Plenty of wine cellars and secret passages in these Seacliff homes. The folks in Seacliff took their privacy seriously.

I didn't see any cameras but there had to be some. Possibly hidden by the Louie illusionists. I scanned the perimeter of the building, looking for likely weak points to force an entry or exit if need be. Two years on my own here had made me soft, that much was obvious.

I pulled out the lozenges that the Sun Emporium custom blended for me. Eucalyptus, peppermint, honey, wasabi, yuzu oil, and a dash of skepticism. The oils were layered and continually stimulated my mouth, sinuses, and mucous membranes to a state of minor annoyance. The ever-stimulating lozenge, coupled with a small amount of imbued skepticism, allowed the taster to fend off charm speakers.

I lifted one of the pair of ornate gold lion head knockers and pounded twice. My father always said once was not enough and three times was rude.

Granted, it was early but I was sure they had a full staff of folks who could answer the door. I cooled my heels another ten minutes then repeated my two knocks.

At last the gate creaked open, and to my surprise Uncle Jimmy himself greeted me. According to my files, Dai Lou's eldest son, Ray Ray, stood to inherit control of the clan. Dai Lou's younger brother, Jimmy, currently oversaw clan operations in light of Dai Lou's failing health. Odd, considering Ray Ray was certainly old enough to take control if needed. Again, the clan politics that I detested. I bowed quickly. "Suk Suk, hou noi mou gin."

Uncle Jimmy's thin face lit up in a beaming smile. Between his slicked-back hairstyle and red cardigan, he looked like an ageless Mr. Rogers. His talent was subtle, just a pink tinge around the outer edge of his aura, indicating tight control or very low-level power. Given his rank in the clan, and the poise of his lean body, I knew it to be the former. In his right hand he carried a stout cane, the shaft made of polished, gnarled driftwood, the head of the cane buttery gold worked to continue the driftwood motif. An elaborate dragon scale pattern wound around the cane, and the golden head of the cane was shaped like a large fang. I suppressed a gasp as the pungent smell of its magic hit me like a truck. Uncle Jimmy was walking around with a Hoard piece, and using it as a cane.

His eyes flashed briefly above my head, no doubt scanning my aura before he inclined his head very slightly in return. "Emiko. What a nice surprise. How is your father doing?"

Guess I didn't need to worry about him not remembering me. I bobbed my head. "Very well. He hopes Dai Lou is in good health."

My father hadn't inquired as to Raymond Louie's health but I knew he would have if he hadn't hung up on me so quickly. I could see behind Jimmy's shoulder to the beautifully tended garden in front of the house. But Jimmy hadn't invited me in yet.

As if on cue, Jimmy took three small steps back to allow me in. "Lai, lai, lai."

Crossing onto the Louies' property, my ears popped. The moment passed and the sounds of a noisy household rose in my ears, the clatter of pots and pans from the kitchens, and the cries of young children along with running feet. All the noise bombarded me at once, a stark contrast to the soothing sound of lapping waves on the quiet street beyond the Louies' gates.

It was well known that the Louie Clan's strength was Black Tortoise, specifically illusion, but the sound muffling wasn't in my dossiers. They must have illusions of sound layered over their gates, essentially soundproofing the entire estate. Wind talents like the Trans could pull off this trick by hardening air to block the transmission of sound waves, but the effect was not subtle. The Louies clearly took security as seriously as I did. No clan business would be overheard by passersby.

The Black Tortoise was almost universally viewed as the weaker school of Dragon talents, due to its focus on the mind as opposed to affecting the world around us. But the Louies had developed their talent in a direction no one else had tried before. What else was hidden behind these walls?

Beyond the double doors lay a massive courtyard lined by creamy bamboo reeds and tall waving grasses. To the north, a majestic rock wall rose twenty feet high with a gurgling waterfall descending the face and splashing into a brook that wound around the perimeter of the house. The house itself was modest in comparison to the lavish landscaping and courtyard. The building was a sprawling single story with moon-shaped archways, reminding me of Hangzhou.

Staff and family members roamed the property, and I guessed that a Realm Fragment lurked within, where the Louie Hoard could remain safely out of Wàirén hands. From what I could see of the Louie staff, very few had strong auras. Mostly píng-level. That was odd.

But on the other hand, this property had multiple layers of magic to penetrate. Maybe they didn't need much security beyond that. I noticed Uncle Jimmy looking intently at me as I took in the estate.

We locked eyes for an instant and I became acutely aware that I could scream my head off just inside the entrance and not a soul beyond this property would hear me.

From the rear of the house came the distinctive sound of staff strikes, the clicks and taps of the waxwood weapons taking me back to the years I used to train with my father's weapons master, and then later with Ogata-sensei.

Uncle Jimmy closed the sweeping double doors and locked them with a click. "Lai, lai . . . you're just in time, Emiko."

He turned and walked across the yard, surprisingly spry for his age, and clearly did not require the cane. I made a mental note of this and hurried to catch up to him.

"Uncle Jimmy, I have to—"

He cut me off smoothly. "Come meet the family."

I chased after him, clutching the Talon in my pocket. "Uncle Jimmy, I need your help."

He ignored me and turned the corner, his long strides eating up the lawn. I rounded the corner and almost got stabbed in the neck with the end of a wooden staff. Instinct kicked in and I snatched it and leaned back, ready to spin the staff down and use the downward motion to pull down my attacker. Luckily my brain realized my attacker was about four feet tall and probably in grade school. Halting mid-yank, I twisted into a butterfly kick over the staff to dodge. The move allowed me to avoid trouncing an eight-year-old.

I let go of the staff and my would-be attacker giggled, her round cheeks as shiny as apples. She dashed off in the direction Uncle Jimmy had headed, pigtails bouncing.

Following them, I found myself in the rear of the house, and a small courtyard used as a training area. Weapons racks lined three sides of the courtyard, holding an impressive array of swords, dagger-axes, and spears. An open cabinet set at one corner held a dazzling range of throwing knives and shurikens.

A square of packed dirt was marked out in the center of the

courtyard for sparring. Uncle Jimmy carried my attacker in his arms, his cane casually draped over his forearm and dangling loose. The girl peeked at me from over his shoulder, her eyes round with amusement.

A few feet away, a young girl stood on the dirt, her black athletic pants dusty at the hems. She did not look up as we entered. The staff in her hands whipped left, then right, striking the muk yan jong with a sharp crack. With each strike, the arms on the wooden practice dummy recoiled and spun about its axis, coming at the girl from the other side. She pivoted smoothly, catching the counterattacks on her staff. The girl set an easy rhythm with the staff, running through the practice that laid down the foundational muscle memory for skilled fighting. My hands and shoulders ached at the memory of my own drills. Normally, my father's weapons master had me start the drills using my hands, and kept me at it until my palms and forearms throbbed from the hits against the dummy. This girl's martial arts instructor had to be a Wing Chun enthusiast, too.

Uncle Jimmy's face broke into a smile and he cleared his throat. "Leanna."

The girl stopped at once, pulling her staff to her side. Her hand flashed out and caught the practice dummy before the arms could swing around. She hurried over to us and sketched a small bow. "Uncle."

Dark bangs slick with sweat framed a round face with refined features. She was younger than I'd initially thought, maybe eleven, just starting to lose the baby fat in her cheeks. Small gold hoops pierced her ears. Her dark eyes ignored me, focused only on her uncle. She held the staff loosely at her side, her hand and knuckles calloused in all the right places.

The girl's aura radiated a surprising bright magenta, open and revealed to all. Surprising because it was unfurled. That wouldn't last for long. Her gāo talent level and the fact that she came from a

Hoard Custodian family meant that Jimmy would teach her to lock it down. Hoard families worked at suppressing how much people could learn about their talent from their aura. Too much visibility meant less training and more exposure. Hoard families were all about minimizing exposure.

I'd had that kind of training once. Before my brother had arrived into the world, my father had spent countless hours with me patiently educating me as his father had before him. In those years, we'd all believed I was an animator talent, too, one destined to be gāo-level. I'd learned then to keep a tight lid on my aura, eager to honor my parents' instructions. Only after my expulsion did I learn something twisted had happened to my aura. Something so bad that my parents had instructed me to hide it from all. I still did today but nothing could diminish the burnished glow it had picked up lately.

Uncle Jimmy bounced the little girl a bit. "Lucy, giu yan. Leanna, giu yan. Jie jie."

This was a time-honored dance, the calling of names that every child had to do with their elders. It was strange to realize I was the elder this time. Lucy opened her mouth and parroted, "Jie jie."

Leanna followed suit obediently, but her eyes had already drifted back to her practice dummy.

Guanxi was the coin my family traded in. Good relationships with Hoard families like the Louies were vital. My father had expanded the clan business into rival territories with a combination of shrewdness, bargaining, and favors. Politeness dictated that I preserve my clan's relationship with the Louies and that I continue the long-winded social greetings. Politeness would waste time I didn't have. I needed answers now.

"Uncle Jimmy, do you know about the robbery that happened at the Japanese tea garden last night?"

Jimmy put Lucy down, setting her gently on the grass. She scampered off to join her sister, who had already moved back to the practice dummy. He swung his cane gently before planting it on the grass. His brow furrowed in confusion. "The garden is closed at night. I'm not sure what there would be to steal."

I noted that neither of those statements was an outright denial. "There is a Gate there, beside the Pagoda."

I placed an emphasis on the word *Gate*. Doors like the one in Popo's spa led to Fragments of the Realm, tiny broken pieces of our ancestral home. A Gate was a Door on another level, anchored on an object of power to open a direct path to entire worlds. Like Yomi. Or the Realm itself.

Thwack. Thwack. Lucy started hitting the dummy with her staff, her technique barely adequate but her enthusiasm high. Leanna moved to the weapons rack.

Uncle Jimmy wasn't very tall but he seemed to puff up and his chin tilted out. "Soong siu ze, I think I would know if there was a Gate there."

Again not a denial. And I hated when elders called me *missy,* like I was some upstart. I rolled the lozenge around in my mouth. It had dissolved to just a bare sliver, the bitter tang already beginning to fade. I shrugged and spread my arms out expansively. "It's been there for centuries, hidden under a warding from the Sugiwara Trust to keep the ghosts of Yomi locked up. Now it's missing and there is an open portal to Yomi in the middle of San Francisco."

Jimmy didn't seem alarmed at the thought of ghosts terrorizing the city. "It would take someone very talented indeed if what you say is true."

He turned and gestured to a slim young man with a gray jacket waiting in the shade. "Har zai, tea for our guest."

The young man bobbed his head, his long hair tied back in a loose bun. Har zai returned in a nanosecond with a tall silver pot and two delicate white-and-blue ceramic cups. The tea set had loose tea in saucers, the dark green hue and its curled shape telling me it was very high quality tea indeed. Har zai set it at the table next to us and carefully tapped the tea into our cups. Then in a dramatic fashion, he lifted the pot high and a river of boiling hot water poured into our cups. Har zai didn't spill a drop. Uncle Jimmy gave a nod of approval and picked up a cup to give it a gentle turn. The fragrance of jasmine pearl surrounded us.

I sighed. I couldn't refuse tea. That would be the height of rudeness.

This was going to take forever if we kept dancing around it like this and I had to stay for tea. How did my father put up with this? The taste of the lozenge had all but disappeared from my mouth. I would need to eat another one shortly but didn't want to do it overtly in front of Uncle Jimmy. I crunched down hard and chewed, then reached into my bag and drew out the Talon.

The gold had barely caught the morning light when Jimmy laid a hand on my wrist and pushed my hand down, and the Talon back into my bag.

His smile was indulgent, patronizing. "Please, I don't think this calls for that, do you? A bit of garden rockery was stolen. That hardly merits a Talon."

He handed me a teacup with two hands. "Please, have some tea."

I accepted the cup. The tea within was the temperature of boiling magma so I blew gently on its surface and considered my next words carefully. Despite my planning this morning, it had never occurred to me that the Louies would refuse our Talon. I took a sip of the tea, finding small comfort in the floral flavor burning across my tongue. I needed help to find the Gate and the Louies didn't seem to want to give it to me. Why?

Before I could say anything else, Jimmy strode over to the weapons rack to join Leanna. He grabbed a long spear off the rack, turned, and tossed it at me. I snagged it out the air, catching it in one hand out of sheer reflex. I set the teacup down.

The weight and length of the spear felt both familiar and foreign. It had been some time since I had sparred with one of these.

I felt a tug at my sleeve. Leanna stood beside me, eyes solemn, spear in her own hands. She made a fist with her right hand and slapped it into her left palm before bowing. "Sifu?"

Jimmy stood behind Leanna and placed his hands on her shoulders. "I believe it's customary for masters to fulfill a request for a lesson?"

I didn't know where Jimmy got the idea I was a master, but the look on Leanna's face was familiar. I'd seen it before in the mirror. Leanna might be a quiet one but she had a competitive streak a mile wide. And maybe giving the girl a lesson would soften Jimmy up.

The thought of Jimmy's approval spread warmly through my mind, easing my concerns. Of course it was a good idea to spend time training his niece. Jimmy was a generous man and it was only reasonable that I help out. Jimmy's face looked beatific now, his smile kind and sincere.

My earlier questions struggled to rise to the surface, but withered in the light of Jimmy's welcoming gestures. I would spar with Leanna, sharing some of my training. It was the polite thing to do.

I tucked the spear under my arm and pressed my fist into my palm, giving Leanna a short bow. "Hoi ci."

I dropped my bag on the grass and followed Leanna back to the sparring square, my adrenaline rising as I crossed the boundary line. I couldn't help it. I loved sparring, even if it was with a kid.

I felt I should press on Uncle Jimmy a bit more for the Ebony Gate theft but I couldn't find the energy to do it. Maybe I was going about this the wrong way. Should I really be bothering Uncle Jimmy with this? He was a busy man.

My concerns about the Ebony Gate and the ghosts of Yomi drifted away as I rolled the spear in my hands, getting used to its length and balance. The spear was a twin to Leanna's, about eight feet long, a shorter practice weapon, possibly unwieldy for someone as short as Leanna. Despite the shorter length, the haft was hardwood, not the willowy waxwood used on ceremonial spears.

This haft was meant to transmit and absorb lethal force. The spear was topped with a single-edged, leaf-shaped blade and adorned with a fluttering yellow tassel. The edge of the blade glinted in the early morning light. I found it interesting Leanna trained with live weapons. I had too.

I cracked my neck as Leanna took her position opposite me. I squared my hips and hefted the spear. I had no idea what she could do, but she was at least a head shorter than me, and had six inches less reach. I'd have to be careful.

Uncle Jimmy stood at the sparring square's boundary, eyes on his niece. "What is the Blade's purpose?"

I drew in a breath, my heart suddenly hammering in my chest. I knew the words. Every child did, but they'd been burned into my bones. There were so few Blades, not even one in each generation, so every house aspired to produce one. The odds of Leanna becoming the Blade of her clan were low, and that was a good thing. My years as the Blade were behind me but I still had nightmares. I wouldn't wish it on anyone.

Leanna said softly, "The Blade—"

Uncle Jimmy's voice was the crack of a whip, all traces of the kindly uncle gone. "Louder!"

Leanna brought her spear head up and bellowed. "The Blade for the Clan! Forever!"

Why was Uncle Jimmy teaching Leanna this? My father had raised me on these tenets and I would have expected Leanna's father to do the same. Then I remembered. Her father, Ray Ray, manned a desk at the family bank. If that pudgy banker had ever wielded a staff or a spear in those soft hands, I'd eat my boots. It looked like Uncle Jimmy was raising Ray Ray's girls, and instilling clan virtues.

Leanna gave a high-pitched yell, her eyes never leaving me. She lunged forward and brought her spear up, aimed at my torso. I took a step back and twisted the spear, wrapping her strike and pressing the spear away from me. Leanna yelled again and pressed her attack, two more high strikes before coming in low. Overhead strikes were a bad idea against a taller opponent. Leanna clearly needed more combat instruction, instead of the artistic form so frequently taught in stylized Wŭshù.

She drove me into the corner behind a flurry of attacks and I caught them all, slowly giving ground. The young girl lunged again, a clumsy thrust at my midsection. I deflected her thrust and sidestepped, letting her stumble past me.

I didn't strike at her unprotected back but flipped my spear and tapped her calf with the blunt end. I put just enough force behind it to force her knee to the dirt. I twisted away, jumping up to evade a low slash at my legs, and resumed my stance in the center of the ring. "An Achilles tendon injury will reduce your combat effectiveness by nearly thirty percent."

Uncle Jimmy grunted. "Sloppy. Slow. Dead. Again! Faster!"

Leanna righted herself and came at me again, her attacks quicker this time, but still sloppy. She had a good foundation, but she needed to learn finesse. Her attacks were wild, too showy. Even a beginner could predict her patterns. Uncle Jimmy continued egging her on from the sidelines.

"She's the Blade of Soong, the Butcher of Beijing, girl! She'll carve you up like a roast pig!"

I frowned at the moniker. Was I now the boogeyman that elders used to scare their kids?

Leanna ducked and sprang forward. I lost track of her as my surroundings blurred. One moment I was looking at a beautiful garden of green grass and my opponent with a sharp stabby spear, and the next moment I saw only a haze of color running together like messy watercolors.

Sheer instinct saved my skin. I'd seen where Leanna started from and when she'd started her lunge, coming in low and fast. I'd learned long ago to trust my instincts for split-second decisions.

I whirled away, blocking high. Through the swirling haze of

color the haft of my spear cracked against Leanna's. She favored the high attacks. Air rushed past me, probably Leanna hidden behind a crude illusion. I spun and held the spear before me, aimed at the fuzzy spot in my vision. I backed away and as I put distance between us, the illusion frayed at the edges and Leanna appeared again.

The scent of apples, bright and tart, tickled my nose.

Her grin went from ear to ear. "So cool!"

I didn't drop my guard. "Cute trick."

If her talent was only effective at short range, Uncle Jimmy was shortchanging her, training her with the staff and the spear. She'd be better off as a knife fighter, staying close to her opponents and taking full advantage of her gifts.

Leanna tilted her head at me, her eyes focused just off to my side. I backed up another step and looked down. The head of her spear had grazed my shoulder, sliced through my shirt, and drawn a fine red line across my skin. A tiny drop of blood welled at the scratch.

Well, well. First blood. I settled back down and smiled. "Let's see you try to do that again."

Leanna grinned back at me and took her position. As she rushed toward me, Uncle Jimmy took his leave, walking quietly into the house.


It surprised me how much I enjoyed instructing Leanna. What she lacked in skill she made up for with enthusiasm. Like any martial arts fanatic, she seemed to live on sweat and praise. There hadn't been a lot of praise for me. The best I'd gotten from Father had been the occasional "búcuò." I'd never earned anything higher than that "not bad" comment from him and I found myself happy to credit my young pupil for each well-executed manuever with more generous praise. We ran through most of the weapons in the racks before her tutor came to collect her. She pouted for a moment, but obeyed her tutor.

I helped her clean up, stowing and securing the weapons and raking the dirt in the sparring ring. She made me promise to return and spar with her again and even gave me a quick, sweaty hug before walking off with her tutor. Cute kid. One of the house guards returned my bag to me and showed me out the front gate.

I trudged back to my Jeep, enjoying the feel of the sun baking the delicious ache from my back and shoulders. My next sparring session with Leanna would be interesting. I wondered how she might improve by then. I found myself mentally crafting training schedules and lesson plans for her. The kid had a lot of talent. It would be a shame to let it go to waste.

I stuck my hands in my pockets, fishing for my keys, and my fingers bumped up against my candies from the Sun Emporium, the wrappers rustling as I touched them. Uh-oh. A cool ocean breeze blew past me, carrying the scent of salt and brine and chilling the sweat beaded on my back.

I turned to look back at the Louie estate. In the distance, the twin golden lion head knockers twinkled in the sun like a condescending wink, some inside joke not shared. The shadows cast by the perimeter walls were much longer than I remembered. Another salt wind rushed by me, the scent of brine thick and cloying enough to make my eyes water.

Uncle Jimmy's charm speak fell away from me like curtains parting in a window. The sun was suddenly a little too bright and my feet nearly faltered, even though I was standing on level ground. I looked around, taking in my surroundings, my thoughts sleep-slow and jumbled. My Jeep was parked where I'd left it, my keys in my hand. I rushed forward and put my back to the driver's door, getting some semblance of security. My mind ran in circles, trying to make sense of things. I remembered everything, but the memories were detached, like I'd spent the morning watching a movie.

I pulled out my phone and checked the time. Almost 11 a.m. Nearly two hours gone, and I'd gotten nowhere with Uncle Jimmy. Somehow he'd managed to deflect my questions, rejected my Talon, and gotten me to give sparring lessons to his great-niece.

No, not *somehow*. He'd invited me into his home and wrapped his charm speak around me, as neatly as a spider netting a fly.

A slow, rolling boil of anger heated my belly and burned away the remnants of Uncle Jimmy's power. My eyes snapped back to the ornate gates closing off the Louie compound. I could do it. My swords were in the trunk. I could strap them, climb the wall, drop into the property, and take retribution for this affront. They had half a dozen guards patrolling the perimeter, all armed. My ballistic plate was in the trunk as well. With those inserted in my haori I would mow down the guards in mere seconds. The main house had a front and a rear exit. I'd go in through the back and work through room by room, cutting down Jimmy's entourage until I had him cornered.

The idea of finding Leanna's room stopped my thoughts cold. Would she have a bookshelf full of martial arts trophies? A favorite stuffed animal? I slumped back against my Jeep and slid down until I was sitting in the shade. I ran my hands over my neck and blew out a long breath, willing the anger in my gut to subside. Like Popo had said, I needed to be smarter. Father had warned me and I hadn't taken it seriously enough. I should count myself lucky that all Jimmy had done was squeeze me for a free sparring lesson. He had won this round. Running through their home chopping off limbs wasn't going to solve my problems.

Why had he rejected the Talon, though? I clutched at my bag, suddenly panicked, and then relieved when I felt the reassuring shape and weight of the Talon through the fabric. For millennia, the use of Talons was the one thing Hoard families had held sacred. Elite Dragon talents, especially those with combat-grade power, didn't trust each other easily. But in centuries of adapting beyond the Realm, Jiārén sometimes needed to call on each other for assistance. The Talon was a favor, and also a contract. Talons could be passed down for generations to be honored in the future.

Though Soong House remained small in number, my father had amassed significant power and held considerable influence over the Council. And my brother's brand of Dragon talent was so horrifying that most families would be eager to have a favor from him in the future. The Tanaka House had redeemed a Talon five years ago and I had honored it. The cost had been high but that was the point.

That begged the question: why would the Louies refuse a Talon from Soong Clan?

Cursed skies. I added the Louie Clan to my short list of suspects and struggled to regroup. Someone had sent a ghost into my home. Coincidence? I still needed to follow up with Andie to see what she had learned. And while I was at it, I needed Andie to do a deep dive into the curious Adam Jørgensen. He was too knowledgeable if he knew about the Lost Heart of Yázì. Between the problematic sword in Adam's possession, his name-dropping of the legendary Jiārén stone, and the Ebony Gate, there were too many coincidences for my comfort level. I let out a frustrated huff. I would tackle the Trans next and circle back to the Louies but with better mental armor in place.

# FIONA AND FREDDY

I plotted the trip from Seacliff to Pacific Heights into my phone. Maybe I'd have better luck with the Tran twins. In Pacific Heights I drove past Edwardians, Victorians, Mission Revivals, and straight-up châteaus. With the tech boom, more billionaires had also made the "gold coast" their home. Of course the Tran estate commanded spectacular views of the bay.

What if the Trans had the same cavalier response as the Louies? The Trans were my last shot at getting some real intel on the theft of the Ebony Gate. The theft was secondary to the location of the item itself. I needed to solve the first problem and get the Gate back. Then I could worry about the why.

Through some miracle, I found parking right in front. I debated leaving my weapons in the car. Not much they would do against talents anyway.

My phone buzzed. Two texts from my father.

> **You should call your brother.**
> **Tatsuya worries about you.**

Translation: I should call my father, he wanted an update on my progress. I sighed and texted back.

> **Have been visiting with people. Will update you soon.**

That should keep Father occupied for a while. He would be burning with curiosity now about who I was visiting and how the visits went.

The stately three-story château boasted a manicured hedge, state-of-the-art cameras, and a majestic black double door. I could feel the buzz of their wards as I walked along the brick path through the tall hedges to their front door. I'd wasted enough time at the Louies'.

I looked at my wakizashi, the promise of violence elegantly sheathed. My lips twisted as I recalled the courtesy I'd tried to show the Louies by leaving my swords in the Jeep. But Fiona was about my age and not officially the Head of her Clan yet. I could afford to be more straightforward with her. I strapped on my swords and tucked my tanto in my boot. Immediately I felt my shoulders relax, the weight comforting me—reminding me who I was.

I took the Talon out of my bag and held it up in front of the discreet white camera near the light post and announced myself.

A small green light flashed on the camera and it flickered to life. A bald, grim-faced man came on the screen, his massive square jaw taking up most of the screen real estate. "Yes?"

"Emiko Soong. I need to speak with Fiona. Talon business."

I heard a small buzz and then a click as the front double doors opened. Square Jaw himself greeted me, and he was nearly as wide and tall as the door itself, incongruously adorned in a shiny shark-skin suit and polished Italian leather lace-ups. He also sported a charcoal tie with small pale blue diamonds. Pretty tie. His tie clip was a gleaming silver bar, its hue telling me this was from the Tran Hoard. Very fancy. He sported a heavy chain of silver links around his neck, as well as heavy rings worked in detailed filigree on each hand.

All the silver on this bodyguard wasn't a fashion statement. The Tran family had an affinity for silver in the same way the Louies garbed all their family members in gold.

Possibly the most stylish bodyguard I'd ever run across. His aura looked a little like Big Bill's aura, but locked down tight. White Tiger, gāo-level, maybe Dragon Limbs. Good talent for a bodyguard and I was sure the Tran family would recruit only the top of the class from the academy.

Next to him stood someone the same height, with a closely shaved head but a small dark goatee. He was dressed like his colleague, but looked a bit older. He sported the same tie clip, but for him it was purely ornamental to signal his clan affiliation. He had the pale, wispy gray aura of a Júwàirén. No talent. No way to draw on the shared might of the Tran Hoard gift from the silver. I felt a brief moment of kinship with him.

Sometimes I wondered what my life would have been like if I hadn't been born into a clan with a Hoard. Maybe I'd be a bodyguard like Goatee Guy, able to navigate complicated Jiārén society norms, but without a lick of useful talent. I felt a moment of envy. Goatee Guy probably thought he'd landed a cushy setup, sworn to a powerful family and with all the benefits but none of the pressure. None of the expectations. Hachi slid against my hip, the gentle weight reminding me that it didn't matter. I had served my clan faithfully, even without any talent. I served them still in this Talon Call. Whatever my father's expectations, I would never meet them, but I had learned to live with that as well.

Square Jaw held the doors open and gestured for me to come in. "Ms. Tran will be with you shortly. She has an appointment so it will have to be a quick visit." I had every intention of making it a quick visit, unless for some reason the Ebony Gate was just lying around in the foyer.

I stepped over the dark threshold to the creamy marble entry. A dazzling spiral staircase loomed at the rear of the foyer. I could feel the presence of oodles of money, but none of the buzz that came from the Hoard. San Francisco was the farthest western reach of the Tran Clan. Fiona had taken control of the operations here directly out of Lóng Kǒu, and she fought tooth and claw to stake out her territory. Her parents were semi-retired, residing at their château in southern France.

For the past two years I had assiduously avoided any social events that would bring me in contact with the Trans, but now here I was.

Goatee Guy headed up the stairwell, presumably to notify the Trans I was here.

I focused on the big guard in front of me. Square Jaw looked at my swords and gestured to them. "You need to leave those with me before seeing Ms. Tran."

I smiled, a mere baring of teeth. "I don't think so."

He paused, taken aback by my refusal to surrender my swords. Then his brows drew together, thick and dark. His massive jaw hardened. To some, that might have looked intimidating. Me, I welcomed the confrontation. After visiting Jimmy Louie, I was just spoiling for a fight.

Fiona's bodyguard was a huge guy, with shoulders that practically burst out of the seams of his tailored suit. I assessed him with an experienced eye. A lapel drag would cut him down to size. Or maybe I'd take out a knee. I zeroed in on the pretty tie. No sense in being fancy, a simple necktie choke would suffice. Given his talent, I'd just have to suffocate him with his tie. Even toughened by Dragon Limbs, he would need oxygen.

I had to give him credit, he was very professional. "Miss, no weapons are allowed in the salon."

I tilted my head, curious. "Is Fiona so weak that she worries about not being able to defend herself against me?"

It was well known that I was the Broken Tooth of the Soong Clan, with no talent to speak of. The tiny gold overlay to my aura was very recent, and somewhat mystifying. But still I manifested no Jiārén abilities beyond being able to light up my blood jade inlay on my sword, or activating Bāo's pendant.

Square Jaw struggled to form words and I watched his hands closely as he began to clench his fists. Oh goodie. I shifted my weight slightly to my toes, ready to spring forward.

A bell-like laugh came from above us. A cheerful voice squealed, "Mimi!"

I winced at the hated nickname. I only tolerated it from my father.

I looked up to face Fiona and was hard-pressed to keep the astonishment off my face. Despite the fact that it was still morning, her tiny form was resplendent in a black sequined mini with a plunging neckline and a fluffy white shag coat. Around her neck was a triple strand of thick silver chains. Her left ear sported a silver ear cuff and chain. Her long dark hair bounced in fat curls, the tips painted an icy white. If I wasn't mistaken, she wore four-inch-high open-toe platform heels that would have us eye to eye.

"It's fine, Franklin. We'll go to the Blue Room," Fiona said as she sauntered down the staircase.

I watched her come down the steep staircase in amazement. Fiona somehow made walking in those heels look effortless. I wondered if her wind talent augmented her strides, never letting her make contact with the marble.

Franklin shrugged his massive shoulders and then picked up a small silver tray and offered it to me. The tray held a bottle of sanitizer. This was new. He gestured to the pump and I gamely sanitized my hands. Did he also want me to wipe down my swords with an alcohol wipe? I kind of wanted him to try.

Instead, the big bodyguard led us to the Blue Room. Virtually all of the upholstery and wallpaper was robin's-egg blue, set off by cream rugs and gold trim. Guess I should have figured that a château would be styled in Louis Quatorze.

Fiona's tightly held aura glowed with a thin border of royal blue that highlighted her hair and offset her wide dark eyes. Somehow, she managed to perfectly match the Blue Room. Perhaps she dressed and accessorized with her aura in mind. According to my dossier, she was a gāo-class wind talent and had won her year's Lóng Yá Tourney handily. She and her brother had been one year ahead of me. Though we'd all been housed together as Azure Dragon class, I was never in their orbit.

I bent my head in greeting. "Please, call me Emiko. Hello, Fiona, long time no see."

She grinned, the big smile causing dimples to flash and her lush falsies to flutter. "Call me Fifi."

Of course she went by Fifi. I suppressed the urge to roll my eyes.

Fiona came in close and I tensed in fear that she would attempt to hug me or even worse, do the European cheek-to-cheek press and air-kiss thing. To my relief, she merely patted me on my right arm. "I haven't seen you since . . ."

Her voice trailed off into awkward silence. Yeah. This was why I avoided hobnobbing with elite Jiārén. Either they remembered me for failing out of the academy or worse, for paying them a visit as the Blade. Neither were good conversation starters. Luckily I wasn't here for polite chitchat.

I pulled out the Talon to burn down the awkwardness. Fiona pulled away from me at the sight of the Talon. I launched into my intro. "Did you know we have a portal to Yomi in the tea garden?"

Those faux fox fur lashes blinked and I watched her face carefully. She shook her head slowly from side to side, and her pearly smile faded. For all her high-glamour persona, my sources told me Fiona was a sharp businesswoman and poised to move quickly up the ranks within her clan. If her clan didn't know about the Yomi portal, then Sugiwara's no-look ward had worked. I sped through the morning's events, keeping the fact that Sugiwara was a shinigami to myself. Fiona's expression went from wariness to calculation as I finished detailing the situation. I knew that look. I'd seen it on my father's face innumerable times.

It was also encouraging because I saw concern in her eyes. San

Francisco was hers as far as she was concerned. She didn't need ghosts messing around in her town.

I didn't have time to wait for her to consider all the angles, to make predictions about where all the players would come down. I skipped to the end. "The Sugiwara Trust is my client. I want to know if anything like the Ebony Gate is moving in or out of the ports, any private transportation requests in and out of the small runways from last night onward. If you find it, hold it here. We don't have much time."

If Fiona was surprised at the simplicity of my Talon request she hid it well. She closed her perfectly manicured hand over the ingot, making a fist. "Spell out the terms of our contract."

I took a moment to consider. A Talon contract was binding, and the wording was important. In the end, I decided I was safer just keeping things simple. My father would have been disappointed. "Tran Clan will offer me and my agents extraordinary physical aid and use of all available talent for the next seventy-two hours to effect recovery of the Ebony Gate to the tea garden and support me with a show of force in repelling possible incursion from the demons and ghosts of Yomi."

Fiona thought over my words for a moment, then nodded. "Consider it done."

She and I pricked our thumbs on the sharp dragon's claw of the Talon, our blood lighting it up briefly in a flash of red light as we sealed our pact.

I stuck my thumb in my mouth, instinctively laving the small wound. Fiona snapped her fingers and Franklin stepped forward with a small gray handkerchief pulled from his breast pocket. "Witness."

Franklin nodded. "So witnessed."

I realized I had been holding my breath after what had happened with the Louies. I finally let it out and my shoulders drooped in relief. For the first time since being summoned by the shinigami,

I saw a glimmer of hope. I needed her help, and she was going to render it. Then I could get back to my old life while Tatsuya was safely esconced as the future of the Soong Clan. I tucked the Talon back into my bag. When this was all over, my family would still be short one Talon, but a Talon to the Trans was infinitely preferable to a Talon to a death god.

Franklin opened a drawer in the elaborate console table and pulled out a package of wipes, opening it and handing it to me. I wiped my hands, the alcohol stinging my small Talon wound.

Fiona handed Square Jaw the bloodied hankie. "Thank you, Franklin."

Franklin walked over to the fireplace, turned it on with the flip of a switch, and burned the handkerchief. The flames flared blue and then flickered back to the cozy preprogrammed level. Lóng Jiārén blood flamed hot. He resumed his silent watch from that part of the room.

Fiona sauntered over to the marble bar and pulled out two crystal snifters. She lifted a bottle of Hennessy X.O to me. "A toast."

"I don't drink."

Fiona unscrewed the Hennessy and poured a splash of amber liquor into one bar glass. Then she popped open a can of soda water and with a flourish used tongs to drop a maraschino cherry into the bubbly water.

"Here." Fiona handed me the glass with the cherry. I felt five years old.

I accepted the glass and watched as Fiona clinked her crystal bar glass against mine and lifted her cognac to sniff with appreciation. She radiated vitality and confidence. No wonder her father had handed over the reins.

"To our success!"

"To our success," I parroted.

I took a sip, the sweetness of the cherry and the fizz of the soda water a welcome palate cleanser from this morning's debacle with

Uncle Jimmy. Fiona tipped her head back and polished off her cognac with a pleased smile. Franklin came and cleared our glasses.

I wondered if Fiona would take me to the docks next.

Fiona turned and punched a call button on the discreet intercom hidden in the wall trim. "Freddy, get up here. Pronto."

I blinked and struggled to keep the dismay off my face. Oh skies, I was slipping. I'd assumed Fiona, Head of Clan operations, experienced businesswoman, and force to be reckoned with in San Francisco, would be offering me her aid. With her at my side, doors would open and people would talk. Fiona had enough clout and leverage in the city to have this problem solved before dinnertime. However, it appeared I would be getting help from Freddy, her twin brother. The lazy Tran who spent all of his time surfing in Santa Cruz.

No sooner had she lifted her finger off the comm button when the air around the dainty chaise longue shimmered. My nose itched from the talent flooding the room, thick with the smell of cold salt water. Sparks flared outward from the shimmer, the air around us pulsing like a living thing. Fiona tapped her pristine shoes and checked her watch, almost bored.

Freddy must be a tunneler. I had been so distracted with my own embarrassment in seeing the Tran twins again that I hadn't bothered to check on Freddy. Careless, sloppy. Ogata-sensei would be beating me senseless.

Sure enough, a swirl of mist obscured the chaise longue further and then cleared in an instant, leaving the trim and tanned Freddy stretched out across it as if he'd been chilling there all along. A small pile of sand pooled beneath his feet, looking out of place on the thick wool pile rug. "What's up, sis?"

He glanced over to the fireplace. "Hey, Franklin."

Franklin inclined his head. "Good morning, Mr. Tran."

Freddy's hair was a little longer than I remembered, and his surf tank revealed hard lean muscles. His skin held the brown tones of someone who spent all their waking hours in the sun and he wore Hoard silver hammered into a cuff around his left wrist. He and I were about the same height, which was nice because it meant he couldn't loom over me when he stood up. More impressive was that he didn't seem tired by what had to be a massive expenditure of energy to tunnel here.

He finally realized I was in the room and he popped up like a friendly Labrador, his windswept hair bouncing. "Hey! Emiko, right? It's been more than a minute . . ." Then his voice trailed off, too, as he recalled just when he had last seen me. His smile faded. I did have that effect on people.

Fiona interrupted him. "Freddy, we have a situation. Emiko brought a Talon." His eyes widened and he let out a low whistle.

Fiona turned to me. "I have a preexisting commitment or I would take you myself, but Freddy is faster anyway. You can fill him in and he'll take you to the shipyard. I'll assist further if that does not prove fruitful." She spun on one heel and flashed the trademark red sole of her Louboutins as her other foot lifted.

Fiona flounced out of the room and I was left with Freddy. I would have rather had Fiona's help, despite her demeanor. As far as I knew, Freddy had little to nothing to do with his clan's day-to-day organization. He cocked his head in interest when I explained about the Ebony Gate, but his thoughtful gaze showed no calculation. I trusted my gut feeling that the Trans were not complicit in the theft of the Gate. Or at least, Freddy wasn't. Now I had to trust that he could get me to the Gate in time, and Freddy could live up to his sister's expectations.

"Are you tunneling or do we take my ride?" I asked him.

He grinned, displaying the matching dimples that Fiona had. "If we tunnel, then you don't have to worry about parking." Good point. Again I marveled at his power stores that he considered it easier to do multiple tunnels in a day than drive. For all his low-key surfer-dude looks, Freddy was packing a metric ton of talent. Okay, maybe Fiona hadn't stuck me with a dud.

I needed to grab supplies from my car if Freddy was our transpo. Namely, weapons and premade spells. I stepped back into the marble entryway, Square Jaw watching my every move. The tang of cut grass and of something else that hadn't been there when I first came in assaulted me. Something I hadn't smelled in a while.

Tiger magic.

My stomach tightened, pain rocketing up to my chest. The Thai Tiger Clan members did not come to San Francisco very often. Most of them preferred to enjoy the comforts that abounded in Asia. Only one of them had lived briefly here.

My steps slower now, I exited the Tran château. There on the brick walkway I spotted Fiona clutching a taller man's lapels. Her face was upturned and her pretty features bathed in sunlight as she looked up at Kamon Apichai of the Thai Tiger Clan, the former love of my life.

# PIER 7½

There was no way through but forward if I wanted to get to my Jeep. But I couldn't move. All I could do was stare at my ex. My chest burned, taking all the air out of my lungs. The skin of my hand throbbed with pain and I realized I had gripped the hard edges of my jade pendant tight enough to cut. I released Bāo's pendant and looked at my hand. Blood welled from a small gash across my palm. The sight of the blood revived me and I sucked in a breath of air.

I could play it off. Nobody needed to know how seeing Kamon still affected me. Especially not Kamon.

I squared my shoulders and called out, "Hey Fiona, Freddy and I are going to head out shortly."

They both turned sharply at my interruption. Kamon looked even better than I remembered. He wore his hair a little longer now, a slight curl to it as it brushed his forehead. It had only been two years, but I had forgotten the impact of seeing his face and those intense dark eyes. Now it smacked me like a two-by-four. I tried to shake it off and keep my cool.

He was dressed casually but every part of his outfit was custom tailored, from his steel blue micro-check blazer to his charcoal wool slacks. The lightweight navy mac trench he wore accentuated the breadth of his shoulders. My memories stripped the austere clothing away, and images of him swimming on our vacation to

Maui bombarded me. Seeing him with Fiona hurt. I knew logically that I had broken it off, and it had been years so of course he was dating someone else. Still, seeing pretty Fiona plastered against him punched me in the chest.

Kamon looked startled to see me and took a step back from Fiona. "Emi, what are you doing here?"

I waved my hand breezily. "Don't let me keep you from your date. I just need to get a few things from my car."

At the word *date,* Fiona snapped to attention and immediately wrapped her arms around Kamon's elbow. "I made reservations at this amazing brunch place, Kamon. Just wait until you try their soju Bloody Mary!"

She moved surprisingly fast given those spike heels and she swiveled Kamon around like a tank driver. He looked confused as he obliged her but his dark eyes stayed on mine a moment longer.

When they were out of sight I sagged with relief. I did not need the complication of seeing Kamon again right now. This was exactly why I'd been trying to stay busy in the Júwàirén world for the last two years. I never doubted that I'd made the right call to leave my old life behind, but seeing what I'd lost still hurt.

I jerked open the back of my Jeep, grabbed extra ammo, strapped on my swords, stashed some emergency Kit Kats, and opened my bag of tricks. There was no use moping over Kamon. I had a death-mark on my hand and my immortal soul was on the line.

Freddy caught up to me and whistled appreciatively at the goods in my trunk. Getting the upper hand in any fight was all about preparation, anticipating what your enemy might throw at you, calculating the best response, and then throwing that back at your opponent, all in the space of a second or two. No problem.

As a talentless dud, with no Hoard gift, I'd had to learn a few . . . unorthodox . . . techniques in order to hold my own in a fight. Martial skills and a wicked sharp sword would only take you so far against an opponent who could rain ice blades down on you, or swamp you in a lake of fire. Over my short but storied career, I'd amassed a laundry list of mundane and canned talent solutions that were versatile enough to prepare me for most anything.

If the Louie Clan was involved in the theft of the Ebony Gate, I'd have to prepare for some of their heavy hitters. Charm speakers who could screw with your perceptions, or outright control you. Just remembering how Uncle Jimmy had rolled me ticked me off again. I picked out flash-bangs to disrupt illusions.

The outer branches of the Louie family provided a lot of the muscle to support the mentalists. Kinetics for the most part, unfortunately. Those guys were a royal pain and I was out of my usual remedy. I huffed in disgust and zipped up the bag.

Freddy quirked an eyebrow at me when I slammed the Jeep shut. His eyes traveled up and down my body, taking in all the hardware I carried.

I scowled at him. "I hate playing catch-up and I feel like I'm still a lap behind. I'm not letting this get further ahead of me. Think you can help out if we run into a kinetic, Tran?"

Freddy just tossed his hair out of his eyes and smirked, his attitude just screaming clan princeling. "They won't even see me coming."

I huffed and nodded. He was probably right. His air talent had a long-range advantage. Freddy took a step back and raised his arm. Reality melted and swirled in the space between us, light bending and running like wet paint. The scent of cold salt spray flooded my nose again and the tunnel widened until a swirling circle of color a meter wide distorted the ground at my feet.

Freddy came to my side, a lopsided grin on his face. "You ready for the fastest ride in the park?"

His corny line broke the ice a little and I laughed. "Do you always open with cheesy pickup lines?"

His cheeks flushed and I realized Freddy was trying to impress me. I put my hand out to him and nodded. "Let's go."

We stepped over the edge and Freddy's talent sucked us into the tunnel. The world was whirled away and I bit down before the scream could escape my throat. Freddy squeezed my hand. He might have been giving me a thumbs-up, but it was hard to tell with my eyes watering like crazy. We spilled out of the tunnel and the world immediately righted itself, even though my eyes told me everything was still rocking back and forth. I fell to my knees and dry heaved on the rickety docks of Pier 7½ while Freddy patted me on the back. Traveling by tunneling was only marginally better than a Crossing for me.

Tourists knew all about Pier 39, with its signature sourdough bread bowls ladled to the brim with thick clam chowder. But the Port of San Francisco had something like fifty piers along the seawall and that was just what the Wàirén saw. Nothing magical went through the ports of San Francisco without the Tran family getting a piece of the action and *all* the action happened on Pier 7½.

Pier 7½ looked just like a Júwàirén shipyard with tall cranes, corrugated shipping containers, and the freight ships themselves. But all around me I could feel the wards around each container and a struggling energy, as if their special contents were vibrating within.

Freddy zipped up a faded yellow hoodie and shivered in the breeze coming off the bay. He scoped out the young Jiārén in a red puffy down coat and dark beanie sealing the green shipping container closest to us. "Hey Raj, did you get any last-minute requests since yesterday?"

Raj looked startled then strode over to us. He had thickly lashed dark eyes and sported a short goatee as if he were trying to look older. I pegged him as a recent grad of Lóng Kǒu, someone with decent containment talent at an entry-level job. "Hey Freddy, I just finished that one because I thought you told the clerk to prioritize it over the others?"

His puffy microdown jacket swished gently as he raised his arm to point to a tall crane lifting a corrugated and rusty gray container less than a hundred meters away. A lone freight-hauling truck sat next to the crane.

Freddy shook his head. "I was in Santa Cruz. This is the first I've heard of it."

Freddy marched toward the office portable, moving faster than I'd thought was possible for the laid-back surfer. I studied the gray shipping container swaying above a moment longer. It was certainly large enough for the Ebony Gate. Could it be this easy?

I hustled to catch up to Freddy. "Who's your clerk?"

He scowled. "We have two, Samantha and Curtis. Today should be Curtis."

Maybe I was wrong about Freddy. He seemed pretty familiar with the ins and outs of this pier. Maybe he was more operational than I'd realized. Freddy yanked open the door to the portable, which was not easy given the wind but hey, air talents. The cramped interior was covered in outdated wood paneling, the space taken up by two utilitarian steel desks. Three guys had their backs to us. Two of them were heavyset with broad backs, and the third man had a taller and slimmer build. I didn't see any familiar markings or tattoos but something about the way they held their bodies told me these guys were local heavies. I drew in their scent, trying to catalog what I was smelling. A younger man faced us, sporting one of the bright orange safety vests I'd seen on the workers outside. Curtis, I presumed.

Curtis had virtually no aura. That wasn't true of the heavies in front of us. The tallest one had on a blue down vest and a black fisherman's cap pulled down low. But none of those dark colors could detract from the way the edges of his aura were lighting up in bright green. The wood paneling was practically humming from all his talent use. I sniffed again quickly. Bright and tart, green apples. Skies, an illusionist. Whoever was behind this was throwing everything at it.

Curtis looked harried as he shuffled through a mess of papers on his desk. ". . . of course, Mr. Tran, right away . . ."

The other men turned to face us. One was built like a bulldog, muscular on top with scrawny little legs in tight jeans. The last one had a shaved head and sported a black windbreaker, much like the ones the Louie Claws wore but minus the emblems.

Curtis looked up as we entered and his face dissolved into confusion when he spotted Freddy. "Mr. Tran?"

He turned back to the illusionist in disbelief.

Bulldog yanked on Baldy's sleeve, gesturing to us. Baldy turned and faced us, his eyes narrowing in concentration. Bulldog clapped his hands together and widened his stance.

The sharp tang of acid filled my senses as Bulldog's aura flared in my mind's eye. I gritted my teeth in annoyance. Why was it always kinetics? Why did those with the most common talent always end up as hired heavies? In a split second the details of the room jumped out to me—staplers, pens, scissors, desk lamps, chairs, waste bins. We were in close quarters with talents who could turn every loose bit of stationery into a whirling blender. If he was a high enough talent, even my gun would be useless.

He splayed his hands in a wide gesture, palms toward us, and all the office supplies on the desk flew at us.

I moved to duck behind the closest desk but Freddy reacted first. He stomped his foot and bellowed from deep in his belly, swinging his arms up across his body, fists clenched. The sweep of his arms formed a swirling portal in the wall to our right, the massive funnel sucking in everything coming at us. An exit funnel opened on the far wall of the office and the flying office supplies spewed out at Bulldog's back. Handy talent.

Bulldog pivoted, spinning his arms wide and lifting one of the desks. The rain of office bric-a-brac clattered against it. He lunged toward us, throwing both hands out, and lobbed the desk at our heads. Cursed skies! The desk rocketed past Freddy's funnel and Freddy and I split, diving for the floor as the desk crashed into the space we'd just vacated.

Baldy lunged forward and with a sweep of his hand, sent a filing cabinet crashing into Freddy, pinning him to the floor. Freddy's funnel snapped closed, the pop of air pressure clearing my ears.

Anything I would normally do, like throw a blade, was not an option. Never give a kinetic something to throw back at you. That left me with the ultimate weapon—my body.

I rolled away from the wrecked desk and launched myself at Bulldog. These guys loved to throw stuff around and usually sucked at hand-to-hand. Bulldog windmilled his arms as he backed away. As I closed the distance he flinched, lowering his arms to shield his face. His concentration disrupted, I came in low and drove hard into him, putting all the power of my legs into a fist to his gut. His breath exploded from him and he fell to the floor, gasping and clutching at his stomach. I socked him in the neck, a dim mak strike that blocked his meridians and scrambled his qì. He rolled into the fetal position, trembling as his qì drained away.

Baldy backed away, needing room to work. I dove for his ankle, taking him down with the same move I'd used on Adam in the gym earlier this morning. Baldy toppled like timber and I hopped on to him and drove my knees into his chest, forcing the air out of his lungs. He gasped, his eyes wide with alarm. I'd be lying if I didn't admit to enjoying his distress. But I didn't have time to savor incapacitating these two. I hooked my fingers into the space between Baldy's neck and shoulder, and tapped a quick, hard sequence into the meridians along his neck. He gasped and his eyes fluttered shut.

The illusionist turned from Curtis, his aura flaring radiant magenta. He was older than I had expected, maybe late forties, with sagging jowls. With a straight jab, he punched Curtis in the jaw. Curtis sagged and slumped to the floor like a rag doll. The illusionist's gaze homed in on Freddy like a laser.

Freddy pulled himself from under the cabinet, his wide brown eyes glazed with confusion. His eyes darted between me and the illusionist, panic spilling over his face. He snatched a letter opener off the floor and held it like a knife. No, no, no, this was bad.

I scooted off of Baldy's prone body and edged backward away from Freddy as I assessed my options. I couldn't use the flash-bang in these close quarters. If I put a bullet in the illusionist I wouldn't be getting any information out of him and I didn't want to risk the ricochet. I reached into my sleeves for the next best thing.

Freddy yelled and took a wild swing at me with the letter opener. I dodged around him and his momentum carried him over a desk and onto the floor. With the speed that came from years of practice, I unleashed two shurikens at the illusionist, the bladed stars spinning at blistering speed. One sliced into his arms, lacerating his bicep. Blood spurted from the wound and he instinctively dropped his concentration from Freddy. The second shuriken sunk into his thigh, forcing him to one knee.

Freddy yelped and dropped the letter opener, his hands scrubbing his eyes. "What the hell?"

He shook his head and came up to his knees, his breath coming in ragged pants now, the delayed adrenaline hitting his system. I knew what it felt like. Having someone screw with your perception was the worst. My recent experience with Uncle Jimmy's charm speak still left me feeling a little raw.

I doubted Freddy had ever been in a real fight before, despite him having been blessed with combat-grade talent from birth. He'd graduated Lóng Kǒu so he'd taken the classes, he had the skills, and he'd competed in the Lóng Yá Tourney in his last year. But for a clan princeling like him, it was never more than a game. A way to flex his power and privilege over his peers, and never for real stakes.

I took a slow step in Freddy's direction. "Easy there, Freddy. It's all over now."

Freddy's head snapped up, his nostrils flaring, eyes red with hurt and anger. He looked at me, his eyes concerned. "I almost hurt you."

He slammed two fists together and I watched in astonishment as the floor swirled to life under the dazed illusionist's feet. His eyes popped wide with surprise as he fell into the funnel. The exit funnel opened in the ceiling and the illusionist fell through, his fall looping and accelerating. His scream staccatoed as he disappeared in and out of the portals.

I lunged forward. "No! Freddy, we need him!" I crashed into Freddy and wrenched his arms down. The air popped again and something wet slammed onto the floor behind me.

Freddy stiffened in my arms and my insides went cold. Uh-oh. I turned, dreading what I would see behind me. The illusionist was crushed into the office floor, back bent at an obscene angle. A growing pool of dark fluid spread through the spare carpeting. My shoulders sagged. There went our best lead, now with an extra-huge helping of headache on the side. It was clear to me that the illusionist had been the brains of the outfit, so now I was left with the muscle.

Bulldog coughed and got to his feet. He froze, eyes wide and sweeping from me and Freddy to the illusionist's broken body. With a sinking feeling in my stomach, I realized I had been too distracted by the fight to make sure that Bulldog stayed down.

Bulldog barked a word of power and clapped his hands together. Everything in the office, including me and Freddy, flew back into the wall. My shoulder hit the wood paneling with a painful smack. I landed on my feet and lunged for Bulldog but he was too fast, pounding out onto the dock as fast as his tight jeans would allow.

I bolted out of the office and chased after him, dodging the wooden pallets and crates he launched at me. There were too many bystanders on the dock and Bulldog was using his kinetic talent to throw everything he could in my way. The distance between us increased as I bobbed and weaved around obstacles and I screamed in frustration as Bulldog reached into the crane operator's window and dropped the container onto the freight-hauling truck, his kinetic wave slowing the fall just before the container settled into the truck bed. Bulldog jumped into the passenger side.

Freddy and I had failed to notice the driver before, more focused on Raj and Curtis. I had stupidly assumed everyone was in the office but these guys had a wheelman. I cursed in three dialects.

I made for the truck but with a wave of his fingers, Bulldog launched the crane at me. Metal screeched as the crane supports crumpled under Bulldog's power. The towering crane arm buckled and swung toward me, steel cables pinging as they snapped under the strain. I put on a burst of speed, angling to duck under the shadow of the crane. I was too slow and the truck was already pulling away.

I pulled a last-ditch effort out of my pocket, a rough triangle of broken glass, and hurled it at the truck along with a burst of my own qì. The glass held a charm, a compressed bit of talent. This one held Whirling Blades, which, when properly ignited, was supposed to hit like a master's sword strike at up to fifty feet, giving it more than enough juice to puncture one of the truck's tires.

If properly ignited. My pathetic qì did little more than make the glass sparkle as it winged toward the truck and stuck into the treads. The truck rolled forward and crushed the glass with barely a puff.

I cursed my blocked meridians as the crane collapsed around me. I dove for the deck as the shadow of tons of screeching steel overtook me. I braced myself for the impact on the deck, and then the crash of the crane on top of me.

The tang of salt water bloomed around me and instead of bouncing off the wood of the pier my arms flailed into emptiness. I opened my eyes to a dark, swirling maelstrom. An instant later the sun returned and I crashed into the weathered planks of the pier, bouncing off my shoulder and rolling to a stop in a heap. Dust and debris flew past me in a cloud as the rumble of the wrecked crane subsided.

I sat up. I'd ended up at the steps to the door of the trailer, a hundred yards from where I'd started. Freddy leaned heavily on the doorframe, his face more than a little green around the edges. He sat down on the door sill, his breathing labored. "You were almost too fast for me to catch you."

My eyes tracked back to the twisted remains of the crane and the splintered pier beneath it. Through the dust cloud, the truck's tires squealed as it raced out of the marina and into traffic. The gray shipping container winked in the noon sun, taunting me. The truck blurred and I watched in disbelief as the truck and shipping container faded from sight, hidden by an obfuscation spell. Their wheelman was an illusionist of gāo caliber. I was cursed. That was the only explanation. The heavens hated me.

I smashed a fist against the wooden pier. "We had it, Freddy . . ."

My voice trailed off in frustration as the enormity of our failure hit me. The shipping container was gone and our one lead was now a pile of meat goop in the portable. I let my head smack back down onto the pier. So many people were urging me to be the Sentinel. Would I have more power as the city's Sentinel? Maybe then I could have done this solo, without involving Freddy. He was clearly in over his head, and it was my own fault for letting him tag along. I should have held out for his sister.

Freddy sprawled out on the wrecked pier beside me, his shoulders and back slumped. "I'm sorry, Emiko. I lost control." His voice was still shaky. He heaved a sigh and pulled out his phone.

"Hey, Fifi. We, um, have a bit of a situation. I need eyes on cargo that just left our pier. Gray container, no markings, probably an unregistered truck. Um, and the truck is hidden under gāo illusion.

The, um, pier got damaged, and one of the cranes is totaled. Curtis got tricked by an illusionist impersonating me. I fell for it, too."

Fiona let loose on the other end.

Freddy just nodded. "Yeah, I know, I know and Fi . . . uh . . ." His voice petered out and he swallowed hard a few times. I took pity on him and took the phone away.

"Hey, Fiona, what Freddy is trying to say is that we need a cleaner. Now. We have one body in your office portable. Also, we need a healer for the other guy and to check out Curtis. Do you have an Advocate on retainer? If not, I will call the one House Soong works with. We invoke the Second Law." There.

Freddy looked up at me in stunned silence, but also with a touch of wonder in his eyes.

Fiona screeched, "What?!"


*Dì Tī Tiáo.* The First Law between Hoard families was: protect the Hoard. *Dì Èr Tiáo.* The Second Law was: kill only when justified.

Justification was a slippery slope.

For Hoard family members, justification was even harder due to the power dynamics. If the illusionist belonged to the Louie Clan, we were going to be in for it. Freddy would have to stand before the Council. Assuming the Louies claimed him. If the Louies claimed him, they'd seek restitution. Or maybe they would disavow him? Freddy would claim justification to save my life. Except I had been the Butcher. Nobody would believe I needed Freddy to rescue me. These Jiārén intrigues always exhausted me. I had left those to Father before. Now I was involved again.

A clan war would erupt in San Francisco if this wasn't handled properly. Freddy would definitely need the Advocate. I would be subject to an inquest. Because of my use of a Soong Talon, Father would get pulled in, too. All bad.

"Freddy, have you ever invoked the Second Law Defense before?" I already knew the answer but I was just trying to ease into it.

He shook his head.

I licked my lips, my mouth suddenly dry as I recalled the truth-seeking power of the Advocate. "You can avoid having a full panel hearing before the Bā Shǒu if you submit to an Advocate's truth seeking."

It was an invasion unlike anything else, and forced you to relieve the trauma of the past violence again. Our justice system was short and abrasive. You could withstand a truth seeking from an Advocate, or you could go before the Bā Shǒu for hearing and judgment.

Freddy seemed so young and vulnerable out here in the wreckage of the pier. I knew he was older than me, but I'd had lifetimes more violence during my tenure as the Blade for House Soong.

"Fiona will get you the best Advocate. You don't have to submit to a truth-seeking session but you must still tell them everything, including the fact that you feared for my life and yours."

I hadn't needed Freddy to save me in the portable when he'd pulverized the illusionist, but Freddy's talent sure had helped me out here from the falling crane. The thing was, Freddy didn't know that. He might know me by reputation but he'd been shaken after being fooled by the illusionist and he thought he was rescuing us.

Freddy's eyebrows drew together, concentrating on my words. "It all happened so fast. I can barely . . ." His words trailed off and I knew he was trying to process what had happened in the trailer.

I chose my next words carefully. "The illusionist tricked you, you were going to stab me."

He winced. "He made you look like one of them, and I needed to defend myself."

Was the illusionist a Louie? Jimmy had rolled me so smoothly, with his aura barely even registering. This guy Freddy had crushed could be a family member. Maybe a dark horse with unregistered talent. That's what I would have been if I hadn't been called to be the Blade of Soong. Someone who worked unofficially for the clan.

I'd been through all of this before. The last time I'd had to face standing before the Council had involved the deaths of a building full of low-level yakuza associates—a consequence of honoring a Talon to the Tanakas. I frowned. Two solid years, free of the Butcher title and the headache of Hoard politics. How in the sixteen lesser levels of hell had I gotten myself into this new mess? Oh yes, my mother gave a Talon to a death god who wanted to use my soul as anchor. My mood soured further.

Freddy still looked shell-shocked. He'd stepped up for me, and while his actions were in line with Talon duty, he'd probably had no idea what it would mean to take on a Talon Call from me. I wondered if he would regret it later.

I tried one last time to guide him without scripting his testimony. "The Advocate can tell when you are truthful. Be honest with them that you were afraid for our lives."

I hoped Freddy would never have to invoke the Second Law Defense again. Once was more than enough for anyone. Unfortunately, I didn't seem to have that luxury.

I closed my eyes in fatigue. The sigil burned in my palm and my eyes snapped open. I'd worry about the consequences later. I had a witness to interrogate.

# THE WITNESS

Freddy sent Raj off to gather the other pier workers and set up a perimeter. We just needed to hold off any onlookers until Fiona showed up. She'd have the clout to close everything off from prying eyes.

I dragged Baldy to the back of the trailer where Freddy had cleared some space and set up an office chair. He helped me wrestle the unconscious man into the chair and secure him with a length of rope. The smell of blood hung thick in the cramped space and Freddy kept his eyes steadfastly on his work as he tied the man's hands together and lashed them to the chair. I patted the man down and retrieved a simple flip phone, a pack of cigarettes, and a disposable lighter. No wallet. No ID. I stowed the phone to examine later.

I was infinitely more familiar with using dim mak to incapacitate someone than to revive them. But in theory, I could use a sequence of pressure strikes to wake up Baldy, too.

Freddy watched me warily as I took a closer look at Baldy's neck. "Can you wake him up?"

I probed the big man's meaty neck, prodding my fingers in until I found the meridian underneath the muscle. "I should be able to. It's not quite doing it backward, but nearly."

Freddy gave a little hiccup. I turned to look at him. Between the dead body behind us, and my fingers knuckle-deep in Baldy's neck, Freddy looked ready to vomit. "It's okay if you need to step outside, Tran."

His mouth set in a grim line. "I'm fine. I'll stay."

Despite being the lazy Tran, Freddy seemed committed to stick it out with me. I turned back to Baldy and continued to probe his neck. "I forgot to say thanks, back there. You pulled my bacon out just in time."

"All part of the Tran white glove service."

I turned back to Freddy and studied his face. Lóng Jiārén as a whole were an unforgiving people. We lived by the principles of the survival of the fittest, and stood by our clans and our honor to the death. Rarely was anything given in our culture. Things were traded, earned, or taken.

Freddy had literally saved my life not moments ago and he was treating it like no big deal. I intuitively understood that his nonchalance was not about his talent, but the act itself. My father would have said Freddy had saved me as was required under the terms of the Talon contract, but I sensed there was more going on with Freddy Tran than I had initially thought.

I must have stared at him too long. "What?"

"Just . . . thank you."

I turned back to Baldy and took a breath. I was pretty sure this would work, or at least not kill him. I placed my fingers against his neck, finding the meridian again and spacing out my fingertips. I drummed a quick pattern against the nerve.

Baldy's eyes flew open and he gasped in a breath. I backed away as he thrashed against his restraints, bucking the chair legs off the floor.

I leaned in and cuffed him across the ear. "Settle down!"

He grunted as his head snapped back. His eyes focused behind me, landing on the remains of the illusionist. His aura flared. "You—!"

I jabbed him in the torso, once, twice, my fingers stiffened like a blade. Baldy's aura faded as he cried out in pain. I had to keep him off balance. Even bound to a chair, his powers would be deadly. I grabbed his neck, pressing my fingers into his carotid. His back arched as he tried to pull away from my grip.

"Where is the Gate being moved to?"

Baldy's eyes darted around the room, a panicked animal searching for escape. I set my knee on his groin and leaned on him, bending his neck over the back of the chair. His heartbeat thrummed under my fingers and he reeked of fear sweat. A typical kinetic who'd never had to face down an opponent in close quarters.

"I know you're moving the Ebony Gate. Tell me where you're hiding it. You know who I am. Talk and we can keep this professional."

The man's eyes bulged and his jaw worked, like he was trying to swallow. I eased the pressure off his neck and backed away to let him speak. He coughed, his jaw still working convulsively. His eyes had gained a strange light, an almost manic—

No! I lunged forward, hands to his face, trying to pry his mouth open. Too late, I heard the capsule crack from inside his mouth. A puff of strongly floral-scented gas escaped his lips as I leapt back, arm up over my own nose. The scent was cloying and unfamiliar.

Baldy collapsed back against the chair, the light already fading from his eyes. "He will rise aga—" His head dropped to his chest like his strings had been cut.

Freddy nearly choked. "What happened?! Is he dead?"

I slapped Baldy across the face, the sound strangely loud in the tiny office. The big man didn't move, didn't even flinch or make a sound. I kicked the chair over. It tipped to the side and Baldy crashed to the floor like a felled tree, his head scraping against the corner of the desk on the way down. He lay in a heap, tied to the chair, blood weeping from the gash on his forehead. Holding my breath, I got my hands on Baldy's neck again. No pulse.

Damn him to the eighth level of hell. I let out the breath I'd been holding. "Dead."

Whatever had been in the capsule had dissipated, and my hopes for finding the Gate had disappeared with it. I growled in frustration. First letting the Gate slip through my fingers, and now losing my best lead.

Freddy patted me on the shoulder, looking like he was trying to calm a rabid dog. "It's going to be okay, Emiko. We'll find it."

I stood and whirled on him. "How?!"

None of this was Freddy's fault, but my hands itched and my arms trembled with the need to strike something, someone. I wasn't made for this delicate dance of intrigue. I was a weapon to be aimed and unleashed.

"How are we going to find it? A gāo illusionist is hiding the trailer. They could be anywhere. This useless piece of meat was my best lead!"

Freddy shrugged, clearly uncomfortable. "But you're . . . you know . . . you're the Butcher, man! I'm sure you can . . ."

I winced at the name and the anger drained out of me. Wasn't I here to get away from all that? All my bloody history? "Don't call me that. I hate it."

I struggled to explain without sounding defensive. "Look, I moved here to get away from all that. After the purge at Pearl Market . . . I . . . needed to stop doing what I was doing." I shrugged, not able to explain how devastated I had felt.

"But you were a Blade, Emiko. You didn't even have to finish Lóng Kǒu to land that gig, and . . ."

I bit off my reply before I could say something I would regret. I looked at Freddy. Really looked at him. When I had been failing out of Lóng Kǒu he and Fiona had been a year ahead of me. I remembered him coasting through classes and holding court during breaks, an endlessly changing swarm of fawning girls around him. It wasn't his fault his life had been easy.

"How many Blades do you know?"

Freddy's brow creased, confusion at my shift in the conversation. I was the first Blade in two generations. That meant Freddy had to dig deep into our history. "Um . . . There was Zhang, Hirabayashi, Kim, and Sisuk . . ." His voice trailed off.

"Right. The baddest of all the badasses in the clans. How many of them retired?"

He gave me an abashed look, understanding dawning in his eyes.

"None of them. None of them retired. They all died doing their duty for their clans. Did you know I was the first Blade to break her sword in over five hundred years? Did it ever occur to you to wonder why a Blade serves for life?"

Freddy opened his mouth to answer but I pressed on, the words tumbling out of me. "Because nothing comes for free, Tran. Not everyone got to coast through school. You think being a Blade is all about the power you're given, but no one who leads a clan gives up that much power without adding strings to the deal. Blades are loyal and obedient, because that's what the power requires. And the power shields you from all the death and horror of what you're doing, so you don't feel the need to question your orders. Being a Blade is no better than being someone's trained attack dog."

Dead silence hung between us as my heartbeat thundered in my ears. The last time I'd been this keyed up was . . . well, it was exactly what I was talking about.

Freddy nodded slowly, his eyes wide as saucers.

I sighed and took a recentering breath. He didn't need this lecture from me. And I still needed his help. "Sorry. I didn't mean to dump that on you."

He chuckled and ran his hand through his hair, flinging his bangs back. "Ah, don't sweat it. I probably had it coming. For what it's worth, I'm sorry you had such a rough time at Lóng Kǒu. And I'm not looking for sympathy or anything, but it wasn't exactly a cakewalk for me, either."

Freddy's eyes lost focus as if remembering. "You got out early enough to miss the backstabbing and the schemes, Emiko. All the buildup to the Tourney. Friends turning on friends, siblings cutting each other down . . ."

He shook his head, a painful sadness in his eyes. "I don't talk to anyone from school anymore. Guys I counted on, thought were my friends . . . So much time and energy, just, wasted."

It was true. I didn't know what school was like for those who had managed to make it through the Tourney. My brother and I hadn't talked about it. Maybe we would need to.

Freddy moved to the east window of the portable office and looked out. "Looks like Fiona's here. And it looks like she brought everyone with her."

I looked through the window as well. A fleet of pearly white Cadillac Escalades blockaded the pier and dozens of private security in dark suits were exiting the vehicles and setting up a secure perimeter. Fiona's Range Rover was parked and I spotted her bodyguard in the driver's seat. I looked overhead, the sun's rays burning away the gray of morning. It was high noon now.

"This day just gets better and better. Come on, Tran. Time to face the music."

Franklin sat in the driver's seat, his eyes hidden behind wraparound sunglasses. He stepped out and opened the rear passenger-side door.

Fiona's delicate hand reached out, steadied by the ubiquitous Franklin. She alighted onto the pier, her glamorous attire looking even more outlandish on the docks. Franklin reached into his pocket and pulled out a squirt bottle of sanitizer. She pumped twice and rubbed her hands together briskly.

The door of the closest Escalade opened, and a trim woman stepped out. She wore the trademark shimmery gray of the Tran security detail. She walked over to Fiona and Franklin, her eyes moving over us in a clinical assessment. She was a study in sharp lines, from the ironed precision of her pantsuit to the razor edge of her pageboy haircut. She was roughly the same height as Fiona, or would be if Fiona wasn't in platform heels. Her face had Fiona's pretty features, but with the sharp chin and straight decisive brows, she managed to look nothing like Fiona. Sunlight glinted off the silver lotus flower brooch on her lapel.

Freddy waved. "Hi, Fifi."

He turned to me. "You already know Franklin. This is Linh, my cousin." Her royal blue aura marked her as a blood relation to the Trans. Perhaps she'd been after me at Lóng Kǒu.

Linh and I exchanged curt nods, one soldier to another.

Fiona stepped closer to us, looking like a lost fairy princess as her wide eyes took in the wreckage behind us. She gestured to the downed crane. "Do you know how much one of these costs? How hard it is to get another in time for tomorrow's shipments?"

Her voice, piercing as a bell, ripped across the pier. Her ire was clearly directed at Freddy. "Uh, Fi, I know it looks bad."

My lips quirked in amusement. Freddy was hilarious. It didn't look bad—it looked catastrophic.

Fiona whipped off her Gucci sunglasses and speared Freddy with a glare. "I can't even take a morning off. You're sticking me with cleanup?!"

I checked the time. A hair after twelve now. Fiona had probably been in the middle of drinking soju Bloody Marys with Kamon. My mood, already in the dumps, soured further at the thought of Fiona having a cozy brunch with my ex. My mood then lightened as I considered their date cut short.

Fiona took a few steps closer to Freddy and took a closer look at him. His hair stood up every which way. His face and yellow hoodie were splattered with blood. She frowned and reached into a pocket hidden in the furriness of her short jacket and yanked out a package of disinfectant wipes. Her four-inch platform heels put her taller than Freddy. She reached over and started dabbing at his face with the wipe, her mouth turned down in a scowl.

"Is any of this blood yours?" Her voice was quieter now and Freddy stood meekly under her ministrations.

He swallowed hard, his throat visibly working. "No."

Fiona turned slightly to address me. "Do we know who he is?"

My lips thinned out in displeasure. "I think they were Louies."

Freddy and I looked at each other, our expressions grim. Freddy had likely killed one Hoard Custodian family member, and I'd managed to drive another one to suicide. But between the two of us, Freddy was the one with a problem. Fiona was savvy enough to know what came with invoking the Second Law but she didn't jump to conclusions. Her voice stayed soft and noncommittal. "What makes you say that?"

"Someone sent two illusionists and two kinetics to your pier today. Who else in San Francisco has that kind of muscle on their payroll?"

Fiona's eyes narrowed at me. If I didn't know any better I'd guess she didn't like me very much. "We do."

Fair point. "Well, I mean, I know it's not you, so . . ."

So my reasoning left a little to be desired. It felt right, though. I knew it in my bones. Uncle Jimmy hadn't rolled me this morning for kicks. The intrusion at my house was unlikely to be a coincidence, either. Something bigger was happening and somehow the mastermind had known I would get involved. That seemed ludicrous though. I stayed out of Jiārén intrigue. Why target me? This was making my head hurt. I focused on the one thing I could concentrate on, which was how to find the Ebony Gate.

Fiona turned Freddy away from me as her entourage of heavies secured the pier. I held back and gave them space to discuss in private. As Freddy spoke, Fiona clenched her fists and nearly shook with anger. I wondered if it was because she was angry Freddy had been attacked and their business violated, or if it was because she'd accepted the Soong Talon from me.

But Fiona was made of sterner stuff. She placed a hand on

Freddy's shoulder and spoke bracingly, conviction radiating from her small frame. Freddy was nodding. Good.

They came back to me and Fiona fired off a set of instructions, her black-suited minions rushing off to do her bidding and attend to the cleanup.

"I'm taking Freddy to our downtown offices so that we can update our in-house counsel. We will of course continue to render assistance. Would you like Franklin and a few members of his team to shadow you?"

I thought about what I needed. "We need to find that missing shipping container. I'm sure the Gate is in it."

Fiona nodded and held out her hand. Franklin took a small black tablet out of his pocket and handed it to her.

She opened the tablet cover. "I'm getting eyes in the sky."

That was interesting. I tilted my head. "You have precogs or seers on the payroll?"

Freddy laughed at me, his voice still shaky, but the kid was getting his feet back under him. "Dude. We use drones and helicopters."

I smacked my forehead in embarrassment. Sometimes I made dumb assumptions, like thinking the folks I left behind at Lóng Kǒu would rely heavily on their talent instead of tech.

Fiona ignored us, quickly navigating on the tablet screen, talking under her breath. Finally she said, "They aren't going to fly this thing out. That leaves the Port of Oakland."

The Port of Oakland was enormous, with over thirteen hundred acres of maritime facilities. Still a needle in a haystack, but at least we had a shot at which haystack since the Tran family operated that channel, too. Jiārén goods went through Berth 35 at the Oakland Seaport so if Fiona was right, Bulldog and his illusionist wheelman would have to make their way through to Berth 35. Bulldog's crew was now down two members, so I wondered what kind of reinforcements would be coming. How much manpower was Bulldog's boss willing to throw at this? Could it be anyone other than the Louies that had this kind of manpower? Was some-one else involved?

I thought about contacting Sugiwara, but then what would I say? "Hey there, I found the Gate but I also lost it, and I don't know where it is anymore." Lame.

"Does Franklin need to take me to Berth 35 now?" I was going to need to load up on my canned tricks to deal with more kinetics.

Fiona shook her head. "No, shipments only go out once a day. Today's departed already. Next departure is tomorrow at noon."

That was a relief. It gave me to time to load up and do some research.

"Could Franklin give me a ride to Lotus Lane?"

# LUNCH ON LOTUS LANE

From California Street, most Wàirén saw an alley that branched off the west side of Chinatown. Just another cramped San Francisco alley with close-set buildings that seemed to lean into the street. Subtle Jiārén illusion and persuasion had been layered over the entrance to Lotus Lane over decades. Nothing dramatic, but enough to give tourists and locals alike a sense that nothing down this particular alley was of any interest, and indeed the store one block over had exactly what they were looking for.

After the first ten years or so, a few Jiārén got smart and opened up businesses just beyond the reach of Lotus Lane's magical compulsion. In this way some of San Francisco's Jiārén managed to benefit from both sides of Lotus Lane's protections.

Passing through the protections surrounding Lotus Lane was a trick every Jiārén learned early. Even someone like me, with almost no qì to speak of, was able to find the keyhole in the magic and thread my way through the illusion. As I stepped past the edge of California Street, I crossed the border from Wàirén San Francisco to Jiārén Lotus Lane. A slight frisson of energy tingled over my skin and the drab buildings lining the dark alley faded away like shadows at sunrise.

Lotus Lane was a riot of color. Paper lanterns swung from wires that crisscrossed the street. Banners and flags flapped in the light breeze. And wherever there was space, there were dragons.

Renderings of the various Eight Sons of the Great Dragon

decorated nearly every storefront. The whiskered, serpentine dragons figured into nearly every business logo, each dragon depicted in dazzling emerald, gold, and crimson. Carved and painted dragons perched above doorways and along rooflines to protect each building's inhabitants and bring luck to the merchants.

The lunch crowd was just tapering off, but a good number of Jiārén filled the sidewalks and moved in and out of storefronts. Here, surrounded only by other Jiārén, many of Lotus Lane's visitors moved about with their auras open, adding even more color to the scene. The usually subtle press of the city's magic in the back of my head went up a few notches, as if I were standing inside a massive tuning fork resonating with the city.

In a sense, I was. At any given moment Lotus Lane had the highest concentration of Jiārén in the entire city. Many lived here, and nearly everyone came on a regular basis to visit and do business. Thousands of people each day, each with unique talents, each adding a small bit of their energy to the blossoming magical sentience of San Francisco. The city would be drawn here like a moth to a flame.

The call of San Francisco went up a notch when I stepped over the border into Lotus Lane. The usual background noise of the city's burgeoning sentience ticked up until it was like a boisterous argument right behind my head. I wobbled a little, as the white noise hit me and I grabbed onto a wall to steady myself. I took a few deep breaths, cycling what little qì I had, and calmed my energy until the clamoring city faded into the distance.

My phone rang, pulling me from my reverie. I read the caller ID and picked up. "Andie, please have some good news for me."

A staccato rhythm of a keyboard hammered away in the background as Andie talked around the straw in her mouth. I had never seen her without an energy drink in her hands. "Mostly. Your server is secure, no breach, no data extraction."

"But . . ."

"Someone was definitely there. Nothing on video, but your proximity alarms were tripped, for sure. Someone . . . or something . . . was in your house." Of all the people I knew in San Francisco, Andie had come closest to uncovering the truth about my past. Her paranoia was not quite on my level, but it was enough, and combined with her computer talents, she had managed to poke a few holes in my cover story.

Even my father had a legitimate cover. The clan enterprises were vast and the Soong jewelry stores dotted some of the world's premium retail spaces. But while my father might simply seem like an elusive billionaire, I barely existed. No credit, no online presence, nothing until two years ago. Normal people left a digital footprint.

I was not normal.

Ever forthright, Andie had confronted me on it, unwilling to let her wife become embroiled with my shady history. So I gave her some of the facts. Essentially that I had been part of an organization from a very young age that eschewed technology. The fact that Andie thought I was a runaway who had escaped from a cult was not ideal, but she did not believe I posed a risk to her wife and that was what mattered.

"Thanks, Andie, I owe you."

"Don't worry, it will all be detailed on your invoice."

Of course. "While I've got you on the line, I need another favor."

"Shoot."

I needed to get an angle on Adam, and Andie was perfect for the job. "This isn't an on-the-books job. I need you to dig up what you can for me on Adam Jørgensen."

"Right, right. The new donor for the museum, right? What do you need?" The keyboard clicks picked up in intensity and speed.

"The basics. Personal and financial history. Known associates. Business dealings."

Andie slurped her sugary beverage. "Right, right. Gotcha. And . . .

There. I just emailed you the whole dump. Standard encryption. I didn't have time to sort out his financials yet, so you'll have to slog through the raw files."

I'd spent my whole life watching others perform extraordinary feats with their Dragon talents, and yet Andie never ceased to amaze me. "Andie, you can't have pulled that all just now."

"Nope! I've been scraping his data since he showed up last month. Did you think I was going to let some stranger swoop into town and pull shenanigans on Tessa and the museum?"

"Oh my goodness, I love you, Andie."

"Too bad! I'm taken!"

"Give me the quick and dirty on him. I'll go over the files later."

More keyboard clicking. "I can tell you that his money is clean, at least. He was born to money and spent his life making more money, all through legitimate means. He lived in Japan for five years after college. Following that, he became quite the aficionado of Asian artifacts. He has personal contacts with every museum of note, and he socializes regularly with well-respected scholars in the field."

I caught the grudging respect in Andie's voice. "Honestly, he would probably be better at Tessa's job than Tessa."

Adam's time in Japan was the root of all my problems with him. Somehow he'd been exposed to Jiārén secrets and he was getting perilously close to the truth.

"You're the best, Andie."

"Yes, I know. It'll be—"

"—on the invoice." I finished for her.

I was about to hang up when Andie cut in again. "Pizza. Saturday."

"Andie, I—"

"Emiko, you can, and you will. You can't hide in your house every night."

Well, I definitely wasn't doing that, but I couldn't explain that right now.

Andie huffed. "You said you came here for a normal life, right? Normal people go out for dinner and eat with their friends, Emiko."

Ouch.

Her voice softened. "It'll be easy, I promise. I'll even buy pepperoni."

"I'll . . . I'll think about it."

It wasn't the best, but it was the best I could do right now.


The Sun Emporium was one of the oldest stores on Lotus Lane. The two-story store sported red columns bracketing its entrance. Four dragons twisted around each of the columns. To someone like me, the dragon depiction was meaningful, an homage to the Eight Sons of the Dragon in the Realm. To Júwàirén, it looked like typical Eastern art.

The front of the store was a riot of color and texture and decidedly kitschy. The street-facing window was crammed with redwood carvings, souvenir T-shirts, and postcards—the typical bric-a-brac found throughout Chinatown. In the rear of the store, a silk privacy screen sectioned off the Suns' private offices, where they kept their Door. Behind their Door, the Suns conducted their true business.

The Suns, father and son, had a talent for compressing energy. Not exactly useful in a dark alley, but an excellent aid to those of us without our own powers. In their Realm Fragment, the Suns ran a very handy business. They contracted with local talent, compressing energy into physical objects. Father had introduced me to them years ago, and I'd been making regular visits to fill up my kit since I held the blade.

The Sun Emporium was also my chief provider of one of the basic food groups: steamed buns. Mama Sun made arguably the best steamed pork buns in the city. I'd almost, almost, had delicious pork from Jorge's pig roast for breakfast, before my day had gone sideways. I'd been counting on the Suns to correct my dietary deficiency, but right now, staring at the black-and-white CLOSED sign hanging in their door, my growling stomach questioned my loyalty to the Suns.

I checked my phone. I was only fifteen minutes early. I could stand to wait that long, growling stomach aside. Baby Ricky was probably out getting his own lunch like a reasonable person. I wandered down the street to kill the time, glancing into the storefront windows as I passed by. A few doors down, the smell of sizzling meat stopped me in my tracks as my stomach seized control of my body. I stared at the elaborate script stenciled on the window. GOLDEN DRAGON POTSTICKERS. I'd heard about this place. I'd read rave reviews of transcendent experiences from potsticker chef extraordinaire, Kelly. Apparently the Potsticker Queen rose at 4 a.m. five days a week to roll out the dough, and her fillings were the juiciest, courtesy of a bone broth gelatin cube.

I almost pressed my nose against the glass, trying to get closer to that delicious smell. Maybe I could get an order to go.

The rush hour appeared to have ended and there was no line out the front. I stepped inside, the chime of the door echoing behind me. A middle-aged woman at the reception station slouched over her phone, scrolling as she ignored the chime of the door. She had tightly permed hair that she'd confined with a flat clip. Dark circles under her eyes contrasted against her pale skin and I figured she had to be the Potsticker Queen herself.

Behind the reception station was only enough room for a few tables and a large stainless steel counter in the back. A young man with a paper cap and a green apron worked in the back counter, wiping it down. A sign over the back wall designated MOBILE ORDERS, which I filed away for future reference. Everything was painted an eye-searing green with loud yellow trim.

I grabbed a paper menu and then wondered why they bothered printing a menu at all. Golden Dragon Potstickers had two items on their menu: pork potstickers and milk tea boba. The potstickers came in orders of eight or twenty. The boba tea offered no flavors, no jellies, no low-sugar options—just black tea with milk, heaping amounts of sugar, and lots of chewy tapioca boba. I admired their brazenly limited menu. Clearly they weren't interested in being vegetarian or vegan friendly, nor did they have gluten-free options. That was a bold choice in this town.

The matronly woman in the reception area finally looked up, and then she stood fully upright. Her bright green apron had a dragon biting a potsticker emblazoned on the bib. A small name tag pinned to her apron read KELLY. I was right, it was the Potsticker Queen herself!

Kelly scowled at me.

I took a quick glance down at my jacket. I'm pretty sure most of the blood got on Freddy and not me. Was I not presentable? I soldiered on, bolstered by the thought of sinking my teeth into piping hot pork potstickers. "Hi, can I get an order of twenty potstickers and a large boba tea to go?"

Kelly shook her head and pointed to the door. "No potstickers for you. Leave."

Maybe they'd sold out? I guess I could try again in the future, if I survived the shinigami. "Should I come earlier next time?"

She snorted, her nostrils flaring. "Not serving the Butcher, ever."

I blinked and took a step back. I didn't have a lot of friends in this town and I'd somehow also managed to piss off the Potsticker Queen. Her narrowed eyes were hostile and her lip curled in disgust. This reminded me of how things had been two years ago, when I first "retired" from being the Blade. Lotus Lane vendors hadn't been the most welcoming. I was grateful to the Sun family because they'd helped me break the ice, and a few other merchants had started to work with me once the Suns put out the good word. Apparently the Potsticker Queen did not fall in that camp.

Kelly pointed to the sign taped low on the reception stand, WE RESERVE THE RIGHT TO REFUSE SERVICE TO ANYONE.

I shrugged. Suddenly I wasn't that hungry anymore.

Behind the reception station people rumbled about, chairs scraping against the linoleum floor.

I turned to leave, pressing against the door handle when I heard "Sifu!" in a high-pitched voice.

There was only one person who had ever referred to me as *master*.

Leanna Louie bounced up from the rear of the restaurant, her cheeks creased into a big smile. She had changed out of her practice clothes, now wearing a cream-colored Gucci-logo polo dress, her hair held back with a black velvet headband. A proper princess. Nothing like the little warrior from this morning.

"Are you here for the potstickers? They're the best! We just finished." Leanna beamed up at me and I couldn't help but smile back.

"Umm, I think they're done selling potstickers for the day." I peered around Leanna, and spotted Uncle Jimmy and his nephew, Ray Ray, making their way to the reception area. *Great.* Not who I wanted to see right now.

In contrast to his slender uncle, Ray Ray was a portly, balding man. His hair was thinning, and he'd opted for the comb-over effect, which didn't do much to obscure his shining pate. His black turtleneck sweater looked soft and expensive, made of the finest cashmere. Ray Ray was like a knockoff Louis Vuitton bag, decorated on the outside, but worth very little. As he gestured, heavy gold pieces flashed on his fingers and around his neck. I hadn't spent much time with him but he did look like his father. Hard to reconcile this paunchy soft-looking man with his powerful father, but the distinctive Louie forehead and wide nose stamped on this man were unmistakable. Unlike his uncle Jimmy, Ray Ray did not have much power to lock down, and his hazy pink aura looked weak to me.

Uncle Jimmy still sported his cozy cardigan, casual slacks, and white tennis shoes. Despite the difference in their dress, it was Uncle Jimmy who drew the eye. The solid-gold cane handle didn't hurt. And the elder Louie's presence hummed with a quiet confidence and an air of command that his nephew only seemed to pretend at.

Three goons in Louie Claw windbreakers loomed behind their family heads, all furrowed brows and dark glowers. The tall one looked familiar. His lips twitched beneath his thin mustache. Mustache Boy, one of the thugs who'd tried to harass Grandma Chen the other night. His eyes widened in alarm when he spotted me. That was nice. At least I hadn't lost my touch in terrifying the local heavies even if I couldn't manage to buy one measly order of potstickers.

To his right was a much younger guy with a shaved head and neck tattoo. This guy barely looked old enough to drive. His aura was interesting, more like a zhong-level talent. Not good enough for admission to Lóng Kǒu, but good enough to run with the Louies' crew. Neck Tattoo's aura had a minty green tinge. Maybe a speedster. The smell of potstickers permeated the restaurant and made it difficult to sniff him out.

Leanna shook her head. "No, I just saw them fry a batch. You have to try some!" She turned to Kelly who was still eyeing me with suspicion. "Kelly Āyí, can we have an order of the potstickers for my Sifu?"

Kelly dropped her phone on the counter, emotions warring over her face. Finally her eyes slid over to the elder Louies. Ray Ray glanced at me like I'd just soiled his rug and shook his head. Behind his nephew, Uncle Jimmy kept his eyes locked on mine and gave Kelly the barest nod. The Potsticker Queen bobbed and hustled to the back to yell in Cantonese at the young man behind the mobile pickup counter. Interesting that she'd ignored Ray Ray.

Ugh. Now I was beholden to Uncle Jimmy for some stupid potstickers. My stomach betrayed me with hunger pangs on cue.

Leanna tugged on my sleeve. "Will you have a boba tea with us?"

I shook my head, but kept my reply gentle. I couldn't let my frustrations with her family spill onto her. "I can't today."

My eyes bored into Uncle Jimmy's but I kept my tone light. "I got a little behind this morning and I still have work to do."

The anger I'd suppressed from this morning simmered in my gut. I'd gone to the Louie Clan home as a fellow Hoard Custodian family member seeking Talon support. To use his charm speak abilities on me was the height of disrespect for my clan. However, none of that was Leanna's fault. I could play nice for now but no way was I letting him get the drop on me ever again. I flashed him a dazzling smile. He returned the smile although Ray Ray glowered at me. One of the Claws, the one with the neck tattoo, had broken away and whispered quietly into Ray Ray's ear.

Leanna missed the interplay. "What kind of work do you do?"

"I find lost things."

Her eyes lit up. "Like treasure!"

I knelt to her level and smiled. "Yes, exactly like treasure."

Uncle Jimmy's friendly mask stayed firmly in place. He stepped up behind Leanna and placed his hands on her shoulders. "Of course, there are some things that should not be found."

Leanna's face screwed up adorably and she looked up at her uncle. "What kinds of things shouldn't be found?"

Skies. Could those potstickers be taking any longer?

I decided to take a chance. "Well, let's say there's something very valuable, hidden away. And it's hidden because it locks away a world of monsters. Something like that shouldn't be found, right? And if it was lost, my job would be to restore it to its rightful place."

Ray Ray cleared his throat, apparently not happy at being left out of the conversation. "There are also items that are owned by powerful men. It would not be wise to cross these types of men."

Broken Claw, the nerve of this guy. Ray Ray might have the family name but he clearly had inherited none of his father's or uncle's competence. Fiona and Freddy's security entourage had a mix of combat-level Jiārén, whereas from what I could see of the Louies, they only had píng- and zhong-level talents around them. As my father would observe, A players hire A players. B players hire C players. Had the Louies gotten so weak to prop up Ray Ray's ego?

The Louies were up to their eyeballs in the Ebony Gate heist. I was sure of it. I just needed to prove it. Then I needed to convince Fiona. I needed to find the Gate first, but I really wanted to nail the Louies, too.

Leanna tugged on my sleeve again. "Would you come visit with us later when you finish your work?"

Ray Ray opened his mouth but Uncle Jimmy cut him off with a look and gave a nod. "Yes, you should come for a visit. All work and no play as they say."

His face wore a benevolent expression, as if he were the kind uncle who handed out candies to the neighborhood children. The thugs at his back told the true story. Mustache Boy remembered me and knew what I could do, but despite all that if his boss ordered him to attack me right here he would. He'd draw back a nub, but he'd attack me nonetheless. That's the kind of outfit that Jimmy Louie ran.

Mustache Boy was taller than me and would have decent reach in a fight. His wide shoulders filled out his Claw windbreaker and I could see that his aura was weak. He'd rely on brawn and weapons to try to take me—not talent.

I eyed the third Claw warily. He looked older, his pale cheeks lean and pockmarked and he stayed close to Ray Ray. His eyes were a little too wide, too jumpy. The kind of eyes that made me nervous. I glanced at his hands. He was missing two fingers on his left hand. His aura was locked down tight but I could see the outline of a dark purple. That was surprising. What was someone with so much yin in his aura doing with the Claws? The Louies seemed more interested in money and influence, things they could wield in the present—not something they'd take with them to the afterlife.

Thinking of the afterlife reminded me why I didn't have time to be socializing any further with Jimmy Louie.

"I must finish my job first, no matter how difficult and no matter who is standing in my way. Lóng zhēng hǔ dòu."

Leanna just nodded. I knew she'd been taught this lesson. Probably by Uncle Jimmy. Even a battle between dragons would yield a winner. That was the premise of the Lóng Yá Tourney that pervaded Jiārén culture. I had never fought in the Tourney but my sword had bathed in the blood of seasoned killers. I had reminded the Louies that I didn't care if I had to fight my way up the food chain to recover the Gate.

Leanna's eyes grew solemn. This fight for supremacy was what awaited her at Lóng Kǒu. Her carefree days of training in the yard and eating gourmet potstickers were coming to an end. "Yes, of course, Sifu. I look forward to when we can train together again."

She gave me a bow and walked past me as Jimmy held the door for her.

Ray Ray traded a look with Neck Tattoo. What was that about? All the Claws looked alert, excited almost. Not like guys who had wolfed down a dozen potstickers and had a cushy escort assignment. Something else was going on but I couldn't put my finger on it.

I stayed put, and as each Claw stalked past me, I took a slow inhale.

The three-fingered man reeked of shoe leather and gunpowder.

# LIBRARY PRIVILEGES

I burned my tongue on the piping hot potstickers. So I started dunking them in the black vinegar to cool them down. Delicious. Somehow the fact that these potstickers were solely from the Louie largesse didn't diminish their incredible taste and texture. I schemed briefly about how to get them on my own. Something told me that the Potsticker Queen wouldn't willingly serve me again. Maybe a mobile order was in my future.

While I ate, I thought about the three-fingered man. There was no mistaking the scent of his magic, and ghost masters were a rare breed. I'd never encountered one other than near the temples. They weren't exactly in high demand by Hoard Custodian families. In all probability, the three-fingered man had broken into my house. Did a guy like that act alone? Seemed unlikely.

Popo's warning rang in my ears. Had I managed to get on Uncle Jimmy's radar from one small scuffle in front of her place? If so, he was running a tighter ship than Dai Lou, or maybe she was of particular interest to him. I hated to think perhaps I was of particular interest to him. But there was no help for it now, I'd thrown down the gauntlet earlier.

Baby Ricky still hadn't reopened the Sun Emporium by the time I wolfed down twenty (yes, twenty) potstickers. Hey, I'd had an active morning. That was fine, now I had a thread I needed to tug on. Namely, I needed to know why the Louies had sent their pet ghost master to do a heavy search of my place. I couldn't let that go unanswered but I didn't have enough information. I needed answers and I knew just where I had to go.

The Library.

Not the San Francisco Library, but the Library within.

Grabbing a rideshare to the San Francisco Library was the easy part. Getting into the Library within was going to be a little harder. I hadn't been to the Library in several years. The last time had been before Lóng Kǒu, accompanying Father on one of his business trips to the city. He'd gained access for me that time, bringing me in with him, as was his right. This time I was going to have to earn my own way in.

The library was a massive, blocky building, the steel-gray facade broken up by towering gridded windows and metallic columns inset in the walls. I stood outside for a moment longer than I needed to, girding my loins for the possibility that I would fail to qualify for the level of access I needed. That I would receive yet another reminder of how I was the Broken Tooth of Soong.

In that moment, I caught something from the corner of my eye. Two shadowy figures lingered by the trees. San Francisco was a city of movement and activity. Stillness was unusual. Had Uncle Jimmy set someone up to tail me? I'd have to consider my exit strategy from the Library after I concluded my research.

I made my way into the center of the building, a vast circular atrium filled with soft natural light filtering down from a glass roof. Staircases spiraled down the perimeter of the column, leading up and down. Everywhere I looked, people milled about or lounged in comfy chairs, books in hand and stacked up beside them in haphazard piles. Small gangs of children capered about, only to be corralled and hushed by their parents.

The movement of so many people sent subtle vibrations through the floor, but the not-so-subtle hum of power that I felt buzzing the soles of my feet had nothing to do with the Júwàirén surrounding me. Like Lotus Lane, the Library was another locus of San Francisco's magic. This time, when the city's call hit me, my vision blanked out, replaced by images of the Japanese Tea Garden. The grounds were turned over like someone had taken a plow to the manicured lawns. A gaping pit dominated the center of the garden, the bottom shrouded in darkness and mist.

Subtle. But I was already fulfilling a Talon. I didn't need anyone or anything else telling me what to do.

I waited under the skylight, my eyes closed and head tilted up, as if enjoying the sunlight. When the vision passed I took the ascending staircase two and three stairs at a time, winding my way up until I arrived at the third floor.

The Chinese library collection took up the east side of the building, set behind a pair of wrought-iron gates. The gates were delicately hammered metal, shaped into intertwined vines of wisteria and jasmine. Hidden within the scrollwork, eight dragons twisted through the flowers, their eyes glowing red like low embers in a fire. These were the gates to the Library within, invisible to Wàirén eyes.

Lóng Jiārén had several Libraries like this, scattered across the globe and hidden in plain sight. The Libraries were a repository of the history of our people, holding nearly every written record since the Cataclysm, everything from birth and marriage records to copies of deeds and contracts between clans. Access to the Library was strictly controlled by the one metric that mattered to every Jiārén—power.

I pushed through the gate, the hinges swinging silently. Beyond the gates stood a round room, the walls covered from floor to ceiling in bookshelves. A wooden circular desk held the center of the room. Books covered the desk, stacked in leaning piles that covered the circumference. As I approached, I saw that the books flowed to the interior of the desk and morphed into listing piles on the ground as well. There was no computer, no tech of any kind, just books.

The Librarian sat in the center of the desk, her feet propped up on a stack of books, a large hardbound volume open in her lap. She was a slender Asian woman of indeterminate age, her features pinched around the nose and eyes. She wore a large black wool blazer over a loose-fitting black silk blouse. Her wide-leg trousers ended with a neat cuff above argyle socks and shiny black wingtips. Her aura simmered around her, a roiling iridescent border that made her look like a mirage. She did not look up from her book as I approached the desk.

Two large scrolls fluttered on the two tall bookcases behind her, the heavy black ink a slash of decisive hanzi against snowy mulberry paper. I didn't recognize the red chop but the poems were clearly inked by a master calligrapher, the strokes bold for emphasis in some parts, delicate and feathery at others.

I'd seen these same scrolls in my father's den, and at the academy.

The last four lines always hit me hard.

"Brothers old and young
All will drown,
All treasures lost,
And the world unmade."

For a thousand-year-old poem, it was a pretty gloomy ending. The poem was called "The Flood," and it had been drafted a century after the Cataclysm. Copies of "The Flood" graced the halls of my father's office, the academy, and the headmaster's office. When I had been getting expelled from Lóng Kǒu, those words had felt especially ominous, their dark strokes staring at me from behind Headmaster Chen's elaborate hat.

For me, getting kicked out of the academy had felt like I was just as wrecked, cast adrift with no purpose or identity. Seeing it now reminded me how lost I'd been after my expulsion. How abandoned

I'd felt when my parents left me with Ogata-sensei. How I'd had nothing after I'd broken my blade. I hated that poem

I stood at the desk, and straightened my shoulders. Clearing my throat to get the Librarian's attention seemed like a bad idea. At my last visit, Father had spoken with the Librarian in hushed, respectful tones, something I had seen only a handful of times in my whole life. As I waited, the Librarian stretched out her arm, an impossibly long and thin arm, her long-fingered hand playing over the books on the desk. Her hand crept over the books, seeming to read the titles by touch. She picked up a slender paperback and her deft fingers opened the book, riffled the pages, her fingers tracing the words. The Librarian frowned, her eyes never leaving the book in her lap, but she made a small noise as her fingers seemed to read the paperback.

Luck saved me from interrupting the Librarian's reading. The bookshelves on the east wall split open, revealing a tiny elevator behind them. Two men in dark suits stepped out of the elevator. The younger man carried a stack of ancient-looking leather-bound volumes. The other man, possibly an older brother, held a yellowed silk scroll protected in a clear cylindrical case. The men stopped in their tracks as they spotted me, the bookshelves closing behind them. Their brows creased with hostility.

The Librarian rose smoothly, placing a bookmark as she stood. "Gentlemen."

She followed the men's eyes, turning until she faced me. "Ah. A new visitor. Wonderful. What can I help you find?"

I tore my eyes away from the two men. I didn't recognize them, but that didn't mean much. They might have grievances with my prior activities as the Blade, but no one was stupid enough to bring clan business to a Library. "Yes, I'm looking for Lóng Kǒu records, specifically Lóng Yá Tourney records for the last fifty years."

The Librarian's arms seemed to move of their own accord, organizing and straightening the books on her desk as she spoke. "Yes, we have those records on the fifth level. Your hand, please?"

She pulled her books back, clearing a space on the desk. From beneath the desk the Librarian withdrew a massive tome, bound in filigreed silver plate, with hinges as thick as my arm along the spine. She withdrew a key from her pocket and unlocked the book, flipping rapidly through the pages. Every yellowed page had only one thing, a large handprint. The book recorded everyone who had ever entered the Library in this Librarian's tenure. Somewhere in the book was my father's print from his last visit. She continued flipping the pages. She'd served here a long time.

The book finally fell open to a blank page. "Place your hand on the page."

At least it wasn't siu ze this time. I stepped up to the book, very aware of the eyes tracking me, and the way the older man's nostrils flared as his breath quickened. Their eyes tracked my movements as well, and traced the grips of my swords. Even the least talented Jiārén could gain access to the first few levels of the Library. Just a drop of dragon blood was enough for that. My father's blood had granted access to all nine levels, where the Heads of the Clans could go. I needed to get to the fifth level for my answers, but even getting there might prove beyond the limits of my stunted talent.

I placed my hand on the page, the sweat on my palm sticking my skin to the paper. An instant of a sharp sensation, like a blade drawn across my palm, and the book flashed with golden light. I stepped back, my bloody handprint now marked in the book. My hand was unmarked. The golden glow on the page intensified and I smelled the faint odor of my blood drying on the paper. As the light faded a stylized number eight appeared next to my thumb. Relief and confusion washed through me. Eight?

The Librarian smiled and closed the book. "Right this way." She indicated the rear bookshelf with a sweep of her arm.

The two suits barely contained their disgust, their noses way out of joint now. The older man shoved his scroll into the younger man's arms and stalked toward me, his eyes burning with loathing—not unlike what I'd seen on the Potsticker Queen's face. Wow, twice in one day. I took a half step back and centered my weight, but before I could reach for my knives the Librarian swept her arm out in a wide arc.

My eyes widened as power blasted from the slender woman. Books fluttered and thumped, flying off her desk and slamming into the south wall. The books piled against one another, creating a horizontal barricade that separated me and my angry suitor.

The Librarian turned to look at both of us in turn, her face still, her voice measured and calm. "Please, no clan business within the bounds of the Library."

The man raised an accusing finger, his lips quivering with rage. "She is the Butcher of Beijing! She shouldn't be allowed here with decent people!"

His aura flared as his talent charged, stoplight red. Hmm. Dragon Limbs, tough to fight up close. Better to take him down with a hold and concentrate on the soft bits. I deliberately relaxed, my stance softening even as the old man took another step forward and placed his hands on the makeshift arch of books.

His aggression surprised me, not because I wasn't used to it but more because of where we were. Our Libraries were sacred, hallowed places that protected the ancestral memory of our people. Every clan, every Jiārén, revered the Library like their own home.

Except for this fool, foaming at the mouth. His hands tore at the books, trying to get to me. "You animal! My niece lost her—"

In an eyeblink the Librarian vanished from her desk and inky black smoke streamed from the arch of books and pooled on the floor. The Librarian emerged from the smoke, her garb now the darkest black that seemed to suck in the light, her eyes also full black and electric with power. She held an open book in her hands and her finger traced across the page as she read aloud.

". . . Chōu dāo duàn shuǐ shuǐ gèng liú . . ."

The older man grunted and his head rocked back. His hand flew to his face, red blood streaming between his fingers. Blood welled from the precise red line slashed across his cheek. He stumbled back into the younger man's arms.

The Librarian took a step forward, her eyes still on the book, her fingers leafing through the pages. Power whorled around her like an angry thunderstorm.

". . . Jǔ tóu wàng míngyuè."

The men sank to their knees, books and scroll tumbling to the floor, prostrating themselves shamelessly before the Librarian. The older man pressed his forehead to the floor and laid his hands out, leaving bloody prints on the tile. "Duìbùqǐ, duìbùqǐ . . ."

The Librarian turned to me, the thrum of her power still making the air crackle with energy, raising the hairs on my arms. Clearly when the Librarian read a Tang dynasty poem about swords, it had a very literal effect on its reader. I very slowly moved my hands away from the knives tucked into my belt and let my arms fall to my sides.

The arch of books collapsed and flowed back to the reception desk, the books arranging themselves into seemingly random piles. The Librarian's eyes were black pools of ink. "Please enjoy your visit at the Library."

I edged around the two chastened men and headed for the elevator.

When I stepped inside the elevator a book icon lit up on the interior panel. I placed my hand on the panel and eight buttons lit up below. A ninth button at the bottom of the panel remained dark. I pressed the button for the fifth level and the elevator descended into the Library.

An image of Leanna, her aura recklessly blazing about her, came unbidden to me. By the time I was her age, I had mastered the technique of suppressing my aura. It had been the only thing Father and Mother had drilled into me. They had never discussed my power, only how to hide it. I'd made the only appropriate conclusions, and learned to hide the shame of my family. Power as weak as mine had to be hidden, lest it be used against our family as leverage.

The lighted buttons seemed to mock me now. I stared at my hands, confusion still roiling through me. I'd expected entrance to the Library, but not nearly full access. Was it something to do with Father? Had he pulled strings? Even as the thought arose I discarded it. He wasn't one to cash in favors for something so small.

The elevator passed through the darkness of the Wàirén building, then the walls of the car shimmered as it crossed into the Lóng Jiārén Library, fading into transparency as I entered the topmost levels of the structure. The Library was a massive column, sunk into the earth. The walls of the Library were white marble, shot through with silvery veins. The pale stone was infused with dragon fire and glowed with soft light that lit the entire Library. Two elevators traveled up and down a clear shaft through the center of the structure.

From the elevator I had a full view of every floor, echoing the open central column of the city library. Narrow catwalks with delicate handrails connected the library floors with the elevator shaft. The only connection between the floors was the elevator. Once I was out, it was my only way back out of the building. The hairs on the back of my neck went up, years of training and paranoia coming to wakefulness. I scanned the floors as I passed them, searching for alternate exits.

The top level had the most people, and the most diverse collection of people, young and old, families with children, men and women in crisp business attire, and working-class people in everyday wear. The crowds thinned as I descended into the Library. Families disappeared, and then the working-class people vanished as well. By the time the elevator stopped on the fifth level, I felt distinctly underdressed. Worse yet, I saw no obvious means to gain exit from the Library other than the elevator. I didn't like places where I only had one way out.

The doors opened noiselessly onto the fifth level. Directly before the open doors, the narrow path jutted out into open air, arcing over the empty space. I shook off my worry and stepped out of the elevator. I needed to find the ghost master, and this was my best option. My instincts had always served me well, but I needed to set them aside for now. I was in the Library. It was the closest thing to assured safety we had.

I crossed the narrow bridge, only giving a passing glance to the precipitous drop to either side. Once on the library floor I followed the signs to the Lóng Kǒu records. The innermost ring of this floor held modern books, and felt like a Wàirén library. As I passed to the outer rings, the books became older, bound in the hides of unknown animals, fluttering bits of silk, and bamboo bindings stitched with coarse threads.

One section was a towering collection of drawers, the structure so long that the end of it curved away from my vision. A wizened woman stood before them, her nimble fingers opening and closing the drawers in rapid fashion. Her eyes darted left and right as the drawers flashed open. Each drawer contained scrolls of yellowed paper, cradled in soft velvet.

The Lóng Kǒu section of the Library was set off with an enormous ironworks dragon head, the mouth open and roaring, at least twelve feet high. Curved fangs of gleaming onyx were set into the jaw, and a pair of rubies each the size of my fist glittered in the eye sockets. To access the records, I had to step into the dragon's mouth. Cute. I rolled my eyes and stepped through.

It took an hour of searching to even find the right neighborhood for the Lóng Yá records. Unlike the Wàirén library above me, nothing down here was organized alphabetically, or in any way that seemed to make common sense. I finally found the Tourney records in a dark corner of the Lóng Kǒu section. They were sorted first by year, and then by talent type and levels, and then by family name. The records were meant for someone who knew who they were looking for. For me, I was stuck doing this the hard way.

Based on my brief glimpse of the three-fingered man, I started twenty years back and began going through the results.

Lóng Jiārén were nothing if not competitive and eager to show one another up. He might have won accolades at the school, or other noteworthy accomplishments. I grabbed as many years of records as I could carry and found an open work desk to begin my search.

Three hours later I had a headache. It may have been from pounding my head into the desk. Repeatedly. Stacks of books and ledgers lay piled across two tables, my attempt at organizing the records into something resembling sanity. It wasn't even close.

I'd read over twenty years of Tourney records and had found exactly zero possibilities for who came close to the yin talent that had sent ghosts into my home. I couldn't believe my luck was this astonishingly bad. I was so sure the Lóng Kǒu records would have something. I'd found several lower-level talents who all had clear records of finishing the academy and entering various temples with legitimate positions. Nothing that pointed at someone bending their talents to more nefarious uses.

My eyes fuzzed out whenever I tried looking at anything within two feet of my face and my neck felt permanently stuck in a bent position. Worse yet, the heavy garlic in Kelly's potstickers was doing a number on my gut. Next time, maybe only eight at a time. I stood and stretched, my back and neck popping as I straightened myself out. There had to be a bathroom on this level. I wouldn't have to go back to the elevator for a bathroom, would I? That would be asinine.

As I moved away from my desk a slim volume on a nearby shelf caught my eye, the copper straps holding the binding glinting in the glare of the overhead lights. My eyes tracked down the spine and as I read the characters my own spine shivered.

*Expulsion Records.*

My hand drifted up for the book before I realized it. The copper bands were cold and oxidized, and protected a cover of dark leather. The front cover of the book was blank except for an embossed image of the four cardinal animals: Black Tortoise, Azure Dragon, Vermillion Bird, and White Tiger.

I sat back down. Crawling dread grew in my gut, competing with the garlic already roiling inside. The copper clasps unlocked easily and I opened the book to the first page.

Blank.

I flipped farther back until I found my name in bright red ink. Guilt and anxiety, both aged to consummate perfection, rose within me. I'd left Lóng Kŏu over ten years ago and yet the memory still had the hot sting of shame.

*I don't know the boy's name, but he comes from a Hoard family. They all do, and they've done nothing but torment me for days now. His friends jeer and laugh as they form a circle around us, trapping us inside. I know what's going to happen, so I just rip the bandage off and wade into the boy, my fists flying in rapid succession.*

*I learned to fight sparring against my overbearing cousin, Tai. I am a Soong. We are a combat house. We never let an insult go unanswered. Hit first. Hit hard. My right connects with his cheek and pain flowers in my knuckles and shoots up to my elbow. I ignore it. Without any talent to call on, my only chance is to end the fight quickly and decisively. A left follows, sinking deep into his soft belly. His breath blows over me and smells like herbal mints.*

*The herbal smell intensifies and I know I've lost. The boy draws on his talent—ping-level Dragon Limbs—and his arms harden. He's young, and untrained, so his arms do not become covered in impenetrable dragon scale, but against a twelve-year-old girl, it's more than enough. His heavy fist slams into my shoulder, and a bright star of agony explodes there. I fall back, gasping and clutching at my now dead left arm. His friends jump and laugh. I want to strangle him and his friends. Above us, on the catwalks, more students have stopped to watch today's beating. No one moves to help.*

*Whatever Lóng Kǒu is supposed to be teaching me, the only lesson I have learned so far is that I will always be weaker, because I am a disappointment, a talentless dud who will bring nothing but shame to her family. I thought I had talent, I thought I was like my father, but my short time here in school has shown me that my life has been a lie. Shame and outrage burns in my belly and heat flows to my arm. The herbal scent flares again and I know another punch is coming but I don't care. I just want to hit this boy as hard as I can.*

*Fire courses down my arm like water and the last thing I see before my fist smashes the boy's face is his wide-eyed look of surprise.*

When they locked me in the headmaster's office I knew my fate had been sealed. I waited there, under the unblinking eyes of the carved Yellow Dragon on the wall. I read the words of "The Flood" on those long scrolls again and again, until my father came to fetch me.

My eyes refocused on the text of my expulsion, and I flipped the page, confused. Had I turned the page? No, I had the right page. But the text did not cite fighting, or injuring another heir as grounds for expulsion. Rather, in the headmaster's precise script, were two short lines of poetry.

"Brothers old and young
All will drown,
All treasures lost,
And the world unmade."

Odd.

I flipped further back and the next entry drove the poem from my mind. Two years prior to my entrance to the academy, the headmaster had expelled another student. Anthony Chow. A yin talent, expelled for disobeying his instructors. Chow's transgressions were detailed in columns of red ink, his Dragon-given talent twisted until it was unrecognizable, the use of his power costing him his very essence, causing his fingers and toes to disintegrate.

Was it possible that Anthony Chow had ended up in San Francisco after getting expelled? Was he in the employ of the Louies? I needed to connect Chow to the Louies. Freddy or Fiona would be a good start. Their San Francisco network had to beat mine by a country mile. Popo's advice floated up out of memory to haunt me. *Yeah, yeah, make more friends. I got it.*

This level of the Library seemed to have emptied out as I was researching. The sounds of other Library patrons drifted down from the upper levels. As I wound my way through the shelves the back of my neck prickled with unwanted attention. The hairs on my arms stood on end and a brief wave of bitter cold passed over me. I kept walking, my eyes darting to a glass enclosure holding a collection of ancient wall hangings. I maintained my walking pace and scanned the glass for any reflections behind me.

The restroom was directly before me now, but no way was I putting myself in such a small place with someone following me. I let my hand trail along the spines of the books like I was looking for a particular one. At the end of the row I turned right and tucked into the next aisle, now heading in the opposite direction. I crouched low and peered between the shelves, searching the aisles on both sides.

Nothing. I inhaled slowly through my nose and got nothing other than the musty smell of dust and old books. No one was lighting up Jiārén talent in my vicinity. Why was I sure that someone was watching me?

A soft noise came from my left, drawing my gaze to the next aisle. It was a soft shushing sound, like fabric dragging along the floor. I edged around the shelf and looked down the aisle.

Again, nothing but books and quiet. I heard the sound, this time right behind me and the bitter cold passed through me again, setting my teeth on edge. I whirled, my wrists flicking back, slender blades springing into my hands from my forearm sheaths. I leapt back, blades up and ready for . . .

Nothing. Again.

Cursed skies, what was happening here?

I backed into the intersection of the aisles, giving myself a clear line of sight in all directions and more importantly, some room to move. Something was going on here, something that my eyes weren't helping with. I settled my weight on the balls of my feet, my knees slightly bent, and took a deep breath and let it out slowly. I let my eyes unfocus, stretching my senses around me in all directions.

As my mind stilled, the faint call of San Francisco's magic arose at the furthest reaches of my perception. I swatted at it like a pestering insect. Not now . . . The last of my breath left me and I was left with the rhythm of my heart and the distant, alien music of the city. I tried to tune out the music, but the gentle throb of the beat wormed under my concentration. My heartbeat skipped and synchronized with the music.

There! I spun to my right, my left arm whipping around in a tight arc, blade held out at chest level, a killing strike that would slide between the ribs and pierce the heart. My strike went wild as my blade passed through empty air. Cold enveloped my hand and a thin film of frost formed over my blade. My hand went numb from the biting cold. I over-rotated and slammed my shoulder into the nearest bookshelf. Books flew off the shelf and tumbled to the floor.

Dark mist bloomed from the open pages of the spilled books and the Librarian emerged from the smoke, clad in a smoky gown of deepest black.

I held up my hands, my knives sliding back into place as the Librarian's jet-black eyes focused on me. "It wasn't me, it—"

The Librarian cut me off with a hand, her head turning, snake-like, to search the aisles around us. A low thrumming sound seemed to be coming from the Librarian, and it set all the books around us vibrating on their shelves. She turned down the next aisle, seeming to ignore me, then stopped and pulled a thin book from her sleeve. She opened the book and traced her finger across the page.

". . . zhàn kū duō xīn guǐ . . ."

Another wave of cold ran through me and my vision blurred, or rather, the space in the aisle blurred and a translucent figure of a man in a tattered suit appeared. Thick white scars crisscrossed his face and neck and his eyes were two black pits. He floated in the aisle, his face frozen in a rictus of anguish. The ghost let out a wail that made me shudder.

The Librarian blew out her breath through her nose and snapped her book shut. She clapped her hands together and power flowed from her in a rush. An invisible wave caught the despairing ghost and pushed it away from us. It crashed into the wall and dissipated like fog in sunshine.

The Librarian turned her dark eyes to me again. "Your visit is concluded."

She clapped her hands again and dark smoke descended on me. I flinched away. I opened my eyes to find myself outside the main

156 Julia Vee and Ken Bebelle

doors of the San Francisco Library, the shadows now longer in the early evening light. I guess there was another way out of the Library.

Acrid smoke wafted to me and I was moving before conscious thought had made the connection. I rounded the corner of the library onto Larkin Street and stopped as the smell of gunpowder and shoe leather hit me square in the face. The street was empty except for a crow pecking at a spot of garbage on the sidewalk. I ran to the end of the block and checked the intersection but found nothing. When I returned to the first corner, the crow hadn't moved, still pecking at the same spot.

I moved closer and the crow hopped away. The garbage it had been pecking at was a small pile of ash, slowly disintegrating in the light breeze off the bay. Skies. The ghost master again. Was it Chow? Whoever it was, they were definitely following me. I stomped on the pile of ash and ground it into the sidewalk. The crow gave a loud caw and took wing.

My chest tightened as I imagined Chow loitering outside my house, mere yards away from Bāo, Truth, and my few Hoard pieces. He'd been here tonight, lurking right outside the Library where ordinary Jiārén came with their children. The Library within was one of our sanctuaries. The ghost master had profaned it. My fists clenched until my knuckles popped. Chow had trespassed in my city, violated my home, and invaded my peace. Whatever else happened, I was going to find this man and make my displeasure known to him.

My phone rang and I picked it up on reflex. "Tran?"

"Who? No, it's Adam."

I suppressed a sigh. "It's late, Adam. What do you want?"

He lowered his voice and continued in a conspiratorial tone. "I have a confession."

"You secretly know your sword isn't a Kunimitsu?"

"What? No, no. Not that. I was poking the bear a little, at the gym. I wanted to see how you would react."

"Well, you got pinned for your troubles."

He let out a huff. "Look, this isn't coming out right. Emiko, I think I found the Lost Heart of Yázì."

His voice sounded deadly serious.

A cold weight settled in my chest as Adam rambled on. If what he said was true, he was in even more danger than I had realized. It was bad enough when I knew he had a prized sword of my people. To know that Adam had somehow stumbled onto the very item I needed for my Talon redemption was almost too much to process. Adam, and anyone in his network, including my partner Tessa, was now a risk to the First Law.

Jiārén had three approaches to First Law. One was gentle—some talents could fuzz memory and perception. It wasn't quite erasure but more like a confusion spell. It was useful for small exposures of limited duration. The second was a cleaning. As in, damage their memory permanently. Brutal but effective. But Adam was in too deep now. It was clear to me that the third approach was how Jiārén would deal with him. How my father would deal with him. How I would have dealt with him when I was the Blade. And that was by eliminating Adam and pruning every branch.

My jaw clenched. I wasn't the Blade anymore. I would not be silencing Adam and his entire family. And I had to protect Tessa. Anger burned in my chest and the resentment rose up again. I raged silently against my mother for getting me into this and at this over-confident man for endangering Tessa.

Through the ocean of rage that was roiling in my psyche, I caught bits and pieces as he talked about his search for answers about the Kunimitsu and how Yázì, a common sword guard decoration, had led to hearing about the legendary stone, and how it had brought him here to San Francisco. It all lined up with Andie's brief. Apparently he had managed to get himself invited to an auction for the piece. Tonight. How in the name of the Dragon Father had he uncovered so much Jiārén lore?

". . . so how about it?"

Skies, I'd gotten completely distracted. "How about what?"

He chuckled. "I know, it's a lot, isn't it? I said, can you meet me in thirty? We can figure out how to get to the auction. It'll be fun."

Right. Fun.

Tessa's big-shot donor was about to jump into a pool full of sharks. If it really was the Lost Heart of Yázì, the auction would be stacked with proxies from the biggest Jiārén clans, each of them backed by a fortune in Hoard gold and Talons. If even half of the stories about the Lost Heart were true the stone held enough power to take any clan's Hoard to another level. Whoever ended up with the Lost Heart would tip the power balance of the Bā Tóu.

How had Adam even gotten himself an invite? There was no way he could pass himself off as a Jiārén. The moment he walked through that door any attendee would be well within their rights to kill him under the First Law.

I couldn't let that happen. I wouldn't let that happen.

The cold pressure in my chest spread out into my arms. I spoke slowly, not really wanting to hear the answer. "Adam, how did you score an invitation?"

"Hey, you're not the only one with connections."

"What's that supposed to mean?"

"Come on, Emiko. Your sword knowledge doesn't come from books. The way you handle them, the way you talk about them. You know swords and you know them up close and personal. That type of knowledge comes from exposure."

He wasn't wrong.

Which meant Adam was more observant that I'd given him credit for. That made him dangerous to be around.

The late-afternoon light faded behind the bulk of the library, leaving me in cold, gray San Francisco dusk as the evening fog crept in. Cool evenings didn't bother me, but the chill air tonight felt like mist pouring from an open grave.

I did not have time for this. But I also had exactly zero leads on the Ebony Gate right now and if I could get close to the Lost Heart, then I'd call it a win. Now I just had to keep Adam from getting himself killed at the same time.

Tessa was going to owe me big and I'd never get to tell her about it. "Fine. Where are you?"

# THE INVITATION

Just after five in the evening I found Adam outside the Ferry Building. In deference to the chilly spring weather, he wore a cream turtleneck sweater and a cream blazer with caramel trousers. Everything looked like cashmere. His outfit probably cost as much as my car. With his tall build and tousled hair, Adam stood out amongst the bevy of folks on the Embarcadero today. I'd caught a rideshare back to the Trans' to get my Jeep and restock my pockets with my few remaining tricks. Now, looking at Adam, I wondered if I should have changed clothes as well.

When he saw me, he broke into a wide smile. The late-afternoon sun was heading toward the Pacific Ocean and the rays bathed him in warm golden light. Adam looked really good. Touchable. I restrained the urge to run my fingers over the soft-looking lapel. While Adam greeted me, I considered how I could remove him from tonight's equation. I needed his entrée into the auction, but I did not need Adam tagging along. Bringing Wàirén to Jiārén functions rarely worked out well for them.

"How did you find out about this auction?" I asked him.

"I have a contact."

"And you somehow got an invitation?" My voice was incredulous.

"I bought my way in." His cool response floored me.

There was no amount of money that would allow him into a Jiārén auction. "How much did you pay for this entrée?"

He shrugged. "Two million."

I closed my eyes and prayed to the Dragon Father for patience. "You paid two million dollars for a ticket to an auction about a mythical item of unknown provenance in an undisclosed location?"

He nodded.

I wished I could just assume he got scammed, but he was smart and he was observant. Odds were high that somehow he had really bought off an unscrupulous Jiārén who knew that he could take Adam's money and Adam would ultimately get silenced for his trouble.

"You don't know what you're getting into. You need to sit this one out."

"Aha! So you admit you do know what we're getting into!"

"Adam, *we're* not getting into anything. As soon as the car shows up you're going back to your place and I'm going to find out what's going on. Give me the name of your contact."

His eyebrows lifted into an arch expression. He reached a hand into his blazer and pulled out a small black lacquered fan. With a snap, he opened it to reveal a shimmering silk rendering of Yázì emblazoned across the fan.

Of all of the Dragon Father's sons, Yázì was the most warlike. Though the Soong Clan did not claim to be direct descendants of Yázì, combat houses like ours revered Yázì. He was a wolf and dragon hybrid, his snarling maw of fangs often used as ornamentation on swords. The artist who had embroidered this fan had rendered Yázì in his full glory, blue and silver scales armoring his long tail and a lupine snout against a black sky and curly white clouds. Adam gently waved the fan and the golden afternoon light made Yázì's yellow eyes glow with menace.

Yázì stared at me. I stared back.

Adam rotated the fan. In a masterpiece of craftsmanship, the other side of the fan was stitched with the most delicate of seed pearls, denoting the hanzi for north. There were four cardinal directions, which told me that Adam's paddle was one of four, possibly five if there was a fan out there denoted as the center.

The spines of the fan connected at the black wooden base, which was embedded with a round piece of mutton fat jade the diameter of a boba pearl.

This fan was clearly the bidder's paddle for the auction.

This guy was going to get himself and Tessa and me killed. "Give me that."

"Only if you agree that we are both going."

"You can't activate the beacon anyway if you don't give it to me."

"It appears we are at an impasse."

"Just what exactly do you think you are going to find at this event?"

"A secret cabal of uber-rich and powerful families that trade in ancient East Asian artifacts and weapons."

I kept my face carefully neutral and turned to him. "That is . . . very specific."

Adam's eyes looked out over the ocean like he was seeking a distant vista. "I've been chasing down rumors and lore for years. It'll probably turn out to be nothing, but it is an entertaining diversion."

An entertaining diversion? Who talked like that? Also, he was lying. He tried to play it off like he was an idle rich guy with a hobby but he had pursued this thing with the single-minded intensity of someone with a purpose. With a mission. But why?

My lips thinned in annoyance. I wasn't going to haggle with him to get the paddle. There was nothing I wanted to give him for it.

I leaned in close and grabbed his lapels. Definitely cashmere. With a kick of my foot and a sharp tug, I disrupted Adam's balance. His grip on the fan loosened and I snatched it from him and stepped back.

Adam righted himself and smoothed out his blazer. He gave me a half smile. "You're really good at that."

"I know."

I was acutely aware of Adam's presence next to me in a way that I hadn't noticed when we were rolling on the mat at the gym. He smelled faintly of clean soap and salt from the sea. Why did he have to both look and smell so good?

Focus, Emiko.

I held up the fan to the light. The mutton fat jade was high quality, going totally translucent in the light. Deep within, I saw the smoky outline of the character for zhong. Perfect. The auctioneer was the center and the bidders were the four cardinal directions. I would only have to fight off three other parties to nab the Lost Heart and restore it to the shinigami's Gate. Not great odds, but not the worst I'd ever faced.

"Tell me the truth. Why are you chasing the Lost Heart?"

Adam tilted his head down at me, his eyes shadowed and serious. "I need to know."

"No, Adam, this is not a reality TV show. You don't get a big reveal at the end."

You got dead.

I looked up at his earnest expression, those deep blue eyes so laser focused on mine. All of his attention was on me now, just like when we were grappling at the gym, but none of it was about me. He wasn't seeing me. His focus was about the Lost Heart.

He spoke fervently, like a zealot. "I know it's more than a legend. I know it's real. Seeing it, touching it . . . I can finally honor Yamamoto-san and fulfill his wishes."

His voice was low, hoarse now as he spoke of this family.

I searched my memory. It had to be an old Jiārén family, Outclan and lost to the diaspora. It happened sometimes, when an old clan fell from power or lost its Hoard or heirs. A clan was like a series of concentric circles, with the Head of the Clan and the Heart in the center. The family members and all the members that made up the clan also were supported by the clan resources. When that system broke down, people scattered. Items got lost. People became Outclan.

This had to be how Adam had ended up with Crimson Cloud Splitter.

Somehow Adam's host family in Japan was descended from Jiārén, their blood thin enough to pass in Wàirén life, their family lore hazy enough to recall only some Jiārén details.

"Adam, some things aren't meant for you to know. And your host family wouldn't want you to risk your life to chase down a rumor."

He shook his head. "Before he died, I sat with him. His spirit isn't at rest and won't be until I get to the bottom of this. I know the sword is somehow connected to the Lost Heart."

There was a connection all right. And I would have to do everything in my power to make sure Adam never found out what it was. It was so ingrained in me to honor the First Law, but a very small part of me wished that I could tell Adam, that I could just answer his questions about the sword. But one question would lead to twenty and no Wàirén could ever know that much if they weren't sworn to the Hoard.

Adam wasn't clan. He hadn't sworn to uphold our laws. I couldn't tell him anything.

He also wasn't going to let this go. But time was running out for me and I needed to recover the anchor. There was no help for it. I pressed my thumb to the jade and fed a steady trickle of qì into it the same way I fed the blood jade on Hachi's pommel. The jade vibrated under my thumb and a low hum filled the air.

Adam heard it and stepped closer. "You did it!"

I had done it. And now I was one step closer to fulfilling the shinigami's Talon Call, and also one step closer to getting Adam killed. An auction meant other Jiārén, likely too many for me to handle on my own. I needed backup. I pulled out my phone and scrolled to Freddy's number.

My finger hovered over his name. I needed real help, not a quick ride across the city. It was time to get the true worth of my Talon.

I texted Fiona. **Got a lead on an auction going down for the anchor to the Gate. Don't know where yet.**

That would have to do for now. Now to deal with Adam.

My mind raced. I couldn't make him go home. I debated hitting a few of his pressure points to disable him. But could I leave him slumped on this dirty sidewalk? He was really complicating my life. I didn't like these feelings of indecision.

I didn't get to think about it very long.

A blacked-out Mercedes sedan pulled up to the curb and stopped. The driver's door opened and a hulk of a man in a charcoal-gray suit stepped out. His shaved head scanned up and down the street as he came around the car to open the passenger door for us. A thin line of red glowed around the driver. A White Tiger talent of some sort along with plenty of muscle. His eyes swept over Adam before settling on me as we moved toward the car.

The driver's eyes narrowed. "I'm here to pick up one bidder." His voice was rough, like he'd taken a lot of punches to the throat.

Adam turned to me, his megawatt smile on full display. "Yes, but I'm sure we could make an accommodation for my guest, couldn't we?"

The driver's gaze drifted above my head, then to my right shoulder, where I knew he could see Sword of Truth's silk-wrapped handle. He finally settled on my face and to his credit, his poker face didn't crack, but his eyebrows drew together slightly as recognition finally landed.

*Yes, you should be concerned,* my eyes told him.

If I had to do this the hard way, I needed every advantage I could scrape up. Once again I would lean on my bloody reputation. A chance at the Lost Heart was worth it. I forced down the discomfort rising in my chest and smiled, baring my teeth. The driver hesitated the barest second before regaining his composure.

"Of course, sir."

The driver reached into his pocket and withdrew a small sphere that looked like it was filled with chalk. He stepped past Adam and then made a small arc with his right foot, creating the boundary. He threw down the sphere and ground it out with his left boot. Wisps rose up behind us and just like that, the throngs of people on Embarcadero drifted away from us. I'd used those dispersal spheres myself on many occasions. Handy for dealing with Wàirén.

Adam didn't seem to notice the thinning crowd behind him, the excitement practically vibrating off every cell of his body as he readied to enter the sedan.

The driver reached into his other suit pocket and pulled out a handful of black fabric. He shook it out and it became two eye masks made of black silk.

"For security."

Nice try.

Adam's hand was halfway to the mask when I pulled Hachi and her steel rang out into the cold air. I leapt into the space between the driver and Adam and hit the driver square in the chest with my forearm. He flinched back, his eyes following the gleam of my sword, and that was all I needed to tip the thug off balance.

I rode the momentum and slammed him back into the car, rocking the vehicle up on two wheels. Before he could bring his hands up I brought Hachi around and rested the cold steel under his jaw. I lifted the sword, putting pressure on the soft skin of his throat and forcing him up onto his toes.

It had all taken about a second.

"Emiko!"

"Shut up, Adam." I didn't know if it was the sword, suddenly exposed from my no-look charm, or the growl in my voice, but for once, Adam quieted.

I flexed my wrist, earning a hiss from the driver as he tried to inch even higher on his toes. I curled the fingers of my left hand, digging my fingertips into his chest, probing for his meridians. "You didn't really expect me to put on the blindfold, did you?"

Perhaps it was unfair to ask the man a yes-or-no question when I had thirty inches of razor-sharp steel against his neck, but playing fair had never been my strong suit. My finger found the meridian and I applied steady pressure. The man's eyes widened as his qì slipped from his control like sand through his fingers. Welcome to my world.

"Emiko, I really don't think—"

"Not now, Adam."

None of this solved my problem, though. I still needed to get to the auction, and killing the driver was out of the question. There was no way I was going to endure another truth seeking for killing some low-level underling. Plus, Adam was watching.

When the driver's aura had dimmed to where I deemed him less of a threat I slowly eased my sword down. He slumped against the car when I pulled the blade away, his head and neck shiny with sweat. If I had to guess, I'd bet that losing control of his qì had defeated him more than my blade to his neck. I grabbed him by the lapels of his jacket, keeping Hachi within striking distance.

"Adam, open the back door."

"Emiko, I—"

"Adam. Open. The door."

Adam pulled the rear door open and I shoved the driver in ahead of me. When we were both in the back seat I kept my blade trained on my captive.

"Adam. Close the door and come around to the driver's side."

"What?"

"Adam. Pay attention."

"Right, right." Adam slammed the door shut and hustled to get himself settled into the driver's seat.

Adam buckled himself in and busied himself adjusting the mirrors and seat. When he tilted the rearview mirror his eyes darted down to Hachi, now held low and pointed at the driver's belly. "So . . . is that—"

"Not now, Adam."

I nudged Hachi's point into the driver's gut and the sharp edge parted his wool jacket like soft tofu. He hissed and pulled away as the edge touched his skin. Good. Now I had his undivided attention.

"Where were you taking us?"

The driver's eyes narrowed and the faint smell of herbs tickled my nose. I was right, a Dragon Limb talent. I let go with my left hand and jabbed him in the throat before he could harden his skin, sending him into a fit of coughing and gasping.

Adam twisted around from the front seat. "I think you're going a little hard on him, Emiko."

I leaned in close until my lips were brushing up against Mr. Dragon Limb's ear, and whispered low so Adam wouldn't hear. "You know who I am. You know what I've done. Do you really think the Second Law will protect you? From me?"

Clammy sweat broke out on the driver's neck, the smell of his fear thick in the enclosed space of the car. I closed my eyes and willed myself not to vomit.

The driver whispered, "The Palace of Fine Arts."

I pulled away but kept my sword in his gut and my hand on his neck. "Adam, you heard the man, Palace of Fine Arts. Now."

Adam turned around and affixed his seat belt. "You are definitely an interesting woman, Emiko."

"Not now, Adam."

Fifteen minutes later Adam turned off Marina Boulevard and the distinctive stone arches and dome of the Palace of Fine Arts came into view. Interior lights made the whole structure glow from within with soft, amber light. A flock of swans floated serenely on the glassy-smooth reflecting pool. The scene was peaceful and beautiful. Too peaceful. My hackles went up immediately.

"Park in the back, Adam. I don't suppose you'll do me the favor of waiting in the car?"

"Are you kidding? After all that's happened so far tonight?"

It had been a distant hope. When Adam parked he came around and opened my door. I backed out of the car and dragged the driver out as well.

"Now what?" I shook the driver.

"The rotunda," he muttered.

I eyed the driver. He outweighed me by at least fifty pounds, was taller than me by at least six inches, and had at least four inches extra reach over me. And he was totally cowed because I'd disrupted his qì, blocking his access to his talent. Because now he was blocked. No talent to call upon. Like me. I gave him a grim little smile.

Some Jiārén were so invested in their talent, they couldn't function without it. The driver had barely put up a fight. This was what I counted on as I had trained my whole life to get close, to fight dirty, and to let them know how it felt to be the one with no talent.

"Adam, open the trunk."

I got a questioning look from Adam before he popped it open. I shoved the beefy driver in and slammed the trunk shut with a noise of disgust. I sheathed Hachi at my waist with a mild feeling like I'd betrayed her, bringing her out only to scare some worthless henchman.

Adam's eyes unfocused as Hachi disappeared from his view again. I wasn't exactly sure how the no-look charm affected Wàirén minds, but after a moment he shook his head as if to clear it, then jingled the keys. "So . . . are we just going to leave him . . . ?"

I grabbed the keys and tossed them under the car. "Someone

will find him. Eventually. Let's go. Stay close and don't wander off."


The rotunda itself was just visible around the edge of the building, a fifty-meter-tall structure that recalled ancient Roman architecture, with towering columns supporting a massive dome. I knew from previous visits that eight arched entries led to an expansive space under the dome. A grand colonnade followed the inner arc of the theater building and separated the rotunda from the theater.

Jiārén were prone to the dramatic. The rotunda, with its grand setting and auspicious number of entrances, was the perfect location for such an event.

Adam stopped and also peered around the corner. "What are we looking for?"

We were in an open area, and totally unprotected. There were Jiārén around me, hidden. Behind me. Maybe even above me. I tilted my head up a notch and then back to scan around me.

In the shadow of the rotunda, a dim outline showed a man sitting motionless in a simple chair. Before Adam could call out I wrenched his hand down to quiet him. The entire area had gone eerily quiet, even the sounds of animals dying away.

I waited.

One heartbeat.

Two heartbeats and then movement.

Tight clusters of people had gathered under each of the archways, all of them facing inward. The archway before me and Adam was empty, and several sets of eyes were turned toward us. On those closest to us, I could just make out the bare shimmer of auras. Oh no, this wasn't ominous at all.

The city seemed to hold its breath.

On some unspoken cue, Dragon talents unfurled all around the

rotunda, blasting me with a chaotic mixture of aromas. Auras unfurled under each archway and illusion and obfuscation dropped
away.

Directly across from us, a pair of men dressed in baggy athletic
wear disappeared for a moment behind a cloud of fluttering bodies. Their illusion charm disintegrated into thousands of miniature
paper cranes that took flight only to dissipate into pale purple mist.
High-necked jackets with long tails emerged, the material dyed the
palest lavender, intricate embroidery studded with amethysts running along the lapels and cuffs.

Both men wore heavy bonguk geom at their waists, the swords
held in scabbards decorated with intricate dragon carvings. The
shorter man sported a dangpa on his back, three wicked points
gleaming wetly in the early evening light, the trident's head decorated with a lavender tassel.

On our right, the illusion hiding a trio in local street wear and
puffy jackets fell apart into wisps of blue-gray smoke. The smoke
swirled upward and coalesced into a miniature storm cloud that
hovered above the trio. Blue-white light lit the cloud from within
and finger-thin jags of lightning cracked outward. The air pressure in
the rotunda dropped and my ears popped like someone had driven a
spike into them. The scent of burnt tea leaves hit me and a lightning
bolt as thick as my arm erupted from the cloud and slammed into
the ground between the trio.

I'd smelled this family of talents before.

If I never smelled it again in this lifetime, it would be too soon.

My eyes adjusted after the flash of light and I gritted my teeth.
Three men in silk haori of deep blue, the jackets offset with bright
yellow lapels. Bā xià, the eighth son of the Dragon Father, master
of weather and water, was painted onto their jackets. The dragon's
head curved up their right shoulders and two stones of imperial
topaz had been set as the dragon's eyes. Matching silk pants, cut

wide through the legs for ease of movement in combat. Each man carried a matched set of swords at the waist, the scabbards inlaid with imperial topaz.

Clan Tanaka, my least favorite Jiārén in all of Japan. Here. In San Francisco. My palms burned with righteous indignation and twitched toward my sword. I reminded myself that Junior Tanaka was in prison and I had sent him there. He was enjoying a nice extended stay in Mohe with a chain around his neck that prevented him from using his talent. He'd killed my cousin Tai and the fact that Junior was not six feet under was a testament to my restraint.

I studied the three men. They weren't as big as most of the Tanaka men. The slimmest one had his long hair tied back with a simple cord. I'd bet money he was one of the numerous sons-in-law that Tanaka Senior had brought into the clan. Who would Tanaka Senior trust to procure the Lost Heart?

The two other men drew their katanas in unison and lunged forward together, performing a simple overhead strike. When their blades stopped a thunderclap ripped through the air, the sound wave pushing my hair back. Those had to be cousins, drawing on the famed Tanaka weather talent.

The slim man ran up the side of the rotunda, practically flying, and then executed a flip. White Tiger school, píng-level Dragon Wing talent. It was Haruto Watanabe. Now I had to contend with lightning strikes and flying swordsmen.

This type of showmanship was part of the game at my father's level. Like peacocks preening for each other, a show of strength that was safe for all parties involved.

Two bidders were here now, the Tanakas and the Byuns. That left one more and we had the fourth paddle.

While everyone had their eyes on each other I grabbed Adam by his shirt and dragged him into the shadows on the exterior of the rotunda.

I didn't think Adam's eyes could have gotten any wider. "What is—?"

I slapped my hand across his mouth and whispered low. "I told you, you don't know what's going on here."

Adam's eyes continued to dart left and right over my shoulder. When they looked down to my right and he gave a muffled cry, a cold weight dropped into my stomach.

The figure in the chair was hidden in the shadows to my right. Now that we were in the same shadow, it was easy to tell that the man was tied to the chair. And that he'd been beaten badly, his body covered with the strangely even bruises that were the hallmark of an expert kinetic striking with precision qì blows.

The man moaned softly, his breath gurgling in his chest, blood-streaked drool and snot running down his chin.

I turned back to Adam. "Your contact?"

He nodded, and I finally saw fear in his eyes. Good. Maybe with some fear in him I could finally get him out of here.

"Haider . . . his name is Haider."

I studied Haider's neck and wrists. A thick black cord with a pendant hung from Haider's neck and a knotted black cord with a gem circled the man's wrists. I needed to get closer to see what the gems were. Who Haider's clan was.

Footsteps scraped on the concrete behind me and an overly cheery voice called out, "Oh look. A few rats seem to have made it through. One of them seems to have our paddle."

The voice belonged to someone who'd lived overseas and studied at exclusive private schools with British English instructors. Someone who sounded like virtually everyone I had grown up with.

The skies darkened around us and the water lapped roughly at the shore. Birds shot out of the lake and bushes, dashing away from predators within.

I held still a split second, and my battle readiness settled around me like a familiar cloak.

# AUCTION ETIQUETTE

The air around us chilled, making my skin feel stretched and cracked. A thin rime of frost spread across the concrete. As I swiveled toward the voice, my eyes a lit on the aura color I was dreading. Streaky yellow meant an ice talent. I groaned inwardly. I hated ice talents.

The slender man in front of us was impeccably dressed in a tángzhuāng jacket of cobalt-blue silk. Dark eyes with slashing brows dominated his face. His skin had the deep brown hue that spoke of hard work in the sun. A thin beard covered his lean cheeks, accentuating the shadows under his eyes. The sapphire studs in his ears and the large rough-cut sapphire ring on his hand told me everything else I needed to know. This ice talent was a Koh, one of many from the sprawling Koh Clan. I doubted the Head of Koh Clan, Old Li, would make an appearance today but then he didn't need to. He had proxies to spare and this man seemed more than capable.

Flanking the ice talent were two slightly older women. Twins with inky-dark eyes, thin lips, and mirrored, malicious sneers. They shared the dark eyes and dramatic brows with the man between them. The twins were elegantly clothed in high-necked blue cheongsam and black high heels. One had a blue wool hat with a fascinator perched high on her head. The other a wide brim with a shiny white ribbon. The two looked ready for dim sum or Derby Day. Fat sapphires adorned their pale wrists and necks. The twins had dark yellow auras, their gāo-level water talents explaining the roiling water around us.

The air crackled with power and Haider twitched. He lifted his head, groaning in pain. One eye was swollen shut, the other eye wide and bloodshot and wet with terror. When he spoke in a rapid spate of Mandarin, blood-flecked spittle sprayed down his shirt and across the concrete.

"Master Koh! I'm sorry! I—"

Haider's voice died as the man in the blue suit raised one manicured finger. "You betrayed your clan. For money."

Koh said the last word like he was trying not to retch on it. His thin, glossed lips turned down just a fraction at the corners and Haider's one eye bugged out even more.

"No! Master!"

The twins moved together, the one in the wool hat with her left arm, the one in the brimmed hat with her right, their motions mirrored perfectly. Water leapt out of the lagoon and reared over their heads like a striking snake. The man in the center clapped his hands and thrust his palms forward. The water swept down and flowed along the man's arms. With a sharp twist of his hands, the water froze and launched forward as a spear of ice. The spike landed with a sickening thud, burying itself into Haider's neck and cutting the cord of his necklace. Haider's scream ended with a high, whistling wheeze.

The twin with the wool hat pointed her toe, drawing a short arc on the ground. A thin tendril of water whipped out from behind her, caught the necklace as it fell, and swept it back into her waiting hand. The sapphire sparkled, the facets slick with Haider's blood.

With a sharp yell, Koh windmilled his arms. As his right arm came down the water hovering behind him crystallized into a heavy axe blade that slammed down on Haider, severing his hand at the wrist. The twin with the brimmed hat drew a little arc with her foot, and her water whip snatched the bracelet from Haider's bloody stump.

The first twin lifted the necklace high and blood dripped from the cord onto her hands. "Haider, we sever you from the clan."

Her sister echoed. "Haider, we sever you from the clan."

A chill that had nothing to do with the Jiārén-influenced weather ran down my spine. I hoped fervently that Adam's language abilities did not also include Mandarin. There was only one reason that they were conducting all of this in front of Adam—they were going to kill him under the First Law. I had to figure out how to avoid breaking the Second Law and still save Adam.

The twins tossed the jewelry to the man between them and he caught them, making a fist over the stones. "Haider, we sever you from the clan. May your Hoard pieces be redeemed by one more worthy."

The sisters spoke in unison, "Witnessed."

My throat tightened as I watched the severing. For all my transgressions, my father had never severed me from the clan. I couldn't imagine anything more terrible. Even an afterlife of service to the shinigami seemed less shameful.

Koh pocketed the sapphires and pulled out a blue silk handkerchief to wipe his hands. He turned to me and smiled. The expression did not reach his eyes. Behind him the twins took a half step back but kept their arms raised, streams of water held at the ready.

Koh's thin lips twisted into a sneer as his eyes went from me to Adam. "Did the little rat really think they'd let him into the auction?"

Oh good. A talker.

"Where's Sabine? Is Old Li losing his wits in his old age?"

"He doesn't need that cow. He has me." He thumped his chest for emphasis.

"I'm sorry, who are you?" This was too easy. The arrogance, the paper-thin bravado—men like this, about the first decade after

Lóng Kǒu, hated to hear their reputation didn't spread any farther than the tip of their nose.

He lifted his chin, defiant. "I'm Awang. At least my clan sent me. We all know your clan didn't send you. You're nobody now. An exile. Your tiny clan couldn't buy into this auction with every last ounce of your pathetic Hoard."

Awang. Firstborn. Contrary to my efforts to needle young Awang, I had extensive dossiers on him and his twin cousins, Nayla and Nur Koh. Old Li brought them out when he needed to drop the hammer. Awang was a blunt instrument, powerful, cocky, and petty. His younger half sister, Sabine, was Old Li's favorite and next in line despite her youth. I was sure that fact chafed at Awang on the daily.

It was odd that Old Li would send the Ice Tsunami Trio to this auction. Maybe the old man anticipated it wasn't going to be a simple bid after all.

I knew this trio were a force to be reckoned with, a well-trained, cohesive unit that packed gāo-level power. But they always acted as a unit, never separately, and I had suspicions about their strategy. In my past as the Blade, I'd never crossed paths with them but today was my lucky day.

During our little chat, I'd slipped the earth tile out of my pocket. I just had to bide my time.

"Poor Awang, you're going to be just like me. How does it feel to know that your little sister is the heir?"

Color suffused his cheeks. He spread his palms out in a deliberate movement, his right foot coming down in a short stomp. The water beneath his shiny black leather lace-ups froze instantly and the streams of puddles between us solidified into hard ice.

Nayla and Nur rotated their arms in a wide, showy circle, first in one direction, then the other. If I'd been trying to kill them, they would be dead already for all the time their movements took.

The once gentle lake now resembled the Pacific Ocean, waves rising high and slamming onto the shore. Splashing water sprayed around the Kohs and formed into a swirling sphere around them. The twins funneled water from the sphere and fed it to Awang. The concrete sidewalk cracked and groaned under the thermal stress as shards of ice as big as my leg sprouted up, spreading from Awang's feet and marching toward us.

Adam thankfully kept his mouth shut, but he took a small step back from the ice. Awang spread his arms and the growing ice fanned out, hemming us in on both sides and pinning our backs to the columns supporting the rotunda. It was now or never.

I pushed my qì again, cramming it through my cursed meridians. The mountain tile in my hand warmed just the slightest bit. It would have to be enough. I flicked out my left hand, sending two shurikens flying. With my right hand I slammed the mountain tile at Awang's feet, shattering the tiny ceramic on the ice.

The mountain tile broke and flashed, a brief spark of pale blue light. The tile had held compressed earth talent, enough to briefly increase the force of gravity, meant to be ignited with a burst of qì. Qì that I sorely lacked. Blood and bone!

My throwing knives cut through the air and passed on either side of Awang's surprised face. They sailed past him and into Nayla's and Nur's shoulders. The twins screamed, more with outrage than pain, and their water talent fell apart as their coordination broke. The ice forming from Awang's hands died away at the same time.

I knew it. Awang was an ice talent but he didn't have the discipline to learn the water control he needed to feed his ice talent. Without the twins to back him up and keep him flush with water, he was barely good enough to keep your drinks frosty. No wonder Old Li had left him hanging while he brought up Sabine.

"Hey Nayla, aren't you getting tired of being Awang's geyser?"

The twins whirled, eyes blazing with anger. Uh-oh. With a screech of rage, they both raised their hands and a wall of water erupted behind them. Without saying a word, Awang stepped back into the standing water and began throwing punches, rapid-fire.

Crystal clear basketball-sized spheres of ice formed as his fists punched through the wall of water and launched at me and Adam. I grabbed at Adam to pull him to cover but he was too big and I didn't have the leverage I needed. Adam hauled back on me and pulled me behind him. We made it two steps before I heard a sickening impact and Adam's body turned into two hundred pounds of Jell-O that bore me down to the sidewalk.

Awang roared, his hands in the air now and the wall of water crested over his head like a wave. He brought his hands down and the water crashed into me, crushing the air out of me. My back slammed against the nearest pillar and I gasped, sucking freezing cold water into my lungs. The combined physical and thermal shock made my vision black out for a moment.

When I roused, I was coughing and retching on the sidewalk, dripping wet and freezing. I rolled to my side and found bars of ice arched over me from the sidewalk to the pillar. Awang squatted outside the ice prison, the little not-smile on his lips again. His shoes weren't even wet.

Adam coughed and gasped for air. He had a cut to the back of his head that was bleeding into his collar and his eyes were unfocused. I pulled off his jacket and wadded up the cashmere to apply pressure to the wound. He hissed with pain when I applied my makeshift bandage.

Awang flicked a finger against the ice bars, setting them ringing. Nayla sent a tendril of water past the bars and plucked the fan off the ground from where I'd dropped it. At a confirming nod from Nayla, Awang stood and dusted off his trousers.

"You should count yourself lucky. And you know, this could be good for your clan. When your father hears how we humiliated you, maybe he'll finally grow some fangs of his own and sever you for good."

Hot, liquid anger ignited in my belly. Second Law be damned, Father could deal with the consequences. I set Adam down and threw myself at the bars, my hand stretched between them in a killing strike at Awang's throat.

Nayla reacted fastest, wrapping Old Li's precious firstborn in a sheath of water and yanking him back from the ice cage. My shoulder slammed into the bars and the shock sent a wave of numbness through the joint and down my arm. My fingers hooked and brushed through the water Nayla had wrapped protectively around Awang's throat.

Awang's eyes were wide and his lips trembled, the smug look wiped from his face as he fell back on his butt. He was older than me by five or six years but now looked like a scared schoolboy caught cheating on a test, scrambling to find his footing. I growled and grabbed the ice bars, ignoring the bitter, sticky cold and the frost crusting around my fingertips. As I looked down on him his eyes tracked me like prey cornered by a hungry predator.

Even without the mantle of the Blade in me, the authority of the office flowed through me like cold, biting rage. "That's right, you coward, run and hide behind your cousins. Without them you're nothing but a glorified bartender, the shame of your family."

I held his gaze and drove the dagger home. "You don't want to admit it, but you're no better than me. One day your cousins will get tired of propping you up and you'll finally see it. You will never be the Head of the Clan."

# THE HEART

Awang sniffed and spat on the ground at his feet. "I honestly don't understand how such a disgrace hasn't been severed yet. Every day you draw breath is a blight on your clan."

Nayla pulled her cousin farther back and after a whispered conference the three turned away from me, heading back to the rotunda. Now that I was contained, I was no longer worth their attention.

When it came right down to it, Awang was right. Breaking my blade was a severing offense, a rejection of clan and duty that could not be ignored. By keeping me in-clan, my father sent a clear signal to other Jiārén that even in my exile, I was still under his protection. I had fled to San Francisco for independence, but my ability to do so in relative safety had been guaranteed by my father, despite my continual disrespect.

My father never discarded an asset. I knew my father believed I was still an asset to the clan because he always tried to get me to come back. In every conversation, he left the door open for me to return in the future. My brother was heir, but too young to take control of the clan. Our clan was small but my actions as the Soong Blade had been legendary. My father was more than happy to leverage that.

I might be firstborn like Awang, but I knew my place. I had no illusions that a no-talent offspring like me could ever be heir. The same wasn't true of Awang. He acted like a man who still clung to the hope of leading his clan. But he was on borrowed time. His half sister, Sabine, was the rising star. Ultimately, Awang would merely be Old Li's errand boy.

The last family arrived with less fanfare. A small group of men in cream-colored suits. Rubies flashed on tie pins and cuff links, marking them as Sengs, associates of the Moks from Malaysia. All the bidders were now present. Well, except for me and Adam stuck in this ice cage.

The air shimmered like scorched desert sand. The rotunda was still there but distorted as if a thousand small mirrors deflected light in all directions. The effect faded and where once there had been nothing but empty space in the center of the columns now stood five figures clad head to toe in black. The red sheen of soft Hoard gold accented each man. Heavy chains at necks, wide bracelets above broad-knuckled hands, two wore spiraled bracers on their biceps.

The Louies were the only family in San Francisco with the resources to deploy so much illusion talent, and so much gold. I didn't recognize any of these heavies, but all the Hoard gold was identification enough for me.

Two of the men, wide-shouldered and brawny, held a small table between them. Atop the table perched a gold filigree cage, a cube of gold scrollwork at least a meter on each side. Inside, a teardrop stone the size of a small fist sat on a cushion of black velvet. Even from a distance, the presence of the stone was like looking into the blinding core of an explosion. The stone seemed to pulse with menace, the color the deep black-red of blood spilled in the dead of night. A single flaw ran across the width of the stone, a jagged line of bright, arterial red suspended within.

Blood jade. A stone so powerful, so steeped in the power of the lost dragons of the Realm, that less than one in ten Jiārén even dared to use it. All the pieces I'd seen in my life had been maybe a tenth the size of this stone, and those were still fabulously dangerous. Those who dared to wear blood jade too long risked madness and death as the raw power of our dragons devoured them from within, but the potential gain in power was worth the risk to some. And this was no mere chip of blood jade. This was clearly the Lost Heart of Yázì. Whichever clan took this stone would increase the strength of their Hoard tenfold.

All around the rotunda, hungry looks tracked the Lost Heart as dreams of fortunes and schemes ignited behind every pair of eyes. Even the Ice Tsunami Trio had left me, drawn by the magnetic pull of the Lost Heart. Everywhere I looked, eyes glittered, hands flexed, and auras strained to break free from iron restraints.

This was why Old Li had sent his heavy hitters tonight. This wasn't going to be an auction. This was going to be a battle.

Either Uncle Jimmy or Dai Lou had miscalculated badly. Did they really think they could summon four Jiārén families, dangle something as significant as the Lost Heart of Yázì before them, and the three losers would simply walk away without a fuss?

No. Not just three losers. Someone else was going to lose. My city especially.

Rage boiled in my veins and I kept the pressure on Adam's wound. I tilted my head up. The ice cage was thinnest there and though my mountain tile use had been ignited with a bare trickle of qì, cracks had formed in the ice. I could break this cage with a few well-placed strikes overhead. But then I'd have to let go of Adam.

I looked back down at the unconscious man in my arms. His skin was ashy now, a far cry from the man who usually looked like he was the sun's favorite subject. As much as I wanted to bust out of this cage and hunt down the Kohs, I did feel somewhat obligated to take care of the unconscious idiot laid out before me. Adam had taken a hit meant for me, and done it without hesitation. An idiot, for sure, but perhaps with a few redeeming qualities.

As if on cue, Adam groaned and his eyes fluttered half open. The wound had stopped bleeding and maybe it wasn't as bad as I had feared earlier.

I pressed my hand to Adam's neck and found his pulse, steady and strong. "Adam. I need you to wake up."

The big man moaned and began to shift around. His hand went to his head and he hissed as his fingers brushed over what was going to be a mean knot on the back of his head. "Ow."

"Maybe next time pick something other than your head to block with."

He did the lopsided smile thing again and it was absurdly appealing. "I figured my hard head would be the best option."

I huffed. "Can you sit up? Are you going to pass out on me again?"

With another groan Adam sat up, carefully keeping his head cradled in one hand. His eyes darted around us, getting wider by the moment. "Why are we in ice jail?"

His voice was awfully calm for a man who had just gotten knocked unconscious after a supernatural attack. Maybe I'd gotten lucky and he didn't remember the spectacle of water talent and ice shards from the Ice Tsunami Trio.

I shrugged. "Climate change."

He snorted and resumed exploring the knot on his head.

I stood and brushed off my pants. Our clothes were soaked from the fight with the Kohs, and the chill evening was stealing in, sucking the heat from my arms and chest. Adam got to his feet, a bit unsteady, one hand holding his balled-up jacket to the back of his head and the other hand braced on my shoulder.

"So, what exactly am I looking at?"

He was literally looking at something that would get him killed. If anyone else here turned our way, they would have no qualms exercising the First Law. The only thing keeping Adam alive right now was the fact that the Lost Heart had everyone's attention.

"What do you think you're looking at?"

The invited clans faced toward the center of the rotunda, and the Lost Heart. Around the table with the blood jade, the Louie goons stood in a loose circle facing out, their protective auras burning hot. Even with the precautions, most of the attendees seemed more than eager to jump in. One of the black suits, possibly the leader, spoke in a deep, quiet voice, laying out the ground rules for the night.

Adam turned to me. "I don't suppose you'll translate Cantonese for me?"

"You suppose correctly."

He sighed and turned back to the scene within the rotunda. Then he narrowed his eyes. "Wait, that's got to be the Lost Heart."

His voice went up slightly at the end. He leaned forward in his excitement. I guess getting bonked unconscious and waking up in an ice cage that defied the laws of nature as he knew it was not enough to curb his enthusiasm for ancient artifacts.

Or more accurately, this minor head injury couldn't derail the elation he had to be experiencing to know that the stories of his dying host father might be true.

I could break us out of this cage, but that would just put us in the middle of the Tanakas, the Sengs, the Byuns, and the Kohs. The Louie Claws didn't concern me, but no one here would take kindly to a Wàirén in their midst, or the fact that I had brought him.

The Kohs had already demonstrated their powers. I doubted Old Li was the only one to realize tonight's event would be anything but peaceful. The Byuns likely had a shrieker in their contingent. The Moks had probably embedded one of their earth talents in with the Sengs, someone who could make the ground swallow the whole amphitheater. I reached into my pocket and pulled out the lozenges of skepticism. I crunched down hard and savored the tang of citrus and powerful mint oils. It was probably useless, but if the Louies had sent a charm speaker, at least I would have some resistance against them, leaving my mind perfectly whole as the other clans ripped me and Adam to pieces.

Adam tore his gaze away from the Lost Heart. "These guys seem a little . . . intense."

I almost laughed. Tonight was not going to go well. I was down to my last few throwing knives and Hachi. Whatever happened next, the only thing I knew for sure was that first I would get out of this ridiculous ice cage.

"Adam, these are the most intense people you will ever have the pleasure to meet. I need you to pay attention, and do everything I tell you to."

I readied my shurikens, sliding them loose from my straps so they would be ready to go. The cracks above me were slowly widening as the ice shifted. If Adam could break the cage, I might gain an extra second of surprise. It was still no good. I needed something else, something outside this cage to tip the odds back in my favor.

The water lapping against the shores began to roil again. I whipped my head to look at the Tanakas and then the Koh twins but they hadn't moved. Why all the turbulence? The people in the rotunda didn't seem to notice the turmoil in the water and indeed, no one seemed to be able to tear their gaze away from the red glow of the Lost Heart.

I strained to hear, but the auction master's words were smothered under the noise of the crashing water. A flash of hot, prickly emotion pulsed through me, the sensation rocketing up through my legs. San Francisco's magic clutched at me, but where the sensations before had been needy, this was different.

The city was angry.

Against the shore, the foaming waves tossed bowling ball–sized rocks up onto the sidewalk. The water surged again and dozens of smaller rocks crested through the surf . . . No, wait . . . those weren't small rocks but claws. My eyes widened in alarm as what had to be a dozen sets of webbed, moss-colored limbs rose up out of the lake water and scrambled onto the shore. The creatures were about the size of a tiger and covered with a rocky-brown carapace. What in the eighteen lower circles of hell was I looking at?

Voices rose in alarm around the rotunda as the creatures lumbered over, some gaining speed by launching themselves with their powerful hind legs. One of the creatures jumped toward us and landed with its webbed hands wrapped all the way around the ice bars. The stench hit me next, a miasma of stagnant water and sulfurous rot. My potsticker lunch nearly erupted from my throat.

The scooped hollow on the head, which should have held a small amount of clear water. The dead milky eyes. It was a kappa but not a kappa . . . an undead kappa? Only I could be so lucky as to have to deal with zombie water demons today on top of everything else. The wrongness of these creatures roiled through me, and I couldn't tell if it was me or the city feeling this way.

"Whaa . . . what are those?" Adam held his arm over his nose.

Abominations. It was time to break out. I pointed at the cracks in the ice. "We have to shatter the bars and get out."

Adam blinked. "Okay."

"On my count . . ."

Adam lunged, slamming his shoulder into the bars. The bars jumped and cracked a little more, but didn't break. The kappa holding onto the bars screeched before leaping away. Outside more zombie kappas emerged from the water and broke for the rotunda. Talents broke free left and right, flooding my senses with colors and smells. Jiārén rallied in small groups that were quickly surrounded by prowling rings of undead water beasts.

The Byuns had indeed sent a shrieker, the older man with the dangpa now held in what looked like very capable hands. He twirled the trident and opened his mouth, emitting a nearly ultrasonic whine that set his dangpa to vibrating like a tuning fork. The bars of the ice cage shuddered with resonance. An invisible blade of force cut through the surging kappas like a plow, throwing bodies left and right. More kappas rushed forward to fill the gaps, keeping the Jiārén hemmed in and on the defensive.

I drew Hachi and held her at low guard. Adam backed up a step, took a breath, and ran for the bars, dropping his shoulder into the heavy ice. The bars splintered with a sound like shattering glass.

Adam stepped out of the cage and picked up a chunk of ice the length of a baseball bat. He sucked in a breath and dropped it. Awang's ice was unnaturally cold. But Adam had the right idea, and having an extra weapon in his hands would be a good thing. I stepped up to him and grabbed the hem of his drenched cashmere sweater in my left hand. I kept my eyes studiously away from the way the fabric clung to his chest.

"Do you trust me?" I hefted Hachi in my right hand.

His blue eyes sparkled. "Holy hell is that sexy."

I flipped Hachi in my hand, reversing the edge, and slid it forward as I pulled the sweater away from his body. Adam's eyes didn't waver, didn't leave mine. Hachi parted the wool with ease, slicing off the bottom six inches of his sweater. Adam held perfectly still, a small smile tugging at the corners of his mouth as I ruined a sweater that cost as much as my mortgage.

He was rich, he could afford it.

As I sliced the wool into something he could tie around the ice I definitely did not notice how his undershirt clung to his narrow waist. Adam knotted the fabric around the ice, hefted the makeshift club, and looked around. "So are we just fighting our way out of here, or are we getting the Lost Heart first?"

I might never get a better chance at this. "Lost Heart first."

Adam grinned and adjusted his grip on the club, tightening both his hands around it. "Shall we, then?"

Despite the swirling talents around us, and the scrum of zombie kappas streaming from the churning waters, Adam's smile calmed me, settling the jagged edge of nerves in my belly. I turned on the ball of my foot, dropped two throwing knives into my left palm, and brought Hachi up across my body with my right. I sensed Adam standing close behind me, our backs together, and I knew in my gut that he would watch my back, allowing me to fully commit to the fight in front of me.

The last time someone had my back like this, it had been Kamon. We had faced similar odds then, too. I shook off the memory and dropped my weight into my knees. "Ready?"

Adam's back bumped against mine. "Ready."


In hindsight, wading into a herd of undead kappas was one of the worst ideas of my life. The smell hit us first, like we were fighting knee-deep in fetid sewer water. On the plus side, Hachi's honed edge went through their tough hides like slicing through rice paper. I just wished she'd been a little longer, so I could keep a wider area clear around us.

Adam wielded his ice club with surprising skill, making quick, precise strikes that caught kappas in the knees or haunches. Those he struck were unable to move, and his side of our little circle developed a pile of disabled kappas that served as a bulwark of sorts against the tide of undead creatures. I was grudgingly impressed.

His head injury was no joke, though. Several times I reached out when I felt him shift away from me, and I hauled him back from tumbling into the snarling mass of undead at our knees. He smiled weakly at me one of those times and gamely went back to kneecapping kappas with his ice club.

Everything was terrible. The stench of rot, the sound of wailing kappas, the slick slurry of melt water, mud, and zombie kappa guts under our feet. We only made it a few feet from the ice cage before the kappas surrounded us as well. We made no progress at all toward the Lost Heart.

The Louies guarding the Heart had fallen back until they were nearly touching the small table. They were hemmed in so tightly that they were starting to interfere with each other's efforts. I'd seen this before. Those men had only a few minutes before they were completely overrun.

Two kappas made it to the guards. One knelt down on all fours and the second one leapt on top and sailed over the guards to reach the table. With two massive webbed paws it snatched up the gold filigree cage and crashed through the backs of the guards who were busy dealing with the other zombie water beasts. The men screamed as they went down in a heap under a three-hundred-pound undead kappa.

"It's got the Lost Heart!" I yelled.

It didn't matter that Awang Koh hated my guts, we were aligned in this. His arms swept forward in a wide arc and sent a shower of ice blades at the beast.

Glittering chunks of ice as thick as my leg slammed into the sidewalk, blocking the kappa's path. The kappa swerved and back-pedaled, and ended up right under another ice blade that came down and cleaved through one of its rear legs. But this wasn't a normal kappa water sprite. This thing felt no pain. Even missing a leg, it continued undeterred. It hobbled along on its remaining three legs and rammed its way out of the would-be ice prison that Awang had encircled it with.

The acrid smell of gunpowder and oiled shoe leather hit my nostrils. Of course! Who else could have summoned the undead kappas? Only the ghost master. But I'd seen him with the Louies . . . and I was sure the Louies were zhong—the ones conducting the auction. None of this made any sense. Was the ghost master working for himself? Was there a division within the Louie Clan?

The army of undead kappas was thinning but they were still making it impossible to wade through to the one fleeing with the Lost Heart. The Byun shrieker was useless now, his talent likely to take out his own clan members flailing through the muck and guts.

I had to make a play and I had to make it now.

Awang and his cousins were on the move, cutting through the

kappas and making a beeline for the Lost Heart. Adam and I were closer. If we moved now we would reach the blood jade first. I needed that anchor.

"Adam! This way!"

Adam appeared at my side, the end of his ice club coated in black gore, his once-pristine cashmere sweater ripped to shreds and covered in muck. His chest heaved with his exertions but his eyes shone and his lips were parted in a wide grin.

"Are all our dates going to be this exciting?"

"What? No!"

"Okay, a quiet dinner would also be nice."

I grabbed him by the shoulder and pointed out the kappa fleeing with the Lost Heart. "That's the one we want!"

I pulled my tanto from my boot and reversed it in my left hand. Hachi slashed from right to left, beheading a kappa and cleaving another nearly in half. Adam stepped in beside me and swung his weapon like a golf club, catching the impaled kappa in the head. The force of the impact ripped the beast apart and sent the head flying.

We danced in and out of the writhing kappas, alternating between striking out to clear space and holding back to defend our flanks. My breath flowed in and out, a steady rhythm set to the timing of our fight. Adam moved around me as easily as water flowing around a stone, filling in the spaces I opened, moving in counterpoint to my attacks.

His club came down in a sharp strike, crushing a kappa to the concrete. His face was flushed, but he looked like he still had plenty of gas in the tank. "Are we almost there?"

The kappa with the Lost Heart was nearing the lagoon's edge, having to fight through its crazed brethren as much as we were.

"Yes! It's just—"

A bolt of lightning crashed into the open space, the flash of light blinding me. Adam grunted as superheated air blew us both back a step. Kappas screamed, tossed in every direction. When my vision cleared I found Haruto Watanabe floating before me about six feet off the ground, his wife's cousins flanking him. Rather than facing the Lost Heart, these three men faced me. Claws and fangs, this cursed clan!

Watanabe held his katana at the ready. Behind him blue fingers of electricity crawled up and down his cousins' arms. They pivoted and brought their arms up, energy building in their palms. Haruto advanced a step and paused.

"We have unfinished business, Blade."

I was pretty sure Adam was fluent in Japanese. He'd have a lot of questions for me if we got through this. I focused on the problem in front of me. "I fulfilled the Talon Call. We have no further clan business."

The power the Tanaka cousins held back built until I felt the pressure on my eyeballs. Their auras lit up, glowing bright orange. Watanabe raised his blade to high guard. "I have pledged an oath to Tanaka-sama. His blood is my blood. His feud is my feud."

He wanted to do this now? When the Lost Heart was running off?

I gritted my teeth. Fine. I'd call it like I saw it. If my father were here, he'd laugh in Watanabe's face.

I lifted my chin. "Funny, I don't see the Head of the Clan here. Just some errand boy. Go home to your master. We don't feud with servants."

Watanabe's face flushed red. Maybe rage. Probably embarrassment.

My hair stood on end as the pressure around us dropped in an instant, the air dry and heavy with electric potential.

Watanabe's jacket flared open as he bore down on me, the lining of his jacket glittering. On the opposite side of the open space, the other Tanaka cousins planted their feet in horse stance and shot their arms up to the sky.

My eyes flicked back to Watanabe and the glittering lines inside his jacket. Glittering rows of kanji written in copper thread and topaz gems. Tanaka Hoard gems.

Power exploded from the Tanakas, lighting up the rotunda like a bomb blast. Two tree trunk–thick bolts of electricity erupted from them and engulfed Watanabe. Crackling energy covered his arms and lit up his sword like a torch.

Okay, this was new.

Runners of electricity rained down as Watanabe bore down on me. He flicked his sword left and right and lightning hammered down, tearing holes in the concrete. I tried to get out from under him but flying concrete and lightning pushed me back. His war cry built to deafening levels and he floated to a stop ten feet above me. With both hands on his blade he reversed his grip as if to stab down with a killing blow. The blue-white electric glow of his sword became a miniature sun. Watanabe's eyes shone with the frantic light of a religious fanatic.

The sword flashed and a brick wall hit me from behind. Wet cashmere engulfed me and the ground rose up to slap me in the face. Watanabe's lightning strike blasted the floor of the rotunda, filling my mouth with the taste of ozone and ash. Adam collapsed on top of me and his weight squeezed the breath from my lungs.

I opened my eyes and blinked back the sunspots swimming across my vision. A high-pitched whine filled my ears and my tongue was thick with the taste of blood. I squeezed my hand and was relieved to feel Hachi's familiar silk knots under my fingers. The sound of voices came back next, the words garbled as my brain tried to reboot itself and get my body working again.

". . . kill her?"

". . . aka-sama . . . her sword and her head . . ."

My eyes refused to focus but the sounds were definitely coming from my right. Possibly my left. Adam's chest rose and fell with his breath, but he was otherwise dead to the world. I struggled to get my heels dug in, trying to bridge his weight off my hips. I was not going to die by the hand of some lowly Tanaka errand boy juiced with Hoard gems.

Feet scraped the concrete, getting closer to my head. My heart thudded in my neck as I caught the metallic scrape of a combat knife being unsheathed.

"... do it ... get her sword ..."

I tightened my grip on Hachi. One thing these guys were about to learn was that there was only one safe place to grab a sword by.

My ears popped and the sounds of the world returned in an instant. The smell of seawater flooded over me like a crashing wave and the voices of the Tanakas were swept away. A warm wind whipped around the rotunda, pushing away the smell of ash and ozone, and the sounds of many stomping feet soon filled the space.

My eyes finally cleared as one pair of feet rang out on the concrete paving: precise, sharp heel strikes set to a metronome, the sound as keen as a headsman's axe. I could only turn my head a little to the side so I barely saw her red-bottomed pumps before Fiona stopped next to my head. I tilted my head up and found myself looking up a vast expanse of knee-length silver silk set off with a white fur shrug. Heavy Hoard silver hung from both of her ears and adorned both forearms.

I had to tell her. "It was here, Fiona. The Lost Heart of Yázì. More blood jade than I've ever seen in my life. The anchor for the Ebony Gate was right here and I let it slip through my fingers."

As I spoke, indignant rage coursed through my veins, making my skin flash hot. Some upstart wing talent had managed to derail my best chance at the Lost Heart. I'd thought I was finished with all the fallout from the Tanaka mess.

Fiona crossed her arms and raised one delicate brow. "You tell me about an unsanctioned auction for a Hoard artifact but you don't tell me where, forcing me to retask my entire drone fleet to sweep the city. After wasting time looking for you I get here just in time to lose a priceless artifact to an undead swamp creature."

Her response took me off guard as much as Watanabe's feud cry. "What? I told you everything I knew at the time."

Fiona rolled her eyes under her thick lashes. "Yes and you hardly knew anything."

I speared Fiona with a gaze. Difficult indeed from my position on the ground. "Well, I counted on the full support of your clan in service of my Talon."

Fiona sniffed and her eyes roamed around us. Her gaze floated around the entire rotunda before settling back on me. "Touché."

A warm push of air nudged between me and Adam and my breathing became easier. The gentle force of Fiona's talent lifted Adam away and placed him gently on the ground next to me. Adam had taken a really bad hit and he'd taken it for me. Without him shielding me, I would have eaten all that lightning and possibly died. Or even if my heart hadn't stopped, I would have been too fried to defend myself when Watanabe came for my head. Adam had saved me. I closed my eyes, exhaustion hitting me. I owed him.

She reached out a hand and I took it, pulling myself to my feet.

Fiona took in the wreckage of my clothing and wrinkled her nose. "I suppose you're hoping I'll clean all this up as well."

I gave her my best smile. "As long as you're offering . . ."

Fiona had brought a full complement of her household to secure the rotunda. I made a note of Fiona's show of strength. Even Freddy was present, using his talent to suck away the piles of kappa corpses. One of Fiona's healers went over my arm and feeling finally returned to my fingers.

Fiona put her hands on her hips and looked down at Adam's prone form. "He's seen too much. My team will have him cleaned as well."

Someone to wipe him. It would be traumatic. Brain and memory tampering always was. He might never recover from the "cleaning." It was gentler than termination though. I knew Fiona was right about what our laws called for but I protested anyway. "He didn't understand what was happening."

Fiona shook her head. "No."

I pointed at Adam's head injury. "Struck by lightning. He won't remember anything."

Adam was laid out on a backboard, his head and neck secured. Other than that, the healers hadn't touched him.

Fiona's full lips turned down into a pretty frown. "Emiko."

My shoulders sagged. I had seen this coming a mile away and avoided making any of the calls I should have made sooner. I looked down at Adam. He was a mess. He'd taken a lot of damage today and that last hit was intended for me. He didn't have to do that. I wished he hadn't but it was hard to argue with the results. Because of his actions, I was standing now and could continue chasing the Gate. I could still save my brother. It wasn't just me that owed him, it was our whole clan.

Adam's head wound had started bleeding again. Fiona had forbidden her healer from even looking at the wound.

Before tonight, I'd seen Adam as someone who was important to Tessa, and therefore someone I should protect. But these last few hours had changed all that. At every turn, Adam had surprised me. Every moment with him was challenging and exhilarating. He had a zest for life that lit him with inner fire. I didn't want to see that snuffed out. That wasn't about Tessa. It was about me. I wanted Adam to continue being Adam. Maddening. Funny. Alive.

But the First Law was nearly absolute. Wàirén that learned of our world were cleaned. Some died quiet deaths. Most had their memories erased, a tricky process that could have bad side effects. Nearly absolute. I couldn't allow Adam to be cleaned. There was one exception. It couldn't be made for me though.

But the exception could be made for my father's daughter.

I squared my shoulders and turned to face Fiona. She read the look on my face and her expression turned serious. I unsheathed Hachi and nicked the thickest part of the pad of my thumb. Then I knelt and did the same to Adam and pressed our hands together.

"This man has earned the respect of the Dragon and all the protection that comes with that respect."

Somewhere in Japan I was positive my father had just paused in whatever he was doing. "The Soong Clan claims this one as our own. On our blood. On our clan."

Fiona's eyes widened as I claimed responsibility for a Wàirén, bringing him under the aegis of our clan's protection. "Witness!"

From across the rotunda Freddy cried out, "So witnessed!" He shot me a wink.

I slumped and dropped Adam's arm, exhaustion catching up to me. "Now can I get him to a hospital?"

It took until just past 7 p.m. to get Adam transported to San Francisco General and checked into the emergency room. I stared daggers at the clock for another three interminable hours until a doctor came in to check on him. Ray Ray had sent his goon to snatch the Lost Heart, I knew it. While I was stuck in the ER who knew where he was stashing the stone?

When the hospital staff started asking me for Adam's information I gave up and called Tessa. She showed up shortly, a puffy microdown coat thrown over her pajamas.

"What happened?"

I was already in enough trouble if Adam remembered anything about tonight. Tessa could not be in the same boat. "Long story, will have to wait."

Tessa held her head in her hands and stared at the unconscious form of her museum's wealthy donor. Her eyes flicked back and forth between me and Adam, and I saw the beginnings of doubt in her expression. "It looks bad . . . ?"

"Tessa, I need you to stay with him, please? I can't stay. It's a . . . family emergency."

"Family emergency?"

I nearly smacked myself on the forehead. I never talked about my family with her.

"Yes . . . my . . . brother. He's in some trouble and I need to bail him out." There. That was nearly the truth.

Tessa's eyes narrowed and she opened her mouth to say something when the doctor breezed back into the room. "Ah, good. Do you have this gentleman's information for us?"

Ever prepared, Tessa reached into her bag at the doctor's question. I took her moment of distraction to head for the door. "Tessa, I owe you, really."

She pointed her finger at me, her eyes glinting. "You do."

I nodded gratefully and bolted out the door.

Now that Adam was under Tessa's care, I could rest easier on that front. I needed to make some progress on the Gate. With the Jiārén world in chaos from tonight's excitement, there was no better time to pick up a clue. Also, dinner would have been nice, too. My stomach was hollowed out and a Mission special burrito, melty with cheese and salty from the french fries inside, would hit the spot.

I'd barely turned to walk away from the hospital when my left arm was unceremoniously dunked into a vat of freezing acid and shards of glass. The pain drove me to one knee, my right hand clamped around my elbow. The sidewalk appeared to pitch and yaw as my vision swam. The agony crawled up my arm and stabbed into the base of my neck. The shinigami's mark on my palm glowed a bright blue, pulsing in time with my heartbeat.

A dull roar thundered in my head, an awful sound like a thousand screaming voices. The scream warped and twisted until it became Sugiwara's low baritone. "I have arrived. Attend me at the tea garden. Now."

I gasped as the pain receded into something a little less than life-threatening. The sound and pain disappeared, leaving me kneeling on the sidewalk with passersby staring at me. I pretended to pick up something from the sidewalk and dusted off my pants as I stood. All that mystical power and the death god couldn't invest in a phone? I pulled out my phone to call a rideshare.

So much for my burrito.

# NIGHT VISITORS

I had the rideshare take me back to the Ferry Building so I could get my Jeep, then drove to the park. The mark on my left hand throbbed the whole way. It was eleven by the time I made it to the park and traffic was thankfully light. The shinigami waited for me by the entrance to the garden, in the same spot he'd been waiting during the Talon Call. As before he was impeccably dressed in a camel overcoat and matching driving cap. Was there a high-end haberdashery available in the underworld? I strangled the giggle before it could escape my lips. I must have been more tired than I thought. He was even taller than he'd seemed on the astral plane. I couldn't have missed him in a crowd, and certainly not considering his glowing red eyes. The little cat yokai stood at his side, scribbling studiously in a small notebook.

He turned those eyes on me as I approached. "Ms. Soong. Have you brought me the Ebony Gate?"

I slowed. Had he really dragged me across the city for a status update? "I'm still working on that."

His coal-ember eyes traveled up and down my body, seeming to take slow inventory of me, and his gaze settled on my shoulder where Sword of Truth rode across my back. He took a deep breath as if scenting something on the air. His eyes widened and brightened like a flame catching alight. He raised a skeletal hand and reached for my sword's hilt.

"Have you come to bargain instead? Your mother promised you

would be interesting, but I did not expect so many surprises in one night."

I took a step back, making some space between myself and the creepy death god. "I don't know what you're talking about, but I wouldn't put too much stock in anything my mother might have told you."

I raised my hand to Truth's hilt, not to draw, but as if I needed to protect it. The shinigami's eyes did not stray from the sword and his voice took on a low, reverent tone. "Yes . . . I can feel them. They are calling to me."

They hadn't called to me in two years. Not since I broke the blade. But no one but the Blades knew about this and we didn't usually publicize it. "Who are you talking about?"

He pointed two skeletal fingers at Truth. "This anchors something already. Old soul energy and something else . . . something that is becoming . . ."

He sniffed dramatically as if inhaling something delicious. His face lit with disturbing ecstasy.

My breath caught in my throat and now I did grab Truth's hilt and twist my body away from the shinigami. I shuffled away a few more steps. "Keep your distance."

Sugiwara's voice took on a decidedly fanatical tone. "Your sword must be a soul artifact. Very rare. I have not encountered one in centuries."

He stepped in closer and I wanted to lean away but held my ground this time. He started to mutter to himself. "Yes, many are bound to it, in eternal bondage. Never to reach Yomi."

Not every Hoard clan could claim a Blade. I was the only one of my generation and pledged an oath to the clan that went beyond the family ties. My pledge bound me to my sword. Wielding Sword of Truth had always been a heady experience, the blade seeming to dance in my hands with a life of its own. The first time I drew her, I had communed with the spirit of my great-uncle, the previous

Blade, his soul an integral part of the weapon. Behind my uncle, in layers of dried blood, was an unbroken lineage of Soong warriors dating back a thousand years. It was not an understatement to say the sword thirsted for blood and violence, and my father had provided that through me. Every assassination, every defense of clan territory, every limb I took with her bound me ever tighter to the mantle of the Blade and the sword itself.

Beijing had been the last grain of rice to tip the scales and send my world into free fall. I'd come to my senses in the middle of Pearl Market to the sounds of pain and anguish, my nose and mouth filled with the thick odor of blood and human waste. Blood and gore covered me from head to toe, and butchered and mangled bodies lay scattered across the walkways and market stalls. I'd felt sick looking around me and knowing I'd been the source of that carnage. How much further would I go for the honor of the clan? Seeing the devastation I'd wrought made me question what honor could possibly come from wielding the blade anymore.

The only clean thing on me had been the sword, the bronze edge gleaming pristine under the streetlights, the blade still hungry for more carnage.

It had taken all my will to turn my back on the mantle that night. Breaking Truth had taken another week spent hiding in the countryside, huddling in trees and living like an animal, screaming and crying in my sleep as the faces of the dead haunted me. By the tenth night, rage at myself and my father had won over and I'd snapped the sword in half. Breaking the sword felt like falling off a building and landing on the sidewalk. I had collapsed, senseless, into a rainfilled trench, not waking up until late the next day. Filthy and in terrible pain, I made my way to my safe house.

I picked up the pieces of my sword before I left.

A sickening mix of emotions churned through me as the death god spoke. The awful truth dawned in my chest as I realized that despite my soul-crushing history with Truth, the horrors that had caused me to flee both my duty and my family, I still could not give her up.

This shinigami had stopped talking. I wasn't sure when. His expression was expectant, eager. Even the yokai at his side had stopped writing, its eyes wide and intensely focused on me. I concentrated and forced my hand to unclench, unlocking each finger in turn from Truth's hilt. I carried the sword. It was not carrying me.

"I'm not here to bargain."

The shinigami could keep his grabby hands to himself. Sword of Truth was mine.

The shinigami's mouth turned down at the corners and the eager light in his eyes died. He turned on his heel and stalked into the garden. "Very well. Make haste, moonrise is nearly upon us."

I hurried to catch up to him, trying to shake off the gruesome memories. "You said I had until midnight tomorrow."

The death god's long strides ate up the gravel pathways quickly and I picked up the pace to keep up.

The tea gardens spanned three acres, but I knew my way around fairly well. I had never paid any special attention to the Ebony Gate. I usually felt a low-level buzz around objects with magical provenance but Sugiwara-sama must have placed a very powerful "no look" warding on the gate.

In the daylight, the tea garden normally bloomed with color from the flowers and the cheerful red of the Pagoda. At this hour, everything seemed shrouded in the shinigami's dark haze, rendering everything I saw in deepening shades of gray.

I followed the death god past the bronze Buddha and the enormous Lantern of Peace. In this heavy fog, the Buddha's eyes seemed to travel with my steps. Looking over at the Moon Bridge, I was glad the shinigami had opted for the pathways instead of the bridge. We made our way over to the Pagoda and to the rock formation that the ebony slab had rested on for over a century.

He stopped before a large rock structure. The face of the structure was a large swath of bare sandstone. Just standing before it for a few moments, my face went cold, my eyes stinging from the chill. "Is this . . . ?"

The shinigami nodded. His eyes seemed to burn brighter as he considered the stone. "This is the portal to Yomi. Unprotected. Open."

He looked up to the darkening skies. "And moonrise is here."

The chill emanating from the sandstone was definitely getting more intense. I backed up a step, rubbing my hand over my face. "And moonrise is bad because . . . ?"

The death god narrowed his eyes, giving me a look that could pierce a steel door. "At moonrise the barrier between this world and Yomi weakens. Without the Ebony Gate the ghosts of Yomi will arise and some will find the strength to pass through the portal. The first few adventurous souls tonight, and more each night after."

His gaze darted once more to the sword on my back before turning back to me. "I take my leave now."

He turned toward the sandstone.

"Hey, wait a minute! Where are you going?"

The shinigami half-turned back to me, looking at me through half-lidded eyes. At his side the cat yokai kept walking, reaching back to tug on the shinigami's coat. "Lord, we must depart. The time . . ."

The shinigami made a show of pulling out a pocket watch. "I have many duties, and demands on my time. My place is in Yomi, tending to the dead. Yomi is vast beyond your comprehending. Some yurei will undoubtedly escape my notice. It will be your job to defend the border. Here."

His eyes tracked over my body again, like he was assessing a used car. "I am sure you will formulate some sort of strategy."

He turned to leave again. "I must go. Contact me when you have the Ebony Gate in your possession."

The shinigami stepped into the sandstone rock face and he and the yokai disappeared in a cloud of white mist.

Well, great. That wasn't ominous at all.

I crouched down to study the spot where the Ebony Gate had rested. Only the crunch of the gravel beneath my boots and the thudding of my heartbeat accompanied my movements. The eerie stillness persisted in the shinigami's wake for many long moments as I studied the ground.

My phone vibrated in my pocket and I pulled it out. It was blindingly bright in the dimness of the park. A text from my brother, Tatsuya.

**Nee-san, what's going on? Father wants you to call him.**

I wasn't ready to speak to Father. All the emotions that roiled inside me from honoring my mother's Talon threatened to burst out. I had to shove them down and focus on what I could control.

I scrolled to the flashlight function and shined it against the craggy rock face. I could clearly make out the outline of where the Gate had rested, the indentation smooth and worn. Despite my alarm that the gate to Yomi was missing, nothing looked back at me other than the aged sandstone surface. I took some photos and put away my phone.

It took my eyes a moment to adjust again without the light from my phone. I blinked a few times and put a hand down on the gravel to steady myself. Wait, was the sandstone outline glowing now?

I raised my left hand and the sigil on my palm flashed to life, sending an icy chill shooting up my arm. As I backed away from the rock face, eerie blue light pulsed to life around the edges of the rock, outlining a rough rectangle. The surface of the stone seemed to warp and sag like hot glass. A gust of wind tossed my hair into my face and the stone melted into sand, swirling in the wind, grit stinging my eyes. The center of the rock face darkened as the sand flowed into the rock like water down a drain. Over the hissing sand a high, keening wail came through the expanding portal.

Uh-oh.

# SERPENT'S KISS

I was not prepared for this. In all my years as the Blade, I'd only dealt with corporeal enemies. Even if I'd brought more than the gun in my utility belt, I didn't have any of my tiles with me, and it looked like I was staring down the barrel of a ghost rifle about to unload on Golden Gate Park.

I shuffled back, head whipping left and right, my nerves screaming at me to get out of here. I had to get back to my Jeep. I still had some supplies from the Sun Emporium in my duffel. My only chance was to find something in there and make it work.

The ghost's scream rose to ear-splitting volume and the remaining sand in the rock face fell through, spewing a cloud of dust. The space inside the pulsing blue light became a tear in reality, a rend in the fabric of this world, connecting directly to Yomi.

The gate was pure darkness that sucked in the light, so black it hurt my eyes to look at it. Menacing energy throbbed from the open doorway. A miasma of death energy flowed out of the gate like a rush of filthy sewer water. It hit me, bowling me over with an overwhelming sensation of rotting flesh and writhing maggots.

The city chose that moment to ripple beneath me, its alarm transferring from the rolling soil up through my body.

My legs buckled and I fell back on the loose gravel. I kicked my legs, pushing myself away from the gate. The dread glow flashed sun bright and my ears popped as I flinched away from the glare.

When I blinked away the sunspots and looked back my heart stopped. A ghost hovered at the mouth of the gate, a skeletally thin woman clad in a kimono of white smoke. Black tendrils curled and twisted down the length of the wispy fabric like strangler vines. The smoke kimono broke apart in sections, revealing an emaciated body covered with knife wounds. The wounds gaped, raw and red. Her form turned away slowly, her hair floating about her in lank strands like rotting seaweed.

I pressed my hands slowly into the gravel, willing the rocks to stay quiet as I regained my feet. Silence hung over the park, thick with dread. I pulled my leg in, my abs burning as I held myself off the loose gravel. If I could get to my feet, I could at least get off the path, get out of plain sight. I racked my brain, inventorying my duffel for something that would banish the ghost. My arms trembled.

My body gave out and I collapsed, the gravel rattling as I fell. The ghost whipped around, eyes gleaming black pools of ink. Her face was ashen gray, her cheeks sunken under brutal cheek bones, cracked lips peeled back over broken, yellowed teeth. Her mouth creaked open and she screamed again, the sound and nauseating energy coursing over me in a wave. I dry heaved as I scrambled to my feet and began stumble-running to the garden entrance.

Wind whipped at me again, stinging my cheeks. I turned back just in time to see the ghost lunging at me, cavernous mouth open, exposing multiple rows of jagged teeth. One of the black vines from her kimono reached out and grabbed me by the neck. Searing cold bit into my skin, making me see stars. I tripped, my ankle turning with a sickening wrench.

I'll admit, I panicked a little. My arm snapped up, muscle memory harkening back to years of lessons as a young girl. My fingers curled into perfect form, a warding, even as my conscious mind dismissed the act as futile.

The barest wisp of ghost smoke touched my outstretched hand. Writhing, crawling power shot up my arm from the point of contact.

The energy rebounded through my hand, materializing in front of me as a wall of shadow barreling into the ghost. The unexpected impact pushed the ghost back and knocked me back as well. I tucked the energy into a neat roll and came up on one knee. I stared in shock and horror at my hand where a few black wisps curled around my fingertips. Yin talent? It certainly hadn't come from me since I had as much talent as a lump of coal. The gift from the shinigami? *Ugh.*

The energy that had lit up my arm was already fading, the sensation falling away like a forgotten dream. Another ear-splitting scream shook me from my reverie. This time it sounded like it had come from above. I lifted my head and scanned the tops of the cherry trees and maples. Nothing. Something from the roof of the teahouse caught my eye. Something man-shaped.

The figure raised his arms and his aura flashed for a split second, brilliant purple. The faint scent of shoe leather and gunpowder rolled over me as a wave of oily talent spread out from the roofline. My skin pebbled in the cool night air but the chill I felt wasn't from the temperature. It was dread. First breaking into my house, then stealing the Lost Heart, and now this ghost speaker was following me around the city? I had a sudden feeling of being in water much deeper than I had thought.

Sparks shot out of the mouth of Yomi, and three startlingly bright spheres spun out and over my head. They unfurled into three massive snakes . . . bloodred, flying snakes. Their bodies had to be a thousand pounds each yet they hovered above me, their black tongues hissing as they bobbed in an eerie dance. Black spikes swirled around their heads like angry moths. I knew what these were. Fù chóng, venomous snakes of the underworld. The fù chóng fed on the ghosts of Yomi, draining away what little life energy the ghosts possessed. Like the ghosts, the fù chóng would be ravenous to the point of madness.

One of the snakes dove at the first ghost, the snake's crown of spikes driving into the dead woman's chest. The snake's crimson body glowed faintly as it fed. The ghost wailed, an ear-grating cry of despair and insanity.

The other two snakes came at me, bodies undulating through the air.

I looked up and despaired at the distance to the garden gates and the thought of scaling the locked gates with a ghost on my tail. As if on cue, the serpents' swarm started buzzing loudly. I was out of options. I bolted for the garden entrance, hobbling over the gravel, taking off my necklace as I went. Freezing wind howled again, tugging at me as I stumbled with my pendant clutched in my hand.

I glanced behind me and tossed the pendant in the air. Before it landed I jammed my fingers into my mouth and whistled a high, piercing note. Bāo burst forth in a blaze of emerald energy that lit up the garden like afternoon sunshine. The smell of sawdust and white pepper filled the air and my foo lion landed on the path with a thump.

Bāo came to his feet, standing a meter tall at the shoulder, limbs and body rippling with taut muscle under fine golden fur. Paws the size of dinner plates tipped with curving claws raked at the gravel.

I slid to a stop in a spray of gravel. "Bāo! Hànwèi!"

My guardian lion faced the deadly apparitions, planted his huge feet on the path, and lowered his head. A rumbling growl grew in Bāo's belly and green light played under his feet. The serpents dove at my cat. Bāo roared, a thunderous cough of a roar that sounded like a jet engine. Golden waves of light followed in a ripple and the roar tore through the wailing ghost and the first serpent, shredding them like wet rice paper. The energy rolled across the garden, cleansing the sickly death talent. The remaining two serpents hissed and split apart, dodging the central burst of Bāo's roar. The portal in the sandstone winked out, the eldritch light dying, and the stone was intact once more.

The two fù chóng flew off toward the lights of the city. Skies.

There was no way for me to contain them now. I turned back to the teahouse, but the shadowy figure was gone.

I sat down heavily on the path, just in time for Bāo to lumber into me, circling me possessively and butting my shoulders. I laughed and ruffled my hands through his thick fur, scratching behind his ears.

"Yes, you did good. Who's a good boy?"

Bāo purred and pranced around me, enjoying the praise. Together we walked over to the teahouse. Bāo stalked the perimeter, snarling softly. I climbed the exterior of the old wooden structure, my body contorting to dodge the sharp spires, and hoisted myself over to the roof. I knelt there and took several deep breaths. There it was, the faintest scent of shoe leather and gunpowder. It had to be Anthony Chow, the Louies' ghost master.

Or perhaps, Ray Ray's ghost master. I could hear Fiona's protests in my head. I didn't have enough to point a finger, not yet. But the ghost master was definitely following me. I just needed to tie him back to the Louies.

Tonight had been too close. The city's magic tingled beneath me, prickly and cold. I shivered in response. Hands shaking just a little, I knuckled away the tears prickling at my eyes. My ankle was killing me. The portal was bound to open again. Maybe tonight. A storm was coming, and I had to be ready.

I limped to my Jeep, my fingers tangled in Bāo's ruff as he braced some of my weight. My mind raced with images of the fù chóng and their swirling black blight of poison spikes. Where would they go next? Were they attracted to ghosts? Jiārén talents? If they were attracted to ghosts, churches and graveyards would be my best bet. They'd feed well in Colma, a city just minutes away from San Francisco that housed more dead than living.

I opened the back of the Jeep and found my .243 Winchester bolt action rifle with its sleek matte profile waiting for me. With federal premium 100 Nosler Partition ammo, it did the job with big game, but would bullets do anything to the fù chóng? They looked corporeal enough. At least they were only undead serpents and the rifle would actually be useful. Would killing the serpent also kill the venomous flying swarm or merely unleash them from their tether? I rubbed my eyes in frustration.

I didn't worry about my ability to nail a huge flying serpent but I couldn't risk unleashing the venomous swarm on the populace. I packed ammo on my belt anyway but it felt futile.

I had a sneaking suspicion by the way the serpents had come after me that they would feed from the living just as well as, if not better than, the dead. If the serpents were attracted to Dragon talent, they could end up on Lotus Lane. The Jiārén community near Japantown was more spread out, not concentrated in such a compact location. Or would the fù chóng make a beeline to the Hoards of San Francisco's elite Jiārén families? But like most Custodian families, the Trans and the Louies were a secretive bunch. Their Hoards could be divvied up amongst their properties around the world, or even if they accreted it all in one place the treasure would be behind a Door.

Even if I managed to find and neutralize the serpents, the portal to Yomi would be weakened until dawn. Who knew what else would waltz through? Or fly through.

How had I managed to get myself wrapped up in all this? I'd fled to San Francisco, where my clan had little influence, specifically to not have to deal with this brand of crazy. When I'd first fled here from Tokyo, I'd enjoyed being alone, away from the clan demands. Even hanging out with Júwàirén, where my lack of talent was . . . well, normal, had been relaxing.

The flip side of my hard-won independence was now I felt totally alone, unable to talk to anyone about the Ebony Gate. I pulled out my phone. Two missed calls from my father. I almost laughed. I definitely did not want to talk to my father about my recent conversation with the shinigami. He would just use it as another opportunity to tell me why I needed to become the aegis for the city's burgeoning magic. As I stared at my phone, it buzzed. It was a text from Baby Ricky from Sun's Emporium, a photo of a flying red-and-black swirl by the Sun's storefront on Lotus Lane. The fù chóng had arrived in Chinatown.

**On my way**

I gunned it, speeding across town to pull onto the narrow confines of Lotus Lane, off Washington Street. I parked right on the sidewalk in front of the Emporium. It was just after midnight, which was late for the rest of Chinatown but not Lotus Lane, where Jiārén liked to do their shopping under cover of darkness.

Now the normally busy sidewalks were devoid of people and all above me I could hear windows shutting. One prone body lay in the middle of the street, limp and covered with black spikes that looked like arrows. Oh no.

I looked up. There against the streetlamps, black dots swirled, blocking out most of the light. The swarm circled the roof of the century-old Central Road Bank. Bāo growled low in his throat. I couldn't see the serpents but I had no doubt they hovered above the black swarm, just waiting for a meal. I dashed into the two-story Emporium and the sensor chimed brightly.

The store was dark, lit only through the front window by the streetlamp, and dim red light from the electric shrine candles in the back of the store.

"Ricky! It's Emiko."

Baby Ricky's round race peeked out from behind the screen, followed by the rest of him clad in a black hoodie with SUN EMPORIUM emblazoned across it, inky-black skinny jeans, and black Converse. Baby Ricky was almost twenty and built like a heavyweight wrestler, but his father was Big Ricky Sun, so Baby Ricky was stuck with his diminutive nickname. He styled his hair with ruthless precision, each black strand gelled to stiff submission. "Emiko! Thank goodness. What is a fù chóng doing here?"

"No time to explain. Who is that lying in the street?" My voice was grim. I needed to focus on killing the fù chóng and training the Lotus Lane Jiārén to deal with them if they kept coming.

Baby Ricky's shoulders slumped. "That's Hon Wei from the grocery store. I was too late to help him. It happened so fast. The fù chóng appeared out of nowhere! One second things were okay, the next everyone was screaming and running."

Yes, two swarming venomous half-ton flying snakes were scary. I doubted there was much we could do for the grocer other than a purification ritual and burial. I patted Ricky's back gently. "We'll take care of him."

Bāo walked up and licked Ricky's hand to comfort him. Ricky gave a small smile. "Cool dog."

Bāo huffed. I couldn't blame the kids, though. Foo lions were rare, even amongst Hoard families. Ricky and Sally had probably only ever seen them in books.

"He's not a dog."

Bāo came back and circled around my legs. I pulled out my phone and called Nakamoto House. As the phone rang I walked quickly up and down the aisles, taking a quick inventory. Despite the kitschy exterior, the Sun Emporium sold a lot of off-the-menu items that were handy for someone like me. Unfortunately nothing on the shelves tonight seemed to fit the bill for taking down hundreds of pounds of flying undead serpents.

No one answered and the posh British Hong Kong–accented voice of Oliver Nakamoto came on, droning on to leave a message. I kept my message short. "Oliver, there are fù chóng attacking

Lotus Lane. Mr. Hon Wei has been poisoned and the Lotus Lane Merchant Association requires your services."

The storeroom door opened again, and Baby Ricky's younger sister, Sally, came out, sporting a petite version of her brother's outfit. Straight bangs brushed the tops of her white hipster plastic-frame glasses that kept sliding down her tiny nose. Her silky black hair was tied back in a loose ponytail. Sally's aura had a soft umber hue, like terra-cotta. She wasn't a gāo talent and she never bothered to lock down her talent so it was revealed to all Jiārén who walked into the Sun Emporium. As always, Sally smelled like the baked goods she made with her mother. "Emiko, you came!"

I nodded, an idea taking shape in my head. "It's good you're here, Sally. We're going to need you."

I went behind the counter, looking for what I knew had to be there. While I searched, Sally knelt to pet Bāo, rubbing his cheek affectionately. "What a handsome boy." Bāo purred.

Sally looked up at me. "You've never brought your dog here before."

Bāo butted her hand in annoyance.

"He's not a dog."

Under the register, behind a false panel in the back of the counter, I found them. I pulled out the two ornate crystal bottles of high-proof, highly illegal BáiJiǔ and put them on the counter. "Hey Ricky, you guys still have the pressure washer?"

His eyes widened at the sight of the bottles. "Oh man, Dad has totally been holding out on me!"

"Ricky. Focus."

He shook his head. "Right. Sure. Yes, I'll get it. We use it all the time for the sidewalk." No joke, the streets got filthy and the merchants were constantly cleaning their walkways and storefronts.

"Okay kids, here's the plan." I pulled the Winchester rifle off my shoulder and set it on the counter. They both gulped at hearing my plan, their eyes wide with apprehension. They were just kids, but I didn't see a way around enlisting their help. Baby Ricky moaned in distress as I poured their father's smuggled hooch into the pressure washer.

"Bāo, you have to stay inside, boy." He nipped my hand in protest, but the serpents had dodged his roar easily. I wouldn't be able to bear it if he was wounded by their venom.

I slung the rifle back over my shoulder and drew Hachi. Sally stared as I drew the sword, her eyes locked on the blade. I waited until she looked back at me. "We're not going to let what happened to Hon Wei happen to anyone else, right?"

Sally nodded, her lips trembling. I squeezed her shoulder then grabbed the handle of the pressure washer to drag it behind me. "You guys stay in the doorway as much as you can. Just do as I say and we'll knock these guys out."

I stepped through the doorway and into the pool of light under the lamppost. The black swarm continued to swirl around the bank's rooftop across the street, the buzz audible from below. Baby Ricky and Sally closed the door to the shop and huddled under the awning, leaning out to peer up toward the fù chóng. I turned on the pressure washer, the motor coughing to life. As one, the swarm spun into tight formation and plunged toward us.

"Now!" I screamed and let loose with the pressure washer, the nozzle set to a wide spray. Two thousand psi of finely aerosolized liquor burst into existence above our heads. The choking scent of alcohol blanketed us in an instant. Sally made a wide tai chi push gesture and exhaled in a sudden burst, her talent launching into the mist. At the same time, Baby Ricky held his arms up like he was picking up a boulder, his face already red with exertion. From the corner of my eye their auras flared to life, swirling hues of burnished orange around Sally, pewter gray around Baby Ricky.

Sally's talent was perfect for her mother's bakery. Like her personality, she projected warmth, enough to warm up food, but not hot enough to cook. She could, however, warm up a lot of food at once. Baby Ricky compressed energy, and wrestling his sister's power down to a pinpoint meant enough concentrated heat to ignite almost anything.

The spraying mist exploded into a terrifying fountain of fire, my improvised flamethrower. The first swarm of venomous spikes flew headlong into the wave of flame, crackling and popping in the fire. Bitter ash rained down on my head. The fù chóng screamed and launched another wave of spikes at us. As they spread apart, I saw the shadowy figure of a man behind them on the roof of the bank. Chow. Before I could switch targets he ducked behind the roofline. Fine. I was happy to take care of him up close and personal when I caught up to him.

I focused on the more immediate problem of the fù chóng.

"Sally!"

Sally ran up behind me and took the power-washer nozzle from my hand. Ricky's power flowed around us, shifting to keeping the flames and heat pushed up and away from us. Eyes wide with fright, Sally swung the nozzle, making a curtain of fire above us. I sheathed Hachi and shouldered my rifle, sighted and fired, the familiar motions flowing from one shot to the next. While Sally shielded me I aimed through and around the fire, picking the fù chóng apart. Chambering, loading, and firing, a symphony of bullets that I knew by heart. Bit by bit, the bullets gouged away chunks of red serpent flesh and rivulets of black blood rained down on us.

The spikes did not stop, proving my earlier theory to be correct. One of the spikes swerved around the flames and Ricky yelled as the spike buried itself in his arm. Heat slammed into us as Ricky's power faded, crisping my eyelashes and scorching my skin.

"No!" I stowed my rifle and grabbed the hose from Sally. "Help him!" My legs spread wide, I stood over Ricky as he writhed on the sidewalk, aiming for the stray spikes, black blood sticky on my face. My hands grew wet and slippery from the mix of serpents' blood and sweat.

Sally ducked down, kneeling over her brother to yank out the spike. Baby Ricky groaned and sat up.

My hands struggled to aim the pressure hose, losing their grip. As the hose lifted up, I saw the man on the rooftop, his arms spread wide. Two spikes shot through the dissipating flames and punched into my chest. I gasped from the shock and dropped the hose. Two needle-thin black spikes protruded from my shirt. They pulsed in time with my hammering heart. I staggered and fell to my knees.

Baby Ricky and Sally caught me before I slammed my head on the sidewalk. I couldn't talk, pain stealing my breath. Sally spoke quickly, her hands strong under my arms. "You got them, you got them all, Emiko."

I wanted to nod but couldn't do more than blink in acknowledgment. My jury-rigged flamethrower had died and the street seemed unnaturally dark now. Sally's voice stretched and warbled. My eyes slipped out of focus.

Sally grabbed Ricky's hand before he could grab at the spikes. "You can't take them out! She'll bleed to death!" Sally kept talking as Baby Ricky's big arms curled around me. I heard Bāo roar and hoped he was okay.

My vision narrowed to nothing as my eyelids gave up and I fought to just breathe. Then I gave up on even that.

# BLOODLETTING

*White smoke fills my vision and curls around me, thin, twisting tendrils of cold smoke blindly seeking my flesh like blood worms questing for warm meat.*

*"No!"*

*The voice is my mother's, but it is not her normal voice, quiet, deep, steady as my metronome. This time her voice has a raw, jagged energy that pricks at the center of my heart. I've heard that sound before in my own voice.*

*It is the sound of fear.*

*The white smoke has found me. It rushes in and engulfs me and everywhere it touches becomes pain.*


My face was wet.

At least my chest didn't hurt anymore. I tried to open my eyes but they were crusted shut.

"Hold her!" Hands pressed down on my shoulders, pinning me to a cold surface. I recognized Popo's voice and relaxed. The kids had done all right, bringing me to the right place.

"Emiko, don't move, I'm almost done," Popo muttered under her breath. "Months go by and you don't visit me, and now two visits in as many days!"

Popo grunted in annoyance and slapped a hot towel on my face.

I reached for the towel and scrubbed my eyes. It felt so good to open them. I blinked a few times and a wall covered in hanging butcher knives came into focus. I was in the meat locker on a metal table. No wonder I was freezing. Sally's concerned face loomed over me. "Oh Emiko, I'm so glad you're okay! You scared us!"

Baby Ricky piped up. "Yeah, your face is covered in blood. It's freakish."

Gee, thanks. That explained the coppery sludge in my mouth. Bāo nudged my foot and let out an inquisitive mew.

Ricky and Popo sat me up carefully. The front of my shirt sagged open, revealing my bare torso. Popo's sharp blades at work to cut open my top. A small price to save my life. Sally grabbed another towel and handed me a small gray plastic bucket. I gagged and spat into it. Then coughed and spat again. Blood so dark it was almost black filled the bottom of the bucket. Yuck.

Sally mopped my face, and then to my chagrin, my ears. Apparently I had been bleeding out of my eyes, nose, mouth, and ears as Popo had bled the fù chóng toxins out of me.

Popo tsked. "The fù chóng venom was very difficult to purge. I had to bleed you so fast, too, because it was spreading." Though her words were gruff, her eyes were shrouded with concern. I had scared her. That alarmed me more than all the blood I had just coughed out.

She patted Bāo. "Such a handsome foo lion. Very unusual." He preened for her, rewarding her with a toss of his thick golden mane. Of course Popo would recognize a foo lion. No doubt she'd studied them as part of her training at Lóng Kǒu.

Popo handed me a dark bitter tea. Likely a blood restorative. I gulped it down, shuddering at the foul taste. It was better if I didn't ask what was in it. She pointed at Baby Ricky's arm, which had only a single bandage marking where the venom spike had hit him. "See that? Easy. You . . . you . . ." She shook her head and waved a hand at my chest and pointed to the bloody bucket.

I looked at my chest. Two giant purple bruises spiraled out from the puncture wounds, with a charming yellow and green edge. The longer I looked at it, the more it hurt. I groaned and zipped up my microdown jacket to cover the unsightly wounds and to salvage the tattered remains of my dignity.

Sally whispered, "It was really bad, Emiko. Your heart stopped on the drive over. Ricky had to resuscitate you."

"Thank you, Sally, Ricky. Thank you both." My voice rasped and my throat hurt. I closed my eyes at the magnitude of Sally's words. I owed the Sun family so much it was breathtaking. I'd endangered their lives fighting the fù chóng and their quick action to get me to Popo had saved my life.

"No, thank you for coming to help us!" Sally leaned in and hugged me gently. Funny, she'd been the one who saved me. Sally's and Ricky's auras flashed again in my mind, vibrant and alive in the darkness of Lotus Lane. Even píng talents such as theirs would be beyond my reach. I was lucky to count them as friends, lucky that they didn't see me as a monster. Perhaps I was just *their* monster.

I hopped off the table and my ankle immediately buckled. Baby Ricky braced me. Cursed skies, I did not have time for this. I took a moment to test the ankle again. It twinged, but held. I could stand. Standing was good.

Popo handed me another cup of the bitter brew. I made a face, prompting instant scolding. "Soong Siu Jie! Look at you, up at all hours and covered in your own blood from helping the Suns. You're already doing a Sentinel's work! Take the mantle and get the credit! If you took it at least I wouldn't have to worry so much about you!"

Sally gasped. "You're the Sentinel?"

"What? No! No." Skies. Not them, too. I hastened to clarify. Bāo huffed loudly and it sounded suspiciously like he was laughing.

"I'm not the Sentinel. Popo is just speaking hypothetically."

Popo snorted. "Humph. It's not hypothetical. Just look at your aura. That gold around the edge is from the city. It's not like you have talent of your own."

Ouch. She did not pull her punches.

Ricky nodded in agreement. "She's right, Emiko. You're the Butcher of Beijing, you're totally the most qualified to be our city's Sentinel. Everyone knows it."

My mouth pulled down in a frown. I did not need a reminder of what I was before. I also did not like being outnumbered like this. I had almost died of a venom attack, was it too much to ask that they cut me some slack? "*Everyone* is an exaggeration. At least half of Lotus Lane would rather see me move back to Tokyo."

Sally patted my hand. "We like you, Emiko. Now that Grandma has mentioned it, I can see that golden edging, too. The city must like you, too."

The city was not a stray dog that had followed me home. I resisted the urge to roll my eyes. My eyes were so heavy even rolling them was an effort. As if on cue, the city reached for me again, singing a quiet melody. I swatted it away and another wave of fatigue threatened to buckle my legs. Gods, I just needed some sleep in my own bed.

"For the last time, I'm not the Sentinel." I held out my hand to Sally for my car keys.

She sighed and shook her head. "There's no way we are letting you drive home. You almost died, Emiko."

Oh *now* she remembered. I wanted to say something, but my thoughts were mired in syrup, spinning in lazy circles. San Francisco's song grew louder in my ears and pulled me down into its dark depths. My hand was still stretched out for my keys and my body followed. The floor pitched and the room pivoted sideways. Sally's and Ricky's shouting voices sounded far off and warbled, like I was hearing them through water. I crashed to the floor and the voices faded away. The city's music swelled, and darkness swept over me.

*Pale white mist binds my limbs like cold bars of iron. The sound of rushing wind fills my ears, nearly drowning out the sound of my mother's cries.*

*Mother never cries.*

*My body clenches, spasms in pain as the mist draws closer to me, invading my ears, my nose, my eyes. Agony builds to a frozen, fragile pinnacle of ice.*

*And then it is gone. Warmth floods back into me, then sound and color returns. The world is swaying and I am again on the steps to clanhome, but something is wrong.*

*One of the foo lions is missing.*

*And Mother is holding me. Her arms clutch at me with panicked strength, and her breath hitches in time to the rocking of her body. The only woman who has ever held me like this is Lulu Āyí, but I can see her on the cobblestone path, collapsed in Uncle Jake's bloody arms.*

*Mother's hand is bleeding as she strokes her fingers over my hair.*

*The sun is high overhead and the warmth soaks into my back, banishing the last vestiges of cold. The white mist hovering over the cobblestones burns away in the sunlight.*

I opened my eyes and found myself on a cloud of softness clad in taupe leather. Slivers of morning light streaked across the picture windows at the front of the shop. Apparently my body had decided for me and shut down on its own last night. And then I remembered the music. Had the city done something to me? I lay still for a moment and listened, but the music was gone for now. Somehow Ricky had managed to manhandle me through the Crossing and into one of Grandma's spa chairs near the rear of the spa.

It wasn't bad, considering. Better than falling asleep on the hard floor of my place. I levered myself up to a sitting position, the leather creaking under my elbows. At the sound, Bāo got up off his sunny spot on the floor and padded over, shaking out his mane. He plopped his head on the chair next to my legs and looked at me expectantly. I sighed and ran my hand through his mane, scratching him behind the ear in his favorite spot. He rewarded me with a purr that could compete with some motorcycles, and set the whole chair vibrating.

Whatever had happened on that day in my childhood, Father had decided that I needed a guardian, and had animated Bāo to be my protector. Bāo had been by my side every day since then. When I had left Tokyo, there were two things I couldn't bear to leave behind. One was my broken blade and the other was Bāo. Both were part of me. With them, I was never truly alone.

My phone said it was barely six in the morning. I'd lost some time but I still had better than half the day to track down the Ebony Gate and get it back to the tea garden. If I made it out of this in one piece, I promised myself to bring as much business as I could to the Sun Emporium. If not for those kids, I'd be a corpse in the middle of the street.

I pulled Bāo in a little closer and hugged him tightly to me. In all my time as the Soong Blade, I'd had plenty of life-and-death situations, plenty of times where my life had hung by a thread only as wide as my wits and skills. Kamon had pulled me back from the brink several times. None of those times had felt as real as last night. As the Blade, dancing along the razor's edge was just another weeknight, a common occurrence that I would shrug off.

If I had died last night, Sally and Ricky might have fallen to the fù chóng as well. Who knows what havoc the serpents would have made of the rest of Lotus Lane? If I had died, Sugiwara would have dragged Tacchan into this mess. I couldn't afford to let anyone down.

The ghost master had already tried to kill me, so the Second Law no longer applied. Next time I saw him, he was fair game. Whoever had hired him wouldn't be happy, I could guarantee that. Was it Jimmy Louie? I didn't trust the guy but I didn't think he would order a hit on me.

Bāo snuggled in closer to me and I winced as a sharp stab of pain shot through my chest. I tried to move him off me and gasped as my chest throbbed with pain. It felt like a truck had driven over me.

Popo walked out of her little office with a tray in her hands. "Good. You're awake. You need to eat something."

A small ceramic bowl with a delicate lid sat on the tray. She set the tray down and brought the bowl to me. Just the warmth of the bowl in my hands was a measure of comfort. I lifted the lid and a cloud of fragrant steam wafted up carrying aromas of ginger, chicken broth, and goji berries. The smell took me back to my dream, and one of the few tender memories I had of my mother. With Lulu Āyí tending to Uncle Jake's arm, Mother had personally made a pot of restorative soup for me and Father. The three of us drank the soup quietly in the kitchen an odd moment of family that had not since been replicated.

I drank my soup in silence, relishing the heat spreading out from my stomach, and trying not to dwell on thoughts of my mother. As the heat spread, the pain in my chest faded a little.

Popo brought me another bowl when I finished. As I drank my second helping she handed me a bottle of water and another small brown glass jar of pills, identical to the magnesium she had given me earlier. Wow, had it only been a day since I'd brought the hibagon to her? It felt like eons had passed since then.

"Emiko, some glucosamine for your ankle. You're very hard on your joints."

That was an understatement. I shrugged and popped two.

Popo handed me a tube of cream and pointed to my neck. "That ghost burn needs something. Try this and also, make sure to practice your qigong to replace your qì."

I rubbed my neck, the rough edges of the ghost burn still tender. I hadn't thought about it last night but it made sense that they fed on qì. I closed my eyes, praying that tears weren't about to burst from them. I closed my hand over Popo's and took a shaky breath. "Thank you."

She batted my hand away. "Ai ya. What was I going to do, let you die on my doorstep? If you really want to thank me—"

I butted in before I had to hear her say it again. "Yes, yes. Sentinel. I know."

She sighed. "San Francisco is growing. More Jiārén come every day. We need a Sentinel. The Sentinel mantle would protect you and you would protect us."

And before I knew I was going to say it, the words just spilled out of my mouth. "I'll . . . I'll think about it."

Popo, Baby Ricky, and Sally had saved my life. I owed them a lot. Thinking about it was a small thing to offer.

Her eyes narrowed, but her mouth quirked up in a half smile. She patted me on the shoulder and reached out to ruffle Bāo's mane.

My phone buzzed. Caller ID said it was Oliver Nakamoto. Popo squeezed my hand and stepped away to give me to space. As I picked up the call she began bustling about, preparing the spa for another day of business.

"Hey, Oliver." What I really wanted to say was "Why are you calling me, Oliver?" But my diplomacy skills were improving.

"Emiko, we have taken care of Hon Wei, and are having a ceremony for his family." Oliver sounded like an austere British butler, his plummy tones rolling through the phone waves.

I exhaled in relief. "Thank you. I'm grateful you assisted them."

"Yes, yes. However, that's not why I'm calling."

Oliver and I were not exactly friendly, just professional colleagues. He was a bit older than I was, but even he'd heard of my spectacular failure at Lóng Kǒu. Normally he treated me like I was one step above the gum on the bottom of his shoe.

"It's about Central Road General Hospital."

Now I was perplexed. That hospital was a short walk from Lotus Lane and treated the Jiārén families of San Francisco. I rarely went there though.

"Yes?"

"Two nurses have been injured and there have been reports of ghosts in the labor and delivery ward."

That was bad. I dreaded what I knew he would say next.

"I assume the fù chóng appearance and this ghostly hospital visitation are connected."

Yeah, Oliver was a smart guy. I made a noncommittal sound.

"It seems only reasonable that you should attend the matter at the hospital, seeing as you have assumed the Sentinel role for the city."

My teeth snapped together in annoyance. "Oliver, I am not the Sentinel. I also fail to see how I would be suited to deal with ghostly apparitions."

"Really, Emiko. You don't have to take that tone with me. Everyone knows you have resources at your disposal." With that, Oliver clicked off.

I stared at the phone in disbelief, wanting to reach through the airwaves and smack Oliver's smug face.

That crack about my "resources" rubbed me the wrong way. It's true that Soong House was powerful. It was one of the eight Dragon Hoard Custodian families, after all. My father had never severed me but I certainly had tried to distance myself from him. I did not avail myself of the Soong family's considerable fortune or worldwide holdings. But Oliver was right. Doors had opened easily for me because of who I was. Even my own hard-earned wealth had been amassed more quickly because of the years of specialized training I had received during my years as the Blade of Soong.

Like it or not, I had resources. One was right next to me, purring contentedly. I would handle it. *We* would handle it. I pushed myself to my feet and gathered my things. The sooner I purged the ghosts from the hospital, the sooner I could get back to tracking down either the Gate and anchor, or the ghost master. It was shaping up to be a lovely day. Would be great if I actually had a shot at surviving it.

# WRAITHS

Central Road General Hospital loomed tall on the corner of Washington and Stockton. Júwàirén thought it was a bank. For Lóng Jiārén, it was a private hospital to treat patients with magical injuries.

I could use the same hospitals as a Júwàirén since I didn't have any talent. However I did find myself inflicted with the occasional talent-related injury that had sent me into the tender care of Central Road General Hospital. This hospital did not accept insurance, credit cards, or checks. Cash or gold payment only.

The first time I'd been admitted here, it had been due to a nasty ice talent–inflicted injury. My then boyfriend, Kamon, and I had been lounging at a bar on Lotus Lane, the Thirsty Tortoise. I'd returned from the bathroom to find a young, busty Koh hitting on him. Suffice it to say I learned I was the jealous type and that I was not impervious to ice shard attacks. I "won" but ended up in the Jiārén emergency room. Good times.

Bāo and I walked down the marble corridor, past the double doors of the bank to the rear elevators. Each step I took rattled my ribs and reminded me of the two giant puncture wounds in my chest. Everything hurt. Walking hurt. Breathing hurt. Popo's soup had helped some but only time would do the rest. Unfortunately, time was the one thing that I had precious little of.

Central Road General Hospital's entrance was on the fifth floor of this modern glass-and-steel tower, which soared skyward as gracefully as the Pyramid building down the road.

Frankly I was perplexed that Nakamoto had contacted me about this ghostly visitation at the hospital. The hospital staff was well experienced at magical containment; surely they could figure out how to deal with the ghosts.

The hospital elevator doors chimed softly and we stepped out into the bright foyer. Picture windows on three sides let the daylight fill the space with a soft glowing light. A beautiful sculpture greeted the hospital visitors, the morning sunlight gleaming off the tall sinuous lines of blown glass in varied shades of blue and indigo. Each twisting spire represented one of the Sons of the Dragon of the Realm. All the dragons held a shimmering crystal globe in their mouths, a sparkling homage to the Hoards.

The dragon sculpture had been cleverly installed so that it seemed to float in midair. I counted the swooping lengths of glass as I crossed the foyer. Nine. It was an unusual choice. Most tributes to the Sons of the Dragon depicted only eight, omitting the ninth as the cause of the Cataclysm that forced Jiārén to flee the Realm. The betrayal was why the Hoard had been divided into eight portions, and why there were eight Hoard Custodian families, and why there were eight councilmembers on Bā Tóu.

Not only did this tribute have nine, but the ninth was elevated above the other eight and carried a gold ball, distinguishing it from the pale blue crystals held by the others. The only group I knew of who revered the Ninth Dragon were Realmseekers, a fringe group of Jiārén devoted to the cause of reconnecting our new home with the Realm in order to reunite with the Ninth Dragon. It did not matter to them that our histories told of unspeakable destruction and the death of the Ninth Dragon, their fanaticism brooked no half measures.

Most Jiārén dismissed the Realmseekers as deluded fanatics, wasting their lives on fruitless dreams. This sculpture told a different story, though. Somewhere in our community, a Realmseeker had resources, and enough discretionary wealth to commission ridiculous sculptures for a hospital. Interesting.

Most of the hospital and this entire wing had been built with substantial patronage by the Louie family. Discreet plaques acknowledging various members of the Louie family adorned the walls. A separate plaque was set in the floor at the base of the sculpture but it did not list the donor. Knowing the Louies and the families who ran with them, the ball in the Ninth Dragon's mouth was undoubtedly twenty-four-carat gold.

My lips twisted in disgust. Whatever. If the Louies felt the need to waste money on fancy art that made some obscure statement about our history, that was their money to waste. Despite all the money they had blown to get their names on all these little plaques, I didn't see any of the Louie Clan here to deal with this morning's crisis, and I had a deadline to meet.

Despite my irritation with Oliver for calling me instead of the Louies, I knew it was right that I should be here. This was my town, and the patients here needed me to deal with the fallout from my mother's Talon Call.

I strolled past the well-appointed waiting room, plush patterned carpets in a soothing green-and-gold color scheme. Bāo padded along quietly, sniffing and swishing his long tail. My Vibram soles made hardly any sound at all on the pristine hallways.

Bāo and I made our way to the labor and delivery ward, a section of the hospital I had never had a reason to visit before. We passed a salt room just off the main hallway, made from many tons of salt, and hardened to form a containment chamber. These chambers were perfect for neutralizing most forms of malevolent residue and likely what I would have needed last night if not for Popo's skilled care. My agitation must have been obvious because Bāo bumped my leg and licked my hand. I patted his mane. "Thanks, boy."

As I approached labor and delivery, the quiet of the hospital finally struck me. When I'd dropped Adam off at the hospital the emergency room had been a study in controlled chaos. This time of the morning the hospital should be buzzing with activity, patients waking, doctors making rounds, nurses checking vitals and dispensing meds. Only two nurses in scrubs ran past me, their eyes wide with fright. Neither one batted an eye at my two-hundred-pound furry companion.

I pushed the large button to open the double doors to the labor and delivery ward. A dark hallway stretched before me lit only by dull red emergency lights. Every door was closed and barred with bright yellow talismans that had been deployed from the ceiling. The wing was silent except for muffled sounds of a crying woman. An automated recording started over the intercom, asking all patients to shelter in their rooms. The hairs on my arms stood up and adrenaline surged into my bloodstream as I suddenly felt the presence of a predator. Bāo shifted his weight and his purr dropped an octave, turning into a rumbling growl. A shrill scream pierced the air followed by an unmistakable wail of an infant. I ran toward it, Bāo at my heels.

I rounded the corner to the baby-viewing room and skidded to a halt. Bāo bumped into my back, and snarled when he saw why I had stopped. Three spectral forms, all female, floated at the baby-viewing window. Tattered hospital robes hung off their thin frames, revealing bony shoulders and deflated breasts. Blood and gore dripped down their legs and spattered on the floor. The center ghost's abdomen gaped open from hip to hip, an obscene red mouth on her belly, glistening entrails sagging through the opening. They all gazed hungrily through the window, eyes manic bright with centuries of yearning.

Above the ghosts, the hatch in the ceiling that should have released the fúlù was jammed. The yellow silk was tangled in the broken hinges.

This was bad. *Really* bad. These weren't just any ghosts. They were ubume—the wraiths of women who had died in childbirth. Robbed of not only their own lives, but the lives of their children, they had made a beeline for a nursery after exiting the underworld.

If I didn't get rid of them they would steal the infants' souls and drag them back to Yomi as their own.

Some lazy maintenance worker had doomed all the babies in the ward.

The three wraiths menaced a young nurse in the viewing room, who clutched an infant protectively against her chest. Two more nurses lay collapsed in the doorway and blocked her exit. Livid red ghost burns marked the necks and arms of the unconscious nurses.

My sword and guns had no power against the ubume. Any attack I unleashed from my bag of tricks might injure the nurse and the baby. But unlike last time at the tea garden, I had come prepared.

I stepped aside and let Bāo come forward. "Okay, boy. Do your thing!"

He stomped, his massive paws striking the pristine floor. A faint green light encircled his paws, giving his golden fur an eerie tinge. His jaws spread wide, displaying rows of shining teeth and fangs. His long purple tongue unfurled and Bāo let out a massive roar, deafening in its volume. Two of the ubume shrieked, a high-pitched, earsplitting sound that pierced my eardrums. Bāo's magical roar had hit them square-on, and their ghostly forms shredded, sparks of silver light dangling in the air behind them.

The center wraith, the one with the cesarean wound, screeched and dove over the bodies of the nurses and into the viewing room, flying directly at the baby in the nurse's arms. I leapt into the room even as the nurse raised her hand in a futile warding. The ubume plowed through the nurse's ward. The nurse cried out as bright red burns appeared on her hand and arm. The baby let out a hitching scream as the ghost dissolved into the baby's open mouth.

The nurse screamed. "No!"

The baby's scream cut short and in an instant, the baby's skin went pale, its lips and hands taking on a blue cast. No, no, no! I reached them and grabbed the nurse by the arms, dragging her to her feet. She cried out in pain as I clutched her burned arm. "We have to dispel the ubume! Now!"

The young nurse managed to nod her head as she sobbed. "S-s-salt . . ."

I reached down and yanked the bodies of her coworkers out of the doorway and all but pushed her out the door. "Go! Go!"

We pounded down the hallway and all I heard was the fading sounds of the baby's labored breathing. I hit the door button with my fist and slammed my shoulders into the double doors, cracking the door against the wall. I made it to the salt room first and flung the door open, reaching back to grab the nurse and shove her inside. The baby's cheeks were blue, lips nearly purple. I slammed the door closed.

The nurse looked at me through the observation window, her eyes mad with fright. "Power the room!"

My heart fell into my stomach like a frozen stone. Of course the salt room needed power. It needed someone with talent to direct the malevolent energy, to expel it from the patient. The nurse's aura was soft, with only the faintest trace of color—she didn't have enough juice to power the salt room. Even worse, I had less talent than she. I stared back at the nurse, the horror of my failure tearing through my chest. I slammed my hands on the door and screamed my anger and heartache. I'd failed. I was going to watch this baby die because I didn't have the power to save it.

The tang of cut grass and musk blossomed around me, suffusing my senses and filling my mind with visions of the rainforest. Strong arms appeared on both sides of me, hands placed on the salt door just beside mine. Tiger magic flared bright and hot and the walls of the salt room thrummed with energy. Inside the salt room the nurse gave a cry of joy, her despair turning into tears of happiness as the baby in her arms pinked up and began to wail in earnest.

I turned and found myself a bare inch away from Kamon's face, his brow knitted in concentration. Memory flared, hot and bright, Kamon's strong arms fishing me from the water and untangling me from the crushing tentacles of a penanggalan, his magic crackling and lighting up the water like a fiery sunset. The memory faded just as quickly, leaving me to contemplate my ex-boyfriend saving my bacon. Again. His aura glowed a solid orange, unique to Tigers. Another pulse of magic flowed out from him, running through me like a hot wind and setting all my nerves alight. His eyes nearly glowed, a rim of gold glittering around his irises. I turned back in time to see the baby cry out and the ubume ejected.

The wraith charged through the window, her ruined face a mass of rot and decay. From behind Kamon, Bāo leapt up, his gaping maw wide as he bit down around her head as if he were biting a biscuit. Her torso drooped, then splintered into fragments of silvery light. Bāo landed gracefully on his paws in a light thump.

The nurse screamed and I worried she would faint and drop the baby. I pulled open the door and rushed in to reassure her. "It's okay, it's over. They're gone now. Why don't you take the baby back and check on your coworkers?"

She nodded and rushed to attend to her small charges.

As she soothed the baby and returned to the baby room to summon help, I looked over at Bāo. I wasn't sure what had just happened. I had never fed Bāo before, or seen him eat. He was animated by talent, and didn't function like most living organic creatures.

Bāo licked his paws in tiny, delicate strokes. "Good job, Bāo. You saved the baby." He stopped licking and nodded, satisfaction evident in his huge leonine face.

The alarm stopped shrieking and the red lights dimmed. The doors to the patients' rooms began to open, and nurses and patients cautiously checked out their surroundings. When they realized it was safe, they began to mill about the baby-viewing room, clearly relieved the babies were safe.

A tall, slender woman bundled up in a fluffy white robe and wearing shearling-lined slippers shuffled out of her room. Wisps of dark hair strained to escape from her messy bun. Her eyes were puffy from crying. I pegged her age to be somewhat younger than mine, but not by much. She came up to the baby-viewing window and pressed her fist against her mouth. She must've been terrified when the ubume were there.

I wanted to comfort her, but didn't know how.

The shinigami's words from last night echoed in my mind. ". . . the teeming life of your city. The yurei will be unable to resist. They will sink their fangs deep into the marrow of your city and drink until it is nothing but a husk."

I shivered. We had to find the Ebony Gate. Sealing Yomi was the only thing that mattered now to protect my city.

Kamon stopped beside me. Just like at the Tran house, I was unprepared for the sight of him—especially here. What was he doing here?

My stomach tightened up at the thought that he'd had a baby. It was stupid and I was stupid for being hurt at the thought that he was visiting a secret love child and dating Fiona on the side. It was none of my business. I had let him go years ago and apparently I was doing a terrible job of remembering that.

He put a warm hand on my shoulder and we shared a look, still reading each other so well even after years apart.

"Are you okay?"

"Sure, why wouldn't I be?"

Kamon blew out a little huff. He strode over to the woman with the fluffy robe standing in front of the viewing room and pressed his palms to her shoulders. "Jessie, everything is fine now. Let's ask a nurse if you can hold your baby." She stifled a sob and nodded. Who was she and what was she to Kamon?

Kamon turned and walked over to me. "Emiko."

Then he acknowledged Bāo. "Hello, old friend."

Bāo left my side, the traitor. The lion circled around Kamon, nudging his hip, his pleasure in seeing Kamon obvious. They'd run together when Kamon was in his tiger form. It was a long time ago, but I still remembered how beautiful they'd been in motion. Bāo probably missed Kamon because I didn't hang out with any shifters or animals now that would be comfortable running around with a two-hundred-pound red lion.

"Kamon, what are you doing here?" I really wanted to ask who the woman was but I started with the more reasonable inquiry.

"I could ask you the same thing. It seems that any time something dangerous is happening, I should expect that you'll be in the center of it." Kamon's words were calm, but his dark eyes blazed with intensity.

He wasn't wrong but I bristled anyway. Just for a moment, then I deflated. He had every right to be angry with me.

My tone was less acerbic than it might have been. "Look, I don't see anybody else here helping out. It's clear the hospital needed my help. Well, they actually needed Bāo's help." Just explaining got me frustrated at Jimmy Louie all over again. The Louies were the patrons of this hospital, but no, Oliver Nakamoto didn't call them. Instead, he'd called me and I'd rushed over here. I was a glutton.

I shrugged. "Why does it matter to you anyway? This isn't your town."

Bottom line, though I was a transplant, I really did feel like it was *my* town.

Kamon frowned at my tart tone but responded civilly. "Remember my best friend, Lucas?"

I nodded.

"He got married to Jessie last year and they just had their first baby, Nijat. I'm Nijat's godfather."

I did remember Lucas, a carefree musician from Malaysia. I had no idea that he'd settled down here in San Francisco. But it's not like we ran in the same social circles anymore. I felt absurdly relieved that Kamon didn't have a secret love child after all, followed by a little thrill that Kamon had a future reason to be here in the city. But that still left the fact that he was dating the lovely Fiona Tran. Then I reminded myself that it didn't matter, I'd caught and released this fish already. Ugh.

"Congratulations. That's great news." I made myself respond like a sane person would.

Kamon gestured over to Jessie, who was now tenderly cradling baby Nijat. Given the green blanket, I guessed boy, but who knew? I had almost no contact with babies and was clueless about them.

Kamon reached out and grasped my hand, startling me. "Emiko, I know we haven't talked in a while but please tell me what is going on. Why were there wraiths here and why did the hospital call you?"

I stared down at our linked hands, my heart pounding. His hands were strong and brown from the Malaysian sun. I had calluses from the sword but his were from his time climbing outdoors. I had loved climbing with him. I swallowed hard.

This closeness with Kamon overrode all my common sense. Not that I'd had much to start with. I tugged my hand away from his and spoke quickly and softly so as not to alarm Jessie. "It's the underworld, there's a portal to Yomi in Golden Gate Park. Until yesterday, the Ebony Gate had sealed it. But the Gate and anchor were stolen yesterday. If I don't restore the Gate, more ghosts will escape." I closed my eyes in despair.

Then more words tumbled out in a rush, and I confessed about the fù chóng incident at Lotus Lane. I managed to leave out anything about the shinigami claiming my soul because of a Talon. If Kamon knew, he would insist on helping. The least I could do was not drag him down with me.

Kamon shook his head. "Why are you doing this alone? We should all be helping you, Emiko."

My lips thinned in annoyance. "I'm not sure how anyone else can help. For now, the Trans have accepted a Talon and agreed to help find the Gate." I had basically placed all my chips on that bet and if anything else had stepped through Yomi last night to invade my city, I was sure I would hear about it.

His eyes searched mine for a long moment and then drifted down to my shoulder. His brows creased when he recognized the sword tied to my back. "Are . . . you . . . ?"

I resisted the urge to lift my hand to Truth's grip. "No!"

My exclamation was far louder than I expected, and a few people down the hall turned to look. I lowered my voice. "No . . . no. I'm not the Blade. You should know better than anyone, there was no taking that one back."

I'd broken things off with him right after snapping my blade in half and walking away from my life. The thought of staying with Kamon had been too painful, the idea of seeing the pity in his eyes, too awful. Neither of us had taken it well. Perhaps he felt that my still carrying Sword of Truth was a little like cheating. Ha ha. Cheating on my breakup. How screwed up was my life?

Confusion, and perhaps betrayal, flashed across his face. "Then why are you wearing it? I thought you walked away from all that."

Oh dark skies, I wanted nothing more than to spill my guts to him, to let him know how much of a struggle the last two years had been, how much I'd missed him. My hands clenched at my sides and I held my arms steady so I wouldn't reach out to him. He was so close to me I could still smell remnant wisps of his magic, the scent heady and intoxicating.

It was impossible to keep secrets from him. My shoulders slumped in defeat. "I just . . . I just need her, okay?" I sounded pathetic. "I don't know who I am without her."

His hand came up and he cupped the side of my face, his fingers tracing a well-worn path up my jaw and into my hair. A shiver went through me and I struggled not to lean into his hand. "Emiko, you're not the things you carry."

That sounded very Buddhist. Very Kamon. I had never been as enlightened. I looked away from his serious gaze, tearing myself away from his comforting hand. My neck felt cold and bare without his touch. I shrugged and stepped away from his hand.

His lips twisted. "You can let go of it just as easily as you let go of us."

Ouch. I couldn't even be mad because he was right. I'd left everything behind, including my heart. I should have left the blade behind, too, but I hadn't.

His words had unearthed exactly the problem between us. Something was wrong with me and I couldn't fix myself. I hadn't figured it out in two years and I wasn't figuring it out today. The clock was ticking and I had a shinigami to deal with. I needed to leave and find the Gate. After that, I could indulge in as much self-reflection as I could handle.

"I need to get going. I'm . . . I'm glad your friend's baby is okay." There, that was how normal people spoke, right?

Kamon shook his head, his frustration with me evident in the set of his jaw. "You need help, Emiko. My number is still the same. Call me." He turned on his heel and went back to Jessie and baby Nijat.

I had deleted his contact card two years ago, not that it mattered since I remembered everything by heart. No, I wasn't planning on calling him. But I did know who I needed to call.

I pulled out my phone and dialed as I walked out of the hospital. Baby Ricky picked up on the second ring, his voice froggy with sleep.

"Hey, it's me, Emiko." I felt bad calling him so early.

His voice perked up. "Emiko! How are you doing? Grandma wouldn't let us stay after you conked out. Thank you, again, for what you did for us."

I didn't understand why people kept thanking me when I was the one getting my bacon saved. "Um, yes, I need a favor . . ."

"Of course! Anything! What do you need?"

My thoughts flashed back to the bloody wraiths, and the massive fù chóng, and poisonous spikes impaled through my chest, and rogue kinetics throwing cranes at me. "Everything you've got."

I made my way back to the main entry of the hospital, the Nine Dragons of the Realm sculpture looking down on me. The jeweled eyes of the Dragon gods followed my steps, judging me. Time was running out but my mind bounced around like a Ping-Pong ball, thinking about Kamon and everything he'd said. I did need help. I had gotten help. Freddy and Fiona had saved my bacon. Baby Ricky, Sally, and Popo had rescued me, too. Even Adam, whom I'd abandoned at SF General, had taken a lightning strike for me. I wasn't worthy of all their help, but Tatsuya was. My brother was the future of the clan. Because of him, I was doing our mother's duty and going after the Gate. I quickened my steps to the hospital entrance.

Now that the adrenaline from dealing with the wraiths had worn off, my chest throbbed with pain, the puncture wounds burning tunnels into my chest. I leaned against a marble column and cradled my torso. Bāo licked my elbow, startling a laugh out of me. Laughing hurt.

A fleet of shiny black Mercedes SUVs with dark tinted windows pulled up around the front of the building, forming a phalanx of cars facing the entrance. Car doors opened and slammed in rapid succession. I stepped behind a marble pillar to watch a parade of husky men in black windbreakers line up behind the lead car, a blacked-out Mercedes sedan with gold trim. The men wore jackets with a colorful insignia I'd seen very recently. My lips twisted in disgust. Louie Claws. This crew was clearly more senior than the ones I'd run into recently. A casual look revealed sparkles of Louie gold among all of them: earrings, heavy bracelets, and lots of coin rings on pinkies.

The passenger side of the sedan opened and Ray Ray Louie

stepped out. My eyes nearly fell out of my head. He'd changed into a bright scarlet robe with yellow accents. The robes of a Buddhist monk? I wasn't particularly religious but this felt blasphemous even to me. I fought down the urge to bolt across the building and knock him out. He sauntered into the marble halls, robes swishing along the tiles, issuing orders in Cantonese like he owned the place. Well, to be fair, he probably did own it.

The Claw nearest Ray Ray turned and clapped his hands twice. Three henchmen stepped forward, each carrying a colorful geometric box woven with many strands of yarn. Yellow, green, and white threads gleamed against red enameled wood supports. *Wow.* Tibetan ghost traps. Was Ray Ray suddenly a devout Buddhist monk who could activate these now? If Ray Ray had become a monk I would eat my favorite work boots. I doubted any monk would be caught wearing gold chains like Ray Ray.

The elevator chimed and a harried-looking woman in a neat suit and sleek pageboy cut came rushing out. "Mr. Louie, thank you so much for rushing over here. The alarms in labor and delivery had been going off all over but have just stopped."

Ray Ray smiled patiently, his round face shiny and kind. "Of course we are always eager to assist the hospital. We are ready to dispel the ghosts."

She beamed up at him. "We are so fortunate to have you as a benefactor, Mr. Louie. Please come with me."

I watched in annoyance as the elevator doors closed, hiding the Louie entourage from my sight.

Ray Ray Louie was a day late and a dollar short. Baby Nijat would have died if Bāo and I hadn't come as soon as we did. I hurried across the parking lot, Bāo keeping pace at my heels. It was almost 8 a.m. If I didn't find the Gate in time, this morning's wraiths would look like a walk in the park.

# SUPPLIES

Lotus Lane looked unmarred by last night's events with the fù chóng. Thankfully the merchants of Lotus Lane had pressure-washed everything, including my bloodstains. The colorful lanterns above us clashed with my memory of the dark fù chóng blood on the sidewalk and the painted dragons adorning the rooftops somehow seemed less capable of protecting my people this morning. Instead of fearsome dragons of unlimited power, today they were simply painted wood and plaster.

Baby Ricky and Sally were waiting for me, leaning on their car as I arrived at the Sun Emporium. Baby Ricky waved to me and began sorting out his keys as I parked and got out of my Jeep with my empty duffel. I didn't miss the dark circles under his eyes when he whipped off his sunglasses. I guessed he'd drawn the unlucky straw to go to the store early this morning and clean the bloodstains. And he'd still agreed to open early for me without hesitation. I didn't know what I'd done to earn the goodwill of the Sun family but I was grateful. It was the balm I needed after seeing Kamon and confronting what I'd lost.

As he unlocked the door to the Emporium he smiled and waved down the street. I followed his gaze and found the Potsticker Queen sweeping her front step and giving me a look that could shatter bulletproof glass. I put on what I hoped was a cheery smile and gave her a wave. See? Diplomacy.

Sally stopped beside me to pet Bāo and frowned at Kelly. She adjusted her messenger bag and squinted down the block. "What's with her today?"

Sally had dark circles under her eyes as well. I really needed to stop keeping the Suns up so late. "It's me. She hates me."

It felt strange even explaining this to Sally. Almost everyone on Lotus Lane had given me a wide berth two years ago. Kelly was not unique in her animosity toward me. I never quite understood why the Sun family had been so warm to me but I wasn't going to look a friendly ammunition dealer in the mouth.

Baby Ricky gave me a puzzled look before rolling back the security gate and locking it in place. I knew those gates weighed a ton but the big guy lifted them as easily as he lifted a fork. After we got inside he checked the sidewalk and pulled the security gate closed behind us, locking us in. Sally pulled the blinds on the windows, shielding us from any prying eyes. Ricky moved through the store, turning on lights as he went. Bāo followed him as if he owned the place.

Sally gave me a gentle hug and then held me at arm's length to take a long look at me. "How are you feeling? Better?"

My chest still hurt like I had been stabbed twice, because I had been stabbed *and* poisoned, but I didn't want to alarm Sally further. I nodded. "You know Grandma Chen. She always comes through."

Sally held my gaze through her chunky glasses. She'd really come a long way since I'd first met her two years ago, when she was still hiding behind her insecurities and a curtain of bangs. Her voice was fierce. "So do you, Emiko. So do you."

Behind the cashier counter Ricky opened a hidden panel on the back wall, camouflaged under a kudzu of calendars, invoices, and "lucky" counterfeit currency. A column of light switches sat inside the panel.

He pointed at the shelf I was leaning against. "Better step back."

I hopped away as his meaty hand grabbed all the switches and threw them at the same time. Hidden motors whirred to life, their whining and clanking jarring in the early morning quiet. Clothing racks along the back wall hung with touristy T-shirts lifted away into the ceiling, revealing an array of tactical combat clothing. A variety of armored vests dominated the display, along with other garments, gloves, and boots.

The adjoining wall held racks of Ghirardelli chocolates, bags of Japanese crackers, and boxes of candy. The wall behind these shelves opened with a groan and the candy slid back with a click, allowing another set of shelves to rise from the floor. This one was lined with glass apothecary jars. Crystals in every color of the rainbow filled each jar, some glowing with their own internal light.

The shelf I had been leaning against, with its neat rows of miniature plastic figurines and tiny Golden Gate Bridges, sank into the floor and slid into the darkness. Another shelf rumbled up from the floor taking its place. Tidy ranks of talent-infused trinkets lined each shelf, some literally buzzing with pent-up energy. There were small clay figures in the shapes of people and various animals, as well as small ceramic tiles the size of playing cards, rows and rows of them. Each row held tiles with a different hanzi character engraved on the surface.

The checkout counter rotated into the wall, and a whole new counter spun out from behind the wall. The glass counter under the register was crammed with the truly special tricks that I relied on the Suns for. Behind the counter, something I hadn't seen last time: an array of knives displayed on the wall.

The last of the shelves slid into place and the hidden motors ceased their protests. I took a moment to turn in place slowly, taking it all in. Every time I came here, Ricky and Sally added something new and exciting. Just seeing all the gear quickened my heart rate and breathing. Gods, I was a sucker for this stuff.

Baby Ricky moved to stand behind the register once the floor stopped moving and placed his hands on the glass display case in front of him, a big smile on his face. "Slice 'em, dice 'em, flash 'em, smash 'em. What'll it be for you today?"

As much as I wanted to stay and ogle the new merchandise, I had to get moving. My detour to the hospital had already eaten up a significant chunk of my day. I ticked off the known threats I'd encountered in the last twenty-four hours on my fingers. "I need a full kit today. The menu is going to include charm speakers, kinetics, and a ghost master. Should count on a few Wàirén bodyguards as well, so guns and knives, too."

Ricky's eyes widened. "Is that it?"

I snapped my fingers. "No. Actually, several . . . no, many ghosts. A lot of ghosts are likely. Corporeal and incorporeal. At least as bad as the fù chóng last night. Maybe worse."

Ricky and Sally met each other's eyes for a moment, some unknown communication passing between them. The moment passed and Sally strode over to the armor rack and pulled down what, at a distance, looked like a sequined blouse. She threw it to me and it sparkled in the light as I caught it.

I draped it over my arm to get a closer look. Small blue discs had been woven together into a tight yet flexible matrix. The discs shimmered, their edges iridescent.

"Our latest armor. Each disc is ceramic plate reinforced with carbon fiber and bonded to titanium, then imbued with Dragon Scales. Stops all blades and rifle rounds. Impenetrable."

I whistled as I let the scales flow over my arm like water. I rarely wore the armor plates I already had because they were so heavy and bulky. I tended to ditch anything that slowed me down or hindered my mobility. These scales though . . . I felt my heart quicken with sheer unadulterated lust.

*Want.*

I tried to play it cool but I'm sure Sally and Baby Ricky had already seen me for the sucker I was for this stuff. I petted the scales covetously before placing the scale vest on the display case. Armor

like this would certainly have been handy before encountering the
fù chóng.

Baby Ricky laid out several items. The first item was a nonde-
script jar of what looked like face cream. He opened it and I nearly
sneezed from the sharp odor.

"High-potency skepticism. Rub it in along the edge of both ears.
Lasts longer than the lozenges and should protect you against gāo-
level charm speakers."

He paused a moment, his expression uncomfortable. "It . . . has
been known to cause skin irritation. And a rash."

I brought the little jar closer to me and sniffed carefully. "Well,
I guess if the smell doesn't keep them away, then the rash certainly
will."

Baby Ricky moved down the counter, clearly ready to move on.
"Against kinetics your best bet is to neutralize their ability to throw
things at you."

He pointed at a row of ceramic tiles, each inscribed with sān.
"One of your favorites, Might of the Mountain. Be careful with
this batch, though. Dad's been tinkering with the compression and
these have more kick than you're used to."

Ricky picked up what looked like a frozen soap bubble the size
of a golf ball. "These are new. Sally's idea, actually, made special
for you. Steel Wind. Along the lines of a privacy bubble, but with
a ton more compression. Should deflect most projectiles, but we
haven't had a chance to try any rifles on it yet. The only downside
is you're limited to the air you trap inside the bubble."

Sally beamed. "Yes, well, I'm just tired of seeing Emiko get
poked full of holes!"

She joined Ricky behind the counter carrying two large glass jars
filled with glowing crystals, one gray, the other a deep bloodred.
"Good all-around utility here. Fists of Stone and Dragon Breath."

The blades mounted behind the register caught my eye. Ricky
turned and pulled down a set of slender kunais held together with a

leather strip through the rings on the handles. Even from a distance I smelled the saltwater scent of the talent.

Ricky laid them down next to the earth tiles. "Hurricane Blades. Imbued with wind talent to fly faster and farther."

I ran my finger over one of the blades, feeling the edge. "This is all great, but what do you have for the ghosts?"

He snapped his fingers. "I think I have something in the back that will work. Hang on."

As he headed past the silk room dividers in the rear of the store Sally got to work packing up my supplies. I unzipped my duffel, laying it out flat and exposing dozens of Velcro pockets and pouches sewn into the interior.

With the ease of practice Sally began loading my bag up. We'd done this enough times that she even knew how I liked the bag to be packed. "You know, Emiko, you should really just have a subscription box from us."

I rolled my eyes. Sally was always trying to sell me an ammo subscription. "I'm not sure I need something like that." I was retired from being the Blade. I really shouldn't need so many weapons.

She laughed. "You go through a lot of shurikens and ammo. With a monthly box, we would deliver it to your doorstep."

That was kind of tempting. But I responded lightly, "Then I'd miss out on seeing all this cool new stuff."

I examined the display of knives behind her as she worked. One of the blades at the bottom caught my eye and I pointed to it.

"That one. Did you sell another one like that recently?"

Sally raised an eyebrow and picked up the leaf-shaped blade, laying it on the counter. "I don't think this is for you, Emiko, it's the cheapest blade we have here. Nothing special, just a simple edge enhancement. Beginner's stuff."

I'd seen a twin of this blade two nights ago behind Grandma Chen's spa, in the hands of the newly minted Claw. I turned the knife over in my hands, anger from that night rumbling deep in my belly again. "You sell many of these?"

She held my gaze for a heartbeat. "One to every new Louie Claw."

I read Sally's expression and my anger evaporated. Gods, I was an idiot. I turned and took a good look, a real look, at all the merchandise the Suns had built up in their secondary business. I knew most of it on sight, and I also knew that I would never buy most of it. How far was my head up my own butt if I hadn't stopped to consider who else the Suns were selling to? I considered Popo's warning, and wondered for the first time if I wasn't doing the Suns any favors by shopping here.

"Do you guys . . . ah, do you do a lot of business with them? The Louies?"

Sally returned to packing my gear, her tone brisk. "Ha! You're just lucky my dad isn't here to hear you ask that. We'd be here until lunch just waiting for his rant to end."

Finished with the crystals, I helped her carry the jars back to their places on the wall.

"Lotus Lane is crawling with Claws these days. Honestly, there are too many of them. Most of them are just bored out of their minds," Sally continued.

I didn't miss her eyes darting to the closed and locked front gate, as if checking for eavesdroppers. Her voice lowered. "Dad is really stressing out these days. Merchant taxes keep going up, but Uncle Jimmy won't allow us to raise our prices. It's hard to stay afloat."

The more Sally talked, the colder my chest felt, as if my heart had stopped. Was I really this blind? The Suns had been nothing but good to me, in a part of town where I could count the number of friendly relations on one hand. I had sworn off clan politics and schemes. Had that made me oblivious to the Suns' plight? I wasn't going to get back into clan business, but the Suns were different.

They were good people and if they were hurting, I couldn't turn my back on them.

"Do you know if there is a yin talent working for the Louies? Gāo-level?"

Sally paused, her hands still on the counter. She thought about it for a moment then shrugged. "Hasn't come in here."

That would have been too easy.

I opened my mouth to speak just as Baby Ricky returned from the rear of the store with a large box cradled in his arms. "Found it! It's not a ghost trap, but the closest I can get for you."

That sounded interesting. "A ghost trap?"

Ricky began unpacking the box. "Oh, that I definitely don't have. You'll need to find yourself a Daoist, or a Buddhist. Someone who knows the rituals and can create a ghost trap for you."

I should have stolen one from Ray Ray's entourage. Of course, I would still need someone who knew the ritual. Then Kamon's face popped to mind and I squashed the idea before it could take root. Yes, Kamon was a devout Buddhist, or as devout as you can be when you're a meat-eating tiger. No way was I calling him though.

Ricky stopped what he was doing. "Wait, don't you help out at the temple? You should ask Brother Meng if he can spot you."

I grabbed onto the idea like a drowning man clutching a life vest. Yes, Brother Meng. I'd have to find the time to visit him. Somewhere between finding the Ebony Gate that I hadn't located, and avoiding the growing list of Jiārén who seemed intent on hurting me, and preventing the city from being overrun by ghosts. Right. Piece of cake.

Ricky pulled a lacquered wooden box from the lake of foam peanuts inside the cardboard box. He set the wooden box on the counter with surprising gentleness. An intricate carving of a dragon encircling a globe covered the top. Fine calligraphy, a poem of some kind, covered the sides in neat columns. A blob of blue wax impressed with the Sun hanzi sealed the box. Ricky pulled out a box cutter and began carefully cutting through the seal.

"Dad only made one of these. I don't even remember who provided the talent, but he was only in town for a short time. It was so complicated Dad swore he would never do it again."

The seal broken, Ricky opened the box and pulled out what looked like a fine net of spun gold. He spread the net onto the countertop. Small discs of jade had been worked into the netting at regular intervals, each disc carved with a stylized dragon head, jaws open and roaring. The woven gold seemed to glow with its own light.

Baby Ricky traced a finger over one of the jade stones. "Dad called it a Demon Cloak. The gold is imbued with Dragon Limbs. The stones with Dragon Will."

I sucked in a breath, my eyes going wide. Dragon Will was a rare talent indeed, the ability to cancel out other talents. I held my hand over the Cloak, feeling the subtle hum of energy. It was like standing next to a hot engine, full of dangerous potential. If the Suns had done their work correctly, the netting would act like a lightning rod. I was looking at a one-of-a-kind artifact, something that had taken Big Ricky's immeasurable skill to create. And Baby Ricky was offering it up to me like a normal transaction.

"Wow. Ricky. This is . . . I can't take this."

Baby Ricky's head popped up, his face incredulous. "What are you talking about? You're about the only person I would trust with this!"

I opened my mouth to protest but Ricky shushed me. "Emiko. You've trusted us for years now to get you the gear you need. Trust me now. You need this. If you don't buy it, it's going back into the box to be hidden in the Fragment again. When Dad made this we knew we couldn't sell it to anyone, much less let the Louies know that it even existed. That was then. Things have changed. After the fù chóng, none of us are safe without you taking care of Yomi. You're meant to use it, I'm sure of it."

He exchanged a look with Sally and she nodded back. "We couldn't live with ourselves if we didn't give you all the help we could, Emiko."

I closed my mouth and looked back and forth between them, a matched set of determined expressions, standing on the hill they were going to die on. The Cloak was a one-of-a-kind item and should have been an heirloom for the Sun family. I'd need a day to even guess at its value. They shouldn't be considering handing it off to me. Skies, I doubted I had enough qì in me to activate it. It was a little embarrassing to have such implicit trust from them, especially when every time I dealt with them I felt like I was the one who owed them.

And if I were honest with myself, I needed every advantage I could get. I'd honed my skills as a blunt instrument, thriving when my targets and enemies were clear. Charm speakers, clan intrigues, invading ghosts, and whatever the Louies were planning was not my strong suit. It would be stupid to leave the Demon Cloak. I would just have to work harder to make things right for the Suns.

A thought occurred to me as Ricky repacked the Cloak. "You guys don't seem all that thrilled about doing business with the Louies. Why don't you move? Maybe over to where Grandma Chen has set up?"

Baby Ricky and Sally shared another loaded look, as if carrying on some sort of silent argument with their eyes. This went on for a moment before Ricky broke off, making a frustrated sound. He dropped his eyes and returned to carefully wrapping the lacquer box in a sheet of bubble wrap. "It's . . . complicated, Emiko—"

Sally cut him off with a huff. "It's not complicated, Emiko. Ricky's too scared to tell you that we need a Sentinel if we want to move. The city needs a Sentinel!"

Ricky looked aghast. "Sally!"

His sister shot right back at him. "What? You think she doesn't know?"

Sally turned her fire-bright eyes on me. "I know you feel it. My mom remembers how it was. She says things are starting to go bad, just like they did before the truce."

My body went cold as Sally spoke.

"I spoke with Grandma, after you conked out. You know what she's going through all the way in Inner Sunset. Those Claws aren't out there on their own. Uncle Jimmy has his fingers in everything. They're expanding, making a move for more territory."

Sally seemed to take in my shocked expression and took pity on me, lowering her voice. Her eyes lifted, tracing the faint gold aura around my head. "Grandma Chen is right. The city likes you. You'd be perfect as the Sentinel."

A small part of me wanted to say the things I knew Sally wanted to hear. But most of me, the me that had emerged from Pearl Market covered in innocent blood, wanted nothing to do with it. I had left Tokyo and everything I knew for a reason. I'd spent the last two years here making a new life for myself. There was no way I was throwing all that away for some mystical deal with a new master. I had to do better by the Suns, but I needed to find another way to do it. My way.

I forced myself to smile. Despite my misgivings, the last thing I wanted to do was to bald-faced lie to Sally. My phone chirped, saving me from sticking my foot in my mouth. I excused myself to a quiet corner and answered the call.

A cheery voice boomed through the phone. "Good morning, sunshine!"

I rolled my eyes. "Good morning, Tran. What do you have?"

"What do I have? What do I have?" He sounded far too perky for this time of day. "I've got it! Next arrival to Port of Oakland and your best bet at finding your Gate!"

I hoped he wasn't going to be like this all day. "Okay, I'm on Lotus Lane but I'm almost done. Meet me here. I'll grab some grub, too."

He hooted. "Grub! Now you're talking!"

I found myself physically unable to roll my eyes up any farther. I gave him the address and hung up.

Sally busied herself finishing the repacking of my duffel. I walked back to the counter, unable to meet her eyes. I would find another way to help them, I just needed to figure out how.

I'd brought plenty with me to pay, but hadn't counted on something like the Demon Cloak. I reached into my jacket and pulled out six slender bars of soft gold, each imprinted with a stylized dragon on one side, and the hanzi character lóng on the other. I laid them all on the counter in a neat stack. And then, because I couldn't help myself, I added two bags of Kit Kats as well.

"I hope that's enough."

Sally picked up the gold and made it disappear with a quick motion. "Thank you for your business. Anything else?"

It was past 8 a.m. and I hadn't eaten anything other than Popo's restorative herbal soup. The Kit Kats wouldn't be enough and my stomach growled on cue. This situation was a tragedy that I had to rectify. "Do you have any of your mom's pork buns?"


I spotted Freddy through the blinds, waiting for me on the sidewalk. He squinted up at the garish sign above the Suns' front door. His brow creased and he pulled out his phone, looking confused. I rapped on the window and his head popped up, spotting me.

Baby Ricky unlocked the front door to let me out. I hugged him and Sally, careful not to jar my chest, as I made my way out. "Thanks again."

Ricky waved me off and gave his sister a warning look. "It's nothing. You've been good to our family, Emiko. It's the least we can do."

I stepped out into the sunlight and Ricky locked the door behind me. They still had a lot of prep to finish before their regular opening hours. Freddy's eyes swept back and forth over the Sun Emporium signs and the kaleidoscope of cheap tourist trinkets in the front window.

"What did you need from here?"

I thought about the Louies' stranglehold over the Suns. Per the terms of the treaty, the Trans couldn't transact with merchants like the Suns. He had no idea what the Suns actually sold. Classic move from my mother. Keep everyone in the dark. But today wasn't the day for me to enlighten Freddy.

I reached into the bag Sally had given me and handed one of the warm buns to him. "Best pork buns in the city, my friend. The best!"

Freddy's eyes lit up. "Sweet!"

He took a big bite of the soft white bun and steam poured out. He puffed softly and a swirl of air cooled his bun to the perfect temperature to devour the tender pork filling. As he chewed his face became thoughtful.

I bit into a bun of my own and relished the rich, savory filling. "What's up, Tran? You look like that's your last steamed bun forever."

Freddy took another bite before speaking. "You know, Emiko, you could have called me last night."

"No offense, but I needed your clan's help last night, and I needed it fast."

He downed the rest of the bun and stuck his hands in his pockets. "I'm not really the lazy Tran, you know? I'm the one who started that, actually."

My dossiers on the Trans had very little on Freddy since his matriculation from Lóng Kǒu. He'd kept a low profile since school, seeming to prefer to stay in the background while his sister steered the clan. Other than wasting a strong Hoard gift, he didn't seem to be interested in anything other than surfing and getting tan.

Freddy's face grew serious as he reached for another bun. "After the disaster at the Tourney, I told Fiona I was done."

I stopped chewing. "Done?"

He nodded. "Done with Jiārén rituals. I told Fi that I knew she would be better as the Head of the Clan."

She certainly had the killer instinct. "But why the slacker image?"

His lips turned down. "Fi is the best. Fi is the Head of the Clan we need. But I'm the boy. I can't be too involved or it will confuse the old guard."

I looked down at my half-eaten bao. I knew exactly what Freddy was talking about. I was the oldest, the former heir. Being the Blade meant it was clear I would never be the Head of the Clan, only serve the clan and follow the will of the Head. It was better for everyone. No confusion as to who was in charge.

Freddy and I had a lot more in common than I had realized. But that didn't mean he was my best support for the task at hand.

Freddy was an asset so I wasn't going to turn him down, but I also wasn't going to rely solely on him. Too much was on the line. My brother needed the best. That wasn't necessarily Freddy—the best would be all the Tran resources, which meant Fiona's considerable talent, too.

I tossed him another bun. "What do you know about yin talents?"

Freddy swallowed. "You mean like a ghost summoner?"

"Yes. Gāo-level. A ghost master."

Freddy's eyes drifted and I could tell he was rewinding back to the academy. Finally he shook his head. "Those are so rare. Never encountered one while I was there. When I started at Lóng Kǒu, I'd heard about one before us. Chow something."

It wasn't enough. I needed more than Freddy's vague memories.
"Freddy, I think there's a ghost master working for the Louies."
Freddy gave me a strange look. "Yeah?"
"Yeah. Who else could have summoned all those undead kappas at the Palace of Fine Arts?"
Freddy looked thoughtful but he just grunted and kept chewing.
"Freddy, he took the Lost Heart."
Freddy's eyes grew as wide as marbles. "Seriously?"
"Seriously."
Freddy didn't look entirely convinced but I'd made headway. Somehow the Louies were involved with the theft of the Gate and the auction for the anchor. I didn't know how it all fit together but in some ways it didn't matter. I just needed to retrieve them both and get them to the shinigami. I checked the time on my phone. We had two hours to get to the Port of Oakland, set up, and recover the Gate.

Finally, I was making progress.

# BRITTLE

Freddy struggled to speak intelligibly over a mouthful of pillow-soft dough and pork. "And now, the bad news."

I looked up from the back of my Jeep. The hibagon smell still lingered and I had my duffel laid out to avoid the most obvious stains. When I was positive I was going to still be among the living my poor vehicle could really use a spa day. "What's the bad news?"

Freddy made a mighty effort to swallow his pork bun. "There's a huge pileup on the bridge. The only way we're going to get there in time is if I drive."

And by "drive" he meant his special brand of tunneling. The transport most guaranteed to have me dry heaving after. Not eating all of the pork bun now seemed like a brilliant move. My lips pressed into a thin line and I nodded once to Freddy. My eternal soul was at stake. A few dry heaves against a Bay Bridge traffic jam was a no-brainer. "All right. I'm just about ready."

I picked out a variety of my new tricks and started filling the pockets sewn into the interior of my haori. I slipped a Dragon Breath crystal into a pocket at my right wrist. The Fists of Stone went into the same place on my left. I grabbed a handful of the Mountain tiles and two of the Steel Wind baubles as well. I left the Hurricane Blades for now. If I was going up against kinetics, the last thing I wanted to do was to give them anything else to throw at me. I pulled out my swords and strapped them on. As always, the weight of Truth on my back put me at ease.

Freddy watched me as I secured my swords. His eyes tracked Truth's handle above my shoulder. If only the no-look charm on the swords worked on Jiārén I'd have a lot less of this to deal with. I slammed the door closed on my Jeep with more force than I intended and whirled on Freddy, fixing him with my trademark glare. He had the decency to look abashed.

"Are you done staring?"

He held up his hands in surrender. "Okay, okay. Sorry. I'm sure the novelty will wear off soon."

I tightened my haori and mentally prepared myself for another gut-wrenching transition. Freddy looked almost bored as I stepped up next to him. The corner of his mouth went up in a lopsided smile. "Now remember, don't clench up."

"Why?—"

Freddy's aura flashed a brilliant blue and a swirling funnel spun into life at our feet. Before I could take in another breath he plunged us both into the endless blue pit.


If I had my Jeep, I would have had to fight traffic but at least had the nice drive over the beautiful "new" Bay Bridge. The Port of Oakland had delighted me when I visted as a child, with its tall white container cranes in the skyline. Traveling with Freddy meant I got to see none of it and instead spent a few minutes up close and personal with the asphalt clutching my gut as it twisted in misery. I retched again. Fiery embers of pain seared my chest, the fù chóng wounds reminding me it had been a really winning two days. I vowed to myself I was taking a vacation after this. If there was an "after this."

I wheezed in agony, counting slowly to calm myself. Freddy patted my shoulder awkwardly. I hated anyone seeing me like this.

Finally I got up and spit into the gravel. My mouth tasted sour, a lovely combination of anxiety and wind tunnel travel barfing. I wiped my hands off on my cargo pants. I pulled out my steel water flask and guzzled until the water spilled down my chin. I swished the water around in my mouth and spit again. Better.

Oakland felt oddly quiet. Even with the constant noise of a fully functioning seaport around us, everything seemed strangely muted. It took me a few moments to realize that I had actually gotten used to the constant white noise of San Francisco wheedling for my attention. Out beyond the city limits, San Francisco's voice couldn't touch me, and instead of feeling relieved, I felt like I'd left my house without my shoes. Like something was missing.

Freddy had wisely chosen to stay silent as I got myself back together. Now he pointed to his tablet. "Drones are monitoring the perimeter. We'll know as soon as he enters the port."

He pulled out his phone and called his foreman. "Joey, check everyone's badges. I need you to get two men on the berth to check all incoming vehicles. We are looking out for a gray shipping container with no markings."

Who was powerful enough to divert a vessel for the Gate at the last minute? Who was powerful enough to even utilize a Gate? Bulldog had used a word of power. They didn't teach those at Lóng Kǒu. Those were closely guarded by their respective clans.

I scanned the length of the port, squinting against the late morning sun. Towering skeletal white gantries stood sentinel at the water's edge. This had to be it.

"Freddy, where do you move the containers?"

He pointed to a finger of land jutting out into the harbor. "We use the last gantry out there. Most privacy."

"Okay, tell your guys to let the truck through when it gets here. We're going to get out there first and lay a trap."

We ran along aisles of towering containers stacked up like toy blocks. The run served as a warm-up, loosening the kinks in my back from sleeping in Popo's spa lounger. My chest loosened up. I set a comfortable pace and despite the flippity flip of his sandals,

Freddy kept up without complaint. My estimation of him went up a notch. When we got to the last dock I knelt behind the cover of the gantry legs and searched the waters. Nothing yet. I still had time.

I pulled out my pile of Mountain tiles, a wisp of a plan forming. Whoever they were, they would need the gantry to load the Gate onto the boat. The gantry was the choke point where I could take them. If I hit them after they'd put the Gate on the gantry, at least they couldn't run off with it again. I paced off a large square at the base of the gantry, leaving Mountain tiles buried under the gravel at the corners of the square. The Mountain tiles were my plan B, if things got messy.

Freddy watched me marking out the square for my trap, an odd smile on his face. He reached in his pocket and began patting his other pockets before fishing out a small baggie.

I stood up from the last corner. "What?"

He shrugged.

"Spit it out."

"Nothing . . . Just . . . I didn't figure you for firecrackers, is all."

He turned back to his baggie, his hands whipping out thin white papers that he then proceeded to roll into a fat joint.

Seriously? I couldn't believe I'd gone to Fiona for help and she'd foisted her pot-smoking slacker brother on me.

"We can't all be gāo talents, Tran."

Freddy waved his arm, indicating the trap I'd laid out. "Isn't this just . . . I don't know . . . Isn't it just, silly? We don't need to stoop to this kind of stuff."

Heat bloomed at the base of my neck. I took a centering breath and fought down the urge to punch him in the nose. This was why I didn't hang out with these people. Not two days and it already felt like Lóng Kǒu all over again.

I was twelve, and leaving home for the first time. Second years like Fiona and Freddy had an air of assurance and a cadre of devoted cronies while I'd been struggling to cope with my rapidly dwindling talent. I'd gone from the pride of my clan to a no-talent first year while at Lóng Kǒu. My entire existence had been called into question. I'd thought I was an animator like my father, but in the end it all sputtered and fizzled. I had nothing and the Jōkōryūkai had remade me into a new weapon.

It meant I used every tool I had, whether it was wares from the Sun Emporium or some privileged snot like Freddy.

I plastered a pleasant smile on my face. From Freddy's expression it may not have been convincing. "What would you suggest, then?"

He lit up and took a long drag, the joint dangling from his loose fingers. "I dunno . . ." He shrugged and blew out a slow stream of pungent smoke. "They show up. We knock their heads in. What's so tough about that? I'm me, and you're the Butch—"

My glare went up a thousand degrees, burning Freddy to a crisp where he stood in his leather sandals.

He put up his hands in a conciliatory gesture. "—the Blade. You're the Blade. You're badass. I'm not so bad myself."

He shrugged again, unrepentant despite my withering gaze. Broken Claw. I did not need this to deal with as well today. I should have kept my Talon and done this myself.

"What did you do yesterday to prepare to face the illusionist again, Tran?"

He cocked his head. "What?"

I spoke slowly. And loudly. "What did you do to make sure that you don't get your brain trampled again today?"

I let him stand there, quiet for a moment before I laid into him, my voice going quiet and cold. Freddy's eyes just got bigger and bigger as I spoke.

"Because if it were me on their side, I'd have noticed that there was some hotshot wind talent making trouble for me and I'd make sure that it didn't happen again. I'd ensure I didn't lose another one of my guys to this punk kid. In fact, I'd bring guns. Can you put up your funnels fast enough to deflect 5.56 NATO rounds?"

Freddy's mouth fell open. But I was just getting started.

"Had much practice dodging bullets? Just how many funnels can you put up at once? I'd bring two guys with rifles and extended magazines full of high-velocity rounds, and I'd start pounding lead into you from two different directions. I'd throw in a gāo-level kinetic to catch anything you managed to deflect and send them all back to you until you couldn't keep up and at least one bullet got through."

Freddy dropped his joint, the smoke trailing downward. My breath rasped and I'd clenched my hands into fists during my tirade. "That's what I would do."

I closed my eyes. I'd run so far and sometimes it felt like I hadn't gotten anywhere. "I made my name defeating Jiārén, Tran, on their terms, without any talent of my own. Let me do my job. Do what I say and at least I can bring you back to Fiona in one piece."

I opened my eyes to find Freddy staring at me, his face slack with surprise. Right. Not often you hear someone tell you that they've carefully considered how to best neutralize and kill you. I rubbed at my temples, trying to imagine the blocked qì in my body flowing smoothly and serenely. It kind of worked.

This wasn't Freddy's fault. He wasn't ready for this. Dressed in board shorts and a tank top again, he looked ready for nothing more than a beach volleyball match. Tooth and bone, he was still wearing sandals. Who went into battle wearing sandals?

I put my hands up, placating. "Look. I have a lot more experience with people trying to hurt me. I need you to trust that I know what I'm doing here, and I have reasons for being so paranoid."

Freddy closed his mouth and his dark brows drew together in concentration. "I get that you know your business. But you came to our clan because of what we can do. This is bigger than just you."

He waved a dismissive hand at my tile setup. "I'm a gāo-level combat-rated talent from a Hoard Custodian family, and you're out here setting up party tricks. I've been honing my talent since I could walk. You know what that means."

I did know. My parents had tried to train me and it hadn't gone so smoothly. Which is why I'd spent thousands of grueling hours learning to outwit people without relying on Jiārén talent. He had a point—he had exponentially more firepower in his pinky than all of the tricks in the Sun Emporium added together.

I nodded reluctantly.

He stubbed out the joint with his sandaled foot. "Emiko, you used a Talon because you knew in your gut that you needed to bring in the big guns."

Freddy pointed at himself, tapping his chest twice. As his hand gestured down his torso a swirl of air wound around our feet, a soft whisper. The gravel and dust began to spin as well, and a vortex of air lifted us higher. I wobbled, my muscles trying to stabilize me and failing. I felt like I was on stilts made of rice noodles. We went higher and the cool air brushed my hot face. Freddy kept rising, and I did, too. Soon we could see all the glittering beauty of the San Francisco Bay spread before us. He swirled us three hundred and sixty degrees for the full panoramic effect. I felt the distinct urge to vomit again.

"I'm the big gun." He said it without ego, his voice quiet.

I'd never doubted that he had gobs of power. But my problem at the pier had been his lack of control and combat training. What Freddy was doing now required tremendous control. He was asking me to trust him to be in control this time.

I thought about Tatsuya back at the Soong estate, meticulously drilling his talent, his sweet face tight with concentration. Tatsuya was the future of our clan. He was everything. I couldn't fail and let the shinigami get to Tacchan next. Freddy was right. I needed every advantage, including a gāo talent.

When Freddy held out his hand, I accepted it and he set us gently back on the ground.

We looked at each other, considering our next moves. Tension eased from my shoulders. I knew how to do this. I was good at planning and good at waiting. I leaned in and began drawing in the dirt, showing Freddy the rough parameters of my plan.

Freddy palmed one of the tiles, bouncing it in his hand and testing its heft. In his hands, one of these tiles should work way better than when I used them.

His tablet beeped and Freddy jumped, startled by the sound. The truck was here. I shaded my eyes and scanned the water. It took only a moment to find it. The boat stuck out like a sore thumb, the smallest cargo vessel of any on the water at the moment, and headed straight for us.

"See that boat there? That's how they're getting the Gate out of here. When the fur starts flying, your job will be to keep that boat from getting close to the port. Whatever else happens, the Ebony Gate cannot get loaded onto that boat."

Even though it was the smallest boat on the water, it was still enormous, and there were people on it. I needed Freddy to be powerful enough to prevent the boat from docking, but controlled enough not to toss it and everyone on board to smithereens.

Freddy opened his mouth and I raised my hand to cut him off. "Let me do my job. You've already got an Advocate coming for you. Fiona will kill me if I let you turn it into a twofer."

I pointed at a truck parked next to some equipment. "Hunker down there. You should have a good view as the boat gets closer. Don't start your shenanigans before I do. Go."

He hesitated for just another moment before looking away from my unflinching gaze. In a few seconds he'd hidden himself from the view of the approaching truck. I squatted down beside one of the massive gantry tires. From here I could see both Freddy and the truck, rolling toward us before a gray cloud of gravel dust.

For my part, I didn't like Freddy seeing me set up. The fewer people who knew how I worked, the better. Call it tradecraft.

My square was too small but I didn't have much choice. The larger I made the square, the more diluted the effect would be. But earth energy and I had never really gotten along well. Ha. Well, me and most talent. I had to play my cards to get the most bang for my buck. I looked up into the massive frame, thick steel girders rated to carry tons of weight. I was sure it would hold.

Pretty sure.

As far as solutions went, this one was less than elegant. I tucked the last Mountain tile into my pocket just as a truck rounded the far corner approaching our position. I ducked back behind the gantry.

My well-honed habits as Blade returned to me in an instant as I settled in to wait. My body stilled and my heart rate slowed to a crawl. I opened my mouth to hear better and let my eyes unfocus, taking in the entire field of play. Adrenaline trickled into my blood, not enough to make me jittery, just enough to set my nerves on a hair trigger. I tuned out the pain in my chest, breathing in slowly through my nose.

Click.

Click.

I turned. Freddy sat sprawled on the gravel, his head resting on the side of the truck. He flicked a bit of gravel from his fingers, sending it toward the gray waters of the bay.

Click.

Gravel crunched as the truck neared the gantry. I was going to kill Freddy. Slowly. I picked up a small stone and whipped it at his head. It pinged off his forehead, making him snap up and look at me.

I glared at him, pointed at my eyes, at him, then out to the water. Can you throw exclamation points with your eyes? I definitely tried. Freddy gave me a thumbs-up and turned to the water. He started patting his pockets again.

Was he going to roll another blunt? I really was going to kill him. The truck stopped under the gantry and Bulldog got out from the passenger side. The driver's door opened and a young man hopped out, all strapping muscle and a very obvious gun holster under an open blazer.

Behind the truck a blacked-out Mercedes in tricked-out trims and flashy rims rolled to a stop. No one exited but the car remained at idle. Interesting. Someone had tagged along to make sure Bulldog did his job.

Bulldog pulled a tablet out of his jacket and tapped the screen. The gantry rumbled to life, lowering the clawlike jaws that would grab the container. I bet the Trans had never changed the default password for the hardware. I would have to have a talk with Fiona about their operational security. Andie would have my head if I ever used a default password.

The arm lowered to the container and Bulldog nudged it back and forth with little touches of power. In moments the container was rising into the air. I looked behind me to find the small shipping boat within a quarter mile of the dock. I made eye contact with Freddy and mentally willed him to not do anything stupid.

I counted down, watching the container rise higher in the air. Three—two—one.

I pulled a flash-bang from my belt, pulled the pin, and set it rolling toward the two men. Bulldog surprised me with his situational awareness, seeming to recognize the flash-bang immediately. He turned away just as the device detonated. A brilliant flash of light with a thunderous boom shook the ground. A plume of white smoke blossomed in the center of my trap. I hoped Freddy was paying attention.

I bolted from my cover, making a beeline for where I'd last spotted the new kid. He didn't have a discernible aura but he did have a gun. The last thing I needed was someone taking potshots at me as I dealt with Bulldog. I closed the distance and found him blinking and gasping in the white smoke from the flash-bang, his gun already in his hand. *Idiot.* At this rate he'd be just as likely to shoot Bulldog as me. Where were they getting these guys?

I came in under his gun and swept the new kid's legs out from under him. His head hit the asphalt with a jarring crack and the gun fell from his limp fingers. I kicked the gun and it spun away. I stood, drawing Hachi and turning in place, listening for signs of Bulldog.

A red-hot line of pain sliced across my left forearm and a bright kunai clattered to the ground beside me. I spun and the smoke dissipated. Bulldog stood a good twenty feet from me, legs bent, arms flexed at his sides with fists clenched. His aura flared with restrained tension. His jacket billowed in the breeze and the lining of his coat glittered with more kunai blades.

Just. Great.

Kunai blades were light and deadly, their spear-shaped heads sharpened to razor points with a thin handle for gripping and throwing. Originally a farmer's tool, some genius realized that if they just sharpened the heck out of this trowel, they could use it to stab things. Bulldog's kunai had matte black tape wrapped around the handles to improve his grip. This told me two things. One: he was definitely a pro. Two: like most powerful kinetics, he preferred fighting at a distance, which meant I had to get in close.

Because of the lopsided weight of the speared blade, it took a lot of practice to throw them just so and having strong qì didn't hurt, either. Bulldog looked like he'd had lots of practice throwing kunai and a belly full of robust qì. And that wasn't even factoring in his talent. I was glad I'd sent Freddy to deal with the ship. Now I had to do my job.

Bulldog thrust both his arms out, his aura flashing streaky blue. Two more kunais flashed in the sunlight, hurtling toward me on a wave of sinus-stinging acid. My arms went into motion instantly. Hachi whipped out and deflected the first blade. My left arm swept out in an arc and I pushed my qì down my arm, lighting up the Fists of Stone crystal held at my wrist. Power curled around my hand, hardening my skin to solid granite. It wasn't the best defense against bullets or some jerk throwing ninja blades at me but it was lighter than Kevlar.

The second blade struck my hand with enough force to chip off the point of the blade. A spike of pain lanced through my palm. Okay, only mostly solid granite then. My qì was meager at best. Getting optimal results from my tricks was unlikely, even on a good day.

The freighter drew closer. I had to close this out quickly. I dove straight at Bulldog, Hachi leading the way. Just like last time, he flinched first, shying away from a physical fight. I feinted with Hachi, and managed to get my left hand on the tablet, ripping it from his grip. The tablet fell to the ground and the screen shattered into a starburst of broken glass. The container lumbered to a stop above our heads, cables creaking in the wind.

Bulldog cursed and sent a flurry of knives at me. I ducked and rolled away, one of his blades coming perilously close to my neck. I scrambled for cover behind one of the gantry supports, blades slicing through the air around me.

I edged around my cover and found myself looking at Bulldog through a haze of swirling distortion. The blurry kinetic grunted in pain and dropped to a knee. The distortion vanished and Bulldog reappeared, pulling one of his own blades out of his thigh. From the other side of the dock Freddy gave me a cocky grin and a thumbs-up. Behind Freddy, the boat had nearly reached the dock.

I pointed out to the water. "The boat! Do your job!"

Bulldog spun, looking at Freddy, his head snapping between the Tran scion and the approaching cargo ship. *Oh, no.* His arms shot up, ramrod straight, and above us, the gantry began to moan, the thick steel singing as Bulldog's face reddened. My jaw dropped open as the container began to swing, the thick cables thrumming with tension, the support beams warping as they resisted forces they had not been designed for.

I glanced to my left. The incoming boat was floundering in the water, two enormous whirlpools making it impossible for the captain to steer into port. My eyes widened. It wasn't every day you got to see an A-lister let loose. Freddy really wasn't the slacker Tran. And to think that Fiona was letting him go to waste on the beaches of Santa Cruz. It boggled the mind. I saved that away for later.

I stepped out from my cover and held Hachi at low guard, facing Bulldog. "Give it up! It's over!"

Bulldog followed my gaze, saw the massive freighter pushed off course, and cursed. His aura flared and he thrust his arms at me. The gantry pinged and popped as the stress relaxed. Bulldog's jacket flapped in a sudden gale and half a dozen kunai leapt toward me. Skies, how many knives was he carrying? I swung Hachi and swatted away the first knives as I rolled out of Bulldog's line of fire. More knives followed, chasing after me.

I reached into my jacket and pulled out the little clear golf ball, praying my qì was enough. I crushed the ball in my left hand and spun to face Bulldog.

A translucent sphere of wind energy snapped into place around me, coloring everything in faint silver. I advanced on Bulldog and he screamed in frustration, fingers splayed, veins bulging on his hands. His jacket snapped and whipped as more kunai appeared from what had to be dozens of hidden pockets. The blades crashed into my Steel Wind and punched neat little holes in my shield.

Bulldog cursed and threw blade after blade at me, the acrid scent of his talent threatening to burn my sinuses out. As I closed the distance between us, his blades turned my shield into Swiss cheese and the wind energy fell to tatters around me. Two blades punched through an opening in my shield and drew hot lines of pain across my thigh.

Cursed skies, these were my favorite pants!

It was time. I drove my legs forward and slammed my shoulder into Bulldog's gut, bowling him over. We rolled in a tangle of limbs and came to a stop inside the square of my trap. I came up on one knee, the last intact portion of Steel Wind between me and the kinetic. "Tran! Now!"

Freddy pulled the Mountain tile he'd palmed earlier from his pocket. With one hand still pointed at the water and foiling the ship's attempts to dock, he calmly snapped the tile in half with his other hand, lighting up my firecrackers with more power than I'd ever used in my whole life.

This was a bad idea. In my defense, I didn't have a solid grasp on just how many orders of power Freddy was above me. Or rather, how many orders I was below him.

My whole life I'd never really gotten the hang of Hoard talents. I understood the theory, but the application had always been difficult. I always saw it as a problem of volume. I didn't have enough of my own qì to work with, and no amount of training allowed me to draw any more. What little I had was barely enough to power up my tricks.

I'd set the Might of the Mountain trap with the intent to trigger it myself, so I'd linked several tiles together to amplify my results. The earth energy trap amplified the gravity inside my square. Two, maybe three times. With the barest taste of Freddy's super octane power, gravity in my little square went up by a factor of four or five. My math was a little fuzzy. Still not terrible for someone like me, who does a lot of leg and back workouts—and who was braced for the impact. For someone with spindly little legs like Bulldog? Not so nice.

A ton of extra weight landed on my shoulders in an instant, threatening to drive me to my knees. Something small and sharp popped in my shoulder and a gout of warmth rushed down my chest. The air turned thick and soupy, my lungs struggling to draw breath. Bulldog let out a strangled scream as he went down on one knee and his femur snapped with a crack like a gunshot. He cursed at me from where he was pinned to the asphalt. He threw up a hand and another kunai jumped out of his jacket only to land harmlessly on the ground a few feet from him. The increased gravity threw his shoulder to the asphalt and slammed the side of his face to the ground. One eye, already bloodshot, glared daggers at me as he struggled to lift his head.

I grinned at him through clenched teeth. "Heh. Gravity. It's a bitch."

The groan of creaking metal wiped the grin from my face and I turned to look up at the dangling multi-ton container above our heads.

Uh-oh.

I turned and ran, the increased gravity making it feel like I was slogging hip-deep in sucking mud. The world's biggest rubber band snapped above my head with a sound like a cannon shot. I dove over the border of my trap and overshot my landing by several feet thanks to the resumption of normal gravity.

The shipping container hit the ground like a bomb, the container itself ringing like some hellish church bell. I rolled away from the spewing dust and dirt, arms clamped over my ears, eyes squeezed shut.

I coughed dust and grit from my throat and got up on wobbly legs, my ears still ringing from the impact of the container. My chest felt like raw meat. I was scared to even look down at my torso. Gray concrete dust filled the air in all directions. Tires crunched on gravel somewhere in the haze. I hobbled through the cloud, cursing myself for forgetting about the Mercedes. I nearly ran into it, stumbling into the young man I'd knocked out earlier. This time he got the jump on me, shoving me to the ground and diving into the open back door of the black Mercedes.

I caught a glimpse of another passenger, gaudy gold jewelry shimmering in the light, before the door slammed shut and the car took off, spraying me with gravel. The rims spun, a glittering gold as well. I blinked. I'd seen gold rims just this morning at the hospital. Coincidence?

I didn't like coincidences.

Well, at least I had the Gate now. That had to count for something.

I limped over to the main gantry supports and found Freddy huddled behind the wide beams. Under the coating of dust he looked a little peaky but otherwise okay. He got up on shaky legs and followed me back to where the container had landed. The container itself was just barely still a rectangle. It had landed on the cab of the truck, smashing that flat and exploding the tires beneath it. A gory rosette of blood sprayed out from under the container.

Freddy whistled low, his gaze traveling up and down the wrecked and twisted metal. "Wow. Did you know it was going to do that?"

The gantry looked like a total loss, steel legs bent and twisted like putty, the whole structure leaning to one side like a lamed animal. I groaned. Between the crane at Pier 7½ and the gantry here, I was not going to be Fiona's favorite person. "Not really."

I looked up to where the gantry had been, dozens of feet above us. "That trap has always been a local effect. Maybe six to ten feet from the ground. I may have miscalculated a bit."

Freddy wiped the dust from his face, his shoulders shaking. It took a moment to realize he was laughing. His stifled giggles burst into a full-blown belly laugh. "A bit?!"

It was infectious. Giddy laughter bubbled up from my gut, tinged with the jagged energy of leftover adrenaline. The wound on my chest throbbed, robbing me of breath.

Freddy bent over, hands on knees, gasping for breath between gales of laughter. He stood, hands over his belly, struggling to regain his composure.

"Ah, man. A bit? That's awesome!" His eyes twinkled and he held up a hand to me.

A normal person would have responded instantly. My stupid brain took a microsecond too long to realize Freddy was offering me a high five, and I left him hanging awkwardly in the air. Oh gods, I was making this awkward. Should I do it now? Was it too late?

Freddy took it with remarkable aplomb, lowering his hand to my shoulder and giving me a pat. "That's cool. Too soon. I get it."

He looked closer at me and then his eyes narrowed in concern. "Emiko, your jacket . . ."

I looked down and winced. Blood had soaked through my clothes, spiraling into a dark gory stain on the front of my haori. I'd ripped Popo's neat stitches.

"It's fine." It wasn't the first time I'd soaked this haori in blood. It hurt like crazy though and I wished I had more of Popo's curative soup. I pulled out a gauze pad from one of my many pockets and peeled off two strips of gaffer tape I had lining the inside of my jacket for just such an occasion. Freddy watched with unrestrained interest as I wadded the gauze into my now-open wound and then wrapped the gaffer tape from behind my shoulder and under my arm. A passable pressure dressing. At least I wouldn't bleed to death before anyone else got a chance to finish me.

Freddy looked skeptical but he stepped back and surveyed the wreckage of the container and the bloody mess beneath it. "Man, I guess you got him, huh?"

That sobered me up. "Got one of them, you mean." I described the blacked-out Mercedes that had gotten away. The passenger with the gold jewelry had to have been Ray Ray.

Freddy's brow creased. "Really? Ray Ray? Y'think?"

My thoughts slogged as my adrenaline crashed. I was not up for another argument with Freddy. "It was him. I recognized his car from the hospital earlier today. That Benz had gold trim! Does anyone else decorate their ride with that much gold?"

Freddy shook his head. "Jiārén all like gold trim, Emiko."

I scowled.

Freddy patted his pockets, searching for his weed bag with trembling hands. "It's still a win, though, right? I mean, the boat turned tail, we've got the Gate. Go us, right?"

I wondered what it would be like to live life so optimistically. I drew my gun and held it at the ready as I unlatched the container door. I wrenched the door open and shuffled back, bringing the gun up, my arms tight to my body, praying to the Dragon Father that Ray Ray hadn't stashed any more kinetics inside to protect the Gate.

The shipping container's rusty door creaked open, letting in the glow of early-afternoon light. No assassins awaited us inside. Only the Gate. Or what was left of the Gate. It had been smashed to a thousand pieces. Sunlight glittered across the bottom of the container, winking off fragments of shattered ebony. I sank to my knees, all the adrenaline crashing at once.

Behind me, Freddy's weed bag dropped to the ground with a plop. "Oh man, oh man, oh man."

Despair threatened to drown me. I gritted my teeth. The only way through it was forward. I saw no reason to wait any longer. I clapped my palms together twice, icy blue light spearing through the death mark. The smacking sound echoed within the shipping container as I summoned the shinigami.

# A FAVOR

The death god took it better than I was expecting. Or maybe he just had a really good game face. He merely said, "The Gate will not hold Yomi in this condition."

True.

The shinigami's yokai companion prowled over the broken pieces of the Gate, appearing to catalog the pieces in its notebook. As it moved, the faces on its robe seemed to move, eyes and mouths opening and closing in silent agony. I told myself it was just a trick of the light. If Freddy could see the yokai, he made no indication.

Numbness had set in. I couldn't feel the pain from my injuries, and my brain had stopped working. All I could think about was the horror of that ghost rushing at me from the underworld and Jessie, crying about her baby being menaced by wraiths. Images of the crying mothers and the prone nurses at Central Road General Hospital piled up, taunting me. I couldn't fail them.

But I also didn't want to spend eternity as a garden fixture. There had to be a way out of this mess. If only my brain would work correctly.

Freddy took a long drag on his joint. "Hey, the Gate is made of wood, right? Do you think an earth mender could fix it?"

I looked at Sugiwara, not yet daring to hope. Menders rarely came so far into cities, preferring to live closer to nature. Some lived in the borderlands, working to keep the cities from encroaching into the wilderness. Menders viewed cities as an inexorable cancer eating away at the earth. All menders sought harmony with nature and used their talent to protect and restore nature.

The shinigami's head tilted to one side, his unblinking eyes fixed on me like a carrion bird examining a fresh kill. I ignored the shiver of cold that ran up my back and kept my eyes fixed on his. After a long moment the death god turned away, looking into the battered container.

Sugiwara lifted his skeletal hands and a dull pulse of bitter-cold energy spread out from his fingertips. I blinked, half expecting frost to break off from my lashes. The cat yokai jumped off the pile and took its place at the shinigami's feet. Pieces of the shattered Gate began to move, shifting and sliding over each other, the hollow rattling sound like splinters of dry bone. He closed his eyes and the pieces swirled into a slow-moving vortex, the closest edge passing under his outstretched hand.

Freddy sidled up to me, his voice low and hoarse, pungent white smoke spilling from his lips. "What's he doing?"

Despite my varied and storied adventures, this time I was at a loss. "I honestly have no idea."

"Hmm. Right, right. He's not from around here, is he?"

The crushing sense of defeat in my chest was so great that I didn't even bat that one down. "No. Definitely from out of town."

He took another drag. "Wow."

I couldn't decide if slightly stoned Freddy was an improvement over optimistic Freddy. Stoned Freddy would turn into hungry Freddy later and eat all my pork buns. I sighed and reached into my bag to pull one out. It was time to eat defensively. I had a bad feeling that these buns were going to be breakfast, lunch, and dinner for us today.

The Gate shards clattered to a stop and Sugiwara turned to face us. "A mender may work. It is within the realm of possibility."

The yokai flipped through its notebook and presented a page covered in closely packed numbers. The shinigami nodded with satisfaction. "Nearly everything that made it a Gate is still here, albeit in pieces."

A dull ache bloomed behind my eyes. I knew what was coming. "The anchor is missing."

The shinigami reached into his robe and pulled out a small satchel of glowing white silk. With a wave of his hand the shattered remains of the Ebony Gate leapt into the air and streamed into the bag. When all the pieces had vanished, the bag was still no bigger than a grapefruit. The silk material bulged and flexed, as if the pieces inside were still moving, crawling over each other to get out.

"Yes, the anchor is missing. All the pieces to reassemble the Gate, the physical Gate, are here. A talented mender would indeed be able to restore it."

My gut sank into my shoes as Sugiwara droned on in his low monotone.

"Without the Lost Heart of Yázì, the creation of a new anchor will be necessary in order for the Gate to function as anything other than a garden decoration."

His red eyes turned to me. "Happily, I know exactly where to find an appropriate anchor."

Freddy slapped me on the back. "There! See! Everything's going to turn out okay!"

Despair and anger roiled through my chest, warring winds tearing at my mind. I fought to retain control, to not let myself slip into the maelstrom of emotion. I stood on the edge of a precipice, looking down into a valley of churning chaos. I had to save the city. I needed the Gate to save the city. I didn't want to lose my soul to the shinigami. I needed the Gate with the anchor to save my soul. I needed Tacchan to be safe.

Freddy's mouth moved. He looked like he was saying something, his eyes intent on me. Worried? I didn't hear him, in fact, I couldn't hear anything. The breeze off the bay, the raucous seabirds, the hum of trucks and machinery. It had all faded under a high-pitched tone ringing in my ears.

My hands clenched and unclenched, knuckles popping one after another. Two days ago my life had been as normal as I'd been able to make it in years.

In just two days, the forces I'd spent the last two years avoiding had upended everything, throwing my purpose-built life into mayhem. The shinigami. The Trans. The Louies. Ray Ray.

My eyes widened. Ray Ray Louie.

The whine in my ears stopped and my hearing returned. Freddy snapped his fingers in front of my face, his brow creased with worry.

"Emi? You okay in there?"

I felt the faint glimmer of hope trying to emerge. I turned slowly to the shinigami. "If I can find the Lost Heart of Yázì, we can anchor the Gate with it?"

The demon cat flipped through its notebook. The pages fanned past in a blur with a smell like stale spices and dry sand. The shinigami knelt to examine the pages as they passed. He nodded to the cat and the yokai snapped the book shut, then disappeared in a swirl of white mist.

The shinigami straightened. "Yes, if I had the Lost Heart of Yázì, the Ebony Gate can be restored to its original purpose. However, the chance of regaining the Heart by tonight is vanishingly small, even for someone of your reputation."

He was right, finding a gemstone the size of my fist in the entire city of San Francisco was the proverbial needle in a haystack. Unless I knew where to look.

Ray Ray was well known to be a weak heir. He played at being a powerful Jiārén but in reality he fixated on the material things his station brought to him. My mind flashed back to Ray Ray outside the hospital, puffed up and preening, bedecked in sparkling gold and jewels. Could his greed have gotten the best of him?

I'd seen him with a ghost master, and a ghost master had been tailing me since this whole debacle started. It was beyond unlikely that two ghost masters would be in San Francisco at the same time. I'd been working the problem in the wrong direction. I didn't need to find the ghost master. I needed to find Ray Ray and squeeze him like a ripe mango.

"When I get it back, can you reset it into the Ebony Gate while the mender repairs the Gate?"

"Yes, of course. However, the anchor must be specifically tuned to the Gate's purpose, and if—"

I held up my hands, not even caring right now that I was so rudely interrupting a death god. "Right. You can do it."

I looked up at the sun. "I have until midnight. The terms of the Talon say I have until midnight to deliver the Ebony Gate to you in functioning order. It says nothing about what I may or may not do with my time until then."

The shinigami held my gaze a moment longer before tucking away the silk bag with the Gate fragments. He put his hands into the pockets of his overcoat and turned away from me, as if I didn't exist anymore. "Very well."

I grabbed Freddy's arm and headed for the main gates. His pupils were wide and black, and there was no way I was letting him "drive" us back to the city in this state.

He stumbled along beside me, his voice a little mushy now. "Where we goin'?"

"Where people keep their jewelry, Tran. We're going to the bank."


The shinigami insisted on coming with us, making comments about protecting his investments. I mostly ignored him and shoved him into the front seat of the rideshare. I figured he was intimidating enough to keep the driver quiet and out of my hair.

As the car crawled north through traffic on 880, I pulled out my phone and rang Fiona. She picked up on the first ring and I skipped past all the pleasantries.

"I need a hand."

Fiona hesitated the barest fraction of a second. "My brother is already lending all available aid to—"

I cut her off. I didn't have time for this dance. "No. You foisted your brother on me, figuring he was the least amount of commitment you needed to satisfy the Talon."

From the other side of the car, Freddy mumbled, his eyes half-closed. "Hey man, nobody *foisted* me . . ."

I continued railing into Fiona. It felt good to direct my anger somewhere. I got Fiona caught up on events since last night. She gasped when I described the ghost attack at the hospital and groaned when I explained what had happened to the crane at the Port of Oakland. I left out the part about seeing Kamon at the hospital.

"Your brother's got heart and nerve, but this is beyond his depth. The Louies are up to their necks in this and I'm going to keep shaking this tree. Things are going to get worse and your brother's going to need more than just an Advocate."

Silence stretched before Fiona spoke again. "You don't make a very convincing case, Mimi."

I snorted in frustration. "Don't play games with me. Ray Ray was here! In Oakland! And don't call me Mimi."

She harrumphed. "Did Freddy see him?"

I turned to find Freddy snoring, his head propped against the window.

"No, he didn't. But that doesn't mean Ray Ray wasn't there."

Fiona gave a light laugh. "Things move so fast in battle. You said yourself that the car drove off. I think you can agree that another Hoard family is entitled to more than mere speculation."

"The Louies have had someone named Anthony Chow following me for the last two days. Why would they do that if not to keep me from finding the Gate?"

"And you're sure this Chow is on the Louie payroll?"

"I believe they were together for lunch on Lotus Lane."

Fiona sniffed. "Many of us eat lunch on Lotus Lane. A Hoard family deserves the benefit of the doubt, don't you think?"

My teeth ground together so hard I was afraid I'd crack a molar.

Hoard family nonsense. Right. I should be grateful that Fiona didn't let me forget who I was dealing with. I hardened my resolve and channeled my father. "You do not get to dictate how I conduct my investigation. You will render aid to me at the bank or I will declare forfeit and cry feud on your clan."

Feuding was extraordinarily costly in terms of human capital, and to be avoided by any means necessary. Despite my self-imposed alienation from my family, I knew my father would never suffer an insult like the Trans' shoddy response to a Soong Talon Call.

Fiona tsked. "There's no need for that. Of course we will continue to render aid."

"Mm-hmm." I waited.

She sighed. "You know I am bound by the terms of the treaty."

The treaty my mother had negotiated. Even in absentia, she continued to interfere in my life. As per usual when I dealt with her. I growled. "I am not asking you to break the treaty."

Fiona shuddered. "Yes, we wouldn't want your mother to have to come to town, would we?"

No one wanted to see my mother here. If she was here, it wasn't for pleasantries. She would drop the hammer and if the Louies and Trans had thought the treaty was bad, my mother meting out the Council's justice would be far worse.

"I just need you to go to the bank, Fiona."

Silence stretched for a long, tense moment. We were in a gray area here on the Talon duty but I knew I needed her backing at the bank.

Fiona's response came slowly. "Well, I have been unhappy with the level of service at their bank. I will bring a cohort with me to withdraw my holdings from the Louies' bank. If what you say is true, you can flush them out there. If you were mistaken, then no harm done and we can walk away."

This was a major concession. If I had to bet money on it, Fiona was thinking about what had happened at the pier. Someone had messed with her employees. With Freddy. If that someone was Ray Ray, it was worth a little visit to the bank to find out. "Deal. See you in twenty minutes in front of Central Road Bank."

I clicked off, irritation like an itchy coat against my skin. Unfortunately, the next step was going to be worse. I needed to find a mender. The closest one was maybe in Vancouver and if she wasn't available, then Taiwan. I surrendered to the inevitable.

I was going to have to call my father.

I quickly did the math. It was almost two in the afternoon here, which meant it was morning the next day in Tokyo. Father would be awake. I sighed, took out my phone, and huddled into the corner of the car, trying to buy a little privacy from Freddy. Even after all the attempts to contact me, my father still made me wait for five rings before he picked up.

"Bàba, it's me."

I pictured my father in his garden, sitting on the stone bench overlooking the koi pond. Maybe he was having his second cup of Iron Goddess tea by now.

"Mimi, bǎobèi." I heard the gentle reproof in his voice.

Guilt nagged at me for always dodging his calls.

I summarized the events of the last two days as quickly as I could, leaving out anything that didn't relate to my immediate needs.

I pushed on and finally got to my ask. "So you see, we're going to need an earth mender."

Father grunted. "Not many around."

I knew that. But I also knew that Father had relationships with *everybody* so I waited. With Father, patience was always a virtue. In the background I heard the soft sounds of Sugi prowling around, the clicks of wood on stone. Finally he said, "I think that Lin-Lin Chang in Taiwan is your best bet. Better than Ah Wing in Vancouver."

I sighed. "Bàba, Vancouver is a lot closer. Is there a reason we can't call them both?" Father never did anything without weighing the political cost. No doubt there were favors and obligations that would be tied to this for everyone involved afterward. But San Francisco was worth it.

"Of course, of course. I will call them both for you."

I knew he would. The only issue would be what he would expect for it. I waited again. Experience had taught me to offer as little as possible when speaking with my father. I only needed to wait for him to fill the silence.

"Tatsuya would like you to come home for Lóng Yá." And there it was. He wanted me to come home. Lóng Yá was the dragon's maw that we made all our elite talents run through at the end of their years at the academy. Not every student had to run through this particular gauntlet but ones with something to prove did. For every hundred students at the academy, there might be only two or three that would go through the final Tourney. Hoard families required their young to run the Tourney. My brother was more than capable and everyone would expect him to take first in the Tourney . . . unless there was another Hoard family in contention.

My father had couched it as a request from Tacchan, but I could read between the lines well enough. I didn't doubt that Tatsuya had asked Father to inquire after me, and maybe he'd even wondered aloud if I would return in time to watch his Tourney. I did, however, doubt that Father would ask it of me if it didn't benefit him in some way. My father never did anything for free, and he rarely did anything in one step when he could take three or four and squeeze some profit out of it.

I had mixed feelings about watching my brother's Tourney. I'd never endured that particular gauntlet because I'd failed out of Lóng Kŏu the first year. Based on everything I had ever heard about the Tourney, I didn't feel as if I'd missed anything. But on the other hand, I'd spent most of my adult life taking out magical targets using just my smarts and sharp steel. A part of me wanted to know if I could've taken out powerhouses like Fiona and Freddy.

The idea of being there as Tatsuya competed and cemented his place as the next Head of our Clan was surprisingly appealing. I didn't regret leaving Tokyo, and never felt homesick, but now the thought of going to Tokyo and to the Soong estate filled me with bittersweet longing. Knowing my father, he had already considered everything that had just gone through my head and asked his question in just the right way to ensure that he got the only answer he was looking for.

I closed my eyes, silently cursing my meddling father. "Of course, Bàba."

I could practically see him on the other end, pleased as punch. "I will send tokens." It was definitely faster to use a token to travel by portal but for a split second I wished I could just take a commercial flight to visit my father. It was so much easier on my stomach.

"Thank you, Bàba. I will let you know what happens." I hung up with a sigh of relief.

It would take some time for my father to make arrangements. Neither Vancouver nor Taipei had a portal nexus that could bring them to San Francisco. Transportation, fast transportation, would be a tough problem. But my father excelled at tough problems. I liked to think I'd inherited that trait from him. In any case, I hoped for a few hours leeway until the mender arrived. It was still early afternoon and there was plenty of time left before midnight. For now, everything was moving along ahead of schedule.

The thought of confronting the pompous scion of the Louie family on his home turf sent a shot of adrenaline through my system. I was getting that anchor back no matter what it took.

Despite being half-baked or maybe because of it, Freddy was an easy companion. Minus the pot, Freddy reminded me a little of my brother, Tacchan. They both had that carefree demeanor and quiet confidence.

It had surprised me when Freddy had gotten so rattled on the pier, but then the illusionist was probably his first real fight beyond his rounds in the Tourney. I finally let myself voice my concerns about Tacchan getting through his Tourney.

"Hey, Tran, you completed Lóng Yá, right?"

The smile on his face faded. "Yeah, it was rough."

I thought about Tatsuya, who had combat abilities even more frightening than our father's. Tacchan would be fine. He had to be. I'd left home two years ago, but really, I'd stopped being at home since I left at age twelve. The last time I'd spent any amount of time with my brother we had both been so small. I tried to imagine him, nearly grown and ready to finish at the academy. I couldn't do it. My mind kept putting his pudgy baby face on a taller body. It didn't work.

If Tacchan did well in the Tourney, my parents would finally have what they wanted. My brother would be a worthy heir to secure the Soong Clan and safeguard our Hoard for another generation. Tacchan would get down to the nitty-gritty of learning Father's role and eventually shopping around for a suitable marriage. Maybe my parents would finally stop pestering me about coming back to the nest, leaving me free to live my life without Jiārén interference. My tenuous foray into freedom was stretched thin with the entrance of the shinigami's Talon Call but I had to get through this and find the Gate. For my sake and for Tacchan's sake.

"My brother Tatsuya will be heading into the Tourney soon."

Freddy didn't respond.

I looked back and Freddy seemed unusually subdued. "Come on, it wasn't that bad, was it?"

He looked up and his mouth quirked up at the corner. He seemed to think for a moment before he spoke. "You didn't make many friends there, did you?"

I'd made exactly zero friends there. "Well, seeing as I was there for less than a year . . ."

"No, I mean, you don't even hang with other academy brats afterward. I hear all about your little brother through the grapevine, Emiko. I don't ever hear anything about you."

After my failure at the academy, my parents had fostered me out to a secret society of assassins, so no, I didn't socialize much.

I turned to look out the car window and thought of a way to answer Freddy without having to explain about my time with Ogata-sensei. Our car crawled through the Bay Bridge toll plaza and melded into the myriad lanes merging beyond the toll plaza. "I guess hanging with the cool kids was never really my scene. Not even the Black Tortoise talents would be caught hanging out with a dud like me."

Freddy laughed, the sound utterly without humor. "Man, most of those cool kids were just poseurs. You just didn't see any of this, Emiko. The lead-up to the Tourney? It's brutal. The instructors get inside your head. They know what you're most afraid of. They use it all, turning you against who you thought were your friends. And in the end . . . what was any of it good for?"

Tacchan was entering the Tourney. How might it change him? Our family was small, and Tacchan's future was already set. He had almost nothing to gain from competing—well, other than fulfilling our parents' high expectations. Of course, our parents' expectations were also our society's expectations. I sighed. I looked up to find Freddy looking at me intently.

Freddy gave me a tight smile. "Tatsuya will be fine. He's strong and he doesn't need to win. If I were you, I'd tell him not to get caught up in the game because that's all it is. A big game."

I hoped he was right. Freddy leaned back against the headrest and closed his eyes.

We cleared the new half of the bridge and traffic loosened getting through the Treasure Island tunnel. A subtle tingle of energy through my limbs let me know that we had crossed back into San Francisco, the city's magic once again able to reach me. Ahead of us, the sun began to move lower to the horizon, an ominous countdown to the gate to Yomi opening after sunset. I willed the traffic to move faster. It was going to be a long day and night and I had so much legwork ahead of me. The few hours of sleep I'd gotten at Grandma's hadn't put much of a dent in the beating from last night. As our car sped across the bridge, the tires thumped rhythmically over the seams in the bridge like a metronome set to the music of the city. For once, the sound was a soothing balm and lulled me to sleep.

*I am kneeling on an old and worn tatami in a centuries-old dojo. The tatami is shiny from the shuffling of thousands of feet, and has seen the rise and fall of dynasties. Faded black-and-white photographs of old masters hang in plain black frames along the walls. They turn their stern eyes to me and judge me. I feel displaced and disgraceful, kneeling on this revered surface clad only in street clothes.*

*In the center of the longest wall, a single blade is displayed, a simple tanto, the handle wrapped in black, the tsuba and the scabbard both flat black. I have never seen a blade like this, with no ornamentation at all. And yet in this environment, its presence feels right, a minimalist stroke of art.*

*The mat creaks as someone else steps onto it. A whisper-quiet shuffle of feet across the aged straw mats. Father and Mother take*

*their places on either side of me and kneel. Ogata-sensei kneels be-*
*low the tanto, facing us, his face devoid of emotion, his eyes boring*
*into mine. He is dressed in a plain black gi, the borders worn to*
*pale gray from years of use. Despite the wear, the garment is still*
*clean and tidy, obi tied with exacting precision. His face is lean, all*
*hard lines and angles, his hair cut brutally short, jaw clean shaven.*
*A ragged, white scar runs along the right side of his jawline, from*
*ear to throat. A killing wound. He sits as still as a stone and does*
*not speak for a long time.*

*I fidget. My legs are going numb, the creases of my pants dig-*
*ging into my shins. I hear the slightest exhalation of breath from*
*my father, to my right. I look at him and recognize the expression*
*on his face. The one that says,* Do not shame me. Not now.

*The guilt weighing on my shoulders redoubles.*

*The silence in the dojo stretches on. I am nearly ready to break,*
*to scream at my father, when Ogata-sensei finally speaks, his voice*
*a low, rumbling rasp. I wonder if his voice is the result of the scar*
*on his neck. "She has no patience, no tranquility. The Jōkōryūkai*
*has only trained one woman before, a most unique exception."*

*My train of thought careens off the rails at the mention of the*
*Jōkōryūkai. I have only heard stories of them. The Association. Wild*
*rumors from the darkest corners of the internet whispering of deadly*
*assassins for hire, a secret society of killers trained in dark arts. My*
*mind whipsaws between the idea that the Jōkōryūkai are not only*
*real, but that my parents are somehow associated with them.*

*My surprise increases when my father bows his head until his*
*forehead touches the mat. Father never bows that low to anyone.*

*Father speaks without rising. "She can be taught, sensei. She*
*must be taught. She will be your greatest student."*

*Ogata-sensei huffs an indignant half laugh. "A kunoichi? My*
*greatest student?"*

*Father rises from his bow. "The Jōkōryūkai have already trained*
*one with an aura like hers. No one else can do this."*

*Shame flushes up my back and neck, and my face grows hot. My parents bid me unfurl my aura so I do. I tense thinking of what Ogata-sensei must think. I have never seen my aura, I only know it is not like Father's or Mother's. Their auras are glorious, aching in their beauty and power. I am their shame, a daughter with no Hoard gift. My short tenure at Lóng Kǒu has trained me to keep my aura masked at all times, my terrible burden to carry for all my days.*

*I look at the torn skin on my knuckles and laugh bitterly. I am definitely finished with Lóng Kǒu. My meridians are a tangled mess and I have no talent to speak of. What will become of me now? Of my family? My clan?*

*I look at my father but his gaze is implacable. I turn to my mother. She faces forward, staring blankly into the middle space. Why would I have expected help from her? I swallow, my throat hot and thick. My skin prickles with heat and I stare at the tatami, trying to find a pattern in the worn straw.*

*Ogata-sensei's calloused feet appear before me. I look up the expanse of his gi to his hard, dark eyes. "Stand."*

*When I stand he takes me by the wrist and leads me to the center of the mat. His grip is surprisingly gentle, but his touch moves me like he has command of my faculties. Mother and Father have not moved from where they kneel at the side of the tatami; their eyes do not meet mine.*

*Ogata-sensei turns me to face him and he raises his right arm to chest level.*

*Oh gods, no.*

*He frowns at me as I hesitate and just the look in his eyes is enough to terrify me. I raise my right arm to his, dread like a writh-ing ball of worms in my gut.*

*When our arms connect, Ogata-sensei pushes into me. I have not performed this exercise in some time, so my response is slow, awkward, clumsy. If Ogata-sensei is disappointed at my lack of skill it does not show. I accept his push, redirect it, and push back, now leaning into him. His response to my lackluster energy is graceful, like free-flowing water.*

*We cycle like this, with no variation, until I have regained some semblance of dignity. When Ogata-sensei senses my stability he alters the movement, going higher or lower, forcing me to pay attention, to adapt.*

*It takes a few more cycles to understand what he is doing, and by then it is too late. As surely as he drew me onto the tatami he guides my movements now. It is as if my arm is glued to his. With each cycle his qì pushes through our connection and into me. My insides burn as qì is forced through my wrecked meridians.*

*My shame is revealed. My qì flow is a disaster, making me unable to perform even the simplest expression of a Hoard gift. Connected as I am with Ogata-sensei, I know he can sense the deformity within me. Why are my parents subjecting me to this? Haven't I suffered enough?*

*Ogata-sensei grunts, a sound of surprise, and our impromptu lesson comes to an end. I sway on my feet, feeling strangely off-balance. I retake my place between my parents. The sensei walks across the tatami, stopping before one of the oldest picture frames. The wizened old man in the picture is bald, his face serious. Ogata-sensei appears to consult with the dead man for several minutes before speaking. "Her Hoard gift is . . . dangerous. I myself had hoped never to see it."*

*The mat creaks to my left. I turn and my jaw nearly drops. Mother looks at me and then bows her head to the mat.*

*"Ogata-sensei. If you train my daughter. I would consider it . . . a favor. To me."*

*Mother is a member of the Bā Shǒu, but anyone paying attention knows that she is on the short list to ascend to the Bā Tóu—or she*

*would have been if my father wasn't already on the Bā Tóu Coun-*
*cil. Between that and her legendary talent, she is powerful. And*
*dangerous.*

*Ogata-sensei frowns but the expression does not reach his eyes.*
*His eyes are curious, questioning. "Her talent could destroy your*
*clan. You would trust me with this secret?"*

*Father answers before I can ask what he is talking about. "There*
*is no other we would trust with it."*

*Mother chimes in. "She will need protection. Protection that*
*you can provide, along with training to defend herself in the future.*
*Her path will be treacherous."*

*Ogata-sensei seems to make up his mind. He returns to stand*
*before us. My parents rise and I follow them. My head is spinning.*
*Why is Ogata-sensei talking about my nonexistent talent? How*
*can that be dangerous? My knuckles burn and I try to remember*
*that the fight was only this morning, a few hours ago. Mother has*
*vouched for me, in some way. Something I would never have ex-*
*pected. I have no idea what is happening and everything is moving*
*too fast.*

*A hand grabs my arm, the grip firm. I can feel the strength in*
*those hands. Ogata-sensei stands before me, his gaze assessing*
*me. His expression is that of a painter examining a blank canvas.*

*"A favor from the Hiroto family is much appreciated, but I think*
*what you are asking of me requires something more." Ogata-*
*sensei's raspy voice says the words slowly, ending on a ponderous*
*note.*

*My mother reaches into the sleeve of her robe and withdraws a*
*Talon, the gold catching in the light. Without pause, she pricks her*
*thumb on the sharp point and I gasp. She smears her blood across*
*the engraved hanzi and proffers it to Ogata-sensei with two hands.*

*Ogata-sensei bows over the offering, and pricks his right thumb*
*as well. "I will train her as Jōkōryūkai's finest. Witness."*

*My father echoes, "So witnessed."*

*He nods quickly, once, and turns on his heel, dragging me with him. He marches me to an open door at the far end of the dojo. I look back. Father and Mother have not moved. Father's eyes follow me. Mother has returned to looking into the empty middle space.*

*It is the last time I will see them for many years and I will have time to curse my mother for her help.*

# THE BANK

My nap had been too short and far from restful. Talking to Freddy had rubbed the scab off my old wound of failing out of Lóng Kǒu . . . and what happened after. I stepped out of the rideshare and flexed my neck from side to side, getting a satisfying pop as I did.

I looked down at my jacket. Most of the blood had dried now, making the stain less obvious. The bleeding seemed to have stopped, which was good. Although the tape restricted my arm and shoulder considerably, which was bad. Maybe Popo would take pity on me and stitch me back up later. If there was a later.

We stood in front of the bank on Lotus Lane. It wasn't just any bank, it was Central Road Bank, the preeminent banking option for Jiārén on the West Coast. Under one name or another, this bank had served its clients for over a hundred years. Within these walls, the Louie family owned every last brick, and every ounce of gold, and had used their wealth to power their influence up and down the West Coast of the United States. Today, the man in charge of the bank was Raymond Louie, Jr., aka "Ray Ray," acting CEO, the not-so-secret shame of the Louies.

The graceful building soared three stories, a monument to classical architecture, with white Corinthian columns and surrounded by tall, old-growth redwoods. It was a hidden oasis of calm, just off the corner of California Street and Lotus Lane. Even the city's constant clamoring for my attention seemed muted here, calmer. Maybe it was an effect of the trees.

EBONY GATE 295

The bank building, which took up nearly a third of the block, had been built toward the end of California's Gold Rush and was the only building in Chinatown to survive the Great Earthquake and Fire of 1906. It helped that the Lóng Jiārén had a fair number of water talents to protect their holdings. After the Great Fire, the Louie Clan had hired metallurgist talents who had woven a powerful filigree throughout the frame, reinforcing the structure and allowing it to flex and survive more earthquakes. Central Road Bank was a testament to Dragon power and money, providing a trusted vault and confidential transactions for its clientele.

To me, the building itself also reflected that the Louies were pragmatists, willing to pay for other talents to complement their own charisma-based skills. In that, we had something in common.

Fiona stepped out of a pristine white Range Rover, resplendent in a tan Burberry trench over a clingy pink knit dress and black Chanel platform slingbacks with gold logo clips. Her lips were painted red, full and matte. She'd opted for a smoky eye. Everything about her screamed money, power, and haute couture. I wondered if this was her usual business attire. I envied her the certainty and status she possessed in our world. I wanted to dislike her but I couldn't fault her for holding onto her station with an iron grip.

Like me, she chose her weapons with care. She wielded her looks and clothing the way I used my swords. I wasn't a fan of fashion for fashion's sake, but I understood the power that clothing had, whether it was to dress to fit in or dress to stand out. Fiona chose to stand out and it worked for her.

I spotted Franklin at the wheel of her Range Rover, his distinctive jaw chiseled from rock. He turned to look at me and even from behind his dark aviator shades, his disapproval washed over me like a hot wind.

A small fleet of pearlescent Escalades surrounded the Range Rover, disgorging an army of the finest dressed henchmen I'd ever seen. Claw and fang! Fiona's entire fleet of cars sported brilliant white leather interiors. When this was all over I would need the number to wherever she got her cars detailed.

All of Fiona's men wore fitted gray sharkskin suits with mandarin collars. Lotus blooms embroidered in silver thread ran up each man's left lapel and over his shoulder. Roughly half of Fiona's crew were women, dressed in matching gray suits as well, accented with deadly-looking Louboutin pumps. The women wore hammered silver lotus blooms pinned to their hair. Doors slammed and Fiona's crew gathered around her in a loose circle, affecting casual poses.

A quick glance over Fiona's team told me that her entourage had been with the family for many years, earning their silver through loyalty and service.

Two stood out as Fiona's senior lieutenants. Franklin cracked his knuckles and used his linebacker build to begin shooing away the midday shoppers. Sunlight glittered off the rings on his thick fingers. On the opposite side of the group, a compact woman in a pageboy cut gave terse orders in a quiet voice. Fiona and Freddy's formidable cousin, Linh. In addition to the lotus brooch on her lapel, she also wore stacked silver bracelets on both arms. Quiet but intense power thrummed from them like they were made from banked embers.

Fiona's lieutenants deployed her entourage with practiced efficiency, using the fleet of SUVs to blockade the entire block and establish a perimeter. Technically there wasn't any parking in front of the bank, but of course, Fiona's team ignored all the NO PARKING signs. Hoard family privilege was handy sometimes.

I didn't miss that they managed to arrange themselves to put eyes on all the surrounding buildings. Despite the casual air, every one of Fiona's goons radiated danger. Some of them held tightly controlled auras. Others carried a slight tension in the hips and shoulders that indicated a propensity for violence. I noted a lot of crossed arms, which kept hands close to sheathed weapons.

Goatee Guy stepped out from the Range Rover as well and shadowed Fiona as she walked toward us.

Upon seeing Freddy, Fiona rushed forward to give him a big hug and then hauled back and smacked his head. I was impressed that she didn't launch into the both of us for leaving multiple dead bodies on the Tran business premises and sticking her with the cleanup. Again. That was another thing that made it impossible to dislike Fiona—she was genuinely caring toward her brother and she demonstrated that her priorities were his well-being and honoring the Talon. A class act.

She obviously did not appreciate being summoned across town to the bank, but came nonetheless. I admired the way she handled her business.

Goatee Guy reached into his pocket and pulled out a bottle of hand sanitizer. My eyebrows shot up. Really?

Freddy held out his hands and Goatee Guy squirted a blob of minty-green gel in each hand. "Thanks, Willy."

The sharp scent of alcohol tickled my nose. Willy gestured to my hands. Fiona looked at me expectantly. Fine. I gamely held out my hands for Willy to dose me. I had no idea Fiona was such a germophobe. How would she react if she knew my jacket was covered in dried blood?

Fiona tilted her nose up and waved a hand at her fleet of shiny Escalades. "Okay, I'm here. It's high time we moved our assets anyway. I don't know why I put up with Ray Ray in the first place. So far, I'm only here to make a very large withdrawal, unless I am convinced otherwise." Fiona put a hand on her hip, her impatience clear.

I pulled out the phone I'd taken from Baldy and showed it to them. I'd hit pay dirt with the recent calls list. "See these?"

Multiple calls from the same number, which ended in two zeros. I tapped the number to dial it back. After two rings, a pleasant young man's voice greeted us. "Central Road Bank, your business is our business. How may I assist you today?"

I clicked off.

Fiona's eyes narrowed. "Mimi, everyone banks here."

The connection was thin, but my gut told me the Louies had their fingers in every pie in town, including this one. "Don't call me Mimi. Who gets this many calls *from* the bank?"

I ticked off my arguments on my fingers. "I spotted a ghost master with Ray Ray yesterday on Lotus Lane. I'm positive that same ghost master has been shadowing me all day. Who else but the ghost master could raise the army of undead kappas we saw last night? Ray Ray was at your port in the company of the Gate. Do you really think Ray Ray or Uncle Jimmy would let this ghost master stir things up like this if they weren't ordering him to do it?"

Fiona wasn't dumb, and I suspected she didn't like where this was going. I closed the phone and watched the wheels spin in her head. I'd watched my father do the same thing, calculating the political fallout of one path versus another, holding the fate of fortunes and lives in the palm of his hand.

Linh silently materialized at Fiona's side with a folded paper in her hand. "Data dive just found this, Fi."

Fiona took the paper and opened it. She scanned it, her face a stony mask. Fiona would be a hell of a poker player. She looked up and her eyes speared through me, as if trying to decide what to do with me.

"What?"

Fiona turned the paper around. "Is this him?"

The printout was black and white, and grainy, but the lean, pockmarked cheeks and wide eyes were a sure thing. I nodded.

Linh took the printout back and tucked it away inside her blazer. "Mr. Chow has an extensive record with the Wàirén authorities, so he was easy to find. Despite many run-ins with the police, he's never spent any time in lockup. His legal fees and services are always handled by Kawamoto and Yuen, who also happen to be the Louie family law firm."

Fiona smirked at my shocked expression. "What, did you think that because I pooh-poohed your assertion before that I wasn't going to follow up on it?"

My estimate of Fiona went up a notch. I had chosen correctly when allying with her.

Her eyes darted to Freddy. He still had concrete dust in his dark hair and dark circles had formed under his eyes. The kid was exhausted. Fiona's eyes softened for a moment before becoming imperious again.

"Well? Anything to add?"

Freddy looked around, apparently surprised to hear Fiona addressing him. I guessed he wasn't used to it. "Hmm? Well, there was a blinged-out Benzo at the port. Could have been Ray Ray's."

His eyes flicked to me and then to his feet. "I didn't see Ray Ray, though. Didn't see anyone inside the car."

Freddy met my eyes with a shrug. "Sorry, Emiko. You told me to watch the boat, so I was watching the boat. Then the crane came down on us and . . ."

He trailed off as Fiona's cheeks turned three shades redder. Freddy looked back and forth between me and his sister. "That one's on me, Fifi, not Emiko. I got a little carried away . . . For what it's worth, I think Emiko's on the right track. Something's fishy. If it's the Louies, we need to know. One way or the other."

My eyebrows just about crawled up into my hair. I hadn't expected much from Freddy, given his unwillingness to get involved in clan politics. Maybe Fiona sticking me with her brother had turned out to be in my favor after all. I kept the smile off my face and turned to face Fiona.

Fiona's sharp eyes flashed between us, a lioness who didn't know what to do with her unruly cubs. I chose discretion over valor and kept my mouth shut, letting her stew for a moment.

If I was right, the Louies had infiltrated the Trans' shipping office, making Fiona an unwilling accomplice in their crime, and one of their heavies had taken a serious swing at her brother. She must have concluded the same. Fiona's mouth settled into a hard line and her eyes darkened. I nearly cheered. Fiona's hackles were up, giving me a powerful ally.

Fiona brought out a compact to check her makeup. "Fine. I'll get you inside. From there you're on your own."

Sugiwara-sama had remained silent since our arrival, keeping his own counsel. But now was the time to lay all our cards on the table.

I looked pointedly at the death god. "Now would be a good time for you to tell us why anybody would want to take the Ebony Gate."

The shinigami rose to his full height and his illusion fell away, his camel topcoat disintegrating into streamers of white mist. Cries of alarm went up throughout Fiona's entourage. Freddy backed up a step, his eyes wide and staring. Only Fiona seemed to be unfazed, continuing to touch up her powder.

Sugiwara spoke slowly, his words careful. "A century ago, another placed a powerful no-look ward on the Gate for me. I believe that recently someone was able to see through it and realized what it was." He paused, then added, "There are always those who wish to unleash the power of the underworld. Powerful death talents are always attracted to the underworld."

I wanted the shinigami to say more but he stopped talking.

Freddy rubbed at his eyes and then stared at the shinigami. He looked at me in shock and made gestures behind the shinigami's back. I interpreted them as Freddy saying, "Really, dude? You didn't tell me about the death god?!"

I shrugged.

Fiona seemed less impressed by the fact that a shinigami was gracing us with his presence. She cocked her head. "What use do the Louies have for a Gate to Yomi?" That was the million-dollar question. There were very few known Gates and they were keyed to certain locations. The Ebony Gate had been used more as a seal but Jiārén typically treated a Gate as a means of rapid transport that connected us through the Void. At least, that was how I understood Gates and their anchors to work.

Freddy grabbed my arm. "Emiko, the container only had the Gate, not the anchor."

Something in my head clicked like a switch and little details from the past two days flashed across my mind, including the Ninth Dragon sculpture at the hospital.

I turned to Sugiwara. "Could the Ebony Gate be connected to a new destination with a different anchor?"

The death god nodded. "Yes, of course. This is the nature of—"

I was stunned. I was also an idiot. It had never crossed my mind that we were dealing with a Realmseeker. They were rare and secretive . . . and quite frankly, insane. I ran through what would be the perfect storm. The known Gates were heavily guarded. A Realmseeker would have to find an unattended Gate since it would be suicide to storm a heavily guarded one. Check. They'd have to be crazy enough to think they could survive a journey to the Realm. By definition Realmseekers were zealots who believed we should return to the Realm. Check. They would have to work a powerful rending spell on that Gate to tear the fabric of this world to reach the Realm. Only one of the eight Hoard families might have the power to work such a rending. Were the Louies in cahoots with Realmseekers? Was it too far-fetched?

I nodded. "Someone in the Louie Clan is a Realmseeker."

The silence that followed my pronouncement would not have been more awkward if I had declared that I was a panda. It wasn't every day you accused a Hoard family of harboring a lunatic amongst their numbers.

Fiona was the first to react. "Mimi, come on, that's—"

"Don't call me Mimi. Fiona, after everything you've heard today, can you afford not to investigate?"

I knew my father would, and that meant Fiona would. As the Head of the Clan they were both driven by the same set of priorities. I was tired of letting the Louies steer the ship. It was time to bring this to a head and Fiona's fury would be the catalyst to do it.

I pulled out the little tub of Baby Ricky's skepticism cream and opened it. The pungent cream smelled of spice and citrus and warmed my skin as I rubbed it along the curves of both my ears. The lozenges hadn't been enough for Jimmy, but Ray Ray's talent was a cheap imitation of his father's and uncle's.

The Tran twins looked at me with raised eyebrows, their elitism showing. "Look guys, I know it smells weird, but it works."

Fiona shrugged and dabbed a little cream behind both earlobes. She rubbed her fingers together, inhaling the scent of the cream. "How quaint."

Freddy declined the cream when I offered it to him. Guess he still thought he was too good for my herbal remedy.

The shinigami watched this with interest and I wondered how often he spent this much time in the presence of the living. No doubt he was studying our expressions and mannerisms, cataloging them for future use. In the absence of our attention he had again clad himself in illusion.

Fiona signaled her guards to remain with the vehicles and then she marched up to the building and pushed in the double doors to the sprawling white marble entryway. Gold dragon fixtures clawed their way across the cornices. Dark wood paneling trimmed the walls and doorways. A white granite counter flecked with gold leaf ran the perimeter of the central lobby, dotted with teller windows. The tellers stood behind bulletproof glass. I squinted and a shield aura appeared, parallel with the glass, rendering it fire- and hex proof as well. *Very nice.*

Dozens of paper lanterns hung from the high ceiling, casting the room in warm light. Faint power drifted down from the lanterns carrying the scent of black sesame. The bank hummed with the quiet, machinelike efficiency you only got with massive wealth and tight management.

A dizzying wave of sensation swept through me as I stood in there. The city's Jiārén clustered here and this bank's protection had been reinforced with generations of talents. I gritted my teeth and stepped forward.

A cross section of San Francisco's Jiārén population waited patiently in line to do business with the bank. Lotus Lane merchants clad in rough work clothes stood elbow to elbow with businessmen in crisp, custom suits that could only have come from the tailors of a Hoard family. The merchants carried satchels of cash, the businessmen briefcases that might contain anything from gold bars to ancient artifacts. No one fidgeted in line, and not one raised voice disturbed the quiet sounds of clinking coinage and scratching pens. I eyed the lanterns again. Interesting. The Louies had canned their charm speak as security measure.

As I walked past the entryway and into the main room, electric sparks coursed up my back. I slowed down, stifling my reaction. A bank of this pedigree held not only vast sums of liquid assets; there were sure to be a significant number of Hoard artifacts here as well. The bedrock below the bank was saturated in magic, a heavy overflow from the accumulated wealth of several Jiārén clans stored in one place.

The city's call to me had been loudest on Lotus Lane. But here, it was screaming directly into my brain. The power beneath my feet nearly set my teeth to vibrating. The stone had been unearthed from a local quarry and the massive framing pillars sourced from local old-growth trees. I stood inside the city's bones, atop a wellspring of its power, and the city's magic threatened to drown my senses.

With my senses being bombarded, I didn't notice the security guard until he tapped my shoulder. Six feet of brawny muscle stood behind me, packed into a gray work shirt that strained at the buttons.

The broad expanse of his chest seemed to meld directly into his heavily jowled face. The embroidery on his chest proclaimed that Sam with no neck was a valued member of Golden Dragon Security. "Ma'am, we're going to have to ask that you leave your swords and any other weapons in our custody while you bank here."

Fiona gave me an impatient look as I made my way back to the security office. I wondered why they were singling me out when half the people in this building were capable of bringing the roof down with a thought. I eyed the lanterns again.

Freddy followed and let out a low whistle as I withdrew my pistol from my side-draw holster. Security Sam gestured to my left ankle and I sighed for effect and pulled a knife out of my boot. I stood at the counter and waited. If he asked for my shurikens, they were using millimeter scanners. If not, then just regular metal detectors.

The security guard's aura was faint, barely any talent at all. Many years ago, he may have been fit and strong. He certainly still had the bulk of muscle under that soft layer of fat that spoke of a sedentary life and too many noodles. But his eyes remained keen and he sighed and pointedly looked at Truth's finely wrapped handle where it cleared my shoulder, and Hachi at my hip. I pulled Hachi off my hip and held it loosely in both hands.

Security Sam reached for the scabbard. I snapped my left hand out and grabbed his wrist, stopping his hand just inches from the lacquered wood. My thumb dug deep between his tendons and I applied a bit of pressure to the nerve. With a gasp he collapsed to the countertop. I did not release his hand. This was the closest any stranger had come to touching my swords in a long time.

His left arm flailed, trying to reach across his body for his sidearm. I increased the pressure on his wrist and he groaned in pain. I knew exactly what it felt like. He gave up on the gun and his left hand came up, readying to strike me. I whirled Hachi and jabbed the end of the scabbard into his solar plexus. His eyes bulged as his breath left him in a whoosh. His left hand closed over my left wrist, trying to free his hand. I didn't move. I'm a lot stronger than I look.

I heard Freddy's footsteps behind me and I warned him off with a glare. I pulled my arms in and dragged Sam across the counter until his face was scant inches from mine. "Do you know what this is?"

His dark eyes, bright with pain, widened in confusion. "A sword?"

The souls of generations of swordsmen howled in fury within me at the guard's ignorance. A part of me ached to draw Hachi, leap over the counter, and slash my blade through his abdomen, spill his entrails, and leave him to die in miserable agony like a butchered animal.

But I wasn't that person anymore. I was trying not to be that person.

I took a breath and held it a heartbeat, then let it out slowly. It helped me keep my voice soft when I next spoke.

"My swords are centuries old and have sent more souls to Yomi than some wars."

I twisted my wrist, dancing the reflected light from the scabbard across the guard's face. "The skills and techniques to make swords of this caliber were forgotten long before either of us was born. The skills with which to wield such a blade have been passed down in an unbroken line of swordsmen that ends with me.

"The last time I drew my blades in anger I took the right hands of over thirty people who had the temerity to insult my name and my clan."

I let my anger show on my face. My disgust at this lowly Louie minion even daring to put a finger on my sword. I smiled and bared my fangs. "Do you know who I am?"

Security Sam swallowed hard, recognition dawning in his eyes. "The—the Bu—the—"

I pulled him in closer and gritted my teeth, part of me hating myself for doing it. "Say. It."

The guard's voice was barely a whisper. "The Butcher?"

My eyes swept over the guard's regulation buzz-cut hair, rumpled shirt, the spreading sweat stains at the armpits. Security Sam was probably a vet, working for beer money, gone soft at a cushy security gig. This was so far above his pay grade and he knew it. He stood motionless and I knew it was fear of my reputation that held him still more than my hand on his wrist. He was just one more Louie pawn in my way. Regret flared in my chest at what I had done before to people just like him and what I was still doing now. Despite two years of saying I was no longer the Blade, when push came to shove, I always fell back on this. All the things that made me what they called me—the Butcher.

It would never stop until I was dead or until I truly stopped being the Butcher and started being something else. After this Talon Call, I was done. It was time I was something more than the Butcher.

My lips flattened in disgust at everything that had brought me into the Louies' den today. I would get the anchor for Tatsuya and our clan, and then I would never set foot in this cursed place again.

"Your job description does not extend to minding the Butcher's swords, Sam." He flinched as I said his name. "I will return for my guns and other knives shortly. Do you understand?"

Sam nodded briskly, his Adam's apple bobbing. I forced my fingers to uncurl from his wrist. A bright red crescent marked where my thumbnail had dug into his skin. Sam backed away, cradling his injured wrist. I spun on my heel, resecured Hachi, and stalked away before I did anything else I might regret.

Freddy fell in beside me. "Jeez, Emiko, went a little hard on the guy, didn't you?"

I ignored him.

We rejoined Fiona and walked into the main lobby of the bank. She lifted her nose in the air and tapped her foot, speaking into the room to no one in particular. "Why is no one assisting me?"

Two bank tellers rushed over, one tall and bald, with delicate features, the other shorter and younger with apple-round cheeks and short, pomaded hair. The young teller smiled obsequiously. "Ms. Tran, did you have an appointment today? How can we help you?"

How gratifying. The Trans must have significant holdings here. I just stayed quiet and watched Fiona work. My fingers still tingled from the adrenaline. From atop her Chanel heels Fiona looked down her delicate nose as if she had found a bug on her immaculate slingbacks. Her expression changed to a predatory smile. "I'm sorry, you have mistaken me for someone else. I don't deal with underlings. I can't imagine how you made such an egregious error."

The younger teller swallowed hard, their eyes flicking from us to the perimeter of the room where cameras peered down at us, and to Sword of Truth's handle above my shoulder.

"I'm . . . ah . . . I'm very s-s-sorry, Ms. Tran, but Mr. Louie is busy with another client at the moment. If you would—"

Fiona's eyes widened in outrage. "Are you implying there are clients more important to this bank than me, you twit?" A torrent of aggrieved and impassioned Vietnamese and French blasted out of the petite woman, nearly peeling the skin off the two unlucky bank employees. She waved an arm across the room. Other clients turned to look at the commotion in the entryway. "Whose gold do you think holds up these tacky columns, child? Get your boss out here now, before I get cross."

The older teller bowed and spoke without raising his head. "Apologies, ma'am. If we may at least tell Mr. Louie what your visit is concerning."

Fiona lifted her nose again, staring into nothing. "Tell Ray Ray I'm here to shut down all of our accounts."

The younger teller gasped, "Oh Ms. Tran, won't you please have a seat in the waiting area while we call Mr. Louie, I'm sure there's been a terrible misunderstanding."

Fiona sniffed. "You will bring Ray Ray to see me. *Now.*"

The younger teller rushed off, the tails of their gray suit jacket flapping from how fast they hustled. The tall bald one remained. In fact, he hadn't even risen from his bow until now. "Please, Ms. Tran, I am Saburo. Allow me to escort you and your guests to our private conference room so that you can be more comfortable."

Fiona gave a negligible shrug. "Very well."

Saburo led us behind a screen of tasteful bamboo plants, through a locked door that he opened with his palm on an access screen. We followed him down what felt like miles of identical hallways, past an endless array of offices, each decorated with dark walnut paneling and a plethora of money tree plants. His aura had the same hue as Sally's, but only the barest hint. Maybe a low- to mid-level fire talent. Unusual talent for a bank teller. Saburo didn't walk like a teller. I studied the lean lines of his back. There was a smooth ripple of muscle under that well-tailored suit. If he was just a teller, I'd eat my boots.

Along the ceiling, I spotted more small cameras marking our progress. More paper lanterns dotted the ceilings here as well.

Bank drones filled the offices in ones and twos, all of them dressed nearly identically in severe dark business suits. To a person, each sat quietly at their desks and worked robotically at their computers or paperwork. Other than our footsteps, the only sounds were clicking keys and scratching pens. No chitchat between the workers, no music, not even an inspirational cat poster. *Weird.* I knew the Louies ran a tight ship, but this was ridiculous.

We passed through another security door opened by Saburo's palm print. There were fewer employees in this section of the bank, and the soft tapping of computer keys was replaced by the sharp ticking of abacuses. Here, in the bowels of the bank, was the bank's true master—twenty-four-carat gold. No paper money made it to these offices—that was for small accounts in the public areas. Pure gold and precious artifacts were the true lifeblood of this bank.

We descended a long flight of stairs and I slowed my breathing to compensate for the increasing density of the city's magic. It flowed around me like molasses, getting thicker as we descended. Between the city's magic and the Louie lanterns my senses were getting hammered. No one else in our group seemed to notice.

Saburo navigated the hallways with an assured stride and an economy and precision of movement that I associated with well-trained waitstaff and well-honed fighters. The idea of him being some lackey bank teller for Ray Ray was laughable. He was clearly someone of importance to the Louie Clan, but for what? The thick soup of the city's magic made it difficult for my senses to discern anything of Saburo's aura.

I decided to stir the pot a little. "Hey, Alfred. Where are you taking us?"

It took Saburo a moment to realize I was speaking to him. His bald head turned the slightest bit, just enough to bring me into his periphery. The corner of his mouth turned down. Apparently he didn't approve of my humor. I couldn't imagine why. "Someone of Ms. Tran's status should not be made to wait in the lobby. We have private meeting rooms for our esteemed clientele."

"Right, right. So is being Ray Ray's gopher a good gig for you then?"

Fiona's eyes widened at my comment but Saburo only sniffed and didn't deign to respond to my jibe. Good restraint. His aura was locked down so tight only a bare sliver of color outlined his profile. He definitely wasn't a mere bank teller.

Freddy tapped my shoulder. "Let up, would ya?"

I rubbed at my earlobe and widened my eyes, willing Freddy to get it. He bugged his eyes out at me, clearly not getting it. I gave up and marched on.

We were headed to an unknown destination, buried beneath one of the most secure buildings in the city, and I had left half of my weapons at the door. It made my skin itch. Freddy and Fiona seemed content to take the situation at face value, and the shinigami simply followed us in silence. The longer we walked, the more uncomfortable I became. I doubted the client conference rooms were down in the bowels of the bank.

As we continued to march downward, I could smell the mélange of small items now, possibly some old relics that had been part of a Hoard before.

Though it was rare in modern times for Hoard pieces to leave a Custodian family, Hoard pieces had been more freely exchanged in earlier eras, when the diaspora had been less populous. And of course, when clans died out and items ended up with Outclan. I had earned a steady reputation for myself recovering those Hoard pieces from various wreckages and private collections of Wàirén.

As we walked steadily downward, the smells of the Hoard items grew stronger and the air grew colder. I checked my cell phone. No Wi-Fi and no cell service. Finally Saburo stopped and led us to the lavishly furnished waiting room outside the vault. He pressed his palm against the sensor and I finally got a real glimpse of his aura, a flash of burnished orange. Definitely not a bank teller, unless he was smelting gold taels, and gāo talents of his sort were rare. I kept my guard up. Even if he were only a píng talent, he moved like someone hiding coiled danger. Saburo tamped his aura down and the door unlocked with a click. He held the heavy door open for us and we entered the waiting area. Antique tables and high-back leather chairs awaited us inside.

Down here, practically underground, the city's magic hummed louder in my blood, trying to lure me. I took a deep breath and tried to cycle my qì and hold the city back.

Saburo poured tea from a delicate Yixing clay pot and bowed to Fiona before vanishing, the door closing behind him with a gentle pneumatic click. The cups were tiny, like a shot glass size of tea, perfect for cooling and drinking quickly. Freddy drank his tea, then Fiona pushed her cup over to him and he slugged hers down, too.

Freddy looked at me. "You gonna drink that?" I pushed my tea-cup over to him, too.

He asked Sugiwara, "You thirsty?"

The shinigami lifted his brows. "By all means, young Tran, help yourself."

Freddy slurped down the remaining tea. "Thanks, I'm super thirsty from all the tunneling today."

He had expended himself today tunneling to chase after the Ebony Gate. And then created enormous whirlpools to hold off a shipping transport. The qì expenditure was staggering. "Will you be able to tunnel again today?"

Freddy made a face. "No way. I'm tapped out."

Fiona looked at him with concern. I got the impression that Freddy rarely had to stretch himself. She looked at me with a different kind of concern. "When Ray Ray gets here, let me handle it, okay?"

Before I had a chance to argue with her the door opened quietly and the portly figure of Ray Ray Louie entered the room. "Fifi, please pardon my delay. I wasn't expecting you this afternoon."

Fiona's game face snapped back on. "Humph. I'll bet you weren't."

Ray Ray came closer, but didn't sit down with us. He ignored me, Freddy, and the shinigami, which gave me plenty of opportunity to scrutinize him. At least now he wasn't profaning Buddhist robes. He'd changed into a custom-tailored suit and a deep red tie with a gold diamond pattern. His chubby arm sported a wide gold Rolex, and he had a large gold coin ring on his pinky. The coin was surrounded by a circle of sparkling diamonds. It was likely a baby gift, later forged into a ring and encrusted with diamonds. Around his neck hung an immense tear-shaped jade pendant dangling from a thick gold chain. The pendant caught the overhead lights and glinted, deep red. A single flaw ran down its center. It was stunning, and familiar. I had seen it before, at the auction. I squashed down my reaction. I couldn't believe that Ray Ray was blatantly wearing the Lost Heart of Yázì.

Bold, or insane?

My eyes flicked to Sugiwara and the death god gave the barest nod of confirmation. Hope surged like a powerful wave in my chest. The missing piece to the Ebony Gate was within reach. I wanted to punch the air and then knock Ray Ray's sweaty head off his neck. I knew I'd seen the slimy dog at the port. And he had the absolute gall to wear this stolen anchor for the Ebony Gate right in front of us.

But no one else seemed to notice. Fiona and Freddy were oblivious. Had Ray Ray put a no-look ward on it?

That's what I would have done. Then I realized something. The death mark on my palm. The shinigami's mark had granted me a very small amount of immunity from the ghosts of Yomi. It seemed it also gave me an affinity to see the Lost Heart of Yázì, even now.

Was Ray Ray making a play for power in going after the Gate or was he merely Jimmy's pawn? The negligence with which he was flaunting his pendant threw my thoughts into chaos. What was his angle here? Blood jade artifacts were zealously hoarded. Small chips and pieces for augmentation were more common for members of Hoard families, such as the phoenix on my tsuba, but this was different.

The pendant was massive. A fist-sized stone that probably weighed as much as ten normal pieces. Blood jade was powerful, and finicky. It derived from the blood of dragons and in thousands of years no one had determined how any one talent would react to it. It could just as easily have no effect as it could turn one's mind into coagulated porridge. No clan would commit so much jade to one piece. It was a terrible risk and a garish waste of resources. A significant piece like this pendant belonged in a vault or a museum, not on some pudgy banker's neck.

Ray Ray's entire focus stayed on Fiona. Given that she was fairly vibrating with annoyance, it was a wise move. "Fifi, my staff tells me you seemed terribly upset. What can I do to address your concerns?"

His aura was the same soft pink-tinged hue as Jimmy's. Charisma talent rarely flared. Instead its users pulled on it at a slow and steady rate throughout their interactions with people. He tried to soothe Fiona but she fiddled with her earrings and frowned at him. The citrus scent of the skepticism cream wafted up.

"You're letting things slip around here, Ray Ray. I can see it everywhere." She waved a hand around the immaculate vault. "I just don't feel the same trust in your bank as I used to."

Ray Ray sat at the head of the table, next to Fiona, and laid his hands on the table. "Fiona, let me assure you that I am here to listen and regain your trust. The Central Road Bank and the Louie Clan pride ourselves as members of the community that all can turn to for security."

I was having a hard time following the conversation, my gaze drawn back to the blood jade at Ray Ray's neck. All I needed to do now was to get that stone and get out of here. The mender would meet us at the tea garden and my soul would be safe from an eternity of guard duty. The shinigami would leave my brother alone. Win, win.

Ray Ray seemed to just notice Freddy and he extended his hand with a warm smile. "Freddy! It's good to see you, son. You look like you've been getting a lot of sun. How's life in Santa Cruz treating you? I'm still waiting for you to open an account, you know. You can't stay under Fiona's accounts forever, son."

Freddy grinned and shook the big man's hand. "Yeah, been a little busy, y'know?"

Fiona slapped her hand on the table. "He's not opening anything, Ray Ray. I've been hearing things. Reports of Louie Clan members engaged in terrible things."

Ray Ray placed his hand over Fiona's. "Fiona, dear child. Our families have abided by the treaty for two generations. Between our families, we own this city. You and I have worked too closely for wild rumors to come between us. If you've been hearing things, you know you should come to me. Whatever misunderstanding has occurred, I know we can find a way to make it right."

As he spoke, the pudgy banker stroked the back of Fiona's hand and I watched the impetuous fire in Fiona's eyes wither and die. I was only half out of my chair when Fiona closed her eyes and her jaw clenched. A tiny breeze swirled around her, fluttering the fat curls of her hair. She inhaled deeply and her eyes opened, once again clear and bright.

"I don't think so, Ray Ray. I'm going to need to see some hard proof that you've got things in hand here."

Ray smiled sadly. He let go of Fiona and folded his hands on the table. His eyes never left Fiona's. "Freddy. Be a good boy and show your sister I've got things under control."

Freddy stood, knocking the chair over as he rose. Ray's aura blazed to life like a gasoline fire, filling my nose with biting black sesame paste. All my anger fizzled out, doused by confusion and a suffocating calm.

I watched with detached fascination as Freddy stepped to his sister's side and calmly smashed his fist into the side of her head. Fiona crashed to the floor, a trickle of blood running down from her ear. She hadn't flinched, hadn't made a sound as she toppled, or lost the faraway, distant smile on her lips.

Fiona lay in a heap under her chair, arms and legs at awkward angles. I should have gone to her, but Ray Ray didn't want me to do that. It was very important to me to make Ray Ray happy. Making Ray Ray happy suffused me with a warm, golden glow of contentment. The necklace he wore helped make his intentions crystal clear, as if Ray Ray were speaking directly into my brain. It shone like a sun in my mind, the golden light extinguishing everything else. Everything except for Ray Ray.

Ray Ray looked at me with his kind eyes. "Sit. Down."

I sat, delighted that I could do something to please Ray Ray.

Ray leaned over the meeting table to look at Fiona. "I trust this demonstration has been adequate?"

He shook his head, and I quailed inside. Was Ray Ray unhappy with me? "You of all people, Fiona. You should know better. Really, associating with the Butcher? You simply cannot be surprised. You Trans think you're so clever. Before all this is over, you're going to learn what real power is."

I would have jumped for joy if Ray Ray hadn't asked me to sit still.

Ray Ray carried on. "Freddy, where is the Gate now? We need to get going."

Freddy spoke in a dull monotone. "Sugiwara-sama has the pieces with him."

"Excellent. Be a good boy and get them for me?"

My eyes barely moved. Freddy passed behind me to where the shinigami sat across the table from me. His motions robotic, Freddy held out his hand. "Mr. Sugiwara, my friend Ray needs the Gate, please."

The shinigami stood slowly, his illusion falling away. The natty suit disintegrated, morphing into a billowing robe swathed about his gaunt figure, brilliant white. Gone were the mild-mannered brown eyes and the death god's blood-red eyes glowed, flashing between Freddy and me.

The shinigami seemed to come to a decision and turned to face Ray. "Raymond Louie. You will not be in my sphere of influence for at least another three years. I have one requirement."

Ray's face turned gray at the shinigami's dire pronouncement. He nodded, jowls quivering.

With measured, slow movements, Sugiwara-sama withdrew the silky white satchel from his misty robes. The soft material of the bag bulged around the broken pieces within. He reached a skeletal hand into the bag and pulled out a handful of glittering ebony shards. The shards glinted in the light as they fell back into the bag. "Your mortal concerns are of no import to me. I am the Custodian of the portal to Yomi. You will leave Miss Soong in my custody, unmolested. In return, you may take this."

I screamed at the shinigami from inside my head. No! I didn't want to go with him! I wanted to stay with Ray Ray! Bony hands deftly retied the satchel and held it out to Freddy, as the death god looked a question at Ray Ray. Sweat had beaded up on Ray Ray's brow. I seethed with anger. How could the shinigami treat Ray Ray like this?

Ray Ray shook his head and the calm demeanor returned to his eyes. "Sure. Sure. Get the bag, Freddy, we're leaving."

Freddy took the bag and walked back toward Ray Ray.

"On second thought . . ." Ray's eyes focused on me again. Freddy stood behind me, close enough that I could feel his breath on my neck.

Hands roughly clutched at Truth, wresting the sword off my back. My anger flared. No one touched my swords! My ire died away, though, when Freddy handed my sword over to Ray Ray. Oh. Well, if it was Ray Ray who wanted my sword, then that was okay. I hoped it would make him happy.

Ray Ray held the bronze blade almost reverently, examining the intricate wrapping around the handle, his fingers tracing over the delicate inscriptions. "Beautiful. The Butcher's blade." His dark eyes snapped back into focus and he spun on his heel. "Come, Freddy. It's time we left."

The vault door closed behind them with a soft click. The bitter stink of burnt black sesame disappeared and the howl in my lungs burst out, echoing back to me from the thick steel.

# THE VAULT

My scream tore through my throat, ripping something essential out of my chest. My insides felt used, rubbed raw, and covered in itchy slime that I couldn't wash off. I'd been so focused on the blood jade that I hadn't felt Ray Ray's power until it was too late. Nothing in my research said anything about Ray Ray being capable of these levels of power. He wasn't a major player—that's why he ran the bank and Uncle Jimmy ran the family empire.

The whammy I'd gotten from Uncle Jimmy had been subtle, elegant talent born from a lifetime of diligent practice. Ray Ray, with all the grace of a tacky knockoff Rolex, had stuck his grubby hands into my brain and used me like a sock puppet. I almost felt a small measure of pity for Uncle Jimmy having Ray Ray as a blood relation. Almost.

I'd seen talents boosted by blood jade before, and fought them. Nothing I'd seen had been like this. This was an astronomical increase in power. The blood jade on Ray Ray's neck was the equivalent of showing up to a fistfight with a tanker full of napalm and a flamethrower. Whatever else happened today, I had to get that rock away from him.

Fiona moaned and I whirled, knocking my chair back from the table. The shift in my balance brought me up to speed as I finally realized the lost weight across my back. Cold fury ignited in my gut. Ray Ray had abused me and committed an inexcusable offense. Truth had been a constant presence in my life for years, never far from my hand and forever reliable, especially in times of dire need. Even though I'd broken the sword to free myself, it still was an essential part of me. Knowing Ray Ray had walked out of the vault with Truth in his hands gutted me.

I launched myself over the conference table and bolted for the locked door, knowing it was futile. I slammed my fists against the door, screaming in frustration. I palmed the security scanner and as I suspected, the system checked for palm prints as well as auras. I cursed fickle gods and slimy bank tellers as my eyes scanned the vault door, searching for an answer. The door was well made, the seams barely a hair-thin crack at the edges. The face of the door was smooth except for the palm scanner.

I stumbled back to Fiona and eased her off the upended chair and to the floor. Her eyes were still glassy and she moaned softly as I whipped off my jacket and laid it under her head. The blood from her ear had slowed to a bare trickle. ". . . Freddy . . ."

Sugiwara-sama's ghostly robes stopped at the edge of my vision. The death god looked up, seeming to peer through the earth. "Sunset is in less than an hour."

I stood and stalked over to him, lifting my chin to look him in the eyes. I needed to hit, to strike, to hurt something, anyone. Blood pounded in my ears and my vision tunneled down to the shinigami's inhuman eyes. "What in all the hells was that? You just gave it away? We need that to seal the portal! We had a deal!"

His red eyes seared into mine and the death god just stared at me, silent. Childhood lessons burned into me cried out for me to kneel at the shinigami's feet and apologize profusely for my impertinence. I clenched my fists and locked my knees, trembling from anger and frustration. The dense earth packed around the vault seemed to crush in on me, smothering the air from my lungs.

The shinigami blinked slowly. Once. "*We* do not have a deal. *You* have a deal with *me*. I have made this abundantly clear. Sealing the portal is my only concern. Without the Ebony Gate, I will make use of whatever is necessary to fulfill my duty."

He reached into his misty robes and withdrew another silk satchel. "However, if you are distressed by the loss of the Ebony Gate, you need not be worried. Even in its condition, I cannot allow this artifact to fall into the hands of those who would abuse it. First and foremost, the Ebony Gate is an opening to Yomi, and that is my responsibility."

The shinigami had pulled a switcheroo on Ray Ray.

For once I had nothing to say. I shouldn't have been surprised. Gods were notoriously incapable of playing straight with mortals.

The shinigami put the satchel back into his robes. "The illusion I gave young Tran will fade at moonrise. We would do well to leave and attend to the portal by then."

Fiona groaned and coughed. I pointed an accusing finger at the death god. "Like hell we are."

I moved to Fiona's side and helped her sit up. She cursed and ran a hand over her ear, looking astonished at the crusting blood that came away on her hand. She looked questioningly at me.

"Ray Ray charmed us. All of us."

The look of confusion on Fiona's face deepened, a furrow creasing her delicate brow. "What? Ray Ray's talent isn't like that. He plays with babies, makes old ladies feel special. He doesn't . . ."

"Did you notice the blood jade pendant?" Her look of confusion morphed into simmering anger when I described that Ray Ray was literally wearing the Lost Heart of Yázì and had used it to roll Freddy.

I had shaken the trees and a steaming mess had fallen out. There was no rug in the world big enough to sweep this under. The Louies were up to their necks in this. Well, Ray Ray at least. He might be Uncle Jimmy's pawn, or he might be angling to unseat Jimmy. Either way the fallout would upset the status quo on the entire West Coast.

Without knowing Ray Ray's angle, we couldn't go to Jimmy or to the Council with this. The Ebony Gate was a powerful artifact. I still didn't know who was after it and why, but I had a feeling this went a lot further than the Louie family. Maybe all the way up to the Council itself. I had to speak with my father. We had to get out of here.

Fiona was back on her feet again. Still a little unsteady, but every inch the regal family leader from atop her stiletto heels. "So, what's our next move?"

Before I could answer, a small whirring sounded above us. Jet nozzles lowered from the ceilings above us and a fine mist sprayed down on us. A sharp, floral scent filled the room.

Fiona wobbled and grabbed for the back of the nearest chair. Her voice was breathy. "Mimi, I don't feel so good . . ." She collapsed back to the floor, dragging the chair with her.

I held my breath and backed into the corner, looking up at the gas nozzles. I should have realized that the bank had safeguards like this. Think, Emiko!

Sugiwara-sama lifted his face to the ceiling and sniffed delicately. "Hmm. A slight paralytic. Floral based. Interesting. They've managed to distill kanashibari into a drug."

My eyes narrowed. "They bottled sleep paralysis? Why isn't it affecting me?"

The death god's eyes flared red, the light piercing through me again. "I suspect because the mixture is tuned for talents, and your talent is—"

"Nonexistent." I finished for him.

A half smile twisted the shinigami's face. "That's not what I was going to say. In any case, I suspect you have a few moments more before you succumb to the elixir."

"Don't worry about me. It's the Gate they want. They can't hold you here, so get yourself back to the tea garden and reseal the portal. The mender will meet you there and repair the Gate. I'll deal with the Louies."

The shinigami's predatory smile returned. "Oh, but I do worry about you. The Ebony Gate is shattered. If it cannot be repaired, you are my only alternative. I cannot allow you to come to harm."

My vision blurred around the edges and I leaned back heavily against the cold vault wall. How deep underground were we? It was getting hard to string thoughts together. "Um, thank you? So you'll get us out of here?"

"Yes, I can leave this place with ease. As soon as you succumb to the kanashibari, you and I will take our leave and return to the tea garden. Have no fear, I will reseal the portal."

Thoughts bumped around in my head like big, ungainly balloons. "Fiona. We can't leave Fiona behind."

"The Tran woman is no concern of mine. I only need you to anchor and reseal the portal."

The chill of the vault behind me sank into my bones and the ground beneath me began to vibrate, shaking me out of my stupor. I blinked rapidly, trying to process the shinigami's last words. I remembered our first meeting at the tea garden.

He wasn't going to help me escape, he wanted to use my life force to seal Yomi. The warm jasmine-scented mist drifted to fill the room. I backed into the farthest corner from the door and held my arm over my nose. My eyelids felt leaden, my movements sluggish. I reached into my bracer and pulled out a shuriken and sent it spinning to the security panel. The ceramic blade shattered on the high-impact glass.

I fought to keep my head up, to keep an eye on the death god. He hadn't moved. Were his robes getting bigger? He seemed less like a tall figure in a robe, now more like an amorphous mass of white smoke accented with a pair of glowing eyes. He . . . It . . . It wasn't a person, and had never seen me as a person. To it, I was just another tool, like the Ebony Gate. I tried to laugh. Emiko Soong, cosmic doorstop.

My knees buckled and I slid to the floor, sitting wedged into the corner of the vault.

Skies. I'd left Adam at the hospital. I hoped he would be okay. I needed to tell my father about our clan responsibility to him. My mind spun, a kaleidoscope of my future and my present.

I'd barely made it two years since leaving my family, and all the crazy had caught up to me. Despite my new life, I'd fallen right back into the chaos of Jiārén politics. I cursed all the dragons above me for my bad luck, but I knew I was the only one to blame.

If I wanted a quiet life I wouldn't have rolled those thugs harassing Popo. Instead of focusing on the Gate, I'd spent half my time chasing ghosts all over the city and getting burned for the privilege. I thought about Popo, the Suns, even silly Freddy. Jiārén, all living precariously on the edge between two worlds, the same place I was trying to make room for myself. All of us, getting pushed around by old powers with old agendas, old grievances.

I was tired of getting pushed around. I thought breaking my blade had freed me, but I was still confined by the same boundaries in San Francisco. The Louies, and maybe even Fiona, they wanted to use me for their own ends. I was a tool to be utilized. I wasn't free, I'd just traded up to a bigger prison cell, one with two wardens instead of one.

Popo had sent me to the Trans. Stupid me, sleep-deprived and exhausted from taking down a hibagon, had assumed she wanted me to make friends. Smart me, showing up late to the party again, realized Popo was gently prodding me to make allies. To pick a side.

The peace treaty my mother had imposed on the Trans and Louies would soon be history. It was plain as day now and I cursed myself for not seeing it sooner. The Louies were up to something, and it would throw San Francisco into chaos, maybe worse than the turf wars in the seventies. The Louies were bringing war to the city. To my city.

A thrill of adrenaline rushed down my arms, making the hairs stand on end. The surge of hormones shook off the kanashibari enough for me to stand up without wobbling. The shinigami took a step toward me, then stopped as it met my eyes. Even the shinigami was using me for its own ends.

I'd left my family to start making my own life, my own choices. I'd come to San Francisco and found not only a life, but a new family. New Jiārén. I wasn't going to stand by and watch as the Louies and Trans carved up my city.

Popo was right. It was time to pick a side. My side.

I'd been fighting it for months, not realizing it had been the key to my cell the whole time. I took a deep breath and flung my senses out into the room, past the walls of steel and concrete, into the bedrock of the city. Beneath my feet, deep in the earth, tree roots quested through the darkness. I called out to them and they twisted through the earth, searching for me. The city whispered its siren song, audible to only my ears, and ringing in my soul. This time I sang back to the city, my small talent ringing in counterpoint, calling the city to me.

I loved the city, had loved it from my first visit as a child. I owed the city a lot. It had sheltered me when I had sought sanctuary, provided me not just with a living, but with a life. I had tried countless times to give back to it, ridding it of magical nuisances, helping the Jiārén community with their various and sundry problems. And I had been doing it with the equivalent of having two hands tied behind my back.

No more.

I breathed deep, exalting in the energy stored in the heartwood of the ancient redwoods, the bedrock, the water in the soil, the very air I breathed. The earth throbbed and the frame of the building seemed to flex around me. I cleared my mind and took another breath through the trees above me, my lungs taking in the fresh air from outside the bank, the scent of the earth, the warmth of the sun. I took another breath and listened. The city spoke to me and for the first time since hearing her whispers, I stayed still, and listened.

A deep, basso thrum of energy began in the rock around me. The shinigami backed away from me, a look of awed curiosity in his eyes. I closed my own eyes and focused on the city that had accepted me into its family. Liquid warmth filled my limbs and my chest filled with cool salt air and fog. I leaned my head back and sensed heavy stone and soil, felt ancient roots following hidden lines of water to me. I stood, knees loose, ready to fly at a moment's notice. I flexed my wrists and clenched my hands into loose fists. An image appeared in my mind. I stood on the rocky northern point of the city at the base of the Golden Gate. I faced the swell of the gray ocean, the tide coming in. Cold wind blew past me carrying the scent of danger and malice. It would not linger. Not while I was here.

The walls of the vault groaned, metal creaked and screamed as ancient redwood roots shattered the vault walls and tore them apart. Gnarled roots burst through the ceiling, raining dirt and rocks down on us. Latent power, bright and golden, glowed through the roots as their fractal ends quested through the air, looking for something. Looking for me.

I stood straighter and something in my core called out to the city. The roots tangled together and shot toward me. They hit my chest like a hammer blow, rocking me back until I met the vault wall. My breath exploded out of me even as my chest caved to the force of the impact, the twisted tree roots piercing my body, just to the right of my heart.

Pain tore through me as the roots writhed, pinning me to the wall. My right arm was useless. With my left I tried to push myself up, fight back, but it felt like trying to lift an airplane. The golden light in the roots pulsed and intensified, filling the vault with shimmering light. Time seemed to pause and hold its breath.

The shinigami whispered, "Fascinating."

Power and energy exploded into me like a crashing tidal wave, coursing into my body through the tree roots and spreading out from my chest. My eyes watered. My skin itched and tingled. My teeth shook in my jaw, threatening to come free. I clenched my jaw down and screamed through my teeth, my left hand on the root, straining to pull it from my chest.

Slowly, the roots moved, coming away from my body. With each small movement the heat in my chest subsided and my breath came easier. The dazzling light died as the roots came free from my chest. I gasped in a breath and looked down, dreading the sight.

A clean, neat hole about an inch in diameter punched through my shirt, the edges of the fabric smooth, the fibers fused together. A pale, circular scar marred my chest, closer to my shoulder, the skin smooth and shiny. What the hell was that? I rubbed my hand over the wound. It didn't even hurt—the bone felt intact. It looked and felt like an old scar.

The ground shook and rolled like a wave of water, and although the heavy meeting table slid across the room, my footing remained steady. The crack in the ceiling split wide open and bright sunlight lanced into the vault along with a rush of fresh air. Motes of dust and pulverized rock floated in the golden beam of light. I rubbed at my chest again. I had claimed the city, and the city had claimed me. I felt like I had been branded.

There was no time to worry about this right now. I walked past the shinigami and picked Fiona off the ground. There was no more pain in my chest from the fù chóng venom, and no pain from where the city had pierced me. Instead I felt strong, filled with righteous anger and resolve.

Fiona's eyes fluttered open as I slung her arm over my shoulder and made for the crack in the wall. "Mimi? What happened? Where are we going?"

The seething anger in my throat sparked anew, running flashes of heat and gooseflesh down my arms and back. "We're getting out of here. Then I'm going to hunt Ray Ray down and get my sword back. And don't call me Mimi."

# SENTINEL

I climbed through the crack in the earth, convenient juts of stone
and root providing hand- and footholds as easy as a ladder. Everything around me pulsed with life and I could hardly breathe
without getting light-headed. Beneath me, Fiona gingerly picked
her way up the crevasse, with the shinigami following. Fresh air
washed over me as I neared the bright light at the top. The comforting moisture in the air tickled my senses. The fog would be thick
and heavy tonight.

Golden sunlight dazzled my eyes as I crested the exit of the
crack. My hand slapped down onto warm concrete and I hoisted
myself up to the sidewalk. I had come up just off to the side from
the main entrance, closer to Sacramento Street. I took a breath and
the city took a breath with me, warmth flowing around me like a
swirling blanket. It was a strange but not unpleasant sensation.

A lot of people were milling about on the street. Hopefully some
of them were the guards that had accompanied Fiona.

I turned and offered my hand to Fiona to help her up. Climbing
out in her ridiculous platform slingbacks couldn't have been fun. I
grabbed her arm and pulled her up until she had her feet under her
on the sidewalk. The shinigami made his own way up, his illusion
back in place.

Fiona flicked her fingers and a swirl of air circled her, dusting
off her trench coat until it was pristine once again. She fiddled
with her belt, then looked up at me. She seemed to have shaken off

the effects of the kanashibari mist. She tilted her head, squinting against the afternoon sun. "Let's not do that again. So now—"

Her words choked off and her hand flew up to cover her open mouth. "Ohmygod. Mimi! Your hair!"

I ran my hand over my head, sure that the braid had started to unravel. "Don't call me Mimi, Fiona, I'm not—"

My mouth stopped working as I brought my braid around. What had been a thick French braid of glossy black hair was now shot through with a brilliant streak of silver that ran the entire length of the braid. Of all the ways the city could have marked me, this is what it chose? I looked like a cartoon villain ready to don a dalmatian coat.

I looked up to the sky and wondered what in all the Realms had happened to me.

"Mimi, that's not all." Fiona stared at me, then gestured to my neck. "Did you always have that tattoo?"

Umm, no. I pulled aside my collar where Fiona was pointing. Fiona's eyes only widened more. Great Dragon Father, was I going to be stuck with turtlenecks from now on?

Fiona's head cocked and her eyes softened, still staring at me.

"What now?" I dropped my arms. People on the street had started to look our way. A pair of women crawling up out of the sidewalk wasn't exactly an everyday occurrence, right?

Fiona stepped close and put out her hand. She held her hand a few inches from my face, her fingers following some unseen contour. Her eyes sparkled with joy and wonder, a strange expression on her usually haughty face. "It's beautiful, Mimi. I've never seen a gold aura before."

A crowd of people had gathered in the middle of the street, most of them staring at me with open-eyed wonder. Fiona's team split, with half of them coming to surround Fiona and the remainder hanging back near her fleet of double-parked Escalades. As I scanned the crowd, I finally took in the scene around us. About half of the crowd wore severe suits and serious faces, maybe employees who'd fled the bank.

The main doors of the bank hung askew, and a deep crack ran up through the stairs approaching the doors. Several windows on the front of the bank had shattered out of their frames. The fissure we had climbed out of ran up the wall, going clear up to the third story. Wow.

The redwoods on either side of the bank seemed larger than I remembered. On both sides of the bank, the bases of the trees had swelled, stretching their roots under the foundation of the building. Energy hummed through the trees like high-voltage electricity. In fact, now that I looked for it, the energy flowed under the concrete like a river, springing up with every tree on the street.

I felt them before I saw them. Dozens of people moving toward me, their footsteps hesitant. Merchants and residents of Lotus Lane, people I had come to know these last two years. I felt them approaching me, sensed their small talents deforming the shape of the field of magic that was our proud city.

Big Ricky broke away from the crowd, his steps gaining confidence as he moved into the empty space between me and the crowd. His wife and kids followed in his wake. Big Ricky and his son would never be mistaken for anything but father and son, both cast from the same mold with a thick barrel chest and meaty arms perfect for hours of hard labor. The elder Sun stopped ten feet from me, his face beaming with paternal pride, a small smile curling the corner of his mouth. He clasped one calloused hand over his opposite fist in front of his chest and bowed deeply at the waist. Behind him, his family followed suit.

From his bowed position, Big Ricky said, "Blessings for our Sentinel."

Beside me Fiona shook herself like she was waking from a dream, looking from me to the Suns. After a moment she seemed to come to a decision and she stepped away from me, not quite as far as the

Suns, but out of my personal space. Fiona straightened her clothes and met my gaze, a strange look in her eyes.

Before I could say anything Fiona winked and bowed deeply, matching the Suns. "Blessings for our Sentinel."

Oh no. After Fiona's display, it became a wave. Dozens of people coming up to a respectful distance to bow deeply and intone the blessing. This was not what I wanted. I just needed to get out of that vault and make Ray Ray sorry he'd ever gotten out of bed this morning. I needed to make sure the Louies didn't hurt anyone else. I did not need a crowd of fawning onlookers everywhere I went.

While some of the Lotus Lane merchants approached, I noted that nearly all of the bank employees stayed back, many of them gathered in tight knots and talking quietly, casting quick glances over hunched shoulders at me. Great. Another thing I didn't need was a host of new enemies.

The odor of black sesame paste tickled my nose and my head whipped around. At the far corner of the bank, toward California Street, Ray Ray Louie stepped out from an unmarked door with Truth clenched in his fat, grubby fist. Freddy followed behind, hustled along by Saburo. A long black Mercedes sedan waited for them at the curb, engine idling, doors open. My vision narrowed down to my sword, sullied by Ray Ray's hand.

My voice snapped, a whip crack. "Fiona!"

Fiona's head popped up and she followed my gaze. Murmurs spread through the crowd. I took off at a dead sprint to retrieve my sword.

# BATTLE ON LOTUS LANE

Broken Claw! My feet pounded along the pavement. I had a handful of shurikens strapped to my arms and Hachi at my side. All my other weapons were inside the bank. If my hunch was right and Saburo was one of the Louies' hired hitters, well . . . then I guess I'd get a chance to test my skills against a combat talent. The key would be getting close enough.

Ray Ray spun, surprisingly agile for his size, and pointed a finger past me. "Stop her!"

A sharp pulse of power flowed past me, the heavy scent of black sesame paste filling my nose. Ray Ray's aura shone like an angry star. I turned in time to see two of Fiona's bodyguards, Willy with the goatee and a young woman, lose focus in their eyes and take off at a run directly toward me.

Skies above! This was not good. How many people could Ray Ray charm at once? I had to break his concentration. I pulled a throwing blade out and threw it on the run. The blade flashed in the sunlight as it crossed the distance and buried itself in the meat of Ray Ray's shoulder. He screamed and cursed me.

I shot him the finger. "Fiona! Kill the car! Don't let them leave!"

From behind me Fiona's strident, high-pitched voice called out, "Ai!"

I stumbled to the side as air swelled behind me like a wave. My ears popped as the pressure wave swept past me in a rush. Saburo moved fast, his long arms shoving Ray Ray to the sidewalk. Saburo dove in the opposite direction, dragging Freddy to the ground with him. As they fell down Fiona's wind blade passed between them and sliced into the car.

Metal squealed and shrieked as Fiona's power ripped through the engine compartment. The car bucked up onto two wheels, the force of the gale lifting the passenger side. It crashed back to the asphalt and the car split in two, fluids pouring out of the massive rent in the metal.

And then Willy and the young woman were on me, tackling me to the asphalt. I tucked as we went down, covering my head with my arms and cushioning most of the impact. Either Ray Ray's new power didn't extend to his victims' talent, or he was too distracted to take advantage of them, because Willy and the young woman went to work on me with just their fists, pummeling me like a side of beef, all the while with nothing more than a blank look in their eyes.

Apparently Fiona trained her charges well, especially the young woman, whose sharp knuckles pounded into my shoulders and arms, rapid-fire as I tried to keep my guard up against her assault. My upper body was going to be one giant purple bruise if I made it through this. These were Fiona's people and they weren't in control. I wouldn't hurt them if I could help it.

Someone screamed as a howling wind kicked up, probably Fiona's work, showering the street with dirt and grit. I squinted against the gale. Two more of Fiona's guards had caught up to me and tore Willy off my lower body. With my legs finally free I bucked my hips up and jackknifed, kicking my leg up and around my attacker. I rolled up and over, pinning her knee with my arm and rolling her onto her back.

I got my hands on her shoulders and pushed her down. "Stay. Down."

With each word I uttered, the vibration carried and the asphalt beneath us bubbled and flowed like water in rhythm with my voice. The city's magic rippled around my hands and the young woman sank into the street until her arms were buried. My eyes widened as the asphalt resolidified and locked her in. Well, that was new. The young woman continued to struggle, her eyes still a blank stare.

I turned my focus back to Ray Ray.

I stood in the thrashing winds. Onlookers had found shelter in doorways and the rest of Fiona's people sought cover behind their vehicles. Fiona floated in the middle of the street, a whirlwind swirling around her, the tails of her trench snapping like whips. The winds sprayed the entire street with debris and dirt, stinging faces, forcing everyone to shield their eyes. Except for me and Fiona. For some reason, her winds didn't touch me.

I walked up the street through the windstorm and found Ray Ray huddled against the side of the bank. Ray Ray stared, his stricken gaze going from the wreck of his car to Fiona's fury. Saburo towered over him, one foot on Freddy's back. Freddy seemed to be trying to get up.

Saburo hissed, "Focus, Mr. Louie! Get it together!"

As I rounded the corner Ray Ray's wide eyes found me and narrowed, blazing with anger. "Leave us!"

The blood jade around Ray Ray's neck flared like a miniature sun again. White-hot lines of Ray Ray's talent coiled around me. Black sesame paste flooded my nose, the scent burnt and acrid. Before his charm could clamp down I snapped my arm out and my shuriken flew. At this distance I could hardly miss. I misjudged it a little in all the wind, though. The tumbling blade flew low and buried itself in Ray Ray's groin, drawing a high-pitched cry from him. Oops. Truth fell from his hand and clattered to the concrete. Ray Ray's talent faded like wisps of smoke in the wind. Freddy yelped and he started struggling.

Saburo cursed in Japanese, looking from me to Ray Ray, and then to Freddy struggling under his foot. As Fiona's winds calmed and she floated down, Saburo made up his mind. He dragged Freddy to his feet and snaked his left arm through both of Freddy's, pinning

Freddy's shoulders back. Freddy's eyes popped open with pain and he lunged forward. Saburo hammered his fist into Freddy's thigh, buckling his leg.

Saburo's face peeked out from behind Freddy's body, giving me no target. "You have grown much in your power and skill."

He spoke like he knew me but I had never seen him before today. The man's voice sounded measured and calm. It was the voice of an experienced fighter. I was sure I had never faced him before, whether in practice or in a more serious skirmish. As I moved to the side, Saburo pivoted with me, keeping his body hidden behind Freddy. Defending against another shuriken. The man's actions clearly pegged him as a security operator—a curious choice for bodyguard for Ray Ray. And he hadn't taken the lid off his talent yet. I wondered what he was waiting for.

Saburo pulled Freddy in closer and Freddy yelped in pain, his face going white. "I have no need of this young man, but I'm afraid I must protect my charge. Would you be willing to trade?"

The bodyguard seemed to think he knew something about me, and maybe he knew of my reputation as the Blade. But he didn't seem to realize that I had never made trades. I didn't negotiate—I executed.

But I wasn't the Blade anymore. People like Freddy were counting on me. I kept my response measured, despite my urge to leap and twist Ray Ray's head off his neck, consequences be damned.

"Any trade we make is only for time. Ray Ray owes me and I will take my retribution, if not now, eventually."

As I spoke, Fiona moved behind the wrecked Benz and out of Saburo's line of sight. Clever girl.

It was funny. Fiona was the one with all the talent—she'd sliced their car in half—and Saburo seemed focused on me. I had as much talent as a stick of wood and I felt naked without Sword of Truth on my back. In fact, that was how the dean at the academy had labeled me, Mù meaning *wooden*. The lowest of the low. But now I had a little bonus from the city and it was time to put it to work.

I inhaled slowly, drawing in my breath through my nose. My mind reached for the city's roots, the ones that had punched through my flesh, tasted my blood, and freed me from the bank. I just needed a little love tap to buy Fiona some time. I exhaled from my mouth in a burst and the ground began to tremble, slowly at first, then a large rumble.

Saburo turned his head quickly from side to side, scouting his exit. Too late.

Two giant tree roots punched up from behind Ray Ray, one wrapping around his neck and the other around his ankles and pulling him away from Saburo and Freddy. That would keep my prey in place for me.

Fiona leaped into action, sending the steering wheel ripped from the Mercedes into a speeding collision with Saburo's head. He ducked away, throwing Freddy to the sidewalk. Freddy rolled away and scooped up my sword. He sprang up from the asphalt and tossed Truth to me, a puff of his talent keeping the sword aloft.

The lacquered wood slapped into my palm, the weight and heft satisfying and comforting. I strapped the scabbard over my chest, glad to feel my sword's presence again. Fiona rushed into the opening, sweeping Freddy up in her arms before Saburo could recover. She wrapped him up and pulled him away from the bank in a gale of wind.

I pulled Hachi, her shining steel glittering in the sunlight, and when I opened my mouth the words just poured out.

"Ray Ray Louie! You have wronged the people of my city! I am the Sentinel and I will have retribution!"

# RETRIBUTION

Ray Ray only whimpered in response.

Whereas before I had worked to shut out the call of the city's magic, now I opened myself to it and let it permeate my body. I would use everything at my disposal to shut down Ray Ray's attempts to break the treaty and recover the Lost Heart of Yázì. And if I happened to also mete out some justice for his wrongs against me and the Trans, that was just gravy. Anticipation curled in my belly. Ray Ray would pay. I just needed to get through his stalwart bodyguard.

Stale grave air wafted over me. I turned my head the slightest bit and found Sugiwara-sama standing at my elbow. The seal on my palm flared and burned.

"We will leave now, Sentinel. The portal awaits."

The death god's timing sucked. I ignored him and gripped my hand tight around Hachi's hilt, my fingers finding the familiar contours of the wrapping. I squeezed my left hand into a fist until the burn left my palm. I walked away from the death god and approached Saburo. I flicked my wrist once, loosening my sword arm, and stopped a good twenty feet from Saburo.

"That man has wronged me, my clan, and my city. Step aside."

Saburo took a centering breath and settled his weight into his narrow hips. "This man is my charge and I will not allow harm to befall him."

My gaze flicked over Saburo's fighting stance, trying to puzzle the man out. He was capable. He wasn't stupid. He was likely about to wield his talent. His weight shifted slightly from foot to foot.

I studied his face, which showed no emotion, not even a tightening of the jaw. Refined features with angular cheekbones, head shaved to spotless precision, the stubble on his chin shot through with flecks of gray. His dark eyes glittered with anticipation. Maybe late thirties or early forties, possibly from a mid-tier clan pledged to the Louies. His suit stretched and flowed with him, clearly tailored to allow movement while masquerading as everyday business attire. He carried no weapons I could discern, which only made him more dangerous.

I put both hands on Hachi and settled my own weight. "You know who I am."

Ray Ray whimpered on the ground. Saburo didn't even spare him a look, only raised his arms, his hands loose and ready, his aura still tamped down to nearly nothing. His feet touched the ground though, and his lungs breathed my air. His presence deformed the magic of the city, tickling my senses like a mosquito landing on my arm. Saburo quietly built power behind his locked walls as we stared each other down. He blinked once, slowly. "The dragon's flight is righteous, the path true to all."

I blinked. To those around us, if they understood Japanese, Saburo's response would make no sense. To me, a former student of the Jōkōryūkai, it meant everything.

The tickling in my senses bloomed into surround sound and Technicolor. My perception pierced his shields, laying his aura open to me like a book. My focus dropped for a moment as I staggered under the deluge of information pouring into me. The bottomless power of my city coursed through me like a river and reality crystallized into razor-sharp clarity.

In an instant, I knew almost everything I needed to know about this man. The shape and scale of his talent lay exposed to my senses. I fought the instinct to look away from what I knew to be intensely private information. Saburo was a gāo-level fire talent. Small wonder he was keeping his aura locked down. So how in the eight great levels of hell had Ray Ray gotten paired up with this elite-level talent?

"Since when does the Jōkōryūkai work for sniveling dogs like Ray Ray?"

"His interests are our interests. His goals serve the true path."

The hell they did.

My lips thinned in irritation. The Association had drilled into us its reason for being, which was to preserve the quality of life for Jiārén here outside the Realm. The Association did not answer to the Council, nor did they answer to any single clan. Each member took an oath to sever their clan ties, which was why I had run away. I had worked faithfully for the Association, and I believed in their vision, that we should live among Wàirén, and to keep our ways secret. They served the Hoard, but without the Hoard clan dynamics. The Association meddled in Wàirén and Jiārén affairs equally, but always for the First Law. For making it possible for us to live among Wàirén without disruption.

There was no conceivable way that Ray Ray's power grab could serve the Association—could protect our way of life here.

I moved my bottom hand to the end of the hilt, for maximum leverage in a killing stroke. "Step aside. I must exact recompense from your client."

Saburo shifted his stance slightly in response to my own shift. "And I will do what I must to protect him. I bear you no animus. We are but two warriors, well met on a narrow bridge."

One corner of his mouth lifted in a small, sad smile. Then he rocked his weight back and I felt the shift through the sidewalk, his feet pressing through his shoes, readying himself to launch forward. His talent morphed in my mind, sharpening itself to a point, set to burst free from his shields. I read his power as it deformed the city like a pebble dropped into a pond. Our duel played itself out in my mind. He would leap toward me, leading his attack with a shaft of fire aimed at my chest. I saw it all and I knew exactly how I would counter.

Saburo had no chance.

We threw ourselves at each other. Saburo's talent blazed into the open, his burnished orange aura finally flaring to life before my eyes. A chorus of gasps went up from the onlookers behind me. A spear of white-hot fire blasted out from his hand, the heat so intense the sidewalk cracked and the blast of hot air blew my hair back.

As weapons went, fire was a good one. It was fortunate fire talents of his caliber were rare, or else the cyclical nature of clan battles would have burned all the major cities down twice over already. I needed something to redirect Saburo's fire, a massive heat sink, before he cooked me like roast pork. The city would provide me with exactly what I needed.

Cold, wet fog, damp and cloying like soaked wool, swirled around my body. Saburo's fire lance crashed into a wall of San Francisco's thickest spring fog, turning it into a blast of superheated steam. A chill wind roared past me, nothing like Fiona's delicate touch. This was a mountainside of air, moving past me like a rumbling freight truck, pushing the steam away from me.

Saburo grunted as the wall of steam barreled into him. Gray mist and steam covered the street, obscuring everything. I felt Saburo's footsteps on the pavement as he ran toward me. I waited, absolutely still, until he committed to his leap, and then I stepped to the side.

Hachi flicked out and found its target in the hazy mist. I felt the blade bite home and Saburo gave a small exhalation of breath. He landed on the pavement and rolled to a stop. I swept my arm and the wind rose up to clear away the fog and mist.

Saburo lay on his back, his right hand pressed to his side. Livid red burns mottled his face, neck, and hands. Bright red blood pumped through his fingers and pooled under his body. Hachi had found his liver, and he would bleed to death without treatment. I looked in his eyes and saw the same grim understanding. I stepped up to him, my sword at my side. His eyes never left me, unflinching. I inclined my head to him, a salute. From the ground, Saburo did the same. "Keep pressure on that wound."

I pitched my voice so all could hear. "Rick Sun!"

The elder Sun approached. "Yes, Sentinel?"

That title chafed but I tried not to let my discomfort show in my voice. "Take this man to the hospital. Tell them . . ." I stopped, aware that all eyes on the street were focused on me. ". . . tell them the Sentinel requests this man be treated at once."

Big Ricky bowed low. "At once, Sentinel."

I turned away from them. The Suns were good people. I was confident they would get Saburo to the hospital. Big Ricky was probably already calling Popo to meet him there. Saburo had just been doing a job. He didn't warrant death for that. Ray Ray, on the other hand . . .

I found Ray Ray where the tree roots anchored him, curled up on the sidewalk, clutching his wounded arm like a security blanket. He laughed as I approached, the sound thick with scorn.

"Sentinel? What a joke. Don't fool yourself, girl. Gong saan ji goi, bun sing naan ji."

I exhaled, purging my rage. In the past I would have agreed with him. A leopard doesn't change his spots. But I had spent the last two years fighting back decades of trained instinct. I had gone two years without taking a limb or snuffing out a life. I had even made a friend. I had changed.

Ray Ray leaned back, looking up at me. "You'll never be more than a thug doing your father's dirty work. You've always been a simple tool, for simple problems. You're out of your depth here, girl. Best run home to your father, this is one game he did not teach you to play."

It was true. I had been the tool of powerful people. During my tenure as the Blade I had learned many things. One of which was to use what I had. I watched Ray Ray's aura flicker and surge and the Lost Heart of Yázì glowed with a deep fire. In my mind's eye, the city lent me her vision and I saw through Ray Ray's charm speak.

"Let me out." His aura was blinding in its intensity. Despite that, I felt nothing. Heard nothing. I couldn't. The city was louder, flooding my senses with all of her reach. Ray Ray's charm was a small thing in comparison. The Lost Heart of Yázì was powerful to be sure, but it couldn't compare to the ascendant power of an entire city filled with Jiārén, steeped in centuries of Jiārén power.

"No."

He pitched his voice higher. "Help me!"

I realized my mistake when the rock hit me on the shoulder. I turned to find a ragged half circle of Lotus Lane merchants around me, all of them hefting rocks and improvised weapons. To a man, woman, and child their eyes were vacant and unblinking, their mouths curled up in manic smiles. On the other side of the street, Fiona and her subordinates stood in a loose circle, protecting Freddy and the unconscious forms of the two who'd attacked me. A similar grouping of smiling merchants surrounded Fiona's group. Skies. This is what I got for letting Ray Ray bloviate.

Ray Ray's power radiated out from his body. While he was talking to me he had charmed all the civilians within the sound of his voice. The blood jade wasn't just an amplifier, it gave him the kind of raw power most talents needed a lifetime to develop. Just putting the blood jade on lifted him to world-class gāo talent.

Two men in bloody butcher aprons walked up to Ray Ray, cleavers in hand. With drooling smiles they hacked away at the tree roots, slowly digging my prey from my trap.

"Best put that sword away, siu ze. Wouldn't want any of these nice people to get hurt."

I sheathed Hachi. My breath hissed, anger coiling my body so tight I felt like I would explode. I couldn't believe I'd let this . . . bank teller get the drop on me. He dared to lay hands on Truth. Bloodlust pulled at me like a deadly undertow, threatening to drag my head below waves of unending blood. I looked around. Ray Ray had surrounded himself with civilians, spreading his talent in a wide net over easy prey. His talent needed intense concentration to control a powerful target. I hadn't expected him to go low like this, scooping up buckets of minnows to throw at me.

No one in the crowed carried any weapons. I could cut through them like tofu in seconds and make that arrogant banker taste my steel. But I wasn't the Blade anymore, and I had rules that I lived by, no matter how much harder they made my life.

In moments, the two men finished hacking through the tree roots and helped Ray Ray to his feet. He brushed down his suit coat and pulled at the wrinkles.

All traces of the kindly uncle vanished from his face and the civilians took two steps toward me.

I gauged the distance to Ray Ray. I could make it. And I would be drenched in the blood of innocents again. It was Pearl Market all over. The mantle of the Blade had driven me to exact retribution on all who opposed me, to send a message that the Soong Clan were not to be trifled with. No. I had to find another way.

I pulled Hachi off my hip, keeping the sword sheathed, my hand gripped over the tsuba. I thumped the biggest man in front me with the end of the scabbard, striking him in the solar plexus. He went down with a whoosh of breath and I jumped into the opening. Ray Ray's eyes widened into saucers as I covered the distance between us. I stayed low and moved fast, throwing shoulders and elbows to keep the crowd at bay.

I was almost to him when hands clawed at my hair and jacket. I struck with my fist and scabbard, tapping meridian lines just to disable. I didn't want to hurt any of these people but I wasn't going to let Ray Ray hold them between me and his punishment.

A blacked-out Mercedes squealed around the corner down the street and gunned the engine, heading straight for us. Ray Ray's head snapped around at the sound of the car. "Hold her!"

Arms and legs flew as the grinning civilians dogpiled me. Ray Ray edged along the wall, heading to meet the approaching Mercedes. No! My anger spilled over and a basso rumble filled the air. San Francisco raged with me, seismic fault lines grinding like gnashing teeth. The sidewalk pitched and yawed, undulating like water. Ray Ray was thrown from his feet by the temblor. The attacking citizens fell to the ground in droves.

I burst free from the crowd, my feet steady on the rocking pavement. I reached Ray Ray and grabbed him by the lapels, hauling him to his feet and slamming him against the side of the building. His head connected with the wall with a crack.

His unfocused eyes found me, his words slurred. "See? You're just a blunt instrument. Why do you think your father only used you when he needed someone mutilated?"

Hands latched onto me again, pulling me away from Ray Ray. I wound my hand into his shirt, but there were too many of them. The hands wrenched me away from Ray Ray, his shirt ripping as the buttons gave way.

I fought, but the mob pulled me away by sheer force of numbers. My eyes fell to Ray Ray's shredded banker's shirt, his tie hanging askew. Among his layered necklaces hung a delicate gold chain with the blood jade pendant. It was old. Very old. It had anchored the Ebony Gate for a very long time.

But it wasn't the invaluable blood jade that had my attention. His shirt had torn open from the collar, exposing an intricate tattoo that covered the entire upper left side of his torso.

Black ink traced the figures of nine ornate dragons with serpentine bodies and hooked claws. Long whiskers trailed around mouths filled with sharp fangs. Eight of the dragons entwined amongst themselves to form a complex circle, with each dragon

Julia Vee and Ken Bebelle

facing outward. The Ninth Dragon sat in the center, its eyes depicted with bloodred ink.

My heart stopped. I'd been right. Ray Ray was a bona fide Realmseeker. A member of a death cult driven by a mad thirst for power, that wanted nothing more than to return to a land that had been ravaged by dragons, reduced to bone and ashes, and resurrect the Ninth Dragon. The dragon that had betrayed its kin and precipitated the Cataclysm. Broken Claw, Ray Ray Louie was completely out of his mind.

Ray Ray clutched his shirt together when he saw what I was looking at. He hissed at me as hands tore at my hair, my clothes, and rained punches down on my head. The merchants of Lotus Lane dragged me away from Ray Ray as he screamed at me.

"I told you, you have no idea what you're dealing with. Everything is going to change! And when it does even your father won't be—"

The Mercedes roared onto the sidewalk, jumping the curb and causing everyone to scatter. I jumped back as well and ended up looking at Ray Ray over the car.

The passenger door near Ray Ray popped open and a gravelly voice from inside said, "Ray. Shut. Up."

Ray Ray's eyes burned but he lowered his head and got into the car and slammed the door. The car peeled away from the crowd, leaving tire tracks on the sidewalk.

# PEACHWOOD

The citizens of Lotus Lane returned to normal once Ray Ray was out of their line of sight. Thankfully, they stopped beating on me fairly quickly, and multiple hands pulled me to my feet. Franklin took charge of the civilians, getting the severely injured to the hospital for treatment. Fiona set up a medic station between two of her SUVs and had her people take care of those with minor injuries, taking advantage of the Louies' absence to build a few bridges on Lotus Lane. I saw more than a few red envelopes being discreetly pressed into palms. Reparations for damages to storefronts and lost business. Say what you wanted to about Fiona, that woman was smart. For the price of some bandages and plate glass, she was sowing doubt in the heart of Louie territory. A bargain at ten times the price.

I felt like I could breathe again now that I had Truth back. I patted the pommel to reassure myself. I recovered the rest of my weapons from the rubble of the bank lobby. Security Sam had been knocked unconscious by a falling statue. Lucky for him he'd fallen over the security box, protecting my items with his massive body. On my way out I filled out a customer comment card commending him for his attentive service. I slid the card into the battered collection box.

Fiona took charge of Freddy to have Popo check him out, along with Willy and the girl with the sharp knuckles.

\* \* \*

With the high of accepting the Sentinel mantle still on me, I pulled the girl from the asphalt easily. I even managed to restore the road to its original condition. Without these powers, the fight with Saburo would have been a dicey affair. Jōkōryūkai did not kid around, but they were among the rarest of the rare. Running into one here was not a coincidence. I wasn't sure yet what it meant, but I would need to look into it.

The rest of Fiona's crew dove into the remains of the bank and within moments they were making a conga line, exiting the bank in twos and threes with locked briefcases and ornate trunks. Fiona assigned one of her drivers to take me anywhere I wanted. She spared a second glance at my clothes and instructed her driver to take the car in for detailing immediately after. She promised to meet me at the tea garden shortly. Her last words to me were both vindicating and alarming.

"I believe you now about the Lost Heart and the Louies. We will render extraordinary aid to you and afterward, regardless of the outcome, we will cry feud on the Louies."

Her words punched me in the gut. I'd finally brought her irrefutable evidence that the Louies were involved in the Gate heist and taking the Lost Heart. And now Ray Ray had wronged her and Freddy to such a degree she could not back down without losing face.

My mother's treaty had lasted decades. The irony wasn't lost on me that fulfilling my mother's Talon Call would now be the undoing of the treaty. I wondered if my mother would be proud of me for fulfilling the Talon, or angry that I'd precipitated a clan war she'd worked so hard to avoid.

Before dropping me off at my Jeep, Fiona's drivers made one extra stop for me. It was getting late in the day, and I still didn't know when the mender was arriving. At best, I was cutting it close. At worst, I needed a better solution for fighting ghosts. If I reached out far enough, I could just feel the spot in the tea garden where the

Ebony Gate had stood. The space felt like a deep, open well. Cold, malevolent energy seethed at the bottom of the shaft, waiting for darkness to arrive. With my new Sentinel senses, the approach of sunset was a ticking clock in my head.

It was time to talk to someone who actually knew something about dispelling ghosts.

Unsurprisingly, the shinigami chose not to enter the Daoist temple with me. I bowed to the attendant and a smile creased her weathered cheeks. Wong Āyí knew me since I made it a point to visit Tin Tong Temple every month. It was one of the oldest Daoist temples in the country, founded during the Gold Rush. The temple had always comforted me and it was established by Wàirén for Wàirén, so my lack of talent was a non-issue here.

Walking in as the Sentinel, when my very skin felt sensitive to every breeze, made me look at the temple with new appreciation for its very normalcy. Here, I could just be a visitor and not the Sentinel and I welcomed the respite.

Before me stood a tall sculpture of Mazu, the sea goddess. The white marble was smooth and worn at the pedestal where many had touched it to seek a blessing for safe crossings. Today I did the same because I sure could use a blessing today.

After bowing my head to Mazu, I walked past the altars and followed the quiet chant of prayers whispering through the hanging red lanterns. I stepped out onto the balcony where Brother Meng stood, his distinctive silver hair shining in the late-afternoon sun.

Brother Meng's tall frame was clad in a plain blue cotton jacket with frog closures over shiny blue athletic pants. His white pristine sneakers were in stark contrast to my crud-encrusted boots, which had stepped in brain goop earlier.

Whenever he looked at me, I wondered if he could see all the stains on my soul. But he was always kind enough to ignore the sad state of my spirit. This temple was one of the few places where I felt like I had a shot at redemption. Like me, Brother Meng could see auras and his own was only the barest hint of peach, unsurprisingly a Black Tortoise talent for foresight. But unlike me, Brother Meng was Outclan. That meant he did not have a clan, and he did not worship our Dragon gods. He was not subject to our Council's edicts. Brother Meng lived among Wàirén, but had that slightest bit of Jiārén talent that set him apart.

I never asked what clan he was descended from. That would be beyond intrusive. But I had my suspicions. It was rare for someone from a clan of fading size and power not to merge into another by marriage, adoption, or alliance. But it did happen. Some of our Jiārén diaspora faded to obscurity. Others like Brother Meng found a way to live amongst Wàirén but still be in contact with other Jiārén.

I envied him his peace and today I had a big ask.

"Emiko, I see you've made a decision."

I blinked. "I did?"

He gestured to my aura.

"Oh."

I bit my lip and gave him the abbreviated version of how in my efforts to recover the Ebony Gate, I'd finally answered the city's call.

"The city chose well for its Sentinel."

I didn't know how to respond but I appreciated Brother Meng's support. I got to the reason for my visit. Brother Meng didn't even raise an eyebrow when I asked to borrow the blessed peachwood sword.

The sword gleamed in the light, its golden wood carved with precision and polished to a high sheen. A gorgeous qílín was scrolled down the blade, the Chinese unicorn that adorned almost all peachwood swords. Delicate script flowed along the scabbard. A pretty sword made of peachwood wouldn't cut down your average opponent but was a time-honored method for dealing with demons. I hoped it would work on the ghosts of Yomi.

Brother Meng polished the sword, read the characters out loud for me, which I recorded on my phone, and then wrapped my hand around its pommel. "Emiko, you are not a Daoist and for this to have the most effect, we must prepare."

I thought that was what we had been doing. But I nodded and waited.

He placed both his hands above the sword and closed his eyes. He began to chant softly, the sounds vibrating in my ears. As Brother Meng hummed, I swore I could hear the chiming of bells around us but it was only the two of us with the sword. I watched his aura but it stayed steady and faint. Instead, a cool wave of energy spread out from his palms. An otherworldly blue light surrounded the peachwood and it practically floated within my grip.

What Brother Meng used was not Jiārén talent but the power of his faith. It was humbling to watch and also horrifying to imagine doing this without him.

When at last he looked up from the sword, the sword had stopped glowing and again felt heavy within my grasp.

"Please, Brother Meng, would you join me in this battle?"

His lips turned down slightly and now I did see his aura deepen in hue. "This is your battle, Emiko, and I believe that arming you with that peachwood sword is the limit of my role in this affair."

My eyes closed in despair. I didn't know if this was enough. If I was enough. I thought about my brother, Tatsuya, anxiously preparing for the Tourney. I thought about the Suns, who had been scared out of their minds the night the fù chóng had attacked Lotus Lane. I owed them. A whip of air slapped my face. When I opened my eyes, several crows flew past our balcony, their caws snapping me out of my funk. A familiar wave of coolness wrapped around my body, making my skin tingle from the contact.

It was the city, giving me a little boost, and a wave of gratitude washed over me for the city lending me its strength, giving me what I needed to break out of the bank vault.

With the gentlest of gestures, the city had reminded me why I was here and what I needed to help keep the city safe from the undead.

"Thank you, Brother Meng." I bowed over the sword.

He gave me a jovial smile. "Before you leave, I wanted to remind you about the Silver Hornets."

Ah yes, this was clearly more pressing for Brother Meng—the Chinatown youth basketball team he was coaching. I didn't need his sales pitch, but I let him do it for form's sake. I agreed to sponsor the uniforms and gym rental costs on the condition it be anonymous.

I paused by the altar on my way out. Dozens of clay jars surrounded the altar, each with several smoldering sticks of fragrant incense.

I bowed three times and asked for guidance for dealing with Yomi's angry spirits. This was my last chance tonight to restore the Gate. I let my breath out slowly and stepped into the dying sunlight.

Sugiwara took one look at the newly acquired sword tucked under my arm and nodded. "Good choice."

I hoped so. Because I didn't have many other options for the evening ahead.

# YOMI UNLEASHED

I parked my Jeep outside the tea garden just as the day's sunlight started to deepen into twilight. Ray Ray still had the blood jade, but we had the Gate. By now, Sugiwara's illusion would have vanished. If he really was a Realmseeker, Ray Ray would be back here tonight, before the shinigami sealed the portal and locked the Gate away again, this time maybe for good. The prospect of another chance to serve Ray Ray a steaming bowl of retribution sent a thrill of anticipation down my arms.

Opening my duffel, I began loading myself up with every bit of gear I had. The vest of dragon scales hugged my chest and moved with me like a second skin. I fell in love immediately and started budgeting for more dragon scale armor. I pulled a clean haori from my pack, shrugged it on, and began packing every hidden pocket with all the goodies Baby Ricky and Sally had sold me. Even with all my fighting gear, I managed to find space for a handful of emergency Kit Kats. Matcha and strawberry. I kept the Demon Cloak in its ornate box, unwilling to take out such a rare artifact until it was necessary.

I quickly rebraided my hair, ignoring the bright silver streak running through it. There would be time to deal with that later. Maybe. I coiled the braid at the back of my neck into a low bun. The peachwood sword was the last addition to my ensemble. I tied it into my belt just below Hachi. If I went down tonight it would not be for lack of trying.

The evening light lengthened the shadows around us, turning the peaceful garden into a sinister warren of dark shapes. Through my new Sentinel senses the portal to Yomi stood out as an island of cold, silent energy in a park that burst at the seams with vibrant life energy. I couldn't believe I'd never sensed it before. In less than an hour that silent energy would wake again. I had to close it tonight.

I put on my earbuds and played my recording of Brother Meng reading the sword characters from earlier. My lips shaped the words and I committed them to memory. I didn't know what they meant really, and I wasn't a monk, but the peachwood sword from Tin Tong Temple was old and had been blessed by many monks. I trusted in Brother Meng's faith and that would have to be enough.

Sugiwara-sama had donned his illusion again. He wore the same wool cap and camel coat as yesterday evening, dapper professor out for his nightly constitutional. The shinigami's gaze wandered back and forth between the rising moon and staring holes through my back. I ignored him and concentrated on memorizing Brother Meng's recording.

Fiona's arctic-white Range Rover pulled in and parked alongside my Jeep. Freddy practically bounced out of the passenger side, looking no worse for the wear. Maybe Popo had given him a booster. Fiona climbed down from the back seat and strutted toward us, her white leather trench coat brushing the tops of her black suede thigh-high boots. She had a gray cashmere hat with a fluffy pom-pom pulled over her hair. Perhaps this was her version of combat wear? When had she found time to change clothes? Maybe she stored an extra wardrobe of outfits in the back of her Range Rover.

No other cars pulled in behind Fiona and I shot her a look. "Did I understate the number of ghosts we would be facing? Where's the rest of your crew?"

Fiona arched an eyebrow back at me. "I left them to oversee the cleanup at the bank. Same as I've been doing for the last two days. Cleaning up after you and my brother."

Well. Touché, then.

A few steps behind Fiona, another tall form emerged from the SUV. My shoulders tensed. Kamon. Just what I needed to make an already fun night even more memorable. I still felt raw inside from our encounter at the hospital. I wasn't ready to be in close quarters with him so soon. I didn't know if I ever would again.

Even at a distance, Kamon's magic pulled me like a magnet and I took a step toward him involuntarily. Kamon was a tiger shifter. They didn't wield magic, they *were* magic. It emanated from them like a solid disk, a corona of orange light. In the daylight it was less obvious but in the dusk and fog, it was a brilliant beacon.

Franklin got out last and took up his station just behind and to Fiona's left. He settled his hulking form at parade rest, looking ready to stand there until the end of the world.

Kamon stopped a few feet away. His dark brows drew together in consternation as he took in the shinigami. I knew his heightened shifter senses told him that everything about "Mr. Sugiwara" was not as it seemed.

The fog rolled in, wisps curling around the shrubs and the trees. Sugiwara moved his arm in a slow sweep and all at once, the black mist rose up from the ground to surround the walls of the tea garden. The mist closed across the broken entrance, thick tendrils of smoke crisscrossing the gap and sealing the ghosts inside the tea garden. With us.

Freddy's eyes opened wide. "Whoa, man."

Sugiwara-sama lifted his head, eyeing the darkening horizon. "At sunset the portal to Yomi will open. My barrier will keep most of them inside the garden, but it will not withstand all of them."

Kamon opened his backpack and took out four small wooden torches and a ball of orange yarn. "We need to build a spirit trap."

The shinigami assessed Kamon, weighing the notion, and then nodded slowly. "That could work."

I had heard of the spirit trap in Tibet but never seen it done. If this spirit trap required any sort of devotion or belief, I would definitely not be the candidate for that task. Instead, I drew the peachwood sword and hefted it. I knew what my task would be.

Kamon turned to me, his eyes homing in on the wooden sword. "Emi, what do you think you're doing with that?"

The deep timbre of his voice brought back a cascade of memories as well as the attendant emotions. Was there an accusation in his tone? I shoved the bubbling feelings back down. Now was definitely not the time. I looked over his shoulder to the fading sliver of sunlight on the horizon.

Beyond the walls of the garden, San Francisco spread over the tip of the peninsula, a densely packed city full of quirky shops and quirkier people. A city that had seen fit to take in a lonely stray and give her a home that she didn't deserve.

"Build the trap, Kamon. Build it fast. I'm going to do what I'm best at."

I turned away before my emotions got the best of me. Freddy caught up to me and we stopped halfway to the gaping hole in the sandstone. At least he seemed to be taking this seriously as he'd put on his Hoard silver, a matched set of antique bracers on his forearms, the metal dull with the patina of time. Tightly set kanji flowed around the metal, something poetic about dragons and standing to the last man. The scent and gleam confirmed that Freddy's silver was an old Hoard piece, passed down through generations.

Freddy had gotten his wind back but he still looked a little peaky. His eyes kept darting between me and the sandstone. "So . . . we got a plan, or what?"

I opened the wooden box and stared at the glittering gold and jade within. "A bit of a plan."

With Freddy's help I got the Demon Cloak out of its box and carefully spread out to its full span. The gold mesh barely covered the stretch of sandstone where the Ebony Gate had once stood watch over the portal to Yomi.

Freddy whistled with awe, his eyes tracing over all the jade medallions. "What does it do?"

I looked up to the faint rising moon. "If I'm right, it should prevent some of the yurei from crossing the portal tonight. I hope I'm right, because I don't think the mender's going to get here in time."

All artifacts needed power, a kickstart to get the juices flowing. Based on our debacle at the Port of Oakland, I knew Freddy had power to spare to activate the Cloak, but something held me back from asking him. It was an itch in my palms and a feeling of depth in my chest, like I could take in a breath, and just keep sucking in air. I felt like I was poised on a cliff edge, ready to jump off. Becoming the Sentinel had changed me. My fight with Saburo, if you could call it that, had sealed it. Now I needed to figure out what that meant.

I knelt and placed my hands on the mesh, half of me wondering what the heck I was doing, the other half eager to see what would happen. Any other time, the thought of activating such an intricate artifact would have been daunting. Now my arms felt electric, brimming with power I'd never had before. I pushed the flow of power into the Demon Cloak and the gold chain began to heat under my palms.

The power felt like the city, but it also felt a little like Freddy's, and oddly, also like Kamon's. I looked around, but only Freddy was watching me, transfixed by the Demon Cloak. Kamon stood with his back to me, talking to Fiona. From the way his arms moved, I could tell he was annoyed. Probably at me. I shut them all out and tried not to think about how closely the musk of Kamon's tiger magic seemed to hang over me.

In a few short moments the gold mesh of the Demon Cloak shimmered with heat and the jade medallions glowed with eerie green and gold light. I sat back on my haunches, wondering at the sight. Not only should that much power have been impossible for me, but I should have been physically and spiritually exhausted from the effort. I felt no more taxed than if I'd walked up a short flight of stairs. If this was a boost from being the Sentinel, I couldn't complain.

The shinigami appeared beside me without warning. Pale white mist drifted from the collar of his overcoat. He looked down his nose at the Demon Cloak. "An interesting gambit."

He turned to me, his eyes flashing red as his illusion slipped. "Tell me, have you prepared yourself for the inevitable outcome tonight?"

Something about the death god niggled my brain. The sound of his voice, or perhaps the color of his coat. I reached for it, but the thought slipped away like a live fish. I shook my head to clear the image and refocus.

"We have the Gate. The mender is on his way. Ray Ray wants the Gate, so he will come to us. He will bring the blood jade. We will repair the Ebony Gate."

The death god's smile was completely devoid of humor. "That is not the inevitable outcome."

He waved a hand at the Demon Cloak. "This . . . bauble . . . cannot hold the hordes of Yomi. You should prepare yourself, young Sentinel. I will await your earth mender, but when the time comes, I believe I will take your soul for the anchor to the Gate."

With that the shinigami turned on his heel and strode away. He stopped next to the portal and pulled out the white satin satchel with the Gate fragments. Without a word he upended the bag, spilling the shattered pieces to the grass in an unruly pile. He turned back and gave me another humorless smile. I had to admit, relying on Ray Ray's arrogance was not optimal. This had to work. If not for me, then for Tatsuya.

Freddy moved to stand by me and we watched the shinigami begin working with Kamon. "That is one seriously weird dude."

It broke the tension. For all his shortcomings, Freddy had been an admirable ally over the last two days. Whatever happened tonight, I was glad I'd had the chance to meet him. I clapped him on the shoulder. "You got that right, Freddy."

His eyes widened and his grin creased his whole face. I couldn't help but smile back. He pointed at me. "There it is! So, what's my part in your plan?"

I dug through my bag, pulling out my box of salt and a handful of bagua mirrors. Behind us, Kamon and the shinigami laid out the torches in a square pattern while Fiona walked the perimeter, stringing the yarn between them.

I didn't have a Buddhist's faith for protection, but I did have some time-honored recipes. I walked a circle around Freddy, laying down a thick trail of salt. "The plan is for you to stay inside this circle."

"What?! Emiko, I can—"

I cut him off with a look. Freddy had done so much for me, with little complaint. I owed it to him to keep him as safe as possible.

He deflated under my glare. "Fine."

I arranged four of the mirrors, propping them up in the salt. Hopefully it would be enough to keep the ghosts off Freddy.

"You stay here. Watch my back. It's going to be a madhouse, so keep them off of me, hear? As soon as Kamon and Sugiwara have the trap ready, start funneling them over there like your life depends on it. Because . . . it kind of does."

Freddy gave me a thumbs-up.

The last slice of sunlight died and a discordant, keening chorus wafted up from the open portal. I shivered, the sound grating on my nerves like nails on a chalkboard. I turned back to the portal and found Fiona at my side, pale white mist cascading down her arms. The harsh tang of seawater surrounded her.

As shadow crept over the sandstone, the stone caved in like it had the previous night, imploding in a spray of sand, grit, and stale coffin air. Everyone lifted an arm against the fetid air and squinted against the spray of sand. Except for Sugiwara-sama, who stood as still as a statue in a calm breeze.

A wave of choking energy bloomed from the portal and the wails of the dead increased until it felt like the sound was etched inside my head. Another gust of dust-filled air and the Demon Cloak bowed upward with some invisible force pulling it taut across the opening of the portal. One by one the jade medallions brightened, the script on each one glowing bright yellow. The mesh heaved like a bellows, straining to resist the forces of the dead. I stood on the balls of my feet, my senses tuned to a razor's edge, my palms itching to grip or hurl a weapon.

The first ghost popped through the mesh, an amorphous blob of black energy, the surface slick like oil. The ghost screamed as it was pressed through the mesh, the gold chains cutting it to pieces even as the spelled jade consumed the ghost. The screams continued, and the ghost pressed through the Demon Cloak like a jellyfish through a cheese grater. It reformed as it passed through the portal into a headless man in a tattered suit, carrying a rotting head in its arms. The face on the head screamed as the body lunged at Fiona. Fiona spun on one toe, delicate as a prima ballerina, and flung her arm out, mist trailing like streamers. Power surged from her, pressing in on my new senses. A wave of pressure arced away from her outstretched arm and slammed into the ghost, ripping its spectral form in two at the waist. The two halves of the ghost fell apart, dissolving into ribbons of dark energy. Impressive.

A second ghost squeezed through the gold mesh, this one's head wreathed in black flames. Black fire gouted from its mouth as it screamed and bore down on me. The peachwood sword danced in my hands, striking out gracefully as I dodged aside. The ornate dragon carved into the wood glowed like hot embers as the sword pierced the ghost's form. With only the barest resistance, the sword cleaved through the specter, reducing it to billowing ash.

The wailing dead quieted and silence descended on the tea garden like a blanket.

Fiona arched a finely wrought eyebrow. "Is that it? I got all dressed up, for this?"

Before I could answer, Kamon shouted. "Here they come!"

A flood of undead energy burst from the Gate like a geyser, the shock wave throwing Fiona and me to the ground. The Demon Cloak glowed red hot and one of the jade medallions crackled with a spray of green sparks. One by one the light in the other medallions died. Another torrent of death energy blasted upward and the Demon Cloak tore off the stone and disappeared into the night. The sickly sweet scent of death and grave rot poured out of the portal as dozens of ghosts shot through—a ghastly parade of the unsettled dead. Skeletal men with heads covered only in tiny fanged mouths. Screaming women with skinny, elongated necks covered in sores. Floating heads dragging glistening ropes of entrails. Amorphous clouds of shadow.

The stench of rotting flesh and decay washed over us like a tide. Inside his circle, Freddy fell to his knees, dry heaving. Fiona staggered, her glossy complexion going a little green around the edges.

I gripped the peachwood sword in both hands. I had been the Blade of Soong and, as much as I might regret it, the Butcher of Beijing. I had faced and beaten countless gāo-class talents. I had fought, maimed, and killed, all for the honor and power of my clan. All of those fights had been for Soong's good name. For business.

This one was personal. Tonight I was fighting for my brother.

Tonight I was fighting for the heart and soul of the city I had come to love like no other.

Battle calm fell over my shoulders, my senses prickling as I unconsciously categorized and prioritized the multitude of threats before me. I noted that Fiona was back on her feet, her body pulsing with latent power. The qillin on the sword glowed faintly and the wood warmed to my touch. I let loose a battle cry and stormed into the oncoming wave of hungry ghosts.

# THE MENDER

Dozens of ghosts filled the tea garden with their piercing screams. More threatened to pour forth from the portal at any moment. Most bolted for the walls of the garden, only to be turned back by Sugiwara's ward. The smoky black barrier sealed the garden, stretching skyward to block the ghosts trying to fly over the walls. The angered yurei turned their frustrations on us, the only living targets available to them.

Fiona and I danced through the tea garden, fighting a containment battle, trying to keep the ghosts hemmed in around the portal to Yomi. Well, I slashed and Fiona danced. As in, Fiona was—literally—dancing. I don't know how she did it, considering those sky-high boots, but she pirouetted and pranced between the ornamental trees, slicing ghosts with blades of air as she went. The white mist surrounding her veiled her like a gauzy cloud. Her dainty, manicured hands breezed through the mist, sending hardened air at her targets. It looked like art.

If Fiona's side was like a ballet recital, then my side was more like a gory monster movie. If ghosts could bleed, my side would have looked like a Jackson Pollock painting. The peachwood sword stabbed and slashed, tearing its way through one ghost after another. More and more grotesque spirits poured forth from the portal, carried on an unending wave of dread energies.

I spun and stabbed the sword up to the hilt into a ghost with the body of a woman and the broken, bloody head of a jackal. A spiral funnel opened up to my left and a headless ghost that had been screaming down on me was sucked away. My head snapped up and I whirled to check on Freddy. He was still in his protective circle, hands together at his chest, eyes narrowed in concentration. The headless ghost popped back into existence ten feet above Kamon's head and fell into the ghost trap. I gave Freddy a thumbs-up. The kid was doing well.

But we should have been doing better. Torches blazed at the four corners of the trap and even across the garden the fiery prickle of magic tickled my senses. That thing should have been sucking up ghosts for a mile in all directions.

Freddy's eyes turned into dinner plates looking over my shoulder. "Emiko! Get down!"

I didn't hesitate. I dropped to the ground and rolled, gravel crunching under my shoulder. I came up in a crouch, sword up and ready, but it wasn't a ghost behind me. The air in front of me shimmered and swirled, an oval slice of air flowing like mercury and showing a twisted reflection of the tea garden. The portal swelled and two bodies materialized and fell to the ground. The portal collapsed on itself with a pop. Thank the Great Dragon Father! I didn't recognize the young woman, but the older man was Ah Wing, our inbound earth mender. He crawled to the unconscious girl and rolled her onto her back gently.

I jumped to his side, sword swinging through the skinny neck of a ghost coming up on Ah Wing from behind. "Ah Wing, you need to get to the Gate!"

The older man shook the young girl, trying to rouse her. "Lilly's drained! Too many jumps!"

Kamon appeared at his side and scooped up the slender girl in his arms. Orange fire danced around his eyes. "I've got her! Go with Emi!"

Fiona danced between us and flung her arms out as she twirled. The hardened air brushed my hair back as it whipped by. She planted her feet and threw both hands toward the open Gate. A gale of wind kicked up a rooster tail of dust and plowed a furrow in the ground leading to the Gate. All the ghosts along the path disintegrated.

I grabbed Ah Wing by the collar and pushed him as I ran, throwing my respect for elders out the window. "Go! Go!"

We bounded over the portal and reached the shattered remains of the Ebony Gate. Ah Wing went to his knees at the mound of ebony fragments. His huge eyes found mine, disbelief plain on his face. "You need me . . . to mend . . . this?"

The peachwood sword whistled through the air and lopped the head off a ghost that had just appeared through the portal. Ah Wing's frightened gaze went from the pile of Gate fragments, to me, and to the slowly discorporating ghost. He gave me a slight nod and bent to his work.

"Freddy! Fiona! Protect the mender!"

Too late I realized my mistake. My yell had drawn the attention of the screaming horde of yurei. The yurei closed in, surrounding me and Ah Wing. Their howls rose, blotting out everything beyond the ring of ghosts pressing in on us. I backed up until I was nearly standing on top of Ah Wing.

Fiona pressed in, her scythes of air wreaking havoc through the ghostly throngs. It would take her too long to get to us.

I pulled off my necklace and whistled a high, piercing note. My father's talent exploded around me in a wave of green, pushing back the suffocating press of hungry ghosts. The scent of sawdust and white pepper stung my nose. Bāo landed at my feet with a thump and shook out his crimson mane, a steady rumble already rolling in his massive chest. The ghosts pressed in around us and Ah Wing plastered himself to the grass, his arms up over his head.

I sheathed the peachwood sword and dug one hand into Bāo's mane, wrapping the other around Ah Wing's shoulders, and ducked my head down. "Now, boy!"

Bāo's muscles tensed under my hand and he let loose a roar that shook the earth beneath my feet. The power of his roar blew my hair back and cleared a radius of twenty feet around the pile of Gate fragments. Ghosts within that radius were blasted to wisps of harmless vapor and carried away by the evening breeze.

I grabbed the old man by the collar of his jacket and pulled him up to his knees, pivoting him until he faced the broken Gate again. "Fix it! Fix it fast!"

Bāo leapt over my shoulder, his jaws stretched wide and roaring, sharp fangs shining in the moonlight. I whirled in time to see him crash into a massive ghost covered in bleeding wounds. I drew the peachwood sword and waded in after my lion, hacking away at the ghost until it shredded away.

More yurei boiled out of the hole in the earth at my feet. The peachwood snapped out again and again. Bāo leapt in and out of the darkness, his claws carving arcs of green light as he sliced through ghostly bodies. Together we created a small area around Ah Wing to give him a safe bubble in which to work on the Gate.

Fighting Jiārén was easy compared to this—at least they got tired. This horde of ghosts was relentless. In an eyeblink, my fatigue got the best of me. I brought the sword up a hair too slow and a ghost, this one's body covered with pus-filled sores, lunged in and grabbed my sword arm. Icy black pain exploded in my arm.

The ghost opened its gaping mouth and swallowed my sword and arm whole, driving dozens of spectral needle teeth into my forearm. A black hole of pain blossomed, draining my qì away. On the other side of the gate, Fiona whirled through a host of specters, cutting them to ribbons. Freddy had gone to his knees inside his circle, sweat pouring down his cheeks. An open funnel above the Gate sucked up the ghosts, almost as fast as they could appear. I dropped to one knee and the tea garden went fuzzy around the edges, the sounds of battle becoming muted and distant.

At my feet, Ah Wing shuddered, his eyes closed, hands held

above the shattered Gate, his fingers intertwined in a painful-looking knot. The broken fragments of the Gate trembled, the entire mound of ebony vibrating, each piece dancing with energy. He would fix the Gate. I just needed to give him more time.

Tiger magic flared, hot and electric.

Kamon burst from the darkness. In midleap his brilliant orange aura flashed. Rippling muscle flexed and expanded across his arms and back. His immaculate dress shirt burst apart at the seams as he added another hundred kilos of mass. Gold and black fur in jagged stripes erupted across his body. Fingers and hands widened into paws the size of dinner plates with hooked claws extended. His face broadened and his eyes glowed yellow as his irises snapped open. His mouth opened, wider and wider, his teeth elongating into man-killer fangs. It all happened in less than a second, a fluid transformation that looked as natural as someone taking off a coat. My ex-boyfriend in full beast mode.

Kamon's leap carried him into the ghost that had my arm. His jaws closed on the ghost's head, massive fangs brushing against my arm. His jaws closed, the muscles flexing under his golden pelt, and the ghost crunched. Kamon shook his head, twisting the ghost away from me and tearing it to ribbons.

My arm dropped to my side, the feel of the ghostly teeth a burning ring of ice around my forearm. Thankfully I still had the peachwood sword clutched in my hand. I'd hate to tell Brother Meng I'd lost his priceless relic on my first night out. Kamon prowled protectively around me as I got my arm to start listening to my brain again. That had been close. At least as close as my run-in with the fù chóng. If Kamon hadn't shown up the ghost would have sucked me dry. I owed him. Again.

Relief and adrenaline coursed through me, sending me into giddiness. Never one to pass up an opportunity, I reached out with my good arm and stroked his back as he passed me. His fur was soft and burning hot under my hand. "Who's a good kitty?"

He froze midstride and that majestic head turned to me, ears twitching in a way that I knew meant he was really annoyed with me now.

Freddy yelped and I turned back to see him pumping his fists in excitement. Ah Wing, visibly trembling with exertion, stood over a partially rebuilt Ebony Gate. Streaks of forest green rippled through his aura and my shoulders sagged in relief. The remaining pieces floated above him as his arms moved in a mysterious symphony above the Gate. Hope rose in my heart. He was *so* close.

Ah Wing gave a small sigh of triumph, his demeanor relaxing a bit even as his hands stayed locked in position. One by one, chips of ebony floated down and clicked into place. With each piece, the pulse of calming energy quieted the mob of ghosts around us.

I relaxed. A little. We still needed the anchor. Where was Ray Ray?

Across the Gate, Fiona dropped her hands to her knees, her chest heaving. I wasn't going to complain about the reprieve, but I kept my sword up. The ghosts milled about, keeping their distance. Very odd.

I elbowed Kamon. "Your trap doesn't seem to be working very well."

Even as I said it the familiar stench of shoe leather and gunpowder hit my senses. Ash and blood! My eyes tracked up to the roofline of the teahouse. I should have known that the Louies' ghost master would come here. He was driving the ghosts, making them insane with hunger.

Nothing on the roof. I scanned the tree line, looking for any hint of his position. The scent of his talent kindled hot fury in my gut. I stoked that feeling higher and higher until it turned into rage. The scar on my shoulder pulsed, as if the city's magic was vibrating within me.

Kamon frowned, his shoulder muscles bunching as he tensed. "I noticed. Maybe we didn't—"

Something twitched at my senses and I whirled. Kamon spun at the same moment, and I knew he'd felt the same thing. Oily tendrils of death talent stretched out from within the trees and expanded into a fine net that blanketed the entire garden with the scent of his vile summons.

The portal to Yomi clenched, like the death spasm of a corrupted heart, and spewed forth a deluge of specters from the underworld. The explosion knocked Ah Wing off his knees and the old man covered his head with his arms as he fell. The spinning pieces of the Gate clattered to the ground like rain. The twisting mass of ghosts rose into the air, a serpentine column of horrors. The end of the mass opened in a silent scream and descended onto the huddling earth mender.

I screamed and charged the ghosts.

More screams echoed from the depths of the Gate, more horrors surged out of Yomi. The portal disgorged a river of souls, adding to the spectral horde. Strikes snuck past my guard, leaving ghost burns on my arms, my shoulders, my back. There were just too many.

This is how it all ends, a small voice whispered in my head. You lose everyone and everything. My mind conjured an early memory of my brother, his small face scrunched in concentration as I showed him how to use chopsticks. If I didn't fulfill the Talon, Tatsuya would never be safe from the shinigami.

I helped Ah Wing up and ordered Bāo to help Fiona protect him. As the mender resumed his work Kamon and I pressed out, reclaiming lost territory around the Gate. The main mass of ghosts twisted around the tea garden, as big as a Muni bus and twice as long. It opened its mouth at one end and a tide of blackness gushed out. The inky black broke apart into dozens of screaming ghosts and streaked toward us.

Franklin melted out of the darkness at Fiona's side and put his body between Fiona and the incoming demons. He set his feet and raised his arms, letting out a guttural shout. I grabbed Kamon by the scruff and we dove behind them. A wall of shimmering blue energy blossomed between Franklin's hands and expanded to ten feet around him. This was much more than just Dragon Limbs. I had underestimated the range of his talent.

My mouth dropped open. Franklin was Fiona's personal aegis. No wonder he never left her side.

The yurei crashed into the barrier and disintegrated into mist. With every impact the shield flashed with brilliant blue-white light. Franklin grunted as each ghost hit, his feet dragging furrows through the grass as his body was pushed back.

The cohort of undead writhed and screamed as it careened inside the shinigami's containment field. It twisted back toward us and the spectral mass slammed into Franklin's shield, causing it to flash with blinding light that lit up the whole tea garden for a split second.

Fiona cried out as Franklin's eyes rolled up into his head and he collapsed. She ran to catch him before he fell, just as the barrier disappeared. Fiona laid Franklin gently to the grass and then whipped around, her eyes bright with fury. Her arms flashed forward and a blade of air whistled across the grass, digging a deep furrow that cut across the lawn and through the spectral horde in one stroke. The horde broke apart, many of the ghosts fading into mist.

Kamon's magic flashed again and he appeared beside me, back in human form, steam pouring off his naked body.

Blood streamed from his wounds but I could see them already shrinking up, the ghost burns healing before my eyes. Handy.

I kept my eyes locked on his and definitely didn't look anywhere else no matter how much I wanted to. He growled and wrested the wooden sword off my hip, his eyes full of concern and exasperation. "You haven't changed. Always crashing through the jungle like a raging elephant."

He unsheathed the sword and handed it to me, keeping the scabbard. The ghosts were rallying, closing in around us again. The scent of his magic filled my head, a musk of raw magic and unbridled power. My shoulder burned where his hand touched me, my nerves on fire as if waking up from being numb. Standing inside the blazing corona of his magic ignited a liquid heat in my belly. I thrust my sword out and skewered a ghost coming up behind his back. Electric tingles crawled across my arm where I touched Kamon's side. "Sometimes the best solution is to jump in and figure it out."

His nose twitched, an expression of annoyance I recognized from his tiger form. It was adorable. "When will you learn to ask for help?"

I half grinned, still punch-drunk. "I had it all under control."

He shook his head, even that motion catlike, and spun me around so we were back-to-back. "Stay close."

The heat of Kamon's body washed over my back like a tide. He was standing close. *Really* close. The pulse of his magic went up a notch as he began chanting in a low voice. In a moment I realized he was chanting Brother Meng's prayer. Tiger magic throbbed around us, surrounding us like humid jungle air. I inhaled the rich scent of newly turned earth, lush vegetation, and fresh blood. I regripped the sword, the qílín glowing again with fresh power, the sword nearly smoking with the heat of it. Once again the peachwood was feather-light in my hands. At my back Kamon growled low and deep in his chest, the animal in him tearing to get out.

I knew Kamon's magic intimately, but I'd never felt it like this before. I blamed the city and my newly acquired Sentinel abilities, which sensitized me to the energies flowing around me. Kamon had always smelled good, a heady mix of cut grass and cool water. My blood was running hot now and when I stood so close to him I wanted to trip him to the ground and take him for a fast ride.

I'd have to settle for a battle with the undead instead. We waded into the ghosts together, his magic wrapped around the two of us like a protective shroud. The peachwood sword flashed out again and again, almost leaping out of my hands as it dispatched the yurei. Kamon protected my back, using the wooden scabbard as an improvised tanbo. The lettering on the scabbard glowed white hot as it clawed through our spectral attackers.

Kamon grunted. "Just like old times, eh?"

My neck twitched and I ducked, barely avoiding a clawing hand tipped with razor-sharp nails. I whipped my sword out and speared the ghost through its abdomen, a lethal liver strike on a human. The ghost simply faded into acrid smoke. "Which old times are you referring to?"

Kamon ducked and swung his tanbo. "Pahang Park."

I grunted in acknowledgment. How had I forgotten? We'd gone hiking while visiting his family in Malaysia but timed it too late. A hive of penanggalan had found us after dark and really, there is just no reasoning with ravenous floating vampires. We'd hacked our way out of the bamboo forest and left a trail of penanggalan organs behind us. Good times.

"There were only a dozen penanggalan then, Emiko. We can't keep this up."

He was right. We were never going to get out of here with the ghost master out there driving the yurei.

I fell in behind Kamon, letting him take the brunt of the fighting as I recentered, listening for the city's magic. Here in the tea garden, teeming with life and, tonight, death, the city's magic was mine to take. I sank into it and light blossomed before my eyes.

Kamon shone like a star, his innate magic like the setting sun. Bāo was the deep green of my father's talent, with a spot of darkness in the center of his chest. The city's magic ran across the ground like underground wiring, the power fading as it rose into the air.

From the tree line, the ghost master's power seeped outward like stink from rotting meat. I followed the stench backward, tracing the lines of power to their source. I gave a small sigh of satisfaction as I found my prey.

Kamon narrowed his eyes. Don't do it.

I blinked, the picture of innocence. Do what?

I tossed the peachwood sword at Kamon. He caught it with a snap and yelled something at me. I couldn't be sure what he said, maybe something about running off half-cocked. I didn't care. I bolted for the trees, the rage in my belly boiling over into bloodlust that made my arms tingle and quiver for violence.

# SACRIFICE

I flew across the garden, heading straight for the silhouette, my steps quick and sure. My eyes drank in what little light we had from the moon and the city, illuminating the trees like a spotlight. There, in the branches of the first pine tree, the shadowy form of my prey. Even at this distance the hollowed lines of his cheek were unmistakable. Anthony Chow. He'd unleashed the fù chóng on me and then Lotus Lane. The fù chóng had killed the grocer, Hon Wei, leaving his body in the street like a piece of trash. Chow had shown no respect for the life of my city and I would exact my judgment. The need for retribution sizzled in my veins as I ran. I wanted nothing more than to sink my claws into Chow's soft belly. Too late, I saw the glint of moonlight off a gun barrel.

I reached into my jacket and brought out a globe of Steel Wind. It wouldn't be enough against a gun but I was also a moving target in the dark. I'd take those chances. With barely a thought, orange flames burst into life around my hand, making the globe shine like a star. I nearly stumbled as I marveled at the power I'd unleashed and crushed the globe between my fingers.

Before I could think about the aberration, the spell globe's effects began. Cool wind blossomed around me and the sounds of ghostly battle disappeared as a perfect bubble of Steel Wind sealed around me. It was quiet inside the power's embrace, making it almost feel like the world outside had stopped.

Sparks showered off the front of my bubble as I approached the tree line. The gun flashed again and again and sound began to leak through as my shield slowly buckled.

I grimaced and drew Hachi. All right, you jerk, Second Law it was again, then. The Advocate was really going to earn her pay tomorrow.

I ran up to the pine tree at full speed, a hunger inside me driving me toward my prey. I planted a foot on the trunk and launched myself up into the branches, my eyes piercing the darkness with ease. I swung Hachi and sound returned in a crash as I shattered my Steel Wind from the inside. I twisted and slashed Hachi, slicing through the branch and into Chow's belly. He gave a strangled, raspy cry of pain as he came crashing down.

I flipped in the air and landed neatly on my feet next to the base of the tree. The ghost master crashed to the manicured grass in a heap of jumbled limbs, the metallic tang of blood thick in the air. He wasn't moving much, but he was still alive. Mostly. I aimed to change that . . . permanently.

I closed in on soft feet, raising Hachi to make a final killing blow and spill his steaming innards.

Firm hands grabbed my wrists and Kamon pressed against me from behind, his arms locking mine and preventing them from moving. I spun, tried to twist away but he held me tight. Bright flames danced around his eyes, his irises glowing gold in the firelight. "Emiko! Stop."

He couldn't stop me. Even from this position I had at least four counters to break free and gut him with my blade. The strength of the city filled my limbs, aching to throw Kamon off me and put Chow down like a rabid dog. I growled. "Why should I?"

His hands flexed around my wrists, his forearms iron cords of muscle. He grunted with the effort of restraining me. His eyes flicked from me to the body at the base of the tree. "Emiko. Stop it. This isn't you."

Two years had passed and he was still judging me by his high standards. I couldn't meet them then and I wasn't about to try now.

I went still, dropped my hand off the hilt of the sword, and elbowed him in the ribs. Hard. He let out a grunt of surprise. His hands let go and his breath wooshed out. I whirled and stepped back, bringing Hachi up between us. "And you know who I am?"

Kamon took a step back and held up both hands, palms out. He didn't even flinch toward the bruised rib. "Why are you doing this? I thought you came here to get away from your father. From your past."

I had. And I had ended it with Kamon because his expectations were also too much. While my father had pointed me at his enemies and set me loose, Kamon had been the other end of the spectrum, a model of peace and iron self-control.

The ghost master moaned, blood leaking from his belly in a slow trickle. He had one fist stuffed into his mouth and he whimpered like a whipped dog. Three of his fingers ended in brutal stumps, the ends cracked and blackened.

The unsatisfied need for vengeance in my belly drove me forward. "He let these ghosts loose in the city. In *my* city! To hurt *my* people!"

Kamon shook his head. "Question him. Leave it to the Council. You don't have to be the executioner. You're not the Blade anymore."

He was right. Of course he was. But I was also right. The roiling emotion at my core burst, filling my limbs with enough power to make my skin glow. I'd spent my whole life locking down my aura and hiding my stunted qì. No more. The city spoke to me in my mind, and I loosed the power from its shackles.

My aura exploded around me, lighting up the trees around us. Kamon's eyes widened, and then his pupils contracted to slits against the light. The power of the Sentinel blazed through me. I opened my mouth and words spilled out, like someone spoke through me. "I am not the Blade. I am the Sentinel of San Francisco."

Kamon's voice was a bare whisper, his eyes filled with sadness. "Emiko."

Power poured through me like a geyser, more power than I'd ever experienced in my entire life. It filled me to bursting, setting my skin to tingling with giddy, electric energy, The city reached through me again. "Your Councils mean nothing to me. Those who wrong my city are subject to my law."

I fought for control, pushing back against the power, and it was like trying to hold back an ocean with just my hands. The city bucked under me and Kamon went to his knees as the ground shook. I clamped my jaw shut and closed my eyes. Behind my lids, the magic of San Francisco burned around me like a wildfire, radiating out from my feet. The flames leapt toward me, eager to burn, desperate to consume me.

No.

I had not traded one yoke for another. I slowed my breaths and calmed my thoughts. The city would not have me this way. I would not be a mindless tool again.

A freight train of emotions barreled through me. This time I took a moment to see what was mine, and what was the city's. I was jaded. Hardened. Focused. The city was young. Impulsive. Impetuous. We were a fine pair. The flames at my feet lowered, guttering out at the edges, the color fading. The power coursing through me slowed as well and I pushed harder. I would not lose myself to the city.

Finally the flames were mere embers at my feet and the city's power was a comforting heat under my boots. I opened my eyes. Kamon knelt on the grass before me, his eyes wide with shock.

I gestured for him to get up. "I'm back. It's me."

He didn't move. "You're sure?"

"As sure as I can be. I think the city and I just had a bit of a disagreement. But I think we're clear on our relationship now."

A wave of emotion flashed across his face. "I thought I'd lost you. Again."

Well, this wasn't the time to open that particular wound. "I'm fine."

I offered my hand and pulled Kamon to his feet. We worked well together, we always had. We'd been a good team, just not the greatest couple. But that had been my fault. There was no reason to drag him over those stones again.

The ghost master groaned and I realized he wasn't whimpering. He was *laughing*. I spun, bringing Hachi up, and time seemed to slow down.

The ghost master cackled and his talent burst forth from him in a wave of nauseating energy. A bright red spurt of blood fountained from his belly. What was he doing? Pushing that hard with that wound would kill him. A manic grin stretched his mouth and tears leaked from the corners of his eyes.

The scent of bitter black sesame nearly choked me. I opened my Sentinel senses and Ray Ray's talent lit up the air around me, twisting lines of sickly pink. The lines blanketed the tea garden and converged on the ghost master, plunging into his chest and infiltrating his meridians.

Chow's eyes rolled up into his head and his laughter died as the remaining color drained from his face. A fresh spurt of blood spilled from his abdomen. As he died his remaining fingers crumbled to ash.

A ghostly chorus screamed in unison, blanketing the tea garden in psychic pain. Freddy and Fiona yelled for help.

The death mark on my hand burned with icy heat and the shinigami's voice boomed inside my head. "The anchor, Sentinel. NOW."

From the trees between us and the portal, Ray Ray Louie stepped out of the shadows, the blood jade at his neck shining like an evil star.

# FRIENDS

Ray Ray gave me an oily smile. "Emiko, be a dear and take me to the Gate."

He truly was the dim bulb in the Louie Clan. The city's magic swelled within me and I swatted down the tendrils of his talent. Beside me, Kamon had found the strength to break Ray Ray's influence as well. Wow. Immune to charm speaking. So unfair.

I threw two shurikens at Ray Ray, aiming to cut the pendant right off his fat neck. A funnel of wind blocked the razor-sharp blades from reaching their target. The tang of ocean hit my nose as Freddy opened a portal in front of Ray Ray, blocking me from charging in with Hachi.

Freddy's face had gone slack, his eyes vacant. Pink lines of power snaked up from the earth, through Freddy's back. "Emiko, Ray Ray is our friend. We have to help him."

Ray Ray smirked behind his new shield.

Kamon growled his frustration. I was frustrated, too—with myself. Sure, I was immune now as the Sentinel, but I'd been so focused on my plan I had neglected to protect Freddy and Fiona, my allies, my friends, from Ray Ray's talent.

I backed up a couple steps. "You want the Gate? It's over there."

I glanced quickly over my shoulder. Fiona stood guard over Franklin's body, her chest heaving, but her ensemble still flawless. Between them, Ah Wing had collapsed atop the now intact Ebony Gate. A trickle of blood ran out of his ear, his face frozen in a grimace of pain. A small hole in the center of the structure remained open, ready to accept the blood jade anchor.

Fiona had to shout to be heard over the wails of tortured ghosts. "What's happening, Mimi?"

Hearing her voice, Ray Ray's face became even more smug. He snapped his fingers. With the city's magic, I watched the pink lines of his talent plunge into the back of her neck. Fiona's eyes widened into blank saucers. Her arm lashed out, a wind blade whipping toward Kamon. My heart stopped as Kamon leapt, grace and power as he shifted in the air. Landing well away from the path of Fiona's wind blade, he swished his tail, almost taunting. Fiona focused on him, intent on her target.

With a lazy movement, Kamon prowled toward her. She raised her arms, gearing up for another round, but Kamon took off like a shot, diving into the thick greenery. Fiona stalked after the tiger, leaving me blessedly without having to worry about one more hostage for Ray Ray.

I had to take Freddy out of the equation. He'd turned that goon at the pier into meat paste. I couldn't afford to take it easy on him. But I liked Freddy and I didn't want to hurt him.

The fire from my power struggle with the city had not dimmed. Heat still simmered from the soles of my boots as if heated by the very dirt below me. I took in a deep breath, flaring my nostrils and inhaling the city's fog mixed with the shinigami's dark mist. The wound on my shoulder throbbed in pain but also in unison with my breath.

I inhaled and let my shoulders soften as I stepped backward to sink gently against the earth. My spine rounded and qì sunk low to my dāntián as I gathered the city's mist around me.

Freddy stepped forward as I stepped back and Ray Ray proceeded cautiously forward, a macabre dance toward the Gate.

I cycled my qì through my body and pressed my palms together. I just needed a little bit more. Each step I took backward, I inhaled to gather the breath of the city within me. I stretched my senses out, feeling around me and deep into the trees. Kamon, hot and electric in my mind, bounded away, darting between the trees and staying just ahead of Fiona.

Ray Ray needed a hard lesson, but I had to take Fiona and Freddy out of the picture first. Without hurting them. Not exactly my forte.

Freddy moved between us and raised his hands, opening two more funnels on either side of me. Freddy's face paled in the moonlight. Skies, Ray Ray was going to drive Freddy over the edge the same way he did the ghost master.

"I'm not some upstart Claw. You're out of your depth here, siu ze."

Oh, Ray Ray was just asking for it now. I cycled my qì faster, pulling harder on the heat in the damp soil beneath me. Cool fog coalesced around my legs, thickening into an opaque soup that spread out ten feet around me.

I squared my shoulders and dropped my weight into my hips. "What do you even want the Gate for?"

Ray Ray smirked. "Oh, you'll figure it out eventually. Soon, everyone will know."

I barely dodged in time. The fog around me stirred, giving me the barest warning. I dropped to the ground and rolled, a hard scythe of air passing through the space where my head had just been. Broken Claw, that was close. I came up on my knees and pulled the city's magic around me like a blanket, thickening the fog.

Fiona stood at the tree line, arms spread wide. The next scythe came in low, flat to the ground to cut me off at the knees. Freddy's funnel opened next to my shoulder, pushing me into the incoming blade. I was out of moves, stuck between two gāo talents with more than enough power to crush me like a grape.

Simple muscle memory saved me. I threw my arm up as if to block Fiona's air blade. The city's power exploded under my feet and surged up my spine. The hairs on my arm stood up and I clamped down, forcing the power to follow my lead.

Tons of earth and sod erupted at my feet, rising in a wave to absorb Fiona's attack. I clenched both my fists and the grounds of the tea garden liquefied. The Trans cried out as they sank into the earth to their knees in an instant. The shinigami floated serenely above the roiling dirt, watching the interplay with an amused expression on his pale face.

All of the city's magic lay at my fingertips and I had claimed it for my own for the limited purpose of protecting the citizens. My control was tenuous, but this was the only way I could think of neutralizing the Trans without hurting them.

It was now or never. I rooted my stance. Exhaling, I swept my hands together in a huge push move. I was not an air mage like the Trans but the city controlled the air all around us and heeded my command. Waves of air rolled away from us like a detonating bomb with me as the epicenter. Freddy gasped and froze, his eyes blinking in stunned fear. Fiona doubled over, wheezing.

Acting on instinct, I sunk low into my horse stance, pouring my qì back into the earth. I shifted my weight and moved my right leg back into a deep snake stance, inhaling as I did so. The air cycled around me, the very air I'd wrested away from Freddy and Fiona. Freddy wobbled, his lips opening and closing like a fish. I pulled again, sucking in the air, swirling the fog around me into a vortex of mist. Freddy and Fiona gasped for air, their faces going blue.

I pulled harder, qì cycling through me like a cool river. The Trans went down to their hands. My limbs burned. Just a little more. Freddy's eyes fluttered closed and his head hit the grass.

Pain flared in my side, white hot and sharp. My qì flow fell away, falling apart like snow in a fire. The swirling air stopped, fog dissipating into wisps of vapor. I went to one knee, agony spiking through my chest and into my heart.

Ray Ray Louie stood frozen behind me, his hand on the handle of what had to be an eight-inch blade, six of which he had currently in my side below my ribs, just below the reach of my vest of scales.

Between the waves of pain, I trembled with the conflicting need to strangle Ray Ray and the need to stay still and not bleed out. This smug banker had gotten the drop on me. Would I die of humiliation or blood loss first?

Fatigue washed over me, and I forgot the pain as I fought to keep my eyes on Ray Ray. I couldn't die like this, stabbed by a lowlife hopped-up thief.

As I stared into his eyes, his satisfaction drained away to be replaced by terror. A cold sheen of sweat covered Ray Ray's face, his eyes rolling with fear.

The shinigami loomed over Ray Ray's back, his power cascading off his shoulders in cold waves of pearlescent smoke. One skeletal hand extended from his pale robes, bony fingers in a death grip around Ray Ray's wrist and keeping his knife from going any farther.

Sugiwara's voice was low and terrible, the sound of waking nightmares. "I will not allow Miss Soong to be harmed."

His eyes dropped to where the knife had pierced my side, blood welling around the wound. "Any further."

Oh, so he was a comedian now.

# THE ANCHOR

The icy power of the shinigami broke through the fatigue. In typical fashion, the death god didn't get rid of my problem. But he had kept me from taking a blade to the heart, so that counted for something.

There was a last bit of my qì cycling in my dāntián. With a soft exhale, I softened my torso and sank low, calling the city's magic to me as I drew in a deep breath. The city answered me, a river of cool energy coursing up through my feet and soothing the ragged pain in my ribs. I wrapped my hands over Ray Ray's hand on the pommel and yanked out the blade, keeping my eyes locked on his.

A dizzying pulse of power burst from my chest, from the point where the city roots had pierced through me, causing my eyes to blink as if burned from the sun. Something inside my chest throbbed and warmth spread down my chest. Where blood had surrounded the blade, my skin scabbed over, itching like a week-old wound.

Ray Ray began to whimper as I took our joined hands and turned the tip of the blade toward his neck. Though I ached to slice him wide open and empty his blood to feed my city, the thought of mingling my blood with his on the blade repulsed me. I flicked the tip of the knife under the pendant's chain and snatched the blood jade in my fist.

The shinigami placed his other hand over Ray Ray's terrified face, weathered ivory bone fingers wrapping around it from ear to ear. "Sleep, Raymond Louie. These events are no longer any concern of yours."

Ray Ray went limp, his eyes drifting closed. Around us the ghosts of Yomi continued to circle the garden, their screams now pitched to an ear-shattering tone. Freddy and Fiona lay unconscious on the grass, knee-deep in the lawn.

Sugiwara held out his hand, his illusion fading away into smoke. His hand was skeletally thin, the fingers impossibly long. Even with the ghosts screaming around us, the shinigami's voice carried with perfect clarity. "My presence will only hold them off for a short while. Give me the anchor."

I placed the blood jade pendant in his palm. The shinigami tilted his head and examined the stone. It lifted from his hand and floated to the center of the Gate. The tear-shaped piece pulsed red once and then melded to the Gate before going dull. The shinigami stepped closer and raised his arm, beams of white light shining from his hand to the blood jade.

My hand clenched around the death mark, the icy pain driving me to my knees. The mark throbbed and agony rippled up my arm, my very bones rattling. It went on for an eternity and then stopped. I nearly moaned in relief.

The shinigami frowned and lowered his hand, the light dying away. The pendant lifted away from the Gate and floated back into the death god's hand. "This item can no longer serve as the anchor. The charm Raymond used on the Heart has . . . corrupted it."

I lowered my head to the ground and closed my eyes. My jaw ached as I ground my teeth and cursed Ray Ray Louie to the deepest levels of Yomi for eternal punishment. The events of the last two days blurred together and the adrenaline drained away, leaving only despair. Despite everything, all that I had done, I had failed.

Gravel cut into the skin of my forehead as I sagged further. I had nothing left.

I had gambled everything on recovering the Gate. I thought about my conversations with my father. I hadn't said goodbye. I lifted my head and wiped the gravel off my face. I would stand for this next part when the shinigami anchored my soul to the Gate. I wished Kamon didn't have to see this. I'd already put him through enough. As if on cue, Kamon stepped out of the trees, steam wisping off his naked shoulders, blood streaming down his chest from a diagonal slash across his ribs.

I smiled grimly at the death god. "How will you anchor the Gate now?"

He seemed to grow an extra foot taller as white smoke draped his figure from neck to foot. Dirty white robes billowed around him, the tattered edges showing the wear of millennia. The chill of empty graves emanated from him as mist swirled around his feet. His gaunt features darkened under a large hood. Bloodred eyes glowed from the dark shadows concealing his face. He seemed to float, reminding me just how unconcerned he was with my earthly affairs. Kamon growled low in his throat, his tiger close to the surface.

More ghosts poured out of the portal, now a steady stream of tortured souls. Bound by the shinigami's ward and unable to escape their torment, the ghosts circled the tea garden, a vortex of the damned swirling above our heads. If they broke through the barrier, they would run rampant through the city.

The shinigami gestured and the blood jade floated to my hand. His words echoed strangely in my ears, as if he no longer bothered to pitch his voice for mere mortals. "The anchor needs a connection to this world, the vibrancy of life experienced."

I looked over to Kamon. He shook his head at me, his expression angry. It was a look I was used to seeing from him. At least I got to see him one last time. With him I'd once experienced a full range of emotion, the vibrancy of life the shinigami referred to.

The shinigami floated closer to me and my teeth began to rattle from the cold. Was this what my afterlife would be like? Eternally cold with this death god as company?

The wails of the dead rose in volume, the sound threatening to buckle my legs. Freddy's eyes popped open and his arms flew up to press over his ears, fingers clawing at them. He might have been screaming. I couldn't hear him. I only heard the ghosts. And Sugiwara.

He leaned in close to my face and I smelled the dry odor of dead leaves in winter. "You are filled with life. Your soul teems with energy. It would fill the anchor to overflowing."

The swirling mass of ghosts thickened, the inner edge encroaching on our sanctuary in the eye of the storm.

Some kind of paralysis held me in place, Sugiwara's voice immobilizing my limbs. Creeping cold locked my legs in place and stole the burning fury that had filled my belly. The shinigami lifted a bony hand as he approached. One skeletal finger reached out and touched Sword of Truth's hilt.

No. No one touched my sword.

It broke the spell. My arm whipped up, batting away Sugiwara's hand, and my hand flashed up to my shoulder. For the first time in two years, Truth's bronze blade sang again, a high, ringing note. Too high. I drew and struck with my sword in one smooth stroke, slashing across Sugiwara's chest.

It did nothing. The smoky robes barely stirred as the broken blade passed through his body with no resistance.

The shinigami smiled, patronizing. "Are you ready to bargain, now? This one, too, contains much soul energy, old and refined." He inhaled deeply, as if savoring a fine wine. "Yes, this would do quite nicely as well."

I blinked in confusion. "What?"

"Your sword is a soul artifact."

I heard the words and I rebelled at the very thought, rekindling the anger in my belly. Sword of Truth was as much a part of me as my very limbs. We were one. I would not be carving off a piece of myself tonight. Not like this. Not when I'd sacrificed so much two years ago just to save what I had left.

I tightened my grip on Truth's grip and shook my head. "No."

The storm of ghosts closed in. I made out individual faces of ghosts, racked with agony, struggling to push through to the interior. Time was running out. The ghosts would overwhelm us in moments. If the shinigami fell, the horde of ghosts would be unleashed on an unsuspecting San Francisco.

Kamon appeared at my side and placed a heavy hand on my shoulder. "Emi, listen to me. If Truth can be the anchor, we can seal the portal again."

Of course, he was right.

It just felt wrong. It sounded obscene.

In the moonlight Truth's sharp edges gleamed with lethal promise despite her broken blade. The blood groove almost smiled at me, my compatriot these many years. Tears fell from my eyes and collected in the groove.

I listened for her song. All I heard were my own gasping breaths.

Kamon wrapped an arm over my shoulders and leaned in close. "Let her go, Emiko."

The protective wall around us shimmered and began to crumble. The ghostly wails notched up again as they began to spill into the interior like a waterfall. An avalanche of spectral forms swarmed toward us.

The ghosts descended on Fiona's unconscious form, sinking their spectral claws and teeth into her. Fiona's immaculate white trench coat disappeared under a writhing pile of ravenous yurei.

Bāo roared and leaped to wrestle Fiona out of the pile. Green bursts of magic exploded around him, sending ghosts flying in all directions. Before he reached Fiona his roar withered and his body shimmered, fading to a dim outline of green sparks. My faithful lion disappeared before my eyes, my father's talent drained. There was nothing left to animate Bāo. My eyes stung with tears. Bāo wasn't gone forever—just until my father could reanimate him—but I needed my friend and guardian now more than ever before.

The shinigami's protection crumbled around us and the ghosts swarmed in, ravenous. I cursed impotently as livid red ghost burns appeared on Fiona. Freddy screamed as ghosts descended on him as well.

I couldn't let Truth go. I'd tried before. "Kamon, I can't. My sword is—"

Sword of Truth was the reason I'd been accepted by my father. She allowed me to be the Blade of Soong, to have a place in my clan. For five bloodstained years I'd carved my niche in Jiārén society, proving I wasn't a dud. After the incident at Pearl Market, I'd lost my taste for maiming and blood but I still hadn't managed to give my sword up. My worth to the clan.

Kamon turned me to face him. He was so close, his warm aura bathed over my face. "Emi, we need you."

I turned away from him. The ghosts whipped into a frenzy, driven mad as they gorged on Fiona's and Freddy's life energy. Sugiwara's ward around the tea garden strained at the seams. They wanted to get out. To get into the city.

My city. Heat from the very ground beneath me soared through my limbs, filling my body and emanating through my fingertips. Gold sparks flashed from my fingers, mirrored in my bronze blade's surface.

The shinigami pointed at the moon, its rise complete. "Decide now, or I will decide for you."

I had a new place now, no longer a hound at the beck and call of the Soong Clan. The city had lifted me from the vault, marked me and restored me. It was my rebirth. I knew what I had to do. I would be making my own decisions from now on.

I drew Truth's jagged tip across my palm, right at the death mark, letting my blood, my Sentinel's blood, run down her edge. My blood would forever tie me to this Gate, as I was now tied to the city. I strode to the Ebony Gate and stood over the dull surface. With a scream I drove Sword of Truth into the heart of the Gate. The ebony opened to accept the broken sword, gold sparks flying from the impact. My sword sank into the wood to the hilt. It felt not unlike a killing blow dealt against a body.

Mist swirled around the Gate, and from the formless haze I saw the unbroken line of the Soong Blades before me.

Their whispers were a ghostly chorus. "The Blade for the Clan."

Tears streamed down my face, hot against my cheeks. I hadn't heard them for two years. No longer would they serve only the Soong Clan. Here they would anchor the Ebony Gate, serving all of my city's people. Forever.

It was done.

# RESTORATION

Gray San Francisco sunlight crested the eastern wall, bathing the tea garden with the new day's light. I had never been so happy to see the sunrise in my life. It would be my first day in many years without Truth on me, but that thought didn't sadden me. I looked to the Ebony Gate where I knew she served as the anchor together with all the Blades before me. Now we served something greater than one clan.

I'd had the last few hours to grapple with these feelings. Instead of feeling drained from my battle with the hungry ghosts and the loss of Truth, I felt strangely energized. The city's magic curled all around me and the skin of my face tingled with every breath I drew in. Somehow, the city was boosting me.

With the ghost master out of the picture and the Ebony Gate restored, the shinigami's powers and Kamon's trap drew the remaining ghosts in like a high-end vacuum cleaner.

To my relief, Kamon had put on clothing. I guess when you're a shifter, you always keep extra clothes in the car.

Fifi roused and whipped up one last mini tornado and restored her white leather trench coat to spotless condition. Despite fighting ghosts for the past six hours, she retained every inch of her poise and picked invisible crumbs of dirt and debris from the hem of her coat. Her skin was pale and drawn but knowing her, she'd treat herself to a day of self-care with her Hoard to recharge. She sniffed at me, looking down her arms at the red ghost burns. "Is it going to be like this with you every time?"

I stayed quiet, for once, and just enjoyed the view of the sun coming up over the skyline of my city.

My city.

Freddy and Franklin had both awakened. Fiona got her shoulder under Freddy while Franklin limped along beside her. She stopped in front of me. Freddy squinted at me, trying to focus. He finally grinned and held up a loose fist to me.

I sighed and bumped knuckles with him.

He splayed his fingers out and wiggled them. "Boom! I'll be your wingman anytime, Sentinel."

Fiona rolled her eyes. "I need to get these two to Central Road General."

I nodded. I'd feel better once Freddy had some medical care.

"Has our Talon duty been satisfied?"

My father would have asked for more. Kamon appeared beside me with my bag in his hands. I dug through the pockets until I found the heavy weight of gold. When I brought it out the sunlight gleamed off the metal except where my blood was smeared over the hanzi.

I was handing over a Talon to a clan ready to cry feud on the Louies.

My father would definitely have asked for more.

I handed the Talon over and Fiona accepted it.

"Witness." My voice rang out across the tea garden.

Kamon echoed me. "So witnessed."

Fiona tucked the Talon into her belt and gave me a final, enigmatic look before turning away with her brother. I watched them leave and decided I could worry about the Talon on another day. Today was mine.

Sunlight crept around corners and over rooftops, bathing the skyline in cleansing light. It burned off last night's fog and soaked

into the sidewalks, taking the edge off the early morning chill. I
felt it all, deep in my bones, and I relished the sensation of the light
inching slowly across San Francisco.

I had spent years doing my father's bidding to protect our family,
our clan's interests, our honor. The title of Blade, and then Butcher,
had always felt . . . off. I knew that in his way, Father was trying
to make me feel needed, feel a part of the clan, even as my lack of
talent left me outside. I had done my best to serve the clan. The
Blade for Clan, forever. I had broken that oath, and thought nothing
would redeem me. But the city had found me worthy.

I had just spent the night putting down ghastly apparitions, en-
during my ex, and putting up with Fiona's ridiculous attitude. For
nothing else than the well-being of people who would never know
what we had done.

It felt great.

I took that as a good sign. But the work for the shinigami was
just beginning. After the ghosts were locked away, he knelt before the Ebony Gate and began the painstaking task of reinscrib-
ing "The Song of Izanagi-no-Mikoto." Luckily the daylight would
make that job much easier.

Ah Wing stood on shaky legs and bowed to me. "Sentinel. You
will let your father know I finished the work, yes?"

I nodded. The poor man was barely standing. Thankfully, the
woman who had transported him, Lilly, had roused and seemed well
enough. In the heat of battle I hadn't had much time to interact with
her. I'd been a little busy trying to keep ghosts from frying her and
devouring her soul. Lilly dusted off her trousers, a dressy hounds-
tooth pattern. Her cream silk blouse was looking a bit wilted under the black cashmere cardigan. No rips or tears though so that
was good. She had beautiful black hair, long and sleek. It was a
bit messy and many strands had fallen out of her loose ponytail. I
felt an unfamiliar stab of envy now that my hair was streaked with
a crazy skunk stripe from the city.

I checked in with Lilly to be sure she didn't need to go to Central Road General Hospital. She yawned and stretched, her voice soft. "I'm fine, I just need to sleep." Lilly had that British Hong Kong accent, a product of years of Oxford-educated tutors.

Lilly's eyes crinkled into a small smile. "I've always wanted to visit San Francisco but I hadn't planned on my first trip being to a dark, ghost-infested park. But I got to meet a Sentinel, so that's a plus!"

Go me. I was the worst tour guide ever.

I called a rideshare for Ah Wing and Lilly to take them to the posh penthouse apartments my father owned downtown at the NEO. The staff there would see to their needs.

Sugiwara bent over the repaired Gate and white mist crawled out from under his coat and blanketed the steel. Kamon and I backed away from the death god as he began intoning in a low voice. Flashes of dark energy crackled between his hands and the Ebony Gate. "The Song of Izanagi-no-Mikoto" was lengthy. He would be at this for a while.

I walked back to the tea garden area where I had left the ghost master. I knelt over him and systematically searched him.

No phone and no wallet, which left the gun. An H&K VP9. Very nice. Customized grip with a stylized dragon. Distinctive. I'd fired this type of pistol before at the range. Good trigger. Precision shooting. This was a gun for a professional. If the Louies had hired this guy, that was a problem. He'd tried to kill me twice. My father would consider that an act of war. But I had no way of knowing who was calling the shots—Uncle Jimmy or Ray Ray.

I contemplated stripping him to check for tattoos, but the smell of his talent still lingered. It repulsed me and I realized having the Louie tattoo or not still wouldn't tell me much. At least he wouldn't be causing any more trouble for my city. Ever.

The crunch of car tires on gravel tore my attention away from the shinigami to the garden entrance. In the gray morning light, a pair of blacked-out Mercedes quietly rolled to a stop just outside the broken gate. I squinted at the figures exiting the cars. A tall figure in a burgundy cardigan stepped out, planting a gold-handled cane in the gravel.

Oh goody. My adrenaline zinged upward. This would be fun.

I walked toward the garden entrance, leaving Kamon behind to watch the shinigami do his thing. I dragged the body of the ghost master with me, his blood still oozing out from the slash across his torso. The city's magic buoyed my steps, filling me with energy and clarity far beyond the means of caffeine. I dropped the dead ghost master on the gravel path, laying him between me and the approaching Louies. I reached out and grabbed Ray Ray's body and dragged him toward me on a wave of undulating turf. I kept my eyes locked on Uncle Jimmy's as I swept my arm forward and brought Ray Ray to a stop at his feet. As I dropped him, Ray Ray's head thumped on the gravel pathway.

I considered sheathing Hachi but decided if I was going to make a statement, I might as well make it as loud as possible. I clasped my hands together, sword pointing down, and inclined my head. Slightly.

"Suk Suk. Good morning."

Uncle Jimmy stopped a few feet from the bodies and his two bodyguards fanned out to either side of him. Behind him, two more goons in dark suits took up positions outside the entrance to the garden. The cars were parked to block the exit. A stony expression flashed over Jimmy's face and was gone, quick as sunlight on moving water. His eyes didn't even move in the direction of his nephew. His mouth broke into his trademark grandfatherly smile and I had a sudden intuition as to Ray Ray's aspirations.

"Emiko. It's good to see you are unharmed."

His gaze lingered for a moment on my hair, then a point slightly above—my aura, no doubt—then scanned quickly over my shoulder to the scene behind me. His shaggy eyebrows went up. "You found the Gate."

I stared back at him in stony silence. This man's nephew had dared to lay a hand on my sword. Their security personnel had tried to kill me. Jimmy himself had rolled me when I went to visit him. He'd turned down my offer of a Soong Talon.

He was not my favorite person right now.

"Yes, it turns out it had been stolen."

If being called out for his blatant lies from earlier bothered Uncle Jimmy in the slightest, he hid it well.

Uncle Jimmy squinted at the Gate. "And the Gate's anchor restored as well."

"Yes." The Lost Heart of Yázì was tucked in my pocket. My ambiguous response was both right and wrong, but I saw no need to enlighten Uncle Jimmy.

The shinigami's rhythmic chanting carried quite well in the chill morning quiet. The intensity of the work being performed distorted the city's magic and brushed against me. I resisted the urge to rub my neck.

Jimmy's eyes traveled down the length of my body. "And our fine city has a Sentinel at last. This is most auspicious." He brought his hands together and inclined his head in a modest bow, deeper than the one I had greeted him with.

He began to pace back and forth, still ignoring his unconscious nephew at his feet. "We will need to determine the best day to present our new Sentinel to the city, yes? Perhaps the main office in downtown . . . yes, the architecture is quite stunning. That would be a good spot. In the meantime . . ."

As Uncle Jimmy prattled on, his talent stretched out from him in careful tendrils like a meandering root system. In truth, compared to Ray Ray, Jimmy's power was delicate, even elegant. Perhaps he thought he was being subtle, but his power cut lines through the air like chalk on a blackboard. And without the perception of the city's magic, I was sure his technique was quite effective. This was how he'd distracted me so easily before. I let his charm speaking get closer, until the faint smell of black sesame paste brushed my senses. I whipped Hachi through the air in a downward slash, cutting through the tendrils. Jimmy stopped pacing and his talent retreated.

I smiled like a child presented with a second helping of dessert. "That won't be necessary, Uncle Jimmy. I'll make my own introductions."

He huffed a little laugh. "Really, Emiko, you're the Sentinel now. That's a big move. You'll need to get to know the major players in the city. I can help you with that."

I took a moment, pretending to consider it. "I've been working with the people on Lotus Lane for years now. Some families did business with me when no one else would even look at me. I like them. I'll start there, and let them know their Sentinel is around to protect them. Then I'll go to Japantown and Inner Sunset."

Jimmy's mouth turned down at the mention of territory he didn't control. "Tread carefully, young Sentinel. Choose well and we can all be winners."

I sneered. "Your nephew had a funny way of offering me a choice."

"Hm. Yes, that business at the bank was unfortunate. We need to move past that. You need friends in the city, Sentinel. You are young and inexperienced. Did you know that most Sentinels die within their first year? Who are you going to ally with, the Trans?" He laughed, an ugly sound that jarred with the patrician look on his face.

Kamon appeared beside me. He pitched his voice low but loud enough for my ears, almost a growl. "Do you know what you're doing?"

I didn't take my eyes off Jimmy and tried to ignore the electric sensation of Kamon's proximity. I whispered back, "Winging it. Like always."

Uncle Jimmy gestured with a small wave behind him and the door of the Mercedes opened once more. Saburo stepped out of the car, moving a little stiffly, but dressed smartly in a slim black suit. Looked like Grandma Chen had fixed him up. One of Jimmy's goons came forward and grabbed Ray Ray's body, hauling him none too gently across the gravel to Saburo.

Jimmy sighed and shook his head. "It is the job of the clan elders to maintain discipline in the family. Even if it pains us to do so. I understand that Ray Ray, by his actions, has wronged you. I would not see this action reflect badly on the Louie Clan."

My body went cold as Jimmy spoke. Saburo knelt and took Ray Ray's hand in his own. He struck Ray Ray sharply across the face, once, the sound ringing across the garden. Ray Ray's eyes cracked open and he moaned in pain.

Jimmy gave a little bow. "I believe this will be appropriate recompense for your trouble, Sentinel."

Saburo's aura flashed and Ray Ray screamed. A white-hot line of fire erupted from Saburo's hand and the man calmly drew it across Ray Ray's wrist, severing his hand. The skin at Ray Ray's wrist blackened and charred, filling the peaceful garden with the sickly smell of burning flesh.

With practiced motions Saburo snapped up the severed hand and deposited it into a red velvet bag, securing it with a red satin thread. Lovely. It looked like Uncle Jimmy was the one signing Saburo's paychecks, then.

I was reluctant to put Hachi away. As if he sensed my hesitation, Kamon stepped forward to take the bag from Uncle Jimmy, proffering a small bow. Uncle Jimmy raised an eyebrow but dropped the red bag into Kamon's outstretched hands.

My eyebrows pulled together in consternation. Kamon wasn't my servant to fetch and carry for me. He didn't need to step in front of me or take any hits for me. But I didn't say anything. He always had possessed a keener political mind than I could claim, forged in the fire of Tiger politics. Whatever he was doing made sense to him. Still, I didn't have to like it.

I watched that red bag like a cobra. Why would Uncle Jimmy think this would satisfy me? When I was the Blade, I had never taken restitution when I could instead exact retribution. Was he bribing me?

Kamon returned to my side and I took the bag from him with one hand, keeping Hachi up. I shook the bag open and looked inside. On the pinky finger of the severed hand was a gold coin ring, the hanzi Lóng carved into the face. Dragon. Around the coin a circle of pavé diamonds glittered in the morning light. Ray Ray's pinky ring. Beneath the sweet stink of charred flesh, the thick odor of Hoard gold. Pearl Market flashed across my mind again: burning market stalls, screaming girls, and blood. So much blood.

I looked at Uncle Jimmy and bile rose in my throat, seeing him in a new light. The friendly manner, the Mr. Rogers persona. It was just a flimsy veneer, a thin layer of shine that covered the steely resolve beneath. A man so ruthless that he would feed his own family to the wolves in such a cavalier fashion.

The kind of ruthlessness that broke me in Beijing, that drove me to maim more than thirty girls because they had been caught up in the schemes of another clan. Because they stole from the Soongs. The kind of ruthlessness that suffered no slights and crushed all dissent. I'd clawed my way out from under the mantle of the Blade and found myself again. I was not going to lose that.

I found my voice. "You know Ray Ray is . . ." I made a little twirly motion at my temple. "I saw the tattoo on his chest. I'm sure everyone on the street saw it. How did you end up with a Realm-seeker in your own house?"

Something flashed across Jimmy's eyes but his facade didn't crack. "Ray Ray is . . . devoted. But . . . he's not wrong. When you've been around as long as I have, Sentinel, you see the ebb and flow of power. Survive long enough, and you can begin to predict the currents and where they will flow. True believers are often the harbingers of change."

I dropped the hand to the grass. "I might be young but even I know you're not a true believer, Jimmy."

Jimmy smiled, a grim expression that showed the hardened man beneath the surface. The man who would go to any lengths for his family. "No, make no mistake. The true believers lead the charge, but the pragmatists are the ones who enjoy the fruits of upheaval. Given your history, you've always struck me as a pragmatist, Emiko. This isn't a difficult choice. Join our movement. Relinquish the Gate."

As if it were mine to relinquish. The shinigami would certainly have something to say about Uncle Jimmy's demand.

I didn't want anything from Uncle Jimmy. Not his gruesome reparations, and not an alliance with him. Not after what Ray Ray had put us through. Not after the night we'd just spent nearly getting killed by an army of ghosts.

My father would make the deal. Some complex arrangement that held the Louies close so he could keep an eye on them. I might not be the Blade, but I was still a weapon, honed to a keen edge to make clear decisions. I wasn't a deal maker and I never had been. I wasn't about to start now.

The scar on my chest pulsed. It vibrated out from my torso and all the way to my fingertips. I was sure even Hachi vibrated. Now what?

As I inhaled, the scar throbbed with my breath. Grass sprouted around Kamon's feet. A vine punched out from the ground between me and Kamon, green and lively. Ivy leaves unfurled and more shoots sprang out from the vines. The tallest shoot reached up and curled around the velvet bag, the leaves splaying over it.

The vines pulled the bag from me and extracted Ray Ray's severed hand. Jimmy's men murmured as the vines twisted through the rigid fingers and dragged the hand into the earth.

The remaining vines curled and tumbled, forming a hedge. The hedge grew at a rapacious rate, eating up the ground and forming a living barrier between us and Jimmy.

Well then. San Francisco clearly had an opinion. I found I agreed with the sentiment. I understood what I needed to say.

"San Francisco accepts your offering. Reparation has been made for the slight your clan made against the Sentinel."

Not to the Soongs. Not to the Blade. To me, and the city. If Uncle Jimmy had been hoping to buy more capital with his nephew's hand, he was out of luck. My father would speak for the Soongs—I had spoken for the city.

Jimmy nodded but he didn't look pleased. He called out, "Witness."

His men echoed in return. "So witnessed."

Jimmy was clearly still waiting for the other shoe. Did he think I would negotiate with him over the Ebony Gate? With my blood on the anchor, I was confident I would know instantly if anyone tried to move the Gate again. No deal. I would never be my father but I could at least face down Jimmy Louie.

"As Sentinel I have decided that the Ebony Gate will stay where it is. If anyone tries to move it again, I will be . . . unhappy."

I sheathed Hachi, signaling the end of our conversation.

Jimmy sighed and shook his head. "This isn't a fight you can win. The Great General is rising in the east and the army that marches before him will sweep across the earth like a tidal wave. When that day comes, Sentinel, there will be no middle ground. All will be subject to his will. Mark this day, Sentinel."

He held my gaze as he spoke, his eyes hard, glinting like wet river stones. I held his gaze, unblinking. He had rolled me once. It would never happen again. Jimmy broke first, turning away from me with a disgusted look. He made a small motion with his hand and his men got back into their cars.

Just before Jimmy ducked his head into his car I called out to him, loud enough so all his men could hear. "Uncle Jimmy!"

He stopped and stood back up, his face once again flashing for a brief second with annoyance. It was gone in a moment and the friendly grandfather returned, his expression expectant.

I gave him my best smile—all teeth. "Tell Leanna our lessons will be once a week. I'll send you the bill."

A dark shadow flitted across Jimmy's eyes and then he raised his hand to me and waved, smiling once again. The car doors slammed and the Louie entourage rolled out of the tea garden.

I finally exhaled. The hedge had stopped growing. It was about four feet high now. Hopefully the Golden Gate Park grounds crew wouldn't notice.

# DEBTS PAID

I looked at Kamon. He didn't budge and looked like he had no intention of leaving. My shoulders drooped. I didn't want him to see my final exchange with the shinigami.

The Ebony Gate looked smooth and aged, as if it had never been shattered. As the shinigami chanted, the characters glowed fiery red before imprinting the ebony wood. We watched in tense silence as the last line of script flashed. Red sparks shot around the ebony, forming a sizzling image that burned into my retinas. Then nothing. It looked like just an old rock. The shinigami waved his right arm in a wide circle and pushed, a smooth movement like he was rolling a snowball with one hand. Then I could almost barely make out the Gate, my eyes skipping over it to the lovely dwarf maple to the left. The no-look spell was back in place.

I felt like a thousand-pound boulder had been lifted off my shoulders.

"Well, Sugiwara-sama, is the seal to Yomi secured?"

The death god stepped closer, the misting white swirls obscuring his feet. It gave the impression he was gliding in smoke.

The musty smell of decay preceded him and I wanted to back away, but I stood my ground. I felt Kamon tense, as if ready to spring to my defense.

The shinigami pressed his hands together and gave me a small bow. "You have completed your task, young Sentinel."

I let out a slow, long breath of relief and then held out my hand. "Then the Hiroto Talon is satisfied?"

His skeletal fingers flashed before pulling something from his murky robes. The gleaming dragon ingot emerged, with the blood-stained crane. Tendrils of white mist crept out of his robes, curling around the Talon, as if he was loath to return it.

"Witness."

Kamon's voice was low. "So witnessed."

I snatched the Talon from the shinigami's bony grasp. As my fingers wrapped around the warm gold, the shinigami's white mist brushed my fingers. My hand spasmed, locking onto the Talon like I'd been electrocuted. Pain exploded behind my eyes and drove me to my knees. Kamon's magic flared like an exploding sun and a throaty roar erupted from his chest.

The shinigami merely smiled, his eyes a hollow darkness.

I reached up and grabbed Kamon, digging my hands into his fur, desperate to pull him back from an unwinnable fight, even as images flashed across my eyes.

*White mist pours down the stairs to the doors of clanhome.*

*Father on the ground, blood streaked across his face.*

*Mother crying, angry, shouting. Afraid.*

*Glowing red eyes set in darkness, the gaze boring into me from over my mother's shoulder.*

*More blood, and a flash of Hoard gold.*

*Pain.*

I inhaled and it felt like I'd been underwater for too long. My vision blurred and spots danced across my eyes. My hand was still on the Talon, fingers in a death grip. I met the shinigami's deep red eyes. "I know you."

His voice was the whisper of wind over gravestones. He released the Talon to me. "Yes. You finally remember."

"What did my mother want for the Talon?" The pain was subsiding, only to be replaced by a dizzying vertigo. I knew what my mother had done, but my mind still would not process it, understand it.

"You were taking your first steps into Yomi, and bringing your father with you."

"And you brought me back."

". . . Yes."

It made no sense. Why would a death god care to trade for favors from Jiārén?

"Why?"

The shinigami seemed to shrink in height as his illusion re-formed around him, banishing the creeping mist again for his traveling-professor persona. "It is true, a favor from a mortal would normally be of little interest to me. But then, the Walker of the Void is a truly exceptional mortal, and I desired the opportunity to meet her again."

I had heard my mother's title before, but never with the reverence in the shinigami's voice. It was usually laced with fear from other Jiārén.

A hole opened in the grass and the cat yokai appeared again at the shinigami's feet, tugging at the hem of his topcoat for attention. It was still adorable, even if it was a demon.

"I had not considered to redeem the Talon in this fashion, but you have surpassed all that your mother said you would be capable of. Your talents are indeed noteworthy."

The whipsawing of emotions and revelations about my mother had my mind spinning.

"Talent? I don't have a Hoard gift."

The shinigami's eyes narrowed. "Is that what she told you?"

The cat yokai jumped up now, digging its claws into the death god's coat, and crawled up to his hip. The shinigami brushed the cat off.

"Yes, yes, fine. We will leave now. No need to be rude."

The shinigami stepped back. "I had thought to use you as the anchor. Much simpler. But your way was much more entertaining. Never did I think I would see the birth of a city Sentinel."

I lived to entertain. "You're welcome."

"One last thing." I held out my left hand, palm up. The shinigami snapped his fingers. The death mark flashed blue, then red, and vanished. An almost imperceptible thread between me and the death god snapped. Everything around me seemed to brighten in hue. All of me belonged again to the living and I aimed to keep it that way.

"Farewell, young Sentinel." The mist around the perimeter of the garden began to dissipate. Beneath the death god a swirl of smoke rose and funneled up around him, then drifted to the Ebony Gate. A moment, and then nothing where the shinigami had stood. Just shrubs and river rock. The knot in my stomach loosened. No longer would this Talon's Call pain me or Tatsuya.

My mother was renowned for the breadth of her travels, but I had never imagined her crossing paths with gods. Of course with my mother, it couldn't be a god of flowers and sunshine. No, it had to be a death god and his demon cat.

Would I see her when I went back for Tatsuya's Tourney? The thought of seeing my mother again after two years made me feel hot with shame and anger. But I was the Sentinel now. Would she finally be pleased with me? I'd saved Tatsuya from risk of the Talon Call by a death god. I loved my brother and I served my clan. With this Talon Call satisfied, would my mother finally see me as having done something worthy?

And did my father know that she had given a Talon to a death god for the both of us? The anger that fueled me these last two days dimmed but the confusion I felt was almost worse. The shinigami said I had been dying, that my father had been dying. Why couldn't I remember more?

Kamon grasped my upper arms and turned me gently to face him. "When were you going to tell me that a death god had your Talon?"

I could hear all kinds of things in the low timbre of his voice. Frustration, anger, and sadness. That made me sad, too. This was a brutal reminder of why I'd let him go two years ago. I was too much to deal with. I'd hurt him over and over again. And yet, standing so close to him, the hot lick of excitement from battling back-to-back with him fresh, I wanted him still. I wanted the fierce warrior who had fought the ghosts of the underworld with me. Unfortunately, I couldn't separate that warrior from the man who stood in front of me now. This one was cool and collected, the dutiful son and accomplished statesman. I didn't want to tell this Kamon anything. I wanted to rage at him until flames licked at both sides of him and the warrior came out. But I knew that was unfair.

Despite two years of silence from me, he'd stood by me through this Yomi debacle. I owed him an explanation. I hunched my shoulders, bracing for the discomfort of airing the Soong dirty laundry to Kamon . . . again, just like before. I held up the Talon. "The shinigami made the Talon Call after Ray Ray stole the Gate. Tatsuya felt it, too. But not Father."

Kamon's eyes drew together sharply. "Your mother?"

My laugh was short and bitter. "As usual, she is traveling and I haven't heard a peep from her."

Then I shook my head. "I couldn't let Tatsuya deal with it."

Kamon loosened his grip on my arms and pulled me in for a tight hug. Tiger warmth surrounded me, and the tension in my shoulders relaxed. He smelled like I remembered. Memories threatened to swamp me. When it had been good, it had been really good. He rested his chin on top of my head for a moment before letting me go and stepping back. The distance between us was only a foot, but might as well have been a mile.

I'd told myself that we were over and I'd moved on. I had been lying to myself. I had been numb. He'd showed up again and my feelings had flared back to life. Tonight, heat had sizzled between us. Fighting back-to-back with him had sparked a raging bonfire. The coals hadn't died, I'd only banked them. I wanted to throw myself back into his embrace. I wanted to tell him I'd missed him. But it was too late—he'd moved on.

He was good at knowing the "correct" thing to do. He was offering me comfort, but the brief contact wouldn't be enough to be mistaken for anything more. He hadn't stepped out on his new girl.

I shivered in the cool dawn air but it was smarter than leaning in to him for any more comfort. Bāo's pendant was back on the gold chain around my neck. I couldn't call him forth anymore, he was out of juice for now. But my fingers reached for the familiar cool stone and I took my solace from knowing I would see Bāo again when I went back to Tokyo for Tatsuya's Tourney.

Our phones pinged simultaneously, breaking the awkward silence. Fiona had texted us Freddy's hospital room number. And the Advocate had arrived.

# VISITING HOURS

We pulled up to my house just as the remnants of morning fog burned off. Kamon leaned down a little to look out the window. "Nice place."

Oh gods. How awkward was this going to get? "You can go on ahead, you know. I can meet you at the hospital."

His eyes scanned my house and yard. "Oh, it's no problem. I can wait."

I huffed and gathered up my things before my brain could make the situation any worse. "All right. I'll make you some tea while you wait."

I felt his eyes boring into my back as I disarmed my security and wards and unlocked my front door. We entered and I pointed him to the living/meeting room in the front of the house. "Please have a seat."

In the kitchen I threw a pot of water on the stove and pulled together a tray with cups and loose tea. Kamon had always liked the oolong blended with osmanthus. I tried not to dwell on the fact that I still bought that flowery blend and just scooped it into the small yíxīng clay teapot.

Kamon called out. "Everything okay?"

"Sure! Just a moment!"

Tea needed something to eat alongside it. I pulled open my cupboards and despaired. My cabinets were still bare in the aftermath of the break-in. All I found were restaurant packets of sriracha and mostly empty bags of Kit Kats. I grabbed all the bags and upended them onto the tray. Sakura, matcha, and dark chocolate. It would have to do.

After pouring the water I sat and simply inhaled the fragrant aromas as the tea steeped. I felt like I'd been running at full speed for days, and just sitting was strangely luxurious. I ripped open a matcha Kit Kat and nibbled on it. Unfortunately, being the Sentinel did not bring a heightened appreciation of the delicate melding of tea and chocolate, but it was still delicious, and the first thing I'd eaten while sitting down in a couple of days. I let myself enjoy the Kit Kat slowly, savoring the flavors until the last bit melted away. When it was gone, both the tea and I were ready to go.

I walked back into the living room with the tea tray to find Kamon standing in the morning sunlight through the front window, admiring the Sì Jūnzǐ from my father hanging over the mantel. The Four Noble scrolls depicted delicate flower blossoms—orchid, bamboo, chrysanthemum, and plum blossom. Knowing my father, these scrolls likely dated back to the original Soong dynasty.

I set the tray on the low elmwood table and tried not to think about how good Kamon looked in the light.

"It's a nice place, Emiko. Homey."

I didn't know if I should be offended or if he was teasing me. The front house had nothing homey at all in it. The living room had been converted to an office consisting of mostly black and gray items. The kitchen barely had food—if you considered Kit Kats food. My interior color scheme inside consisted of an off-white paint the store had called "eggshell" and a few black or rosewood furniture pieces.

The flooring was oak, stained gray. The cushions were gray. The fireplace mantel and trim were gray granite streaked with white. The security cabinets along the back wall were also gray. The leather Barcalounger was gray. Tessa had tried to talk me into a red Barcalounger, which was so far outside my decorating com-

fort zone as to be laughable. Yes, I had the scrolls but they did little
to soften the austere surroundings.

A single large lucky money bamboo sat in the wealth corner of
the room, its lush green foliage a lone hint of color in the austere
space. The Suns had given it to me last Chinese New Year. I liked
that plant—it was hard to kill.

Trying to look at my own place through Kamon's eyes was making me crazy. I needed to stop thinking about what he thought. I
gestured to my wakizashi. "I won't be long."

Kamon nodded. He knew my routine. I'd clean my weapons
first, then I'd clean myself. My usual protocol.

I quickly pulled my remaining weapons from my myriad pockets
and laid them on the breakfast counter. From the rosewood longevity
sideboard, I pulled out the custom-blended oil I used to clean my
blades and several soft gray cloths. I concentrated on my task and the
familiar activity helped me ignore the tiger in the room sipping tea.

Hachi absorbed the oil and when I was satisfied, I wrapped her
in a white cloth painted with black kanji calligraphy. I hung the
scabbard in its place of honor on the wall above the longevity sideboard. I began wiping down my shurikens when Kamon stepped
next to me and picked up Truth's empty scabbard.

It hurt to look at it.

Kamon looked at me. "I wasn't sure you were going to be able
to let her go."

His voice held no censure, just curiosity. It was a far cry from
when I'd broken the sword and we'd had harsh words. Words that
led to me leaving him and leaving Tokyo. Leaving my life.

I swallowed hard. "I didn't want to. I didn't feel like me without her."

That sounded pathetic. But it was honest and nobody would ever
accuse me of being good with words.

Kamon's mouth pursed for a moment and then relaxed. "You're
the Sentinel now."

In the end, feeling that connection to the very magic of the city itself had grounded me in a way I'd never felt before. "Yes. I don't know what that means, but I don't need to carry Truth anymore."

Kamon's face softened and it looked like he was going to lean in. I took a step back.

"I'm going to shower." I fled to the back of the main house, to the master bedroom. I locked the door and covered my face in my hands. What the hell was I doing?

I took a deep breath. Freddy. We were going to see Freddy. Focus.

I started the shower, cranking the knobs to boiling hot, and stripped off my clothes. The mirror in the bathroom stopped me before I entered the shower. My eyes widened in horror at how the city had marked me.

Twisting black lines radiated from a white, starburst scar just to the right of my sternum. The tattoo twisted like a thorn hedge, working its way across the top of my breast, cresting my shoulder and stopping at my neckline. It capped my right shoulder as well. I leaned in close to examine the edge. The lines thinned and split as they approached the edge, fanning out in fractal patterns.

I traced my fingers over the lines. My skin was still smooth, except for the scar where the root had pierced me. I rubbed the heel of my palm over the wound. No pain, but I had the odd sensation that something had been left behind. Something small.

Beneath my rib cage was the wound where Ray Ray had stabbed me. It could have lacerated my liver, a slow and painful way to go. Or it could have angled toward my heart, ending my time here permanently if the shinigami hadn't interfered. Thankfully the city's magic had coursed through me, healing me. Changing me. Now I had another scar. This had been a week for racking up the body count and the scars.

My hands strayed to my hair, fingers combing through the strands. My hair had been the most obvious trait I'd inherited from my mother. Glossy black hair that I usually wore in a long braid, now marred with a stark skunk stripe that started at the crown of my head. The gleaming streak of silver extended the entire length of my hair.

Steam billowed out as I opened the shower door and hopped in. Two days ago life had been normal. Even verging on good. I'd spent the last two days nearly dying from fù chóng venom, dodging ghosts, taking the Sentinel mantle, and now my ex-boyfriend was in my living room. I bowed my head under the scalding water and prayed for the shower and the Great Dragon Father to wash my troubles away.

I finished before the hot water ran out and tied back my wet hair. At least this way, the stripe was a little less noticeable. Back in the front of my house I found Kamon asleep on the couch in a patch of morning sun. Just like a cat. Of course, we'd spent almost the whole night fighting ghosts. Even the best fighters needed rest. My hand found its way to my chest again, pressing over the new scar. I wasn't tired. Or at least, I wasn't as tired as I should be. A perk from the city for its new Sentinel? Just one more thing I would need to look into when I had time.

The living room smelled like jasmine oil. I looked at the longevity side table. Kamon had polished Truth's empty scabbard and hung it on the rack the way I normally did. Considerate as usual.

I closed my eyes for a moment, sadness swamping me. He'd been too good for me before and nothing had changed. He was better off with Fiona. She was a Hoard princess and one day she'd be a queen. She was smart, beautiful, and politically savvy. She'd never come home covered in blood and need to clean her swords before washing her body. She was a perfect match for a powerful tiger.

That image stiffened my spine. I nudged Kamon's foot with my toe and his eyes instantly opened. I nodded to the door. "Come on, we have to pick up something before heading to the hospital."


I was back at Central Road General Hospital. Again. At least this time it wasn't to deal with wraiths in the maternity ward. Kamon peeled off to check on Jessie and baby Nijat. I made my way down the long hallways to Freddy's room. Knowing Fiona, it would be big enough to hold a banquet in.

A 250-pound side of beef dressed in a severe gray suit stood outside of Freddy's closed door, arms crossed and looking generally imposing. I walked right up to the guard and stood inside his personal space.

"Hi. My name should be on the list."

His head tilted down to me fractionally, his blacked-out sunglasses traveling down my body. At least my haori was free of blood. I'd changed into a blue jacket trimmed with black silk over my black latex leggings. Without the threat of a death god hanging over me I felt I could be a little more casual. I waited patiently while he gave me a once-over.

After I passed visual inspection the guard offered me a pump of hand sanitizer. I rolled my eyes and got on with it. While I disinfected, his eyes landed on the bulging white plastic bag hanging at my side.

I lifted the bag and opened it under his nose. A cloud of fragrant, porky steam rose up as the bag opened, revealing a mound of pristine white pillows. His right eyebrow arched over his sunglasses.

I looked into the bag. I'd never bought a get-well gift before. Two dozen pork buns had seemed better than a bouquet of flowers. I could spare one. I opened the bag wider and offered it up. The guard picked out a soft bun with surprisingly delicate fingers.

He bowed his head over the bun and with his other hand he reached behind him and opened the door. "Go on in, Sentinel."

I stepped into the room and shut the door behind me.

Fiona stood at Freddy's bedside, a worried expression pinching her usually smooth features. She'd managed to change her outfit. Again. The white trench was gone, replaced with a high-cut eggplant blazer over a fitted rose charmeuse blouse. Her heavy silver chains flashed against the silk. She really must have a wardrobe in her car. It looked like she'd touched up her makeup as well. Good grief.

Another woman stood at the foot of the bed, facing away from me. We were about the same height. Her hair was dark brown streaked with gray and coiled into a low bun. While I had opted for casual, she was armored in a navy wool suit and skirt so sharp, it looked like Teflon. Her skirt ended at the knee, and she wore red leather flats. An unusual choice for an Advocate. I remembered those shoes. "Advocate Leung, I didn't expect to see you here so soon."

The Advocate turned to face me, and even through her glasses, I felt her truth-seeking eyes boring into me. Those eyes saw everything. "Yes, well, your history is well documented. I opted to give myself the advantage of a few days' head start before you started piling up the bodies."

I grinned at her. "Nothing like job security, eh? Pork bun?"

Leung's eyes narrowed at me. "Your family keeps me busy. Ms. Tran? If you would step into my parlor?"

Fiona squeezed Freddy's shoulder and gave him a smile before stepping away. The two women stepped into the far corner of the room, away from the picture window. The Advocate turned Fiona so that they both faced away from us, and into the corner. No lip-reading.

The Advocate raised her hand, a translucent blue sphere the size of a golf ball held between her fingers. She snapped her fingers and crushed the ball with a pop. A bubble of wind talent snapped into being and all noise from that corner of the room vanished.

I sat on the edge of the bed and plopped the bag of pork buns on Freddy's gut. "For you. If I remember correctly, the food sucks here."

"No kidding! The only good thing they've got here is the pain-killers!" He clapped his hands together and bowed his head, grinning before digging out a bun. His hair had been shaved up one side behind his ear and the scarlet lines of a severe ghost burn ran up his neck and scalp. His hands and arms sported an array of bandages as well, and at least three bags of fluids hung on the IV tree.

Freddy's spirits belied the dark bags beneath his eyes. He ate with gusto and regaled me with a story of the nurse on the previous shift and his bedpan escapades. Even as I laughed with him I couldn't help but notice further ghost burns on his chest as his gown drooped open. I cursed to myself. I had no business dragging Freddy into this mess. I might as well have dragged a civilian into a war zone.

"I'm so sorry, Freddy."

He stopped chewing for a moment, then shook his head and swallowed the bun before laughing. "Dude. This is nothing compared to what I felt like after the Tourney. It's nice to get out there. Now Fiona won't get all the credit for saving the city."

Great. I went from worrying over Freddy to worrying over Tatsuya's upcoming Tourney . . . and my promise to my father that I would return to Tokyo for it.

Freddy took another bite and looked at the corner of the room where his sister spoke with the Advocate. "So, the scary lady is an Advocate, huh?"

It spoke volumes that in a room with two gāo wind mages and me, the former Blade of Soong, Freddy pegged the Advocate as the scary one. "Yes. She's worked on my behalf before. She's the best there is. You're in good hands, Freddy."

He nodded slowly. "I heard in school that they're all truth seekers."

I reached for a bun and nodded. "Yeah. All from the same clan, even. They're the only game in town."

"I've also heard their talent is . . . kind of intense." His eyes drifted back to me, a question on his face.

I shrugged lightly. "It's no walk in the park, but it won't kill you."

As Freddy reached for a second bun the door to his room opened with a knock and a doctor entered. Middle-aged, with thinning dark hair, and dressed in a rumpled lab coat, he pulled the chart from the wall.

Freddy perked up. "Doc! Give it to me straight. Will I ever surf again?"

The doctor sighed and leafed through Freddy's chart before approaching the bed. "Hm. Let's take a look at those burns now. Ah, miss?"

Freddy offered the doctor a pork bun. "It's okay, Doc. She's a friend. She's our new Sentinel, too."

The doctor gazed at a spot above my head. "Interesting aura. Huh. I must have missed that memo." He shrugged and opened Freddy's gown. I froze, unable to look away. Freddy's chest was a mass of angry red burns. My throat threatened to close up as the doctor poked and prodded at the burns over the center of his chest, then listened closely with a stethoscope.

While the doctor examined Freddy I stole a look into the far corner. I caught Fiona looking at Freddy, desperate worry creasing her brow. Advocate Leung had taken me through this process before. I had the first ten minutes of her speech memorized by now. With brutal efficiency and eye-watering detail, Fiona was being apprised of her family's rights if this incident was brought before an Arbitrator. Fiona's eyes locked on mine for a moment and an expression I couldn't read flashed over her face. She turned back to the Advocate, furiously taking notes on her phone.

The doctor buttoned Freddy back up. "You got lucky, young man. A few days in here and the worst of it should be past. I hope you understand I'm not exaggerating when I say you skated through by the skin of your teeth. A few more ghost burns closer to your meridians and we wouldn't be having this conversation right now."

Freddy stuffed the last of the bao in his mouth, talking around it. "So, surfing?"

The doctor sighed and dropped the chart back onto the wall, with a little too much force. He gave me a look like *see what I have to work with?* "No. No surfing. No carrying surfboards. No waxing surfboards. No anything. Just resting. Good day, Mr. Tran. I'll see you tomorrow."

Freddy shrugged and picked out another hot bun. He reminded me so much of Tatsuya. Born powerful, privileged, and carefree. Neither of them understood how deadly our world could be, how unforgiving. I had no such excuse. I was a walking testament to the brutality of life amongst the Hoard clans, and what any family would do to protect their own interests. If Freddy had died, it would have been on me.

As the doctor walked out, the Advocate popped her wind bubble and Fiona returned to Freddy's side, her hands trembling. Advocate Leung had that look on her face, the *I've got bad news for you* face.

Surprising even myself, I spoke up before either of them could say anything. "I'll do it."

Fiona gasped, her hand flying to her mouth, eyes wide as saucers then narrowing, calculating. I looked at her and shrugged, smiling. "Like I said, I've been through this before. I have a pretty good idea of what Advocate Leung was telling you."

Fiona shook her head. "We couldn't possibly . . ." But I could see her heart wasn't in it.

"You need a witness. Someone not in your family. Preferably someone from a Hoard clan. I fit the bill."

The Advocate speared me with a look. "You're sure?"

I looked back to Freddy's guileless expression and the ugly scarring along his neck. I suppressed a shiver. "Yes."

"It will hurt."

I bit into my bun, savoring the meaty filling and not breaking eye contact with Advocate Leung. "Promises, promises."

Pain. Freezing, icy-cold needles of pain danced along my veins and burst through my skin to turn into scalding-hot bands that clamped around my arms, legs, and chest. I clutched the gold disc between my teeth, the soft gold giving way to the intensity of my bite. Advocate Leung sat opposite me in the plush mint-colored chairs, our knees barely touching.

Kamon chose that moment to walk into Freddy's room. "What are you . . ." Fiona rushed to his side and clutched his arm, whispering rapidly. I definitely didn't notice how tight she held his arm to her body.

The rest of their interaction slipped away as Advocate Leung's truth-seeking talent poured over me in waves, and I had to close my eyes against the pain. I inhaled slowly through my nose and gripped the armrests until my knuckles turned white. The thick, sweet scent of honeysuckle enveloped me like fog and I struggled not to gag. The Advocate's talent disrupted other talents, reversed your qì flows, and generally made you feel like you'd been run over by a truck. It also made it impossible to lie. In fact that was the whole point of the truth seeking—pain was truth. If I tried to alter facts, the talent would never resonate with me and no testimony could be given.

I held down the inadvisable bun I'd eaten and relived the events on the pier, my mental testimony coming in fits and spurts, taking a break every few minutes to focus on my breathing and absorb the pain. Advocate Leung continued to cross-examine me, looking for inconsistencies in my prior statement. I nodded when appropriate and shook my head at other times. Mostly I had to continue to unpack the violence of the pier attack in sequence. Rewind. Again.

I'd done this before and if I was a betting woman, I'd say that Advocate Leung somehow had it in for me this time. In no time at all, or thirty years later, Advocate Leung released her hands from my arms and the pain slowly began to fade. She removed the imprinted gold disc from between my teeth. The disc had helped me to not bite off my tongue. My jaws ached. I'd have to see Popo on my way home and get something to help me sleep. Something stronger than magnesium. Stars danced before my eyes and I dry heaved.

The Advocate placed the gold disc with my bite marks into a small cream-colored satin pouch. The pouch reminded me of Jimmy Louie's grisly gift, which only made my stomach queasier. A scryer for the Council would transcribe my gold disc. "That will be sufficient. If this is brought before an Arbitrator I am confident your brother will be exonerated under the Second Law. I'll be in touch, Ms. Tran. Good day . . . Sentinel." And with that the Advocate walked out the door, her footsteps ringing down the hallway.

Fiona sat in the vacated chair and handed me a small towel. Kamon moved to stand behind her as I wiped the sweat from my face and neck. I looked up at Kamon. He looked worried, but all he said was my name. "Emiko."

He probably remembered the last time, after my cousin Tai had died. I had exacted my revenge on the yakuza and given the testimony that had put Junior Tanaka in prison in the Arctic. That truth-seeking session had been awful, too. Kamon had held me after Advocate Leung had finished. I was the worst ex-girlfriend ever to make him watch me endure another one.

I nodded at Fiona. "Freddy should be in the clear now."

Fiona's eyes searched my face, as if seeing me for the first time. She spoke, her voice barely above a whisper. "Thank you, Emiko."

She stood and gave a low bow to me, her face serious, with no trace of the cunning I'd seen on Lotus Lane. "Thank you, Sentinel."

So much had changed in just two days. When I had entered the

Tran Clan home, I had been a supplicant bartering a Talon for her help. She'd fulfilled her end of the deal and for better or for worse, I was now the Sentinel. Technically I didn't have to endure a truth seeking. Most people could go a lifetime without ever having to do it once. Here I was after round three with the Advocate. Go me.

Fiona looked up at Kamon. "Would you come see Franklin with me before we ride back together?" He nodded.

She hopped over to the hospital bed and kissed Freddy on the cheek before heading to the door. Kamon turned to follow her but his footsteps slowed by my chair. "Emiko, do you need anything?"

I need you. I bit my lip to prevent something stupid coming out. What I said instead was "I'm good, thanks. I'll sit with Freddy a bit."

Kamon closed his eyes, as if asking for patience. "Emiko, are you okay?"

I looked over at Fiona, her hand on the door handle. She watched the byplay between Kamon and me and I could see the confusion on her face.

I wasn't okay, and Kamon knew it. But we were both going to have to suck it up. The truth-seeking session had blown open my mind and scrubbed me raw. It would take time to build back up my emotional and mental shields.

I tried for a smile. It wasn't my best effort but I could be excused under the circumstances. "I appreciate your concern. I just need some rest. Really."

He gave a curt nod and turned to Fiona. I watched him walk away from me and leave with Fiona. For a long time after, I didn't say anything and just listened to Freddy eat his bun.

# CLAN DUTIES

I didn't know how long I sat there while Freddy ate. There were so many things I needed to do. I needed to let my father and Tatsuya know that I had satisfied the Talon Call. Well, Tatsuya would already know because he would have felt that nagging tension in his belly finally release. I'm sure he'd told Father already. But I was just looking for reasons to avoid phoning my father.

Freddy set his water glass down with a thunk. "Hey Emiko, you okay?"

I closed my eyes and let my head fall back against the chair headrest. "I'm just tired."

That wasn't exactly accurate. The Sentinel mantle seemed to boost me physically but mentally I was fried. It had been like this last time, too, after the truth seeking. Everything had changed for me then after that first session with the Advocate. Under the relentless lens of the truth seeking, I had seen all the things I was doing as the Blade. The blood that had coated my sword and stained me in ways I had tried to ignore. Even the commands of the Head of the Clan and the souls of my ancestors had never been able to override my own conscience after that. Pearl Market had proved it to me. I'd broken my blade and fled from my clan, my parents, and everyone who loved me because I couldn't unsee it anymore. I'd become too monstrous.

There was so much swirling around in my head and my gut that I didn't even know where to start. These last two days had tested me in a way that nothing in my life ever had before. This recent truth seeking gave me clarity without the revulsion and self-loathing that had ensued last time.

Two years here had been healing. My fledgling relationships with Wàirén had restored some balance. I had value beyond my ability to maim and kill. I had people to protect. This was a redemption beyond what I deserved and I was grateful to the city and the people in it.

Maybe I was content? I felt foolish even trying to label it.

"So what's with you and that Wàirén?" Freddy asked.

Adam. One more I had to protect. "He's my responsibility now." Technically he was the clan's responsibility now. That was another reason I was pushing off phoning my father.

"Yeah, but why do that?" Freddy's face scrunched up in confusion.

"I couldn't let him be cleaned. It wasn't right."

Freddy's shoulders slumped. "It's what we're supposed to do, Emiko." But his voice sounded uncertain.

"Are we?" I surprised myself, but saying it out loud, I believed it in my bones. "It's wrong, Freddy."

Freddy sighed. "I guess I never thought about it before."

I was the Sentinel of San Francisco. That wasn't just for the Jiārén of the city. It was for everyone, Wàirén included. First Law was important but why should it allow us to kill and maim Wàirén with impunity?

That's how I felt but I wasn't sure that was the best approach to take with my father. Instead I would lean on the fact that Adam had saved my life and given me the chance to fulfill the Talon to save Tatsuya.

My phone lit up. It was Adam. Speak of the devil.

"Hi, Adam."

"Emiko, they won't discharge me from the hospital because I live alone." Adam sounded frustrated.

"No problem, I'll be right over. What room are you in?"

"Thanks. I'm in B-132."

I guessed my first duty was getting the poor guy home.


The doctor discharging Adam lowered her bifocals and gave me a stern look before rattling off a list of instructions. Adam had a bad burn on his ribs where he'd taken a direct lightning strike. Red lines feathered out across his skin in angry branches. Adam swore it didn't hurt but he looked pretty miserable. Of course, it might have been the fact that he'd also had a concussion and some paralysis. The paralysis was fading but he favored his left leg as he stood up out of the wheelchair.

"Address?" I buckled him in and prepared to punch his address into the nav.

"Eight eighty-eight Spear Street."

Dismay washed over me. I knew that address. That was the address for the NEO Towers. Each penthouse there had sweeping panoramic views of the bay and cost upward of $7 million. I didn't need the navigation guidance to get there.

We drove in silence. I pulled into the roundabout in front of the lobby of the NEO and silently cursed the fickle Dragon gods who had decided that Adam would have an apartment in the same building where my parents kept a couple of units. I wondered if Ah Wing and Lilly Ma were still here resting after their harrowing night assisting me with the Gate. Knowing my father, Ah Wing would be booked on a private jet home to Vancouver shortly.


Adam opened his eyes as the Jeep came to a stop. "Thanks for coming to get me. I didn't want to bother Tessa since she'd been at the hospital all day yesterday."

Ouch. I didn't think he quite meant it like that, but it still laid out my terrible behavior, and reminded me that I needed to square things with Tessa somehow. "It's nothing, really. I'm sorry I couldn't stay with you."

He gave a rueful laugh. "Well, that and you're the only two phone numbers I have in San Francisco."

That sounded uncomfortably like me. Despite two years here, I had very few locals on speed dial.

I put the Jeep in park. "Let's get you upstairs."

The valet, a short guy in a snazzy gray uniform with orange trim, looked up from his paper and hopped to assist us. "Ms. Soong! Mr. Jørgensen! Here, let me help."

As he got his shoulder under Adam's other arm, Adam grunted. "Paul, you know Emiko?"

I gave Paul a quick shake of my head. "Come on, big guy, let's get you up to your room."

At the front desk, a staff member presided over a spotless expanse of chrome-trimmed glass. She wore reading glasses attached to an orange lanyard. Upon seeing me, she slid her glasses off her nose and set them down on her soft gray cardigan. She had large brown eyes, intelligent and watchful. Her brown skin had an ageless quality but I guessed that Priyanka had to be in her early sixties. Her narrow face softened with a smile. "Ms. Soong! What a nice surprise! And good morning to you, Mr. Jørgensen."

I smiled back. "Hey, Priyanka. Can you get the elevator for us?"

Priyanka called the elevator. "I was just about to call you. I arranged for Mr. Wing's transportation to the airport."

"Thank you." Gods, the elevator was taking forever.

Adam looked back and forth between us, his eyes trying to focus. "Wait, you know her, too?"

The Dragon Father smiled on me and the elevator doors opened. I gave Paul a subtle tap to hold him back and helped Adam into the elevator, slapping at the DOOR CLOSE button as we got in. "Thank you!"

The doors closed, leaving us mercifully alone. "What floor are you on?"

"Thirty-two."

Of course. One floor below my parents' units on the top floor.

The elevator gave a soft ding and the doors opened to reveal a majestic entryway. Even this area had a view. Polished white oak floors, lush tall plants, and soft lighting greeted us. The NEO was truly beautiful.

Adam's unit on the thirty-second floor faced east. I had preferred that side as well when I had stayed at my parents' floor above. He pressed his palm against the biometric door lock and opened the door.

Every unit at the NEO boasted high ceilings and sweeping views. Adam's unit had almost no furniture so the lights of the new Bay Bridge sparkled in the dim interior.

We slipped off our shoes in the entryway. The whole flat felt like a Cape Cod cottage mixed with the interior of a yacht. Beautiful wood trims, a soft color palette, and white quartz everywhere. It was a little stark, but inviting. Also nothing like my parents' place here. I felt myself relax a little at that.

The living room was furnished with a few floor cushions and a giant red beanbag. A low coffee table of gleaming koa wood was the sole resting surface. Nothing else.

No sofa and no television. That seemed odd. I didn't have a lot to go off of but most guys would prioritize a television. Kamon's place had a massive number of couches and sofas but I figured that might be a big-cat thing.

"You're still moving in?" I asked.

Adam shook his head. "No, I just don't have a lot of stuff."

Funny, I didn't think I had much stuff, either, but Adam's place took minimalist to a whole new level. Adam swayed and I clutched at him to keep him upright.

"Okay, let's get you to bed and I'll read through the instructions the hospital gave us."

His voice rumbled above me. "So this wasn't exactly how I pictured you spending the night."

Ha ha. My shoulders shook with silent laughter. Even concussed, he was relentless.

"Save it."

We hobbled slowly down the hallway. I knew the layout well since it was identical to the unit upstairs.

Adam braced his hand on the doorframe. "I don't know how to say this without it sounding wrong, but I only have one bed."

Of course he did. I rolled my eyes. I was surprised Mr. Minimalist didn't just sleep on the floor.

"Hate to break it to you, big guy, but we won't be rolling around in your bed. I'm parking myself right there." I gestured behind us to the living room.

He grinned. "I just want to be a good host."

"Let's worry about your concussion, your ribs, and your burn instead of your host duties."

His lips quirked. "I'll be okay. Just have a headache."

It was a bit more than a headache. The medical staff had discharged him with an instruction for me to wake him every hour for four hours, and then every two hours after that. Adam had no family here and I'd felt entirely responsible for his injury in the first place. Only reasonable that I pay penance by checking on him. Not to mention that I'd taken a blood oath to be responsible for him.

I got Adam settled in on his low futon and propped him up with a bolster. I dashed out to grab him some water and ripped open the pharmacy bag.

Adam popped two Tylenol and drained his cup.

The trek up had taken its toll and fatigue lined his face. His eyes drooped and I cursed that overzealous Tanaka minion for the thousandth time. I hated to keep Adam awake even a moment longer but I had to know.

"How much do you remember?"

His eyes, normally piercing in their intensity, wandered upward as he struggled to recall events. The doctor had warned us that he could have lingering memory loss. Finally, he said, "I remember meeting you at the Ferry Building, and getting in the car."

He met my eyes and asked, "Where did we go after that?"

"We went to the Palace of Fine Arts."

"The auction was there?"

I nodded. "Do you remember anything else?"

He shook his head and his frustration was evident as he tightened his jaw. "I've tried, but it's fuzzy."

"Try to get some rest. We can talk more after."

Also, it would give me some time to figure out what I could, or should, say to him about those events.

I moved the bolster and pulled the drapes closed so that he could take a nap.

Once in the living room, my phone pinged, the sound startling me in the quiet of the penthouse.

Tessa had texted me.

**How is Adam?**

**I got him back to his place and he's resting.**

**When are you going to tell me what happened?**

I paused in my tapping. I owed Tessa an explanation and there were no secrets from Andie.

**Is your invite for dinner still open tomorrow night?**

**Yes!!!**

**OK, but no figs for me. I added a barf emoji.**

**Ha ha, we'll get meat for you**

**OK to bring a +1?**

Tessa responded with a thumbs-up. I'd gone from dodging her invites for a year to showing up with a guest.

I padded out quietly and peeked into Adam's room. He was finally asleep but had managed to twist himself out from under his covers. I watched his chest rise and fall as he slept. Poor guy. He had to be wiped out. I thought about tucking him in, but didn't want to wake him. The waking would come soon enough when I had to check his eyes to make sure they were dilating evenly. I made my way to the living room and crashed into the beanbag. It was ridiculously comfortable. Maybe I could get one of these for the front house. If I could bring myself to get it in red, Tessa would be so proud of me for expanding my horizons.

I set multiple timers on my phone and looked out across the panoramic view. My shoulders relaxed and I went into a state of not-quite sleep. It was one I had used often when on assignments for the Jōkōryūkai. Only on those assignments, I had been wearing Truth and Hachi usually. It felt strange to settle into watchguard mode without my swords. I reminded myself that I wasn't here to take out a dangerous element, I was here to help an injured person. I rested my cheek against the cool surface of the beanbag and waited.

As my mind cleared, the song of San Francisco's magic swelled beneath me. The soothing music further calmed my mind, and my awareness grew until my perceptions expanded beyond the glass of the picture windows.

My senses split. At once I was lying down on Adam's ridiculous beanbag, my limbs bone weary from the last two days, and I was also floating above the NEO, my nerves alight with energy, suffused with golden power radiating up to me from the city below. Sound drifted up to me. Sporadic traffic. Dogs and crows. Whispered, loving sentiments and voices shrill with anger.

San Francisco was young, its magic raw and wild. But now that it had bonded with me, I could mold and shape it, and it would change me as well. I stretched my senses farther and bright pinpoints sparkled around me, each light glittering with purpose. The people of my city, who would look to me for protection, even if they didn't know it. I held out my hands and I could feel them all. I couldn't see them but my mind's eye fed me images to comfort me and I imagined them within the city's gentle cocoon.

Freddy, snoring on his hospital bed.

Leanna, huddled in her darkened room under her covers, her face lit by her phone screen.

Popo, working quietly in the back room of her spa, her talent a pool of serenity in the chaos of my city.

Sally and Baby Ricky, stocking the shelves and bickering over product placement.

Brother Meng, coaching his youth basketball teams.

Even Tessa and Andie, not Jiārén, but still my people to protect.

I opened my eyes. I was here with Adam and as I studied his light, I knew he would be fine, and I would be around to make sure of it.

I settled deeper into the beanbag. It really was quite comfortable. I closed my eyes and let the song of my city sing me to sleep.

I had snuck into countless rooms before, but this was the first time I was going to intentionally wake the person sleeping. Adam had sprawled out across his bed diagonally, his arms flung out.

I sat on the edge of the bed and patted his shoulder. His skin was hot and smooth. Adam radiated heat like a furnace. "Hey, Sleeping Beauty, I need to check your eyes."

He turned toward me and his eyelids twitched. I gave in to temptation and ran my fingers gently over his upper arm and squeezed. "Adam. I'm going to turn on a light."

Adam made a soft sound of protest and mopped his face with one big hand. He opened his eyes at last, still moving slowly.

He gave me a sleepy smile. "Hi."

"Hi." I reached over and turned on the bedside lamp. Adam winced but obliged as I asked him to keep his eyes open. Both pupils were heavily dilated, which was to be expected with his concussion, but they looked even. I turned off the light.

"Thanks for taking care of me," Adam murmured.

A wave of tenderness washed over me. I'd assumed responsibility for his well-being but maybe it wasn't only duty that made me feel protective of him.

Adam patted the area next to him and then closed his eyes. "You're welcome to join me."

I snorted. "Nice try."

He smiled but kept his eyes closed. "A guy can dream."

I pulled the sheet over all that tantalizing skin. "Rest. I'll wake you again in an hour."

Adam's breathing evened out and I turned to leave. I froze as my eyes locked on a gentle sweep of red lacquered wood mounted on the wall. Crimson Cloud Splitter hung balanced on two simple hooks. A tattered length of red silk was tied around the scabbard, and a row of blush-pink pearls dotted the grip. It took a moment for me to remember to breathe.

Just two days ago I'd been dead set on separating Adam from this sword as quickly as possible. I was within arm's reach of it now and all I could think of was how hard it would be to explain it to him. As the Sentinel, as Adam's protector, maybe even as his friend, I owed Adam a lot better than stealing the sword in the dark of night. It wasn't going anywhere, and I would keep a close eye on Adam. I had time. I could find a way to do this right.

I went back out to the living room and looked out at the city below. I cocked my ear to San Francisco's music and let the vital hum of its magic and citizens flow through me.

Dark glass bottles stretched down the aisle as far as I could see, the labels blurring into nonsense as my eyes lost focus. How did anyone ever decide when presented with so many choices?

"Are you sure about this?"

Adam looked more like himself again after resting the entire day, but I noticed how he kept a hand on the shelving to steady himself. "I'm positive. Bringing wine to a dinner party is always appreciated."

"But how do you know which one?"

"It helps to know what we'll be eating."

"Pizza." I made a face. "With figs."

Adam laughed and raised his hand to his ribs. "Ow. Okay, just pick a cab or a big, juicy red."

I threw up my hands. "I don't even know what that means."

This was why I didn't do this. I could prepare for a fight with an army of demons, but picking wine was completely outside my wheelhouse. I did not drink and if I did, wine made absolutely no sense at all. Big, juicy red should be a hamburger.

Adam tapped his chin. "Well, Tessa and Andie are vegetarians. Maybe we should get a white for them, too."

I sighed. Even my brother's Tourney was starting to seem easier than this.

"We're in a wine shop in San Francisco, Emiko. It's scientifically impossible to make a bad choice here. Just pick a white and a red. I'm sure Tessa will be delighted."

"Fine."

I studied the labels. Adam suggested cabernet. The labels all had locations. Napa or Sonoma sounded safe. Finally I picked one with an oak tree on a silver label and held it up to Adam. "This one sound good?"

"That's a nice one. Let's grab a chardonnay and we're all set."

I gave up. "Would you please find one?"

Adam smiled, his eyes crinkling with pleasure. "Sure. Happy to help."

After he nattered on about unoaked chardonnays going well with white pizza, I eagerly paid so that we could head out to Tessa's place in Hayes Valley.

Adam settled himself gingerly into his seat and buckled up.

"Thank you again for inviting me."

I rolled my eyes. "Someone has to keep an eye on you. The doctor said so."

Adam shrugged off my sarcasm with aplomb. "Then thank you for keeping an eye on me as well. I just wish I remembered our first date, so this would feel more like our second date."

"It wasn't a date."

"We spent several hours together. I still think that counts as a date unless you want to tell me what actually happened."

"Slow your roll there, cowboy. Remember, the doctor told you not to force it."

Under the auspices that the doctor said we should let Adam's memories come to him gradually, I'd been given a reprieve from telling him much. I had to keep a close eye on him in case the memories returned. If that happened . . . well, we would burn that bridge when we got to it. I also hadn't told him that while he was unconscious I had sealed our fates with a promise sworn on my blood.

My father had merely grunted when I'd told him the Soong Clan had a new ward. That was as good as I could have hoped for. Certainly expecting praise from Father for redeeming the Talon would have been too much. He merely said, "It is right that you are now the Sentinel of San Francisco."

I'd have to accept that as an accolade from him.

I also gave myself credit for not being surprised when my father casually inquired about the disposition of the Lost Heart of Yázì. Due to its "corrupted" state, the shinigami left the stone in my care, and it was currently nestled behind multiple wards and locks in my house. My small Hoard had grown considerably. I wasn't sure if my father actually bought my glib reply, but the fact that he didn't pursue it was more telling. If he knew I had it, he didn't seem to mind. I stewed on that for a while, until I finally decided that it was impossible to determine if that was a good thing or a bad thing.

Andie's tech business had made it possible for them to buy a charming Victorian in Hayes Valley. Tessa's artistic sensibilities had restored the Victorian into a truly stunning home. The facade was painted mint green and detailed with dashes of gold and white. The inviting porch was a deep turquoise and framed by a graceful arch.

For once in my life, I carried no swords on my person—just two bottles of wine. It felt strange, but also gave me the freedom to feel the city's power and life all around me, beneath me, and above me.

Here, on the doorstep of Tessa and Andie's home, I marveled at how different the city's power felt. They weren't Jiārén, and yet their presence also shaped the city's power in a similar fashion. Tendrils of the city's magic reached out to me and fed me sensations from inside the house. Tessa's jangling nerves. Andie, calm and soothing. I drew in a deep breath and knocked twice.

Tessa answered the door wearing an apron dusted with flour and dabbed with tomato sauce. She'd tied her frizzy blond hair up into a loose bun. The look on her face was worth the price of admission as her eyes ping-ponged between me and Adam standing on her doorstep. The smell of roasting tomatoes and dough wafted out of her door on a puff of warm air.

"Emiko!"

I held out the bottles. I hoped this was how it was done. "We brought wine."

Tessa took the bottles from me and her eyes widened even further when she read the labels. "Wow, Emiko, thank you! Come in, come in . . . Andie, guess who made it?"

Adam smiled and waved me into Tessa and Andie's house. I stepped over the threshold, feeling like I was taking a big step into something new. Andie hollered from the kitchen as she spotted us. "Hey, you two! Perfect timing."

Andie wiped her hands on a towel and stepped out to the foyer. Andie was taller than me, with long dark hair like mine. It up in a high ponytail with a slick undershave. She wore a white tank with a black apron over it that said HOT STUFF in red script. Andie was lean and brown and looked like she ran marathons daily. She pulled me in for a hug and then she pressed her palms against my cheeks. She smelled like rosemary. Her eyes traveled up to the streak in my hair and back to my face without missing a beat. As if I needed another reason to adore her.

"Glad you made it."

I could tell from her tone that Andie wasn't just talking about tonight.

Andie turned to Adam. "And what the hell happened to you?"

He ducked his head and pointed at me. "Ask her."

Tessa's and Andie's heads swiveled my way in unison. "He . . . uh . . . got struck by lightning."

"What?!"

I didn't know what else to say. I mean, it was true. It just sounded insane because it was.

Adam said, "Yeah and all I got was this lousy burn to show for it."

They laughed and the tension was broken.

I had expected taking the Sentinel mantle to feel strange, or alien. Bonding myself with the sentient magic of a city wasn't an everyday occurrence.

Here inside this house, the city's magic thrummed under my feet and seeped upward, mingling and blending with the happy smells and energy of their home. It sent a thrill up my spine that lit up my brain in all the right ways. Being the Sentinel didn't feel strange, it only felt . . . right.

"Can I help?"

Andie laughed. "Girl, we know you can't cook."

True. I mean, I could make rice and that was what was important. After that, everything else was just assembly. Tessa ushered me into the dining room and let me set the table while she and Adam discussed the wine and what needed to "breathe." Tessa pulled out an aerator and I thought it looked like a pretty good weapon for bloodletting but I guess it was for pouring. I didn't know what they were talking about so I just zoned out and soaked up the warmth of Tessa and Andie's home.

Tessa and Andie had both been right. Popo had been right. I had spent the last two years trying to make a place for myself between worlds, trying not to pick a side. By staying on the sidelines, I hadn't been doing anyone any good, much less myself. My place wasn't between the worlds, but firmly in both. Being the Sentinel was testament to that. Both Jiārén and Wàirén were my responsibility. Big, scary responsibility.

It was terrifying, but also good. After two years in San Francisco, I finally felt like I belonged. Like I was home. I was even looking forward to returning to Japan next week to see my brother's Tourney. I had feared returning home, not wanting to face the consequences of breaking my blade. But now I could go home and face my father, maybe even my mother, and know that I had made a place for myself in San Francisco. Best of all, my father could animate Bāo again, and I would have my cat back. Or he would have me back.

I sent a prayer of gratitude and humility to the Great Dragon Father for showing me the way.

And for pizza without figs.

# ACKNOWLEDGMENTS

This beautiful book was the labor of so many wonderful people. We are incredibly grateful for the time, love, and care that our editors Claire Eddy and Sanaa Ali-Virani, along with the entire Tor team, put into this book. Every thoughtful touch in this book came from someone who went that extra mile to make this reading experience special.

Thank you to our agent, Laurie McLean, who always swings for the fences.

*Ebony Gate* had its start in a very different setting. We are thankful to Joe Nassise, who coached us through the first iteration, and taught us so much. You would not be holding this book in front of you in this format if it weren't for Jonathan Maberry, who told us to query it. Joe and Jonathan encouraged us to take this long shot. And a special thanks to Kevin J. Anderson for building our Tribe.

Much love to our dear family and friends who nurtured us on this writing journey.

Thank you Ken, Caleb, and JJ, who will watch any movie with me for "research purposes." Thank you, Karna, for always being our first reader. Kevin, your love and encouragement to pursue my creative dreams means so much to me. Sue and Bret, thank you for always cheering me on. My morning crew, Katie, Wendy, Casey, and Jen, I appreciate our years of friendship and thank you for making sure I don't hibernate in my cave. ~Julia

Thanks to my wife, Ann, and our kids, Nicholas and Isabelle, for being there for me as I found my way into a new life as an author. Julia, thank you for pulling me back into creative writing, after our long hiatus for Real Jobs. ~Ken